Dance of the Jester

By
Koos Verkaik

Outer Banks Publishing Group
Raleigh/Outer Banks

Word of Thanks

My agent in the USA suggested I ask Bill Thompson to read *The Dance of the Jester*.

Bill was the editor of the first books of Stephen King and John Grisham, a charismatic man of great reputation. He read the manuscript and invited me to discuss it with him.

On a scorching hot day, we found ourselves in his office in the Empire State Building in New York and together we revised and polished the manuscript and made changes in the plot. He was more than satisfied with the story, and in the meantime, he has read more of my manuscripts.

I thank Big Bill Thompson for his help and friendship.

Suddenly...

Suddenly, at the end of the twenty-first century, the world changed.

The tycoons ruled and named themselves kings.

They were times of extravagance and decadence, extreme power and richness.

The world was one big party.

And there was chaos!

No one seemed to wonder how this all had come to be.

No one seemed to wonder what was actually happening.

No one seemed to care about anything anymore.

Except for some odd outsiders.

One of them was Oscar Man the illegitimate son of tycoon Otto Man.

Once he was a prince; then he became a pariah with nothing to lose for himself and so much to win for the world.

Chapter One

Paris/New York - End of the Twenty-First Century

Prince Oscar Man was in a hurry to catch his flight out of Paris. He had to go to New York to see the coronation of his half-brother Ferdinand. His eyes sparkled like the jewels on the legs of his pants; his thoughts were still with the wild party he had left. His servants, the twins Richard and Jay Jay sat in the front of the car with Richard at the wheel. Their long, blond ponytails slid over the high collars of their red livery coats. A girl Oscar had met just a few evenings ago during the nightly street festivities nestled against him and stroked his face and neck.

She had joined thousands of Parisians and other assorted pilgrims in lighting two hundred and fifty thousand candles and then placing them around the Eiffel Tower: one candle for every tenth rivet in the iron giant.

Later, they were dancing through the streets in a state of euphoria, cavorting and singing, when Oscar Man himself appeared, coming directly toward them as he walked along in the midst of another group of partygoers. She looked up at him, her eyes wandering from his bright blue eyes to the precious stone that was sparkling in the crown that sat upon his head.

"It is time for us to say good-bye," Oscar said now. "And you still haven't told me where we can drop you off."

"I would really rather go along with you," she replied in a soft voice.

The car was stuck in traffic behind a frenzied crowd. The chrome hubcaps, silvery, shining discs at high speed, were now gaping, silent monsters mired in a sea of humanity. The handles of the doors were also chrome, and the curved silver hood, detailed with broad copper bands, looked very much like a steam locomotive's engine. All the interior dials and gauges were tucked behind walnut panels.

Someone was pounding on the roof, and a woman pressed her large, bare breasts and mouth against the passenger window in a deliciously obscene kiss. Her breasts and lips flattened out grotesquely as a multitude of fun-loving hands began to rock the car back and forth.

"Where are we?" asked Oscar.

Jay Jay leaned forward peering out the windshield through the crowds.

"Prince Oscar!" came the roar from outside. "Prince Oscar, our beloved jester! Come out and dance along with us!"

"We have just passed Montmartre," Jay Jay reported. "Now we'll head up to the boulevard Périférique via the Avenue de Clichy and then turn toward Charles de Gaulle Airport. As soon as this crowd breaks up, Richard can step on it and make some time."

Oscar removed a long golden earring from his earlobe and gave it to the girl. It was in the shape of a finger with a flat, precious stone for a nail. He gave her a quick kiss as he reached past her to open the door. The people mobbing the car moved back to let her step out hoping that the prince would follow her. He quickly pulled the door closed again.

Oscar Man waved and smiled at his well-wishers as they drove along. He loved Paris because the winds of change always blew so strongly here. The city was very old but had recently been rejuvenated and totally absorbed by the love that the populace had been exhibiting since the beginning of this phenomenon that was now being called the Second Renaissance.

As the car continued steadily on its way, Oscar made himself nice and cozy in the back on the soft leather seats.

It was a terrible shame that he must leave Europe on this cool, festive night. He gazed out of the window at the twinkling lights adorning the façades of the houses. He watched the kaleidoscope of colors and the spiraling trails of smoke left behind by the barrage of fireworks being shot off all around the city. Finally, he turned his attention to the people themselves, who, regally attired in their finest party clothing, drifted from one party to the next trying to keep dawn at bay while they made the most of the night.

The spirit of unrestrained revivalism that had been spawned by this New Renaissance had spread over all of Europe. Life, however, had become much more intense, and the befuddled euphoria caused by the endless festivities dragged everyone who got involved into the merry, carefree chaos.

Oscar, the jester, had learned to love Europe. He had been born there and lived there as a little boy. Until the age of seven, he had lived not far from the Swiss city of Interlaken. At the request of his half-sister Johanna, he had gone to live in the United States. He had come back to Switzerland as a man and established the headquarters of his company there.

Oscar could have used his own small plane, stored in Switzerland, or even one of the family jets, but he enjoyed traveling with ordinary people on a regularly scheduled commercial airliner. He felt completely safe sitting between the brothers, and there was little or no chance that anyone would try to start up an unwelcome conversation with him.

Right before takeoff, an excited whisper traveled up and down the aisles of the plane that there was a very special passenger aboard. Oscar had risen and given a friendly nod to everyone who had stood up and looked in his direction. They were now high in the sky. Leaning back, Oscar took some time to look around the plane himself.

A generation ago, male passengers would have worn a suit and tie; now this attire was considered a voluntary uniform from days gone by. Uniformity itself was a thing of the past. Looking around, Oscar saw brightly decorated collars, highly imaginative epaulets, colorful scarves and bow ties, imitation fur-trimmed coats and a wide assortment of hat styles. In the seat in front of him, a woman's towering hairdo, tall enough to make Eiffel itself green with envy, rocked to and fro. Another woman who had stood up to put something in the overhead storage compartment wore countless jewels in her own upswept hairstyle. The lower halves of her ears were covered by a tight collar with diagonal rows of pearls stitched into it. Her dress, which reached the floor, was stitched with ultrafine gold and silver wire.

Oscar himself wore ornately decorated pants, high tight boots made of supple brown leather, a ruffled shirt and a coat of dark blue velvet adorned with gold piping.

He crossed his arms and sprawled out in his seat. As the airplane glided through the black night, high above the Atlantic Ocean, Oscar Man thought about how—and why—the world had changed so much.

How did it all start? What mechanism had turned the world upside down? The First Renaissance--the rebirth in the fourteenth, fifteenth and sixteenth centuries--was a period of renewal and revival of the sciences and the arts and of civilization itself, modeled on the example set by the classical antiquities. The revolution had taken place primarily in Italy and France but exerted an influence on the entire world. The devastating plague in the middle of the fourteenth century had cut the population of Europe in half. The disease, which could strike anyone regardless of class, had brought mankind to its knees. So deeply was the population of the world bowed down from all the misery that it remained to be seen whether anyone still had the courage or the strength to stand up again. Yet rise again they did!

And now, life once again was to be lived with all possible passion and intensity. Money was spent freely, art flourished and fashion was extravagant. The master builders surpassed their previous achievements with flights of unexcelled fantasy. The sculptors showed a marked preference for the naked human body and gave personality, beauty and soul to stone. It was a generation of new morality, and men began to recognize themselves more and more as individuals. The hunger for knowledge and the thirst for adventure grew as ships sailed out once again on voyages of discovery.

History, despite what we have been told, does not repeat itself. Modern occurrences are never exactly identical to events that took place in the past, and any comparisons would yield more differences than similarities.

The Second Renaissance, at the end of the twenty-first century, became fact within the life span of a generation and had its origins in North America this time, rather than Europe.

As far as Oscar was concerned, every flight between Paris and New York was a journey filled with symbolism. Furthermore, one of the greatest symbols of all the Statue of Liberty, which had been a present from France and designed by Gustave Eiffel even before he had designed Paris's tower, was always waiting to greet him. Both monuments had more meaning now that one could look back at the nineteenth century with respect and admiration, just as the people did during the First Renaissance when they rediscovered the civilizations of the Greeks and Romans.

The takeover of smaller companies by larger ones once again was beginning to have a snowball effect. In the United States, conglomerates arose like hybrid octopi on all fronts and flung their far-reaching tentacles all the way to Europe and Asia. A source of power fell into the hands of the industrialists. The food supply was controlled from farmer to factory, from laboratory to distribution. The newly refined microtechnologies and the enormous metal industries were all controlled by the same people. These same companies were also the key players involved in construction and demolition projects. They owned banks, insurance companies and aircraft companies. They were involved in the manufacture of automobiles and were instrumental in the industry that had risen around the ongoing exploration of natural resources on Mars and on the moon. They had started their own investment companies and conducted intensive research so that they could stay ahead of their rivals. They bought up everything that they could get their hands on. It had become a hard commercial world, a world in which efficiency and beauty could not exist together. The cities continued to grow larger with more buildings of the same impersonal structure. A large part of the commercial world now was owned by a relatively small number of people who sat at the top of a few powerful trusts. In spite of this fact, remarkable changes began to occur.

Whenever the tycoons appeared in public, they wore warm, friendly faces, although they were but masks. They wanted to be as one with the masses; they wanted to be known as men of flesh and blood, just as their constituents were. They were the new celebrities, and their lifestyles were imitated with fierceness. There was once again a healthy color to the face of a business world that had become virtually colorless and inhuman. Elegance, style and good manners seemed to be the new terms that people were to do business on, and yet many were aware that this was all simply a charade, that behind closed doors, the bone-chilling struggle for power and wealth continued unabated.

One of these men who pushed and parlayed himself to the top was Joseph Krocht.

Krocht had worked his way up in the business world entirely on his own efforts. When he first appeared on the scene with his live broadcast question and answer television show and an army of press officers, everything he had previously undertaken remained shrouded in mystery and fog.

All at once he was there, suddenly in charge of the gigantic, multinational Cabo de Barra Company. He was known as a philanthropist and as one who walked new paths where others wanted to follow. He seemed to sense the spirit of the times, and while on the one hand he was the reliable father figure who promised and delivered his people to safety, on the other hand he revealed himself as a turbulent rebel who enjoyed turning everything upside down and inside out.

Sporting long, curly sideburns, a three-cornered hat and large, colorful coats, he was indeed a remarkable personality. The extravagant clothing of his wife and her friends was equally majestic and combined the best fashions of many different centuries.

Technical and mechanical equipment became more complex at a great pace. It also became more incomprehensible and greatly smaller, and it was the producers themselves, with Joseph Krocht out in front, who set the tone for the battle of the beauty and simplicity of the late eighteenth and nineteenth centuries' appliances against modern science. The pendulum clock was once again in vogue; letters were written with pen and ink; children played with kits of screws, cogs and wheels, axles and little metal connectors. Here and there steam locomotives were put back into use along with tenders, porters, conductors and luxurious carriages. Houses and offices were constructed with façades of old-fashioned firmness. Architects picked up the old thread and created streets where one thought he had been cast back into earlier times as he passed cast iron streetlamps radiating the glow of gaslight. Artists designed realistic statues reflecting those times, which were immediately bought up by Cabo de Barra and its rivals, who placed them in front of their corporate offices and town parks.

Joseph Krocht threw his money about with the best of them. The parties he threw were filmed so that everyone could see what went on in his life. Fashion designers answered the demand of the public, and what was produced by their hands was seldom extravagant or foolish enough. The interior design of houses began to resemble more and more those of the upper middle classes of the nineteenth century with a great deal of wood, copper showpieces, lavish paintings on the walls and thick carpets on the floors. Although the ultramodern equipment of the day remained indispensable, it was hidden behind the walls or in bookcases. Even though people knew full well that they no longer lived in an earlier time, they still attempted to conjure up an illusion of the past and felt very at ease and comfortable with all that was old-fashioned.

Thus, the Second Renaissance had been built on nostalgic dreams, and everyone knew it, and everyone was satisfied with it.

Oscar Man could not help but smile while he thought this over. He knew very well how much the more intelligent people of the world took advantage of the fear of the general population. The common folk were afraid of a completely automated society in which individual thought was threatened. And then there was the problem of decreasing profits due to the fact that technical equipment, which had previously been mass-produced, could not command decent prices.

A market had to be created for products that required craftsmanship and specialized, custom-made goods for these were the products that would bring in the big money.

The First Renaissance had been a process of slow growth during which the human mind had learned to deal with the horrors of the past and give shape to the future with renewed vows.

The Second Renaissance very quickly became fact and was spawned entirely by commercial goals, and yet the party went on.

Oscar wanted to stretch his legs; he stood up and walked to the front of the airplane intending to pay a visit to the cockpit. Jay Jay followed him wearing a face that radiated pure boredom. Oscar knew the brothers would have preferred to stay in Europe. Just as Richard could find his way through the busy Paris streets to the airport with little or no trouble, the brothers knew many other European cities like the backs of their hands, and they loved to travel around the world with him. In New York, however, they would have to behave within the protocol of the Man family, and the complex royal household there would certainly hinder their freedom of movement.

As Oscar returned to his seat, after a short chat with the pilot and copilot, several passengers began to applaud. Soon all the others joined in, and here and there people rose to their feet. He was deeply honored and returned their warmth with a slight smile and a short wave.

A little girl with long golden locks tucked under a tall, oval, brocaded hat, and wearing a long dress made from the same heavy silken material, sat between her parents and looked up at him with bright eyes. He sent Jay Jay to her to present her with a gift.

"Where do you come from?" asked Jay Jay.

The girl was too shy to open her mouth, so it was her mother who answered.

"We are from Reims, and her name is Michelle."

"That makes me think of wine cellars full of great champagne and a Gothic cathedral from the thirteenth century," said Jay Jay, and a smile spread across his face; he knew the town, for he had been there once. "But now it is also the home of a certain young lady named Michelle, who is getting a present from Man-Manakin a division of Man-Mandate Enterprises. It is a handmade dollhouse with rooms completely furnished in Renaissance period style, and of course, there are also a great number of lifelike dolls included."

The girl responded with delight, but her parents were a bit frightened as they realized the value of the gift. Any and all products made in the factories of Man-Manakin or Man-Man-at-Arts were unique and worth a small fortune.

Oscar Man was certainly generous. The smallest bill he had paid in Paris was the one for the two hundred and fifty thousand candles, and no one knew that he had done so. The largest sum he had transferred through the Man-Manward Bank was enough to pay for the restoration of about twenty buildings, including the famous Notre Dame in the Ile de la Cité.

All the big companies threw a lot of money around; in private they called it commercial manipulation.

Shortly before his death, Joseph Krocht had bought a group of small, insignificant islands in the Pacific Ocean, far from civilization, in the great space between the Philippines and New Guinea. The largest of the islands he baptized Cabo de Barra, the same name he had given to his multinational company.

Joseph Krocht had a passion for the sea and sailors in general, and his heroes were Ferdinand Magellan, Vasco da Gama and Christopher Columbus in particular. He preferred to rule his enterprises from the comfort of his luxury ship that constantly sailed the oceans.

The symbol of Man-Mandate Enterprises was a statue of a man in armor with head down and hands resting on the hilt of a sword that was stuck in the ground between his feet.

The symbol of Cabo de Barra was also a statue—all the powerful multinationals loved their sculpture—a statue of a sailor in knee breeches, long hair waving in the wind, his shirt open showing his chest. His bare, lower legs disappeared into iron waves. His arms hung alongside his body, and in one of his hands, he held an old-fashioned pistol with a short barrel. At first glance the statue seemed to be of a fearless, intransigent sailor, a freebooter perhaps, a pirate in his prime. It was whispered, however, that the statue was indeed supposed to represent all the victims of the cruelty imposed by jurisdiction at sea.

The young man had apparently been convicted of committing some crime and subsequently condemned to be left behind on a sandbar. As his ship headed toward the horizon with full sails, he felt the water start to rise around his calves. This was the hour of his death, and it was up to him to decide whether or not he should use the pistol or let the powder get wet and swim until he drowned.

Out in the middle of the ocean somewhere, Joseph Krocht proclaimed himself emperor and put a crown on his head. When he later returned to his base in Atlanta, Georgia, where Cabo de Barra's main office was located, a feast was held that went on for two weeks. At the height of the celebrations, he passed his crown on to his son Walter Krocht. No one ever considered the possibility that he would name himself emperor of a tiny island in the Pacific; he demanded to be called *The emperor of Georgia*.

Joseph Krocht died on the last day of the celebrations, in the arms of a prostitute. His clothes, found spread on the floor near the bed, would have been well suited for a pirate captain from the sixteenth or seventeenth century.

Other tycoons soon followed his example and had themselves crowned. They, however, took the title of king, stating that Cabo de Barra had the exclusive rights to the title of emperor. In some American states, there now existed royal houses, and in New York all the houses were making preparations for the crowning of Ferdinand Man, who had a cathedral built in his honor to commemorate the occasion. It was to be a celebration for everyone, and there was even a chance that Walter Krocht, currently the most famous man in America, would be present at the ceremony.

Cabo de Barra had previously transferred the ownership of an island to Man-Mandate Enterprises. By doing so, there was now a territory that justified the wearing of a crown. Of course, Ferdinand Man could have bought his own piece of land, but it had become a tradition that Walter Krocht make this particular donation, as if to give the appearance that the multinationals were not archenemies at all.

Oscar had a few different residences in the state of New York. He preferred to stay at his penthouse in Manhattan because it was the only place where he could truly be completely on his own.

All the rooms were furnished with bookcases that reached from floor to ceiling. Where there weren't any books, the walls were covered with New Art posters and paintings. The furniture was all made of dark wood. The ferns that grew around the apartment in large pots were tended to by the only person Oscar Man could stand to have around him Cathy Wheeler. She lived in two of the apartment's twelve rooms, and when he was also in residence there, she kept him company, if that was his wish. She also knew well enough to stay out of his way when he didn't want to be bothered by anyone at all. As far as his moods were concerned, she was unfailingly able to probe his feelings. Cathy had organized his library; she had given each book a place of its own and had developed extensive reference volumes with key words, indexes, cross-references and similarities. She was a historian with an almost perfect memory, especially where details were concerned. She was officially in the service of his Swiss company that, as she liked to express it, arranged the centuries.

The contents of entire libraries had been filed in the memories of the Man machinery. Even books that were centuries old and had almost turned to dust, and might never again be opened, could be fully examined and exact copies of them could be made that would last through years of intensive use.

In his penthouse, Oscar Man kept tens of thousands of copies in the bookcases while in the memories of his machines, there were possibly ten times that number.

It was his half-sister Her Royal Highness Princess Johanna who had assigned him this task, and it was for her that he traveled the world looking for books. He searched the European archives and libraries, looked at private collections and knocked on the gates of monasteries and nunneries and the doors of churches: all in the quest for rare books for his sister.

Cathy resided in one of the largest rooms of the apartment.

She had pushed aside a false panel in a wall decorated with New Art and worked with the apparatus concealed behind it. On the oak table beside her, books were piled high, and pens and a notebook were within easy reach. She wasn't at all surprised when she looked up and saw Oscar suddenly standing before her.

She greeted him with a warm, easy smile.

"Hello, Cathy," he said.

She rose to her feet and embraced him. The scent of her perfume filled his nostrils; he welcomed the familiar aroma. After he kissed her, he stretched her arms out with his own and took a step back so he could have a good look at her. Her long, light brown hair fell in curls over her shoulders. She had a very pretty face, and her large, round eyes were a pale gray, a color he had never seen in anyone else's eyes. Her eyes radiated an inner wisdom, and he usually only had to look into them to know whether or not she agreed with him at any given moment. Cathy Wheeler was a person he could, and did, trust implicitly.

"And the prince came down from the skies and greeted her in the early morning," she smiled.

Instead of laughing along with her, he looked around in confusion and only now seemed to realize that it was still dark outside.

"Have you been working all night, or did you start early?" he asked her.

Cathy walked over to the wall and closed the panel. She was barefoot and wore only a knee-length, green silk shirt with wide sleeves.

"So much new work has been sent from Switzerland recently that I can barely keep up with it. You have obviously tapped into many new sources. I was pleasantly surprised when I received those works from the early seventeenth century."

"You only received the things that seemed of interest to me," he said, "and there is so much more that I don't think our sources will ever run dry. But now, tell me how you are."

"The temperature outside is still okay," she said. "We can watch the sunrise from the terrace. I shall make us some coffee and breakfast. Then we can talk. Off you go now."

Oscar walked through many rooms to the terrace, which lay along three sides of the penthouse. Opening the sliding doors, he stepped outside and leaned over the railing. Slowly it was becoming light over Manhattan. A quickly rising, vaporous mist unveiled old and new skyscrapers. What he saw was massive, grotesque and a bit unreal. In his head, he still had the images of snow-clad villages in the Swiss Alps and the streets of Paris, and now he suddenly found himself in the city again. He saw patches of the Hudson River between the buildings, with Hoboken, New Jersey, on the other side.

Cathy had put a tray on a plastic folding table and was standing next to him. Her hand slid between his chest and arm, and her fingers closed around his biceps. Quite often they had stood there together this way, looking through the buildings and sharing in the knowledge that this island had once been the territory of New Amsterdam. They could still surprise each other with facts from the past that they had found in their books.

"All of Manhattan was bought in 1626 by the Dutch from the Indians for less than the price of a decent meal in a restaurant today."

"What the Dutch named *Het Rode Eiland* (The Red Island) became known as Rhode Island, and they say that Coney Island comes from *Konijneneiland*, which means Rabbit Island. Brooklyn and Harlem are named after the Dutch cities of Breukelen and Haarlem."

Whenever they talked to each other like this, Oscar felt at ease. Even now, after they had discussed all the more important matters, Cathy managed to come up with some new fact.

"Peter Stuyvesant the director-general of New Amsterdam had a wooden leg."

"But of course!" he said. "He had it made in Holland and had it covered with silver!"

"What else do you know?" Cathy challenged him.

"His leg was shot off in 1644 by the Spaniards when he was involved with the reconquering of the island of St. Martin. As I recall, the leg was buried on Curaçao."

"But does anyone know if it was his left leg or his right leg?"

"Well, no. Did you find that information somewhere?"

"Yes, and you know details like this make my mouth water. It was his right leg."

They drank coffee and ate crackers with an assortment of cheeses.

"We're always talking about the past," Cathy said with a smile. "I sometimes get the feeling that I have been busy just a bit too long with books that were written so long ago. The future is always better than the past, for everything behind you is dead, and here, in the present, everything is still alive and kicking."

She took his face in her hands and kissed him on both cheeks.

"I'm so happy to see you again, Oscar. But your stay here will be a short one, I suppose, and then you're expected to be present at the crowning of your half-brother."

Oscar nodded and grinned.

It has become an odd world, Cathy, he mused.

He left the terrace and headed toward the bathroom to take a shower, where he had a chance to think about this collective interest and passion for the past that his half-sister Johanna, Cathy Wheeler and he shared. Johanna idolized her knowledge of the past because it was quite chic to know more about the eighteenth and nineteenth centuries than other women. Cathy Wheeler had been to college, and her love for the history of mankind was pure and sincere.

Where Oscar was concerned, it was different. He was the illegitimate son, and it was not the blood of the Man family that boiled in his veins when he assiduously searched for answers to his questions in the oldest manuscripts. It was his mother's blood that drove his restless and stubborn quest into the past.

He searched and searched. Why he did so, he could not say, but he knew he must. Sometimes it angered him. Other times it made him desperate.

He was still naked when he reappeared and walked across the richly carpeted and inlaid wooden floors back out onto the terrace. He leaned over the railing again and stared into the depths. What was happening here—in all of North America and Europe, for that matter—seemed to be a bizarre fraternization of reality and fiction.

He shivered as the water dripped down his body. He suspected that he had something to do with the present situation in the world but could not put his finger on it. Every time he thought deeply about this, he began to feel dizzy and could get no realistic grip on the idea.

Cathy stood next to him. She had a towel with her and began to firmly dry him off.

"When are you leaving again?" she asked.

"Tomorrow I will have dinner with my sister Johanna and my brother Jimmy. I am expected to appear properly dressed and right on time."

"Then we have plenty of time to have some fun," said Cathy as she dropped the towel on the floor and pressed herself against him. "I think you should be aware of the fact that your sister's nerves are shot with the upcoming crowning of Ferdinand in sight. She takes her mind off things and manages to relax a little through poetry. You'd better be prepared for the worst. During dinner tomorrow she has arranged for the actor Larry d'Ariola to recite "The Raven" in character as a blind, drunken Edgar Allan Poe."

Oscar Man took her by the hand and led her inside where they made love with passionate abandon. Afterward, he sat down at a table in one of the studies, took a pen and paper, and began to write.

Early the next morning, he was picked up by Richard and Jay Jay Wright, and they drove in a sporty convertible downtown to one of the offices of Man-Mandate Enterprises where he had a meeting with one of the members of the board Samuel Higgins whom he filled in on his activities in Europe. Sam poured whisky for them as they sat in his huge office, and Oscar watched Sam pace back and forth in front of a window with a splendid view of the Hudson River. Higgins was short and plump; he wore knee-high boots like those of a musketeer and a long cardigan encrusted with rubies. He only half-listened to what Oscar was telling him about all the special books he had found in various libraries but pricked up his ears when Oscar started accounting for the expenses.

"Sounds good to me, Oscar," he said. "Especially the restorations in Paris. It will certainly make the other parties jealous. Cabo de Barra has invested well in restorations in Venice, and it has brought them much positive publicity."

Oscar was not here so much to give an accounting of either his spending or of his actions but more to keep in touch with the firm in a social sort of way. He didn't even have to justify himself to the chairman of the Man-Manward Bank, who could see by simply pressing a button on a keyboard what he had spent. Sam continued talking about the competition between the multinationals that had resulted in a contest to see who the biggest philanthropist could be. Meanwhile, Oscar smiled as he thought about something Cathy Wheeler once said to him while they were gazing down from the terrace.

"When all that you see here was called New Amsterdam, Wall Street was *walled street*, a long street built along a defensive wall, and Broadway was a broad road where coaches could easily pass each other."

Now Wall Street was the playground of the Man family. And when members of the family went to see a show on Broadway, people gathered hoping to catch a glimpse of them. The family was honored and feared at the same time. Only toward Oscar could one behave less reserved and formal. Oscar was the illegitimate son, the jester, the man of the people.

Samuel Higgins poured another drink, toddled up to Oscar and slapped him on the shoulders.

"I'm so glad to see you again, Oscar. After the crowning, I'll take you out, and we can catch up on all the gossip in a good restaurant. After that, we can go to a party in Little Italy or Chinatown. Believe me, I do have my connections. When you are out with me, you will be surrounded by the most beautiful women. Although we know, of course, that you have chambermaids working in your mansion in the village who are much more attractive than most cover girls—not to mention the girls in Switzerland!"

"We'll do that, Sam," said Oscar. "We'll get away from it all together, you and I. I can't wait to see how you will arrange all this with that big belly and those short legs of yours."

Sam laughed aloud and nodded. They talked on for a while longer and then Oscar rose to his feet and said he wanted to use of one of the helicopters up on the roof.

"I must be on time for dinner with my sister and brother, and besides, I'm getting hungry."

Sam walked him to the door and shook his hand. Oscar and the twins went up in the elevator, and five minutes later they were soaring over New York. Instead of looking down, though, Oscar closed his eyes and napped; he had seen the city quite often from the sky.

All the helicopters that belonged to the Man companies had the appearance of animals. Huge, metallic lions and insects buzzed around town, as did fantasy creatures such as dragons and monsters, looking maliciously down on the world. Oscar Man found himself in the belly of a throbbing lizard. The slightly bent tail and outstretched paws that adorned this particular machine did not make the steering of the chopper any easier, but the pilot Stan Woodring and his copilot Francis Finnigan had no trouble controlling it.

Oscar opened his eyes and looked down. The helicopter, leaving the city, had flown over cornfields and green meadows and now circled above the enormous family estate. The palace, surrounded by ornamental gardens and labyrinths, took up the area of an entire town. On the outside perimeters of the building were the offices, while the family chambers were located in the center, built around a walled-in pleasure garden. Towers of varying heights, colonnades and dome-shaped annexes made it difficult for the eye to find a resting point when one looked at this gigantic structure. Doors and gates made from the same kind of wood and white marble frames on all the windows gave one the impression of a well-thought-out plan.

"Why don't we land?" asked Oscar, a bit irritated.

The co-pilot turned halfway around and looked at him over the frame of his sunglasses.

"You were asleep, Prince," he said. "We thought you needed your rest."

Finnigan's voice sounded flat in the speakers of Oscar's headset. Then he heard the voice of Woodring.

"Now that you are awake, though, sir, we will land immediately."

As the chopper descended, a square landing pad came into sight along the north side of the park.

There were lakes, gardens filled with sculptures, lanes, hills with observation towers, bathhouses and tennis courts. But most outstanding was the steam-driven Ferris wheel, which at five hundred feet tall was almost three hundred feet higher than the Riesenrad from the Viennese Prater. Cabins as big as train cars served as compartments and from the soft cushions of padded easy chairs, one had a view all the way down to New York City and the Atlantic Ocean. Every cabin contained a bar and a kitchen, and there were always personnel in attendance to provide guests with foods and drinks.

Oscar stepped out; the windstorm caused by the still-turning propeller blowing his straight hair into his eyes. The twins followed him, and the chopper took off again.

Automatically, the three men started to walk up to the station.

An elegant solution had been found to check up on everyone who would be visiting the palace. Under a roof of iron and glass, proud, black locomotives were being held under constant steam, and every guest was escorted to a place in a compartment by uniformed personnel. Each locomotive had the head of a bull, a lion, an elephant, a buffalo or a dragon. The station building itself was made of wood and stone with narrow, high windows: twenty towers ending inspires, a hotel and, on the ground floor, a number of waiting rooms.

"Welcome, sir," said a big, stout man in a snow-white uniform.

Oscar had known him for years. He was one of the stationmasters. He smiled so intensely that his screwed-up eyes totally disappeared behind his puffed-out cheeks. On his balding head stood a cylindrical hat with a tassel that swung to and fro as the man stepped up to Oscar, holding out his hand.

"Orville Hood!" shouted Oscar, and instead of shaking the man's hand, embraced him.

Orville had already been working there when Oscar Man was brought to the station for the first time in his life and had been taken to his place in the locomotive known as the Dragon.

"The Bull is ready, sir," said Orville. "Allow me to walk with you for a little ways. It has been so long ago since I have seen you around here. Every time you return, I hope that you have had enough of all this traveling and have finally decided to settle down here. Or do you never get tired of Europe?"

Followed by the twins, they walked to the black Bull, which stood there blowing steam alongside one of the platforms. The trains were always surrounded by a special smell, and Oscar inhaled the air deeply through his nostrils.

"When the time comes that I do decide to come and live here, Orville, we will step into the Ferris wheel together and stay there for an entire afternoon. We will spin around and around, drinking French cognac, and I will tell you all about Europe."

"I will hold you to your promise, sir!" said the man. "I saw the lizard appear in the sky and hoped you would be aboard, but then, of course, I knew you would be present at the crowning. Why did you circle around above the palace for such a long time?"

"I was asleep, and no one wanted to disturb me. I believe I'm getting old, Orville!"

The man shook his head, and the tassel on his hat danced from left to right.

"Now I really must object, Prince Oscar. Yes, you are a grown man, but you are still a young man, too!"

He opened the door of a carriage, and Oscar looked inside. The interior was plush with walnut, gold and copper trim and had an enchanting, old-fashioned beauty.

"You go inside," said Oscar to Richard and Jay Jay. "I want to go up front with the engineer."

"What did I tell you?" said Orville Hood with a smile. "A young man, even a child still."

With quick steps, Oscar walked farther down the platform, bouncing lightly on the soft soles of his boots. Orville walked quickly alongside, struggling to keep up.

Oscar had climbed onto the train and standing next to the engineer when the Bull slowly began to move. Oscar felt the power of the engine, heard its moaning and hissing and looked at all the meters and gauges as he watched the engineer. Orville slowly vanished from sight behind them as they left the platform and the locomotive began to speed along the straightaway that lead to the open gates of the palace.

"Everything looks so fine," said Oscar. "Shining and sparkling!"

"It all has to do with our unquestioning love for the machinery, sir," said the engineer giving him a sidelong glance as he kept his hands busy with the various controls of the train. "Every morning the Bull is born anew when we light its fire and raise the temperature of its water. We bring it to life! We belong to the machine, and the machine belongs to us. Even the softest, slightest sigh of the Bull tells me what's wrong with him, and I put him back in good shape with a few drops of lubricant."

The locomotive slowed down, went through the gates and gradually came to a standstill. The train had traveled throughout the entire complex, along the park and then back to the station. Jumping off the train, Oscar went into the big arrival hall in the center of which stood a square wooden bar with wrought iron stools of the finest workmanship. Several servants were in attendance and walked around the room taking care of the needs of the gathered royalty. Each guest had to wait until being summoned by a member of the court, so at this point Oscar was forced to leave the twins behind. Richard and Jay Jay sat down at the bar and ordered something to drink.

Across marble floors and through broad corridors, he made his way to the high-speed elevator and went up to the fifth floor where his rooms were. He went straight to his own bedroom and removed his boots, rings and crown.

Orville Wood was right when he said it had been a long time since Oscar's last visit. Lying on his bed with his hands folded behind his head, he stared up at the painted ceiling and took some time to become acclimatized.

With no warning, the floodgates of his relaxed mind opened up, and he was deluged with a myriad of unpleasant memories. Jumping up, he rang for one of the maids and asked for a proper massage. He had no permanent servants here and had never before seen the young lady who took care of him. He had already decided to spend the night with her later. He hated to sleep alone.

* * *

"Before it gets too busy around here and I have to deal with our guests, let's go on the Ferris wheel together. Ferdinand just built the cathedral where he will be crowned, and from a high altitude it is fantastic to look at. Really, Oscar, you won't believe your eyes!"

Johanna Man put her hand on his and looked at him with a sweet smile.

He smiled back at her and nodded.

"I'm looking forward to that," he said.

His half-sister Johanna, whom he had always regarded as his protectress, had given him a place at the table right next to her. She was the only person in his life he was accountable to. Johanna was much older than he and had taken care of him from the moment he arrived at the palace for the first time, so very long ago.

They found themselves in a hall of incredible dimensions; the ceiling, which was a blue painted sky with angels gliding past clouds on outstretched wings, was at least thirty feet above their heads. A sunroom with a domed roof of stained glass windows led outside to the pleasure garden. The longest side of the room was three hundred feet in length. On the mosaic floor lounged an odd assortment of dogs, and parrots squawked and flew about everywhere. It was strange, but the birds all stayed way up in the trees that stood in wooden troughs forming a path leading to the sunroom. It was as if they knew better than to commit the social error of mingling with the guests down below.

Not many guests shared the meal with Johanna and her brother Jimmy. The only ones, as a matter-of-fact, who were anywhere close to her and Jimmy were their minions. They wore exactly the same clothes as the princess and the prince. They were favorites with very special privileges. It was another one of the old, revived customs—having a minion—and many of the tycoons and other members of the upper class would go nowhere unless accompanied by one.

There were some major shareholders of Man-Mandate Enterprises present whom Oscar recalled seeing on at least one other occasion but did not really know. The one exception was the immensely rich and powerful Margaret Sharpe, an incredibly savvy businesswoman who had been associated with the Man organization for as long as he could remember. Like Johanna, she had her hair up and wore a dress with a tight bodice that revealed a great deal of her ample breasts. Jimmy Man wore dark blue clothes and a grotesque red tie. He had dyed his gray sideburns gold, and the wrinkles in his face were hidden from view by white powder.

Johanna Man raised her glass and waited until Oscar had done the same.

Then she softly clinked her glass against his.

"Welcome, Oscar! Welcome once again! You have been away for far too long!"

They all took a drink as a group of musicians began strolling around the room playing softly. Doors opened almost silently, and mute servants slid along the table serving the meal.

"You send me the most beautiful books," said Johanna. "And believe me, I'm not the only one who is very grateful for that. My library is so famous now that historians from all over the world come to visit me and read my books and files. When you go back to Europe, I'll give you a number of addresses in Italy. There is a private library in Rimini that should contain dozens of unknown manuscripts, and around Bologna and Ferrara there are several churches that need our help making copies of their oldest texts."

Johanna, like Cathy, was extremely proud of her knowledge of the past; it was very chic to have an intellectual pursuit besides business. Her collection of books and manuscripts provided her with an unprecedented high status.

"I'll do my very best. As always," said Oscar.

He ate slowly and took the time to observe the others. He sat here, at this table, with people who ruled the world, who pulled all the strings and who had carte blanche to feast from the financial horn of plenty. He himself was never allowed to interfere in business, and he knew only too well that he did not have the talent for it. He was tolerated here only because Johanna Man wanted it that way. She had given him the princely coronet and had gotten him involved with the family.

Jimmy Man was obsessed with the art of painting. He had worked on the revival of New Art and was a lover of Magic Realism but was most avid about anything that had been painted from life. All of the art in the palace reflected this taste, from the masterpieces lining the halls and corridors to the murals and decorated ceilings. He also had a passion for steam locomotives, and it was he who had given the order to build the Ferris wheel.

Ferdinand was the man of architectural insight. He knew exactly what he wanted and was able to explain very clearly what he saw in his mind's eye to his designers. The palace was the realization of his ideas of grand-scale construction. Within these walls lived over ten thousand people who all were in some way employed by Man-Mandate Enterprises. The main offices of the company were located here and provided most of the employment, but there was also a very large household staff, and then there were the countless artists and master builders and their families who had all found a roof over their heads here.

Ferdinand had designed an elevator that could bridge horizontal distances. Every part of the palace was accessible but only to those who knew the correct codes. Every time an elevator button was pushed or a code entered, the user and the route taken were registered. Life at the court was complicated, and few things happened that the family failed to notice. Oscar never had felt at home here. He still looked with the eyes of a stranger at Johanna and her minion who whispered in each other's ears and smiled behind their hands. He raised his eyebrows when Jimmy looked at him with his dark eyes glaring from deep within his unnaturally white face.

"You've always been more of a dreamer," Johanna had often said to him. "You don't understand how we can rule our businesses with an iron hand one moment and burst out in tears the next upon hearing an enchanting melody."

Oscar did understand, but he felt little or no connection to these people and their way of life. Besides, he had enough problems of his own. Oscar Man was a mystery to everyone including himself, and undoubtedly he was the most obvious and best qualified person to solve that mystery.

With a simple wave of her hand, Johanna dismissed the musicians and had red wine poured in elaborately designed crystal glasses. Through the glass ceiling that crowned the lofty stone walls of the banquet hall, the lights of a thousand stars shone down. Along the walls lamps had been lit, but at the table it remained dusky. With her next gesture, Johanna sent a manservant to a door, and at the precise moment that he opened it, Johanna said, "And now, ladies and gentlemen, it is time for loftier pursuits! It is high time for the art of poetry! I have sent for Edgar Allan Poe himself, but I cannot guarantee that he will be sober!"

She laughed, and her minion laughed with her; everyone in the room looked with sincere interest toward the man who had appeared in the doorway and was now walking up to the table with long strides. It was not the gait of a man who had consumed too much alcohol.

The actor Larry d'Ariola, alias Mr. Poe, stopped and stared straight ahead with his arms folded across his chest. He wore a wrinkled white shirt with a sloppy tie; a worn-out, old-fashioned army coat was draped around his slight shoulders.

He stood right in front of the table, between Margaret Sharpe and a fabulously rich man named Willis, and with an arrogant, self-assured gesture smoothed down his moustache using his thumb and forefinger. He looked out of the corner of his eye and waited patiently until all the whispering around him stopped. Margaret held out her glass to him, and with a smile made an inviting gesture.

With a firm, strong voice he spoke.

"Madam, it has been a long time since liquid of that sort has moistened my lips!"

After a quick stroke through his tangled hair, he pulled a piece of paper out of the pocket of his torn coat.

"I shall read a poem about the brave Eleanor," he said. "Be happy about this, my friends; this work is so new that you are the very first to hear it."

He began. As soon as he started reading, he seemed to draw back into himself and shut the listeners completely out of his world. Although he wasn't particularly a physically imposing person, he took on an appearance of personality with grand charisma.

What he was reciting now had the same construction as Poe's famous poem "The Raven," but Lenore had undergone a metamorphosis and had become Eleanor of Aquitaine. The terrifying black raven had become Richard the Lionhearted, her famous son, who had died in her arms. As the poem progressed, the actor's voice became more impassioned, and he began to emphasize everything he said with hand gestures.

It was as if he were reading it for himself rather than for this small, illustrious company. The poor poet had been raised above the world of fashion chic and riches, and in his shabby clothes, he was king.

He told about Richard, who earned fame and honor on his crusade and came back from Palestine only to be imprisoned by Leopold of Austria. Eleanor helped to raise and deliver the money for his release. Richard, King of England, second son of Henry II and Eleanor of Aquitaine, died in France from an arrow injury sustained not during a war or heroic fight, but when he tried to claim a treasure he had found in front of the gates of a castle in Aquitaine. Richard had given the archer on guard money to spare his life and let him be but was double-crossed and shot regardless. He died in the year 1199 as his old mother comforted him. She lived on, brokenhearted, for another five years before following him into the valley of death.

The end of the poem was at hand, and Johanna Man gave free rein to her tears; her minion cried along with her. Johanna had a great admiration for Eleanor of Aquitaine, who had devoted herself to courtly companionship, dignity and art. She, too, had recognized, appreciated and exploited talent.

Each time Eleanor's name was spoken, it was all Johanna could do to keep from sobbing. She bit her lower lip and softly shook her head.

The poet was done. With a careless gesture, d'Ariola crumpled the piece of paper he had been reading from and let it fall to the floor. With a short nod and a hardly noticeable bow, he saluted the silent company, turned around and walked away. The shadow of his coat flapped back and forth as he strode away, and in the dim light, it was as if one of Poe's terrifying figments of imagination had taken form and pounced from behind. It was only as he started to close the door behind him that the crowd exploded in applause that continued well after he had left the room. He did not react to it at all. He just kept on going.

"A grand homage to a great American," said Margaret Sharpe with a sigh.

Johanna Man dried her tears and stood up. She walked past the table, stooped to pick up the crumpled up piece of paper and went silently back to her seat.

She unfolded the paper and, eyes still wet from tears, read a few lines. Recognizing the handwriting, she looked up and stared at her half-brother Oscar.

Chapter Two

The Coronation of Ferdinand Man

It took the Ferris wheel one hour to complete a full rotation. Oscar Man and Johanna had been in one of the ride's luxurious cabins for fifteen minutes now and had reached half of the total height of the structure. They were alone in this moving, metal room for the princess had dismissed all the servants. They were strolling past the windows, enjoying the view, when Johanna began talking.

"I know I've told you this before, Oscar, but I truly regret the fact that we don't see each other very often. Sometimes, when word reaches me that you are in Manhattan, I hope you will take a little extra time to come to the palace. It's a pity that you can't get along with your brothers."

He was about to respond to that, but she raised her hands, palms out, and continued, "It has nothing to do with the age difference, I know that. I'm much older than you, but I've always felt able to take you into my confidence. You, though, Oscar—you can close yourself up as tight as an oyster, and I'm sure that does not help the relationship with your brothers. I think Jimmy is a bit afraid of you, and Freddy simply does not have the time to even think about you."

She often called Ferdinand Freddy, or Fred. He was the eldest son and had become involved in his father's businesses at a very young age.

"What does Jimmy have to fear from me?" Oscar wondered.

Johanna turned away from the windows and told Oscar to have a seat. He sat down as she went behind the bar to fix something for them to drink, but she had not gotten very far when she gave him an embarrassed look and returned to her seat beside him.

"Can you please do this for us? I'm not very good at these kinds of things."

Oscar was on his feet in a heartbeat and asked her if she wanted coffee, tea or something else.

Slowly, so very slowly, the Ferris wheel continued to turn.

It was still early in the morning, and the sun shone into the cabin from above a cloudless sky. The floor of the cabin was covered with thick carpeting; the overstuffed easy chairs and couches were covered with upholstery that had long fringes. The windows were covered with heavy curtains that had been pulled back and fastened with ornate, thick ropes. The copper ceiling was skillfully decorated with delicate etchings and set with ivory motifs. A dividing wall was hidden from view by a couch with a high back, above which hung a mirror with a golden frame. Two sculpted copper figures, a man and a woman both naked to the waist with their arms raised and their fingertips touching, formed the arch of the doorway. The wet bar was made of wood that was black as coal. Oscar set up the coffee brewer as he continued to listen to Johanna.

"Jimmy fears the look in your eyes. You never relax, and you certainly never show any emotion, but with one of your steely-eyed looks you can sure scare the hell out of someone! And then with no indication or warning, you reveal a very special side of your personality by doing something totally out of character, such as letting a mediocre actor like Larry d'Ariola recite a poem you have written that moves us all to tears. I know that despite his talent for business, and regardless of how much money he earns for the family business, Jimmy feels small and inconsequential. Fred says you have a lot more to offer than you let on and behind your back calls you a sluggard and the court jester."

Oscar stared at the coffee maker silently. Johanna could not help but wonder why he had no reaction to what she had just told him.

A bombardment of emotions was causing a stabbing pain in his head.

For all his life he had hidden his thoughts from the outside world. Even as a child being brought up by foster parents in Switzerland, he had always been alert and had adapted himself to the life others had created for him. He had developed a unique mechanism for defense that he felt was his only way to survive—and the word *survive* was meant to be taken literally. Johanna was right when she said he was self-contained. But that was how it had always been. Still, he was convinced that he had it figured out right so far.

"Well, if you are not going to say anything, you will have to just stand there and listen," said Johanna. "You know, your brothers don't blame you for your not meaning much to the family enterprises. The three of us, Freddy, Jimmy and I, were always allowed to run our operations in any way we saw fit, just so long as we were involved in the family business. You, on the other hand, have always been allowed to lead your own life and spend a lot of money in the name of Man-Mandate Enterprises. Perhaps if you could at least show some gratitude in exchange for your freedom—"

"Is that it?" Oscar asked, surprised. "Is that what they want? Is that what they need? Would it make them feel better if every time we met I thanked them for the wonderful life the family has given me?"

"You hardly ever see them."

They drank their coffee, and Johanna changed the topic of conversation. She told Oscar a bit about some of the business she and her brothers had been involved in lately.

Half an hour had passed, and their cabin had reached the highest point on the wheel.

Johanna got up, walked through the door formed by the statues and went up a flight of metal stairs to an upper floor. In the room above, the walls and ceiling were made of thick glass. Outside the window there was a walkway with a railing, but at this giddy height she didn't dare walk up to the edge and so sat down in a leather armchair, safely in the middle of the room.

Oscar silently took his place next to her, and she pointed out the cathedral that Ferdinand had built. The cathedral was primarily constructed of metal. From ground level, it was difficult to see how it had been built because it sat on top of an artificial, tree-covered hill, but from the vantage point at the apex of the Ferris wheel, one could clearly see that it was a gigantic metallic skeleton of iron piles and copper plates with peaked towers and stained glass windows.

Oscar turned his eyes away from Johanna and looked at the structure and then immediately closed his eyes. What remained on his retina was the image of a cathedral similar to those built in the Middle Ages: a spectacular work of art created by ingenuity and effort. When he looked again at the cathedral, he saw it as a metal monster. The experience became even more strange when he realized that he was watching the cathedral from the highest point of a structure that was at least as peculiar and probably more unreal.

"So that is where Ferdinand will have himself crowned."

He remembered a winter a long, long time ago when he still considered Ferdinand Man an uncle rather than a half-brother. Ferdinand had taken him to the park and told him to stand in the middle of a field. Then he had proceeded to walk away from him with long strides in a straight line, counting out loud. After one hundred and sixty steps measuring approximately three feet each, he stopped, turned and shouted with his hands cupped around his mouth.

"This is how high the Ferris wheel will be that I intend to build here! If I was able to fly through the air as high above your head as I am standing from you right now, you would understand what kind of colossal project I have in mind!"

Oscar had only understood part of what Ferdinand was saying. Oscar was only a child then; he was an adult now, but still considered a jester, without any business sense whatsoever.

He suddenly looked at Johanna with fear in his eyes, for he realized that although she was still talking to him, she was making no sense! She was talking complete nonsense, looked wild and was making nervous gestures with her hands.

"I should have known what would happen when father passed away," she said. Then she shook her head, laughed and continued in a shrill voice, "Laws have been laid down that cannot be changed so simply or just for pleasure. We must reflect on new steps. Don't you think that the large dining room is much more comfy and intimate when it remains a little dim around the table? I have definitely decided to put candles on the table from now on."

She put her hand on his shoulder, pressed herself against him and said, "Oscar, you must know that I will always love you!"

"It makes me very happy to hear you say that," he replied and wished the cabin would descend faster than it had gone up.

The ride would last another half hour before they would be on the ground again. Although there were emergency elevators built into the thick tubing of the gigantic frame, it undoubtedly was her intention that they would remain in the cabin until the circle was complete. He walked with her along the glass dome, she on the inside and stopping every so often to lean on the cast iron railing. Now he started to talk, mainly to keep her distracted.

"Ferdinand has given each cabin a unique design. This is, I believe, a place for guests to stay who enjoy the feeling of circular motion. There are luxurious cabins with comfortable bedrooms and many cushions under the glass dome. They are there for the business associates he must keep satisfied and happy. They go around and around in their airborne paradise, enjoying the view and even more so the girls. All for free, until the carousel stops and Ferdinand comes by to talk seriously about business."

Johanna seemed to be acting normal again. She didn't seem to have noticed that she had been acting strangely, for she made no mention of her behavior.

"Oh yes," she laughed. "All the great and powerful people have had their fun here. After the coronation, the general public will be allowed to have a look in the cabins as well as take a ride on the Ferris wheel. We are going to open the park to the public, and I'm sure the place will be fairly well ravaged, but with a bit of money and effort everything will be repaired."

"I heard a rumor that Walter Krocht will be present."

"It is still no more than a rumor; the great imperator is obligated to nothing and can simply send a delegation representing Cabo de Barra. Nevertheless, I do hope he shows up. We will have so many distinguished guests, and we take everything that happens here this weekend very seriously."

The wheel had a periphery of about a hundred yards. The cabins revolved at a speed of twenty-five feet per minute. That was enough to constantly feel the power of the steam engines that stood firmly fixed below in a gigantic concrete foundation. There, the connecting rods, piston rods, flywheels, pistons and a complex system of gearwheels and axles kept the colossus moving.

The pair returned to the lower floor, and as they climbed down the metal steps, Oscar felt the trembling of the mechanism.

Johanna now started to dwell on business. She talked almost ceaselessly, and he saw her forehead become moist and the veins in her neck begin to throb. Obviously she didn't expect any comments, for she didn't ask any questions.

The cabin slid into the broad groove of the foundation, and someone opened the door. With her head held high, Johanna stepped out and walked away arm in arm with her minion, followed by her uniformed guards.

"Did you have an argument?" asked Jay Jay, who had waited for Oscar along with his twin brother.

"No, absolutely not," said Oscar with amazement in his voice. "I don't understand her at all, though. Her moods changed every ten seconds, and each time I had to deal with another Johanna. One of those Johannas did not seem to be entirely sane, and another one continuously juggled transactions and figures."

"It seems like the coronation has made everyone a bit nervous," said Richard.

* * *

At what age does a child gain the ability to record and store experiences in his memory so that he can remember them at a later date? Sometimes, memories appear to be unreal. Their sources may be photos, films or stories that have been told to the person about their youth. Oscar Man had never seen photographs or any other kind of evidence from the early years of his life, and no one had ever told him anything about that time. When he was brought to America at the age of seven, he brought with him a treasure chest of memories that always remained distinctly present in his mind. He only had to close his eyes to see the sweet, gentle face of his foster mother and the smiles that widely separated the moustache and beard of his foster father. He knew that Anne and Herbert Vesper had loved him with their hearts and souls.

There had been another child, a girl by the name of Rosanne, who was only a few months older than he. His sharp instincts had turned to the girl, and Oscar always did whatever the girl was doing. He slept when she slept, woke when she woke, fell ill and recovered when she did. Soon he was able to anticipate and predict her moods, and it eventually came to pass that he reversed roles and was actually able to do things before she even started to do them. To the outside world this all went unnoticed. His own emotional life remained a secret. He learned fast, observed the behavior of others around him, recognized the emotions and moods of other people and adjusted easily. Oscar Man was an uncomplicated child with a hearty laugh and a sunny disposition who showed no remarkable character traits.

He did not attract much attention, except through his cleverness. His open, warm expression never gave away the fact that he was always on the alert. He was much different from other kids, although this could not be deduced from his behavior. What made him so different remained safely hidden behind the wall he had put up between himself and others.

Still, he was a person who looked around himself in wonder and took notice of everything life had to offer without ever giving himself away. He knew how to conduct himself openly as a man while still keeping the most important part of his thoughts to himself.

He remembered an incident that had occurred in Switzerland the same summer he moved to America.

Someone he was unfamiliar with had passed away. His foster parents were dressed completely in black. There were more adults in the house where he lived than he had ever seen there before, and everyone was wrapped in deep mourning and sorrow. Rosanne and he had gone along with them on the long car ride through the mountains to the cemetery. At the churchyard, Anne and Herbert Vesper kept Rosanne between them, and a woman he had seen in the house earlier took him by the hand. They had stood outside; he remembered that the warm sun shone down on them from a clear sky, and he could see the mountaintops around him. He even remembered the name of the woman: Laura Langen. Her face remained hidden behind a black veil, but he could see that she had dark gray eyes, and her long blond hair hung over her shoulders. Together they stood among all the others around the grave and listened to the sonorous voice of a priest. Oscar still remembered much of what the man had said and could even still repeat, word for word, some of what he heard that day. What had been said about the hereafter, the beauty of heaven and the horrors of hell, had mostly slipped from his mind. He remembered the things that had touched him personally.

"What remains for us who are left behind are memories," the voice sounded. "Someone has left us, and a gap has been created by their passing that can never be filled again."

The warm hand of Laura Langen held his with unmoving fingers.

"All the wisdom a man has gathered during his earthly existence, he takes with him on his final journey," the priest went on. "That is why the newborn must learn everything all over again, for death wipes out all knowledge. No one can ever draw from the well that has been sealed by death."

Laura Langen's moist fingers squeezed the little hand of Oscar Man, and he could feel her fingers on his skin as her long nails pricked his flesh.

This was a crucial moment in his life. The woman kept staring straight in front of her as the priest gave him a piercing, fiery look.

"All that the dead ever was, all that he ever saw, all that he ever thought, now is gone. The train of thoughts has been stopped, the eyes shut for good. Everyone who is born must learn everything anew from the start. To crawl, to stand, to think and act, to speak and even to remain silent: these are all things that must be gathered again, for one cannot ask questions of a dead person. On our final journey, all our spiritual luggage will be taken along."

Again he looked at Oscar, and again Oscar felt the pressure of the woman's damp hand.

Instinctively, he kept his little hand still. The heat of the summer sun made him dizzy, but he managed to control himself. The sweat ran down his back as his bright blue eyes looked expressionlessly into the dark brown eyes of the priest. The woman stooped and whispered in his ear so that only he could hear her say, "Is this true, Oscar? Can you, for instance, look into the past and see what has happened?"

Once again he felt her tighten her grip

He turned his face toward her and gazed at the face behind the veil. Her slightly red lips had narrowed, and her glance was cold and gray. If he squeezed her hand now, it would be taken as a sign that they understood each other, but he knew he had to say something out loud. So, in a small, soft voice he asked, "Who is that man who is talking for so long?"

With an abrupt gesture, as if she was greatly disappointed and no longer found him interesting, she pulled her hand away from his.

"He was a good man," continued the priest. "And he was not afraid of meeting his creator."

That same summer Oscar crossed the Atlantic Ocean. He knew he had escaped from a great danger that afternoon in the churchyard. How it all fit together was still unclear to him. He was able to use his mind to look over an edge, stare into a depth or simply see things that others could not. Shivering from fear at the mere thought of that unknown world but curious nonetheless, he had allowed himself on several different occasions to open his mind up to whatever was hiding there, over the edge, in the depths. And it was not at all to his liking. It was an eerie, frightening zone he could never quite manage to visit entirely. Strange, how he could stare into a world that was not his, but here in the real world, in the house of his foster parents, he felt like a stranger more often than not.

He let the unknown realms that resided in his head rest. Even now, as an adult, he remained on his guard against everything and everyone and played a game that allowed him to lead his life as pleasantly as possible.

From a balustrade on the third floor of the palace, he had watched a performance in the garden below. A group of more than one hundred naked dancers entertained the guests. At the height of their performance, they climbed up on each other's shoulders and formed a towering pyramid that burst into pieces at the exact moment the music stopped. Oscar turned around and walked through a big, empty hall to an elevator door.

A few moments later, he was sliding horizontally and vertically through the extensive transport system and finally arrived in his own chambers.

When he had stood there by the balustrade a short while ago and watched the dancers, he had thought about that important moment in his youth at the cemetery, and he feared he was facing a night filled with frightening dreams. He stayed away from his bedroom for as long as possible, and when he finally did go, he took two girls with him to help keep his demons at bay.

They were good looking enough and cheerful and more than willing to spend the night with a prince.

Two days later, he went to the west side of the palace where the offices and residences of the work force were. The countless streets, detached houses and small castles that belonged to various shareholders and tycoons, all surrounded by beautiful gardens, gave the area the look of a city. Oscar had been able to arrive at his destination by sliding through the walls in an elevator, but the inhabitants on this side of the palace were not allowed to enter the family chambers.

Not many people recognized him. He wanted to go out incognito and without the twins, so he had made up his eyes in black mascara and had painted the left side of his face green and the right side red. On his head was a cap of white leather. He wore a colorful velvet jacket and black trousers stitched with little red stones. He looked just like a jester, and his fierce grimace made it highly unlikely that anyone would talk to him; if they did, he would offer a funny or sarcastic answer.

He wanted to see the bustle in the park firsthand, and since cars were not allowed to drive there, he had asked for a horse. In the stables just outside the palace gates, a groom stood ready with a saddled pinto. The stables held hundreds of saddle and cart horses, and there were well-kept coaches and even horse-drawn trains that could be pulled over a narrow-gauge railway. He made the grooms laugh by doing odd dance steps, and when he went outside with the pinto, he lithely swung onto the horse's back and stood up on the saddle.

After a bit, he lowered himself and pushed his feet into the stirrups. Tiny bells were attached to the halter and saddle, and the mane and tail were adorned with ribbons.

"Oscar! Wait for me!" came a voice from behind him.

He pulled up his horse and looked back.

Margaret Sharpe, the female tycoon who enjoyed the privileges of a royal princess at the court, came riding up to him on a fiery mustang. Her long dress of gold brocade flew back along her legs. She was the inseparable companion of his sister Johanna and his brother Jimmy; all three of them were still single, and together they organized meetings and feasts in their large halls where metallic nymphs and satyrs portrayed in massive sculptures enjoyed everlasting and obscene embraces.

Margaret was an elderly woman who still had a sprightly, almost youthful charisma. Whoever looked into her sparkling eyes forgot about time completely.

She came riding up alongside him and placed her hand on his arm. The last time he had seen her, at the dinner table in the great hall, she had been wearing her hair up. Now, however, her long locks danced across her back and shoulders. Oscar would much rather have remained alone, but now, since she was here, he found that he did not at all mind the company.

"Are you here without bodyguards?" he asked.

"I am not as famous as the members of your immediate family, Oscar," she answered with a smile. "I seldom leave the palace, and when I go down to New York City, I usually travel by helicopter. What do I have to be afraid of? A kidnapping? How exciting that would be!"

She gave him a wink and a coy smile. "I want to see for myself what is happening in our neighborhood. I believe we both had the same plan, except that I have chosen a far more fiery horse than you."

She allowed the mustang to trot a little and passed Oscar. His little pinto struggled to catch up with her.

Amusement tents had been put up all over the park grounds, and there were stalls and hastily set up pavilions constructed of wood and glass where one could get food and drink. Thousands of people paraded over the paths and through the labyrinths in their most beautiful clothes. At the Ferris wheel, people waited patiently in line for a place in one of the cabins. Margaret slowed her horse down and rode next to Oscar again.

"New York City is a madhouse," she said. "Businesses have been closed down, and everyone is in the streets partying. Imagine, Oscar, millions of people feasting at the expense of Man-Mandate Enterprises, and everywhere the name of your brother Ferdinand is being shouted with joy. Whatever happens in the city is world news! If I could only tell you what it costs to have the security troops standing by, to pay the catering industry to hand out food and drink for free, all in the name of Ferdinand. The parades, the music, the shows! Shall we go there together and plunge headlong into the bustling party?"

She shook her head so fiercely that her long hair whipped back and forth across her face. "No, no, never mind, Oscar. You are probably the least likely candidate for such an adventure. You are much too introverted to let yourself go entirely. Even now, you have hidden behind your painted face to make yourself unrecognizable, and you will almost certainly remain too inhibited to live it up in a never-ending celebration."

She was, without realizing it herself, one of the most representative women of the new times. She clung to life, lived for the moment and with her gorgeous appearance was always the center of attention. Then there was her businesslike side, which had given her such an important place at the court of one of the largest companies in the world.

Margaret Sharpe was an eccentric woman who played character roles in almost every circumstance and thoroughly enjoyed the game.

They slowed their horses as they reached an area where it was very busy. There was even a brief moment when they had to stop to allow a procession of people pass who were wrapped in scarlet garments and made their way through the crowds on wooden stilts that towered high above the ground.

Someone told them that the stilt-walkers had come all the way from Pennsylvania and only came down from their stilts to eat or sleep. Oscar leaned forward and called to one of them, "Why do you travel this way?"

"If you are really a jester, you should know the answer to that question, sir," replied the man. "Why must there always be a particular reason? What counts is the action, the movement, the game. And of course, the visual effect is important."

He made a pompous gesture to the passing procession. The red garments the people wore were all fitted with hoods. With jerky, jolting movements, the men and women passed by like mechanically driven, faceless puppets, and they sang a song composed of words that had no meaning.

The bells of the pinto jingled softly as Oscar maneuvered his mount through the crowd.

A parking lot on the outside of the area, where the road ended, was full of cars. They were decorated with copper, silver and golden ornaments. A group of people sat together in a grassy field enjoying the already warm morning sun. Oscar and Margaret hitched their horses there so that they could graze on the grass and then sat themselves down nearby under an oak tree.

"You see my sister Johanna almost every day," said Oscar. "Have you noticed that she is behaving rather strangely on occasion? Or can it be that she only does so around me?"

She carries so much weight on her shoulders, I think it would be more frightening if she acted normal," answered Margaret. "The big enterprises are responsible for the welfare of humanity in this part of the world and in Europe, along with scattered other territories. Comparatively speaking, there are few people at the top, and it is much more chaotic then you would think. Believe me, Oscar, I go through this myself every day."

Although it still was early, barbecues were being lit, and the stalls that served food were doing a booming business. Drinks were available everywhere. Girls walked around with baskets full of delicacies. On the other side of the field, people sat together on cast iron chairs and listened to an orchestra. The clear tones of violins were lifted and spread by a soft breeze.

"But when we were on the Ferris wheel, Johanna was raving about sheer nonsense! I couldn't make heads or tails of what she told me. After that, she rambled on about important business of which she thought I did not understand a thing. Hell! I couldn't even tell if she was talking to me or to herself. Then she began to feel anxious and nervous."

Margaret had been looking around while he was talking to her, but now, all of a sudden, he had her full attention.

"Oh, is that what you mean? Yes, yes, I have wondered about that too. I have heard her speak in riddles several times and so do Jimmy and Ferdinand. I have no explanation for it."

Directly in front of them, a man had broken through the crowd and was gasping for breath. He pushed forward until he had reached a place where he had a bit more freedom of movement. He wore a black jacket with a turned up collar, dark gray trousers and shoes with flattened toes. He was bald, except for a flossy rim around the underside of his skull that went down his temples, eventually turning into curly sideburns. He was a small man with a sharp nose. His small eyes rolled searchingly from left to right under snow-white eyebrows until he spotted a tall man in wide, purple, clownlike overalls.

Approaching, the small man ticked the taller one on the chest and started to talk to him. The man in the overalls shook his head, looked forlornly at an open bar where people were being handed large glasses of frothy beer and then slowly got down on his knees.

Oscar and Margaret watched as the smaller man climbed onto the shoulders of the other and was lifted up in the air when the big man stood up again. Margaret leaned against Oscar with her head comfortably resting on his shoulder.

"The most idle of all thoughts, I think, is that you see yourself as the center of everything," she said as she kept looking from the corner of her eye at the figure who was now raised above the crowd. "Do you understand what I'm saying, Oscar? You are like the sun, the center of the truth. And at the very moment that you burn out and close your eyes, everything will be gone forever. It is not just an idle thought; it is also a warm, reassuring idea. What you see around you is there only for you, and after your death there is nothing. For why should there be anything there when you are no longer able to see it? Everything exists because you exist; everything stops when you stop."

The tall man walked in ever-widening circles and thus had made room for himself and the man he carried on his shoulders. In this manner, he had caught the crowd's attention. His living burden had seen enough people were ready to listen and began his tirade. He gestured with his arms and then grabbed hold of the thin remnants of his hair with such strength that those watching thought that he would pluck them from his skull.

"Up to doom, with giant steps! Straight ahead to the verge of disaster! We can't wait until it comes to that, until the disaster occurs that has been brought down on our heads by our decadent behavior. Chaos is growing constantly, and we celebrate the final party with hundreds of millions of people gathered together. We flaunt and waste; we do everything in excess, and we find only ourselves to be of great importance. Everywhere I go, I see stampeding herds without leaders, the crying, jeering mass of drunks and madmen, people who have lost their way, unpredictable hordes of jesters and fools going from town to town chasing misfortune!

"Go back to your homes; get yourself together; go to work! Or better yet, first make a bonfire of your extravagant festive attire. You are people without control, people without power. It is the big companies who pull the strings and make all decisions for you. Power is for sale, and whoever has managed to buy enough of it is allowed to put a crown on his head. And yet we cheer for them and are their guests at the feasts of coronation. Not one of us should be here today."

The man did not listen to the crowd's objections. Anyone who actually dared to take him on must also find strong shoulders to be raised up on. For decades on end this had been the rule. After both parties had their say, there would be a fight of pushing and bumping, and whoever fell to the ground first would be ridiculed and abused, regardless of whom one felt the most sympathy for when it had still been a simple verbal assault.

Because the man in the overalls had not stopped for a moment, there was still room that could be used as a battleground. Margaret was on her feet and mingling with the others in order to follow the events that were unfolding. Oscar was still sitting under the oak tree when he saw a second figure towering over the heads of the crowd. He scrambled to his feet and went after Margaret.

A few minutes later, he had worked himself to the front row of the battleground; Margaret reached for his arm so she would have something to hold on to in all the jostling.

A lean, lanky boy stood unsteadily on his feet opposite the man in the overalls. He wore velvet trousers and suede boots on which silver coins tinkled. On his narrow shoulders sat a young woman who had provocatively torn her silk blouse open and with a broad smile proudly pushed her full breasts forward. Her long, bare legs were held at the ankles by the boy. She had curly red hair that hung way down her back. She asked the spectators for their responses by a show of gestures. Cheers went up, and there was a loud explosion of applause. Someone shouted that she must have her say and that the first disruptor of the festivities should bite the dust.

Oscar had seen her before. She was someone who he had not thought of for a long time, but who had always remained in his memory. It would only be a matter of seconds of deep thought before, he knew, he would recall her name. Then he could give her back her place in the parade of people he had met during his life.

Margaret stood on tiptoe, and he felt her warm breath on his ear as she said in a loud voice, "That's Angelina. Orville Hood's daughter. You know Orville from the station, don't you?"

He nodded, but her statement did not fill the gap in his memory. Orville Hood, the stationmaster, the big, laughing, stout man with rosy round cheeks, white uniform, cylindrical hat with tassel. Immediately he had a clear picture of him and, of course, remembered their recent encounter. No doubt Orville was married and had a family, but he had never heard about Angelina. Still, he recognized her. Without twitching a muscle of his face under his painted skin, his mind was shaking! Oscar Man was alarmed but stood strong against his burning emotions.

"Civilization needs a foundation," said the man in black who had finally noticed that he had an opponent. "The basis of civilization consists of knowledge and respect for the past, awe for our ancestors, discipline and spirit of enterprise. Every world has to be built up. Festivities without beginnings or endings weaken the nation as a whole. We have started to stagger, and it won't be long before we fall."

Angelina shook her head, and her beautiful red hair took on a life of its own. No doubt she had recently visited a salon, just as Margaret and all the other women had, to get herself a weeklong treatment that made the hair so long, luxuriant and healthy.

"Why should there be an end to the festivities?"

Her voice was clear.

"We are from the intervening period," she continued while the boy carried her on bent legs through the crowd. "Behind us lies the time of the magnificent machinery we could understand and even love."

Oscar smiled and pictured her father and the twinkle in his little eyes.

"The new technologies have all but taken work out of our hands. We have enough, probably too much, free time at our disposal, and the large conglomerates pay us to keep us satisfied and quiet. Who wants to be a link in a chain and never produce a whole product on his own? Who wants to go through life without ever undertaking something special? Who wants to be eternally replicable?"

"Everyone has his own place!" cried the man in black while he prodded the man beneath him with his heels, as if he were a horse, to go faster. "Every link in the chain is of importance!"

"Only to the owner of the chain, not to the individual link!" Angelina reacted.

The boy and the man began to circle around each other. Angelina crossed her arms in front of her firm breasts to receive the first push.

"Life has been created in the laboratories!" called Angelina. "Like the ancient alchemists, someone working with elixirs and brews suddenly had something swarming on the bottom of a glass beaker!"

She received the hard dig of an elbow and squeezed her legs tighter around the stumbling boy below.

"Now she's really raving!" cried the man and grinned at the crowd.

"On the contrary," Angelina defended herself, "I have already said that we are people from the intervening period. Once there was a time in which people were satisfied with their circumstances. They lived in a world that they could understand. In front of us lies the period and promise of eternal life. Someone already working on the immortality of each and every individual. Beyond the horizon lies a time in which no one has to close his eyes forever. But that period is still beyond our reach and will only dawn when our children's children populate this country. It is hard to accept that we were all born too early to lay claim to eternity. That is why it is wise to continue celebrating and keeping a smile on your face for as long as possible."

From every quarter people took her side. She had managed to put into words what everyone was feeling, and her beauty and spirit had infused her words with a magical glow that lifted them up to reveal instinctive pieces of wisdom. But the game was still not won, and both her opponents rushed forward. The big man tripped up the boy, and the man in black hammered his elbow against her supple breasts.

A few moments later, she lay in the grass being abused and hooted at by everyone. The balding man had himself carried around in triumph until his bearer knelt down and put him back on his feet.

Arm in arm, Margaret and Oscar went back to the mustang and the pinto.

"First, I want to have a bite to eat, then something to drink and after that I want to dance and have fun," said Margaret as she flung herself into the saddle. "Can I count on you as far as that is concerned, my dear friend?"

Oscar nodded, and his enthusiastic laugh bared his teeth between his curling lips. He screwed up his black-outlined eyes and said, "But of course!"

Only when she turned her back to him and he followed her, as he listened to the jingling bells of the horse, did his colored face stiffen. He passed the spot where Angelina had fallen and where people were pushing and shoving, showing off their fine clothes, searching for entertainment. He had recognized Rosanne, Rosanne Vesper, who was supposedly the child of Anne and Herbert from Switzerland: the girl who had been his friend, mentor and primary example of life. Was it possible to recognize a child, last seen at the age of seven, when she appeared as an adult before you? He was sure that Angelina Hood had once been Rosanne Vesper.

Oscar felt a strong need to initiate a thorough examination of this situation, but at the same time he knew he would never do so. He took life as it came to him and stepped aside when things became too personal and danger threatened. He lived a safe, albeit unexciting, life.

And so he ate, drank, danced and laughed with Margaret Sharpe and was part of the seething crowd in the park. As night fell and they waited for darkness, they watched as a twelve-foot tall robot slowly climbed the Ferris wheel. On his back was emblazoned the crowned letter *M,* one of the symbols of Man-Mandate Enterprises. High up in the dark, the robot climbed on top of one of the cabins, stretched his arms and jumped. As he plummeted to the ground, he burst into flames, and just before he hit the ground he exploded in a masterly display of fireworks. The trick was in the fact that the priceless animated robot, which did indeed climb the wheel, disappeared from view for a moment and at that point was switched with a cheap flammable copy, which was ignited and sent crashing down to earth.

Finally, the pair of unlikely compatriots headed back to the palace. Although Margaret had asked Oscar to be her protector for the day, she had managed to sneak away several times to throw herself into the arms of unknown, and uncaring, lovers. She looked tired now, and her clothes were torn to shreds. Soon after dark, the pinto was robbed of its silver bells, and drunken thieves had cast their eyes on the glass beads that adorned Oscar's pants, mistaking them for rubies. There had been numerous fights, which members of the palace guard had to be called in to break up. There were lights and fires everywhere, and shouts resounded above the music.

"I have enjoyed this," Margaret admitted. "I know now to find you when I need a gallant escort."

"And I will always be there for you," said Oscar in a solemn voice as he looked away from her.

Back in the stables, they turned over their mounts to the handlers to be unsaddled, groomed and fed. Because each lift in the palace carried only one person at a time, Oscar let Margaret go first. He bowed to her and waited until the doors opened again, got in and transported himself through the complicated system of metal tubes.

Once in his own apartment, he sat down behind an antique spinet and began to play passionately.

At the end of the eighteenth century, a virtuoso composer from Italy had put a melody on paper giving full expression to his feelings of joy. Over the ages it had never been played again, and the musical notation, the only example, had been lost. Still, Oscar Man was able to play it by heart, although he couldn't explain how it had come to be in his head.

* * *

Angus Sebastian was an athletic man in his forties with a square head and a chin like a brick. His ancestors had come from France, Portugal and Jamaica. He looked more like a fighter than a presidential candidate, and perhaps that was what made him so popular and increased his chances of ever moving into the White House. This democrat was idolized by everyone because he called a spade a spade and was not afraid to take drastic measures. It seemed that he preferred not to compromise and never ran from discussions or debates. But his election campaign was financed by Man-Mandate Enterprises, and if Ferdinand Man asked him to go to a television studio to tell the world that the sun circled around the earth, all pretense of maintaining his principles fell by the wayside and he would, unhesitatingly, obey the request. He knew if he did not his campaign funds would dry up faster than a wet sheet in the noonday sun.

Now he turned his massive head toward a camera, laughed amiably and waited for a sign from the director to begin his speech.

He found himself in a studio in New York City on the great day of the coronation. It was early morning, and he was the first of a large group of politicians and celebrities who were to say many wonderful things about Ferdinand.

Angus sat behind a walnut desk, and behind him was the American flag. It looked as if he was in his own office. The sign from the director was given; Angus clasped his hands in front of him on the desk and looked into the camera with the eyes of a faithful bulldog. It was a live broadcast, and he was being seen in countless living rooms and on gigantic TV screens set up all over New York City.

"This is an unforgettable day," Angus began in his deep voice. "A day for all Americans to be proud of. Our government does much good work and will always do so, but the nation longs for the warmth of a royal house. New York is not the first state to make the decision to reintroduce royal status. Other states have led the way. Now this important day has finally come, and I consider it a great honor to be the first speaker allowed to extend my best wishes to Ferdinand Man and his family. Our society, this gigantic melting pot, whose contents remain liquefied by the flames of hope, trust and love has produced a democratic government. This administration has given us leaders and protectors. The royal house gives us the trusted representative, the father of the nation. I congratulate Ferdinand Man on the great status kingship brings, just as I congratulate all New York on this milestone in history."

Moments later Angus Sebastian found himself in a corridor outside of the studio, which was located on the twelfth floor of an office building. With his hands in the pockets of his blue velvet suit, he looked very much like a giant toddler. Angus stared down at the street below where the celebrating masses flowed through the streets like old, sick blood through a narrowed vein. They celebrated at the expense of Man-Mandate Enterprises, and when everything went smoothly and they were happy, they would raise their voices in tribute to him.

At the end of the street, the face of another speaker appeared on a large outdoor screen. Joey Nadi, a popular singer and movie star, sang the praises of his friend Ferdinand Man from the same studio where Angus Sebastian was. In the corridor he had seen Renzo Copeland and Martha Manolow walking around, the heavyweight boxing champion and the most celebrated hostess in the land, who had come to have their say.

Later there was a parade in Manhattan, and the army had been brought in to prevent the millions of people in the streets from crushing and suffocating each other. The Man family and their friends and confidants rode through the streets of the city in open cars. Earlier that morning during a meeting of shareholders in one of the many office buildings the company owned, Ferdinand, wearing a long coat of imitation fur and gold chains around his neck, had placed a crown upon his head.

Oscar Man was sitting in the back of an automobile with vertical exhausts and high, spoked wheels. He wore sunglasses behind which he closed his eyes every now and then.

Next to him sat the presidential candidate Angus Sebastian, who was enjoying all the attention. He waved and rose to his feet several times to bow to the throngs of well-wishers. Angus shook the hands of many strangers and responded to their cheering by waving his arms.

His televised speech had strengthened his bond with the Man family, but it was Ferdinand Man who would be able to make the most of it. It was the first time that it had been said aloud that this new kingship involved an American state and not just a tiny island in the Pacific Ocean. The magical words re-establishing royalty had been uttered by a presidential candidate, and for Angus Sebastian they were words that might finally give him the presidency.

They left Manhattan in a fleet of helicopters owned by Man-Mandate Enterprises. A second parade started at the palace and proceeded on the horse tramway to the great metal cathedral. Along both sides of the railway stood armed guards, and behind them the people crowded to catch a glimpse of Ferdinand Man and his retinue.

The front tram was moved by twenty colossal black English shires with white stockings. Between its ears each horse wore a small sculpture symbolic of one of the larger enterprises, all of whom had important representatives present. The front horses wore an upright man in armor, the symbol of the Man clan, and right behind them came a horse wearing a sailor with hair waving in the wind, the mascot of Cabo de Barra, paired with a horse bearing the naked nymphs of Richthausen Gold Ltd. Behind these could be seen the rampant wolf of Fenrir International, the Roman god of the underworld and fortune Dis Pater for the European concern of the same name and many others.

The biggest surprise of the day was certainly the appearance of the mightiest man on earth: Walter Krocht of Cabo de Barra. He was well over six feet tall and weighed over three hundred pounds. He had a gray beard and short gray hair. Whosoever had the courage to look him directly in the eye could not do so for more than a few seconds. To look at him was to fear him. His presence and power were unequaled, and people bowed to him wherever he went. Krocht wore an odd, hairy, black coat and high boots covered with precious stones. His numerous bodyguards had trouble keeping up with him when he walked, for he took long, mighty strides. He was in the front carriage on the way to the cathedral talking to Ferdinand Man.

Ferdinand was tall and lean with timid but highly intelligent eyes and an indomitable nature that seldom allowed him to remain in one place any longer than absolutely necessary. During his conversation with Krocht, he drummed his fingers on his thighs and repeatedly looked outside.

A colorful group of men and women passed through the open gates of the cathedral. Filming inside was not permitted as this was a ceremony to be witnessed by only those fortunate enough to have been invited. Oscar Man barely noticed what went on around him, and he hardly understood what was being said by the various speakers; the acoustics in the cathedral were the one thing that had been overlooked, and echoes bounced all around. He stood and bowed when Ferdinand Man had himself crowned for the second time that day.

A deafening cheer burst out when the procession emerged again and gathered near the railway to wait for the horse trams. All the guests were surrounded by bodyguards, and Oscar saw the twins standing amongst the security people who worked at the palace. Richard and Jay Jay Wright wore light green uniforms with high boots that went halfway up their thighs making them look like musketeers.

A helicopter descended from the sky, and the spectators behind the guards had to make space to allow it to land. Oscar recognized the chopper; it was the lizard that was flown by Stan Woodring and Francis Finnigan, who had brought him from New York City to the station near the palace just a few days ago.

Oscar stood next to Margaret Sharpe, who wore a wide hoop skirt and an enormous hat, which flapped in the wind. He was about to say something to her, but at that moment he saw Richard and Jay Jay reach for their automatic pistols.

They fell to their knees, aimed their weapons and fired. Margaret started to scream. Oscar felt as if all the power had vanished from his body, and it was all he could do to keep himself from falling. The bullets hit Walter Krocht. The hairy coat instantly became a bloody mess, and his face became unrecognizable and equally bloody. His bodyguards had reacted much too slowly. There was nothing they could do to save him. He spat blood and landed with a loud thud on the ground. The twins kept on shooting and also hit several men of the guard. Then they began to run, and although they had been wounded by returning gunfire, they managed to hoist themselves up into the chopper that hovered right above the ground.

The lizard took off in the direction of the Ferris wheel, gathering speed. Thousands of marksmen fired pistols and rifles, and there was even the sound of heavier artillery being fired. Riddled with bullets, the machine began to burn, smoke and quiver. The pilot, Woodring or Finnigan, tried to keep the chopper in the air, and for a moment it looked as if they might make it, but then it crashed into the Ferris wheel. A loud explosion ended the lives of the pilots along with those of the twins.

In the chaos and panic that broke out, only Oscar remained standing there motionless.

"I believe I'm going to vomit," he said in a soft voice to no one special.

At the Ferris wheel people had been wounded by the flying wreckage of the chopper. Again helicopters appeared, but this time they belonged to the emergency services from the palace. Bodyguards, members of the Man family, shareholders and tycoons formed a circle around the man on the ground who, curled up in his hairy coat, looked like a slaughtered, bloody buffalo.

"Oscar," said Margaret Sharpe, who still was right next to him.

She looked at him with big, frightened eyes.

"Do you realize what has happened? A greater disaster could not be imagined. Walter Krocht of Cabo de Barra—assassinated! Maybe it would have been better for us all if we had been swept off the face of the earth at the same time. Especially for you."

Her last words made him look up in amazement as if he had been sleeping and had just awakened from a horrible dream.

"Margaret, I—"

He got no further. He could not collect his thoughts, and he did not know what to do now. He understood all too well what had happened. Walter Krocht had been murdered in front of the eyes of the world. There were countless cameras trained on him, and several television crews had been ready for when the procession returned from the metal cathedral.

"Oscar," said Margaret again, and when their eyes met, she moved her head slightly to one side.

Oscar wasn't frightened by the sight of the guns and rifles trained on him from all sides by the guards. What really scared him was the long, lean, trembling finger of Ferdinand Man pointed directly at him.

Chapter Three

The Lawsuit

"It's much safer for you in here than it is outside," said Alec Davis hopping along oddly as he tried to keep up with Oscar's rapid pacing.

Alec was a tiny man, wafer thin. His prison clothes, an ill-fitting T-shirt and baggy flannel trousers, fluttered around him. Oscar was wearing exactly the same clothing and shoes, but a number of sizes larger.

The penitentiary complex where they were being held had been built about three years earlier. It sat on the New Jersey side of the Hudson River, across from Manhattan, but Oscar had never been able to catch even a glimpse of the river.

He was in a cell by himself and each day was given the chance to breathe a bit of fresh air in an exercise yard that was twenty yards by twelve yards and was spanned across the top by a latticework of black iron, which made Oscar feel like a caged beast every time he looked up.

"They would kill you if you went outside," said Alec Davis. "And a bullet would be merciful, if you consider what would happen to you if a mob got its hands on you. They would simply tear you to pieces."

Oscar was always astonished at who his company was when he was walking in the yard. He had walked with a murderer from Boston, a crook from Brooklyn and a businessman from Manhattan who claimed to have poisoned his partner. Alec Davis was a drug dealer from the Bronx, who had become addicted himself and had been in such bad shape physically and financially that an armed bank robbery had seemed to be the only way to pay off his debts. The job was a complete failure, though, and he had been arrested and convicted.

Oscar trusted no one and was well aware of the fact that the other prisoners with whom he was allowed contact were all pawns who had been instructed to try and get Oscar to open up to them. He had the feeling that Alec Davis would not be in a cell that night, but rather in a fancy restaurant somewhere reporting to someone over dinner what he and Oscar had discussed during their exercise period.

The principal person to spearhead the efforts to obtain information from Oscar would more than likely be Algernon Sparks the homicide officer from the NYPD, but Cabo de Barra was certainly mighty enough to have infiltrators inside the prison, and he knew that he could not underestimate his own family as well.

"I know," he responded to Alec's statement with a sigh. "There is nowhere I can go and expect a friendly reception. My lawyer Katja Donahue keeps me informed about the latest developments in the case. There is no place on earth that I would be welcomed right now."

"I long for my freedom more and more," said Alec as he struggled to keep up with Oscar. "I want to go to a couple of wild parties again, get shit-faced drunk and find some strangers to sleep with. And once I had my fling and scratched all my itches, I would move to another town, change my name and start a brand-new life. No one would ever see my face in the Bronx again!"

Oscar turned around as he got closer to the wall and began to walk a little bit slower now, but since he wasn't talking much, Alec continued, "I almost got away with that bank job. I had picked out a real cherry. An affiliate of the big European banking conglomerate Dis Pater. I was armed to the teeth and had taken three hostages. We both know very well—hell, man, you probably know better than I do—what these big companies have done. They've grabbed all the power for themselves, and their owners run the world. They own everything. My addiction was out of control and so was the amount of money I owed. I was so far gone that I wasn't afraid of anything, and lemme tell ya, Oscar, that combination can make a man dangerous. No bank would lend me a penny, so I decided to get the money I needed my way—steal it! I think you know what I'm talking about when I say that none of these big corporations—Dis Pater, Fenrir, Cabo, Fortuna Fund, Man-Mandate, Syrinx Colorado or any of the others—will give anyone a break who won't do things their way. You can do it their way, or you can try and do it your way. And if you try to do it your way, you're gonna lose. Well, I tried it my way, and you see what it got me. When I was in that bank, right before they kicked the crap outta me and arrested me, I probably felt exactly like you do."

Oscar stopped abruptly and looked down at the smaller man.

"What do you mean by that?" he asked.

"If Carl Holdorf himself, that fat cat from Dis Pater, had walked in at that very moment, I would have had the balls to kill him right then and there."

He laughed at Oscar, and his eyes sparkled.

"But of course, he didn't walk in. He was sitting far, far away from there in his fancy office in Vienna or just hanging out comfortably at one of his European estates. I hated anybody and anything that had anything to do with this big money, and I was going to teach them a lesson. I was going to show them that a small fish like me could make a big splash in their pond and get away with it. You have always sat real close to the well from where the power springs forth, and you could take your time and wait patiently. You could wait for your chance to take revenge, and when you realized that Walter Krocht was going to be in your neck of the woods, in your neighborhood, that's when you instructed your bodyguards to—"

He didn't finish his sentence and slowly shook his head.

"I wonder," said Oscar, "if my lawyer would find anything if I asked her to check and see if there had been an attempted bank robbery recently of an affiliate of Dis Pater in the Bronx and if the name Alec Davis was at all connected with it."

"Well, I suppose you could do that," Alec said. "All she has to do is to look for my name on the police blotter for that day and then trace the case through the courts."

Oscar nodded.

"But the man who really owns that name would probably be considerably taller than you, don't you think? A little coward like you trembles at the mere thought of a weapon, let alone using one. You try to get me to say things that aren't true, and you are far too eager to be my friend and confidant. It's true my bodyguards killed Walter Krocht; I was standing right there. It was the first time I had ever been so close to him and, as far as I knew, I had no reason at all to get farther away from him. At the beginning of our conversation you made a statement, and you were absolutely right when you said that it's safer for me inside these prison walls than it is on the streets."

Earlier on in the conversation it was difficult to determine whether or not this little man could get any of the prison guards to appear in a heartbeat if he needed one, but you would have to have been either a blind man or a fool not to realize that it was within a couple of seconds of speaking that he was led inside. Oscar Man never saw him again in the yard or, for that matter, anywhere else.

Now he was alone again, and he walked up and down at a calmer pace with his hands clasped behind his back. Every now and then he looked up at the gray sky through the black latticework. Loud, squawking seagulls flew around, and not too far off in the distance he heard the chugging sound of a ship's engines: indications that the river could not be far away from here.

Outwardly, Oscar seemed relaxed; his face was smooth and friendly, and the look in his eyes was one of calm resignation. But behind those same eyes the constant pressure caused by frantic fear had given him a violent headache.

He had become very fond of Richard and Jay Jay Wright, who had always been a part of the palace guard and had been placed under his command by his sister Johanna. He and the twins had traveled all over Europe, and for the longest time they had been inseparable. There had never been the relationship of a prince and his subjects between them: they were friends. Oscar was the impudent, illegitimate son, the undisciplined jester, and the twins had been his buddies and had shared in all his pleasures.

As he thought of them, he could see them in his mind's eye in countless places and situations: sitting in the front seat of an automobile driving over European roads, laughing together in a restaurant or bar at a full table, walking out in front of him to clear the way through the hustle and bustle of a street party. They had become fast friends, and together they spent his money and enjoyed life. Inevitably, his thoughts then focused on that unreal moment after the coronation of Ferdinand as everyone was leaving the cathedral. He had spoken about this so many times during the interrogations in front of policemen, one of whom was always Officer Algernon Sparks and during which Oscar was quite often connected to a lie detector.

"All of a sudden they had weapons in their hands. They fired at Walter Krocht, and I can recall very clearly the expression of amazement on his face before it was torn apart by bullets. I was physically unable to move and was afraid that I was going to faint. I saw the big man of Cabo de Barra spit blood and heard a gurgling sound as he gasped for breath as if his lungs were filled with blood. Jay Jay and Richard kept on shooting, even as he began to fall, and I am sure they hit other people as well. One was returning fire at them. They tried to bridge the distance between Walter Krocht's dead body and the chopper as the bullets tore into their flesh. They must have been as good as dead when they finally collapsed in the lizard. Shots rang out from all sides. The noise was earsplitting! I stood there watching, paralyzed, as the lizard hit the Ferris wheel.

"From that moment on everything becomes vague, but I remember that I still felt dizzy and had to struggle to stay conscious and on my feet. Margaret Sharpe said something to me, and I realized that I was in danger. My bodyguards had murdered Krocht! Weapons were trained on me from all sides, and a furious Ferdinand pointed at me. I was certain that I would be killed right there, riddled with hundreds of bullets. Choppers had suddenly appeared, coming at us from the direction of the palace. Margaret was still with me, holding me by the arm, as I was led away. To my left, to my right, in front of me and behind me, I was surrounded by guards. I was brought to the palace by helicopter but was not allowed to go to my own chambers. I was kept in a waiting room on the ground floor right next to the reception hall and the platforms where the trains stop. Someone from the police showed up, and I was brought down to the city. It is still a mystery to me what became of Richard and Jay Jay, but I must assume that they are as dead as anyone ever was."

No one could understand why he didn't mind the endless, seemingly everlasting questioning, but the answer was relatively simple. He did not want to have the time to think about his predicament. He looked forward to the visits of Katja Donahue, his attorney, who kept him informed about the state of affairs of his case and brought him the latest news from the outside world. He even enjoyed the conversations with men like Alec Davis in the yard. The scenarios that ran through his mind were much worse than the reality of the situation, and he would even rather talk to Algernon Sparks about the death of the twins then to be left alone in the solitude of his cell.

He had great difficulty accepting the facts as they were, and he feared the finger of Ferdinand Man that had been pointed at him so threateningly, but what happened in his head when he was alone on his plank bed was far worse.

He was besieged by feelings that he could share with no one.

Oscar saw two armed guards enter the exercise yard, and he quickly grabbed a few last deep breaths of cold, fresh air. He was escorted to his cell, and the heavy metal door locked behind him. He kept his face emotionless and expressionless, for he was never sure if anyone was watching him; it was very possible that his jailers could see and hear him even in here.

The cell was bare except for the bed, a chair and a bookshelf.

Oscar Man had never been lonesome. There had always been people around him with whom he could talk. He used to go to parties and stay until he was too tired to stand then he could count on Richard and Jay Jay to make sure that he got to wherever it was he was going. He always woke up in some hotel bed or in his own house in Switzerland, often with a beautiful woman lying beside him. Oscar had been the tireless jester who led a life that seemed to consist of parties and money.

Alone now in his cell, he had only his thoughts for company. There were no longer any diversions or pleasure-filled escape routes. The door remained locked, the window barred and dark. He could do nothing except learn to deal with his tormented thoughts. His nights were long and tedious, and he rarely slept for more than three hours each day. The rest of his time, save for his brief daily exercise period, was spent lying on his hard bed as quietly as possible. When he closed his eyes, his spirit wandered and entered a strange world that was not his own—a world that frightened him and gave him horrible headaches.

Today, back in his cell after his walk with Alec Davis, he was overcome by a choking feeling of claustrophobia. He licked his lips and tried desperately to keep his composure, constantly aware that he was being observed. His mind centered on a vague figure who penetrated his mind and with bold paces crossed the border from the subconsciousness to the conscious. The form became clearer, the face more familiar, and with a shock, it came to Oscar that he knew this man no longer dwelled amongst the living.

In his silent, fevered thoughts a name came to him.

Emlyn Gray.

Oscar closed his eyes and desperately hoped that he had not called the name out loud. He withdrew into himself and, with eyes still closed, was able to focus on Emlyn more clearly. The man had blood on his hands, and Oscar watched it drip down along the length of his fingers as he walked through a field of red, yellow and blue flames. His torn shirt and pants were red with glistening blood as was the bottom of his beard. He was a middle-aged man with beady, peering eyes; thin lips; thick, curly hair and a moustache and beard. Oscar was fairly sure that he knew him personally. The man was forming words while looking at Oscar out of the corner of his eye, but Oscar heard no sound, although, for some reason, he knew how his voice should sound. Emlyn Gray gestured with his hands, and blood splashed from his fingertips. Oscar had the eerie notion that if he sat himself down at a table with a blank piece of paper and pen, he would find that more information would be available to him. He believed that if he grasped the pen in his right hand and kept his eyes closed, he would begin to automatically write what it was that Gray wanted him to know but could not communicate to him now. Although the man disgusted him, he recognized his physical appearance, just as his manner of walking and gesturing were familiar. Still, a barrier remained between them that could not be broken.

Suddenly, Emlyn Gray was engaged in combat with ghostly figures whose faces remained vague. He had a weapon in his hand that could have been either a dagger or a sword, and they were locked in a battle to the death. The flames became waves of dark red blood, and as Oscar swallowed out of reflexive fear, he tasted the blood on his tongue.

He sat up straight with a start and gasped for breath. The sweat trickled down his temples and chin, and his heart beat rapidly. He had always feared that something like this would happen to him, that an evil, sadistic, murdering monster such as Emlyn Gray would find a way into his mind and show him things that repulsed him. It took all of his self-control to keep himself from jumping off his bed and smashing his head into the wall.

Oscar heard the door to his cell being unlocked. He swung his legs over the edge of the bed, gripped the edge as if he were sitting in a rocking boat and waited for the door to swing open. In his present circumstances, it really didn't matter to Oscar who entered his cell; after all, there was nothing he could do about it anyway. But this time he was concerned that whoever it was might have heard him saying the name of his terror—Emlyn Gray.

It was the same two guards who had escorted him back to his cell earlier. Now, however, they led him out of the cell and through the corridors of the prison until they came to and ascended a stone staircase. At the top, he was shown into a big office. The guards retreated to the corridor and closed the door behind him.

He was confronted by an enormous wooden desk with an empty, high-backed, brown leather chair on the opposite side. In one corner of the office sat a few people in comfortable armchairs. He knew all of them.

Elmore Farrell the prison governor was there, as was Algernon Sparks, the homicide officer and Katja Donahue, his lawyer. They were all sitting quietly drinking coffee. Farrell gestured invitingly for Oscar to take the remaining empty seat.

"Oscar Man, the prince," he said. "Take a seat, Oscar, and watch; just watch for a moment. I am going to show you old news, but to you it will be new and hopefully very gratifying!"

A panel in the wall slid silently aside, and Oscar saw a commentator standing in a New York street. It looked as if she were present in the office; she was a three-dimensional beauty with long, dark blond hair that waved in the wind. From behind her came the tumultuous sounds of the passing, feasting crowds.

"Cabo de Barra has informed us that they see no reason to any longer suspect or hold Prince Oscar Man in the murder of their leader Walter Krocht. A spokesman for the multinational corporation has said that even though they have not yet recovered from the loss of their leader and still have not found a successor, for the time being a team of twelve of the foremost tycoons from the company will be working together to replace Walter Krocht. They will do their utmost to get the company back on track with the rest of the world markets. This same spokesman has firmly stated that the prince is *not* guilty of the death of Cabo de Barra's mightiest man. Not long ago, I had a talk with this spokesman Isodore Clement, important fragments of which I will share with you all in just a minute. In the meantime, New York is celebrating once again, and I want to show you pictures of that."

The panel in the wall closed again, and the monitor was once more concealed. Katja Donahue, her hair worn up over her sea green eyes, had risen to her feet, and she now embraced Oscar. She wore a long, gold-colored dress, and around her wrists jingled golden bracelets.

"You are free," she said.

She sat down again, and the governor told Oscar, "Without a doubt, you have been one of our stranger guests. That is what I call all our prisoners—guests because most of them eventually leave here. Some, of course, get to leave earlier than others."

He was a tall and dark man of African and Spanish blood, and he constantly smiled. His big, round eyes were dark brown with long lashes that fluttered continually. His moustache was short with little black curls.

"We have extended to you exceptional hospitality at the request of your sister Johanna. My friend here Mr. Sparks made use of your time here for countless interrogations because Cabo de Barra had put heavy pressure on us to get the truth from you, and until they were satisfied, requested that you remain behind locked doors. Legally, we really did not have a leg to stand on, and your lawyer Mrs. Donahue could have gotten you out of here much earlier, since she is in the service of your sister Johanna, but that is all moot now. Now that Cabo de Barra has publicly stated that you are no longer under suspicion, you are, as Mrs. Donahue has already said, free to go."

Farrell poured a cup of coffee and pushed it toward him. Oscar sighed softly and deeply, took the cup and began to stir it with a little spoon.

"The world really has been turned upside down for a while, Oscar," said Katja Donahue. "There was quite a panic when the various conglomerations adopted a hostile attitude toward each other. Not only Cabo de Barra toward Man-Mandate Enterprises but the other international corporations felt that they had to take sides in the matter, as did all the ranking tycoons. Everyone agrees that Walter Krocht was the most important and influential man of his time, and his death was not taken lightly. Believe me, Oscar, while you spent your time here in loneliness, there was an army of detectives, and an even larger group of lawyers, busy trying to map out your life. Almost every person you ever shook hands with—or for that matter even looked at—was questioned. You, on the other hand, were limited to dealing only with Detective Sparks and me."

"This is where you were the safest, trust me," said Elmore Farrell closing his brown eyes like a contented tomcat. "Your sister wanted to keep you unreachable to everyone, and Cabo de Barra insisted that you remain in one place so that the police could drop in and question you whenever they pleased."

"What made Cabo change its mind?" Oscar wanted to know.

"Some think that it was brought about through intense pressure by a delegation from Man-Mandate," replied Katja. "Jimmy Man went to see them along with Hugh Willis a major stockholder and the presidential candidate Angus Sebastian."

Oscar nodded. He knew both men. Willis had been present at the dinner in the palace after his recent return from Paris. Sebastian had been sitting with him in the back of an automobile during the parade through New York City and was present at the coronation.

"I'm sure," Katja continued, "that it is due to their own investigations that you have been exonerated. While you sat alone in your cell, everyone else was poking around in your past. Your penthouse in Manhattan, your little palace in Greenwich Village, your house on West End Avenue, everything must have been gone through ten times or more. Your servants complained bitterly because everything had to be straightened up over and over again. They followed your tracks to Europe and ended up in Switzerland but never found anything to indicate that you had planned to commit murder."

"So the investigation has stopped?" Oscar asked.

Sparks leaned forward in his chair.

"As far as Cabo de Barra is concerned it is, and the fact that they are giving you the benefit of the doubt is being shouted from the rooftops so that there's no longer any danger for you in the streets."

"Benefit of the doubt?" said Katja Donahue, incensed. "They declared him innocent."

"All right, all right," said the officer. "For us, though, it is far from over. Our investigation will continue, and we may need your time, your cooperation and your memory."

He scratched his short, bristly hair and with his head down looked at Oscar from under his blond eyebrows. He was a sinewy man of medium height and wore a simple gray suit.

"It is striking," he continued, "that all the people we have grilled have pulled together in your defense. Oscar Man, the prince, the jester has gotten away with this murder on all fronts. It seems as if everyone involved learned their lessons . . . and stories . . . well."

He got a look of warning from Katja Donahue, but he could care less.

"Margaret Sharpe is the only exception. I have great admiration for that woman, and I have listened to her very carefully. She is the only one who has been able to find contradictions in Oscar Man's life. Here is a man totally withdrawn into himself, a sophisticated, well-read philosopher who is also the central figure at all kinds of festivities and easily plays the part of a jester. She spent a day with him indulging in the festivities in the parks surrounding the Man palace where she also happens to be living. Oscar was her gallant escort who did his best to please her without really enjoying himself. How can this be explained? With a smile, Margaret offered as a solution that this is the nature and fate of the jester. The sad face behind the laughing mask—the tears of a clown. I am always extra alert when a suspect appears to have a split personality."

Katja Donahue stood up and walked to Elmore Farrell's desk.

"All my client has to do is sign a few papers," she said, her golden bracelets jingling as she pointed to a small pile of papers. "Let's get this over with so he change his clothes and get out of here."

* * *

Katja Donahue now sat behind the wheel of an inconspicuous car. In front of and behind them were cars carrying security personnel who worked for the Man family. They drove from New Jersey back to New York, headed in the direction of the palace. Oscar, wearing a leather cap and sunglasses, sat beside her and listened to everything she had to say. She told him all about the impressive funeral of Walter Krocht, which had been held in Atlanta, Georgia. She had told him about it before while he was still being detained, but each time she told the story she remembered something else. She had been there herself as a member of a large delegation sent by the family. Everyone, especially Ferdinand and Jimmy Man, had been afraid of another murderous attempt on the royalty. Even around the grave an uncomfortable atmosphere hung over them. Nothing had happened, however, and everyone had returned safe and sound, deeply impressed by all the ceremonies.

After Katja had finished retelling the story and had been silent for a while, Oscar said, "I want to return to Europe as soon as possible. It seems to me that I would be much safer there. I will stay in the palace for a while so I can consult with Johanna, and then I'm off to Switzerland and—"

"It won't be that easy," Katja interrupted him.

Her voice sounded unexpectedly sharp, and he was immediately on the alert.

"There is going to be an internal lawsuit. It is the intention of the family that you go to Fenrir City in Nevada."

He raised his eyebrows and thought of the symbol of the rampant, monstrous wolf.

"I have no business there. And what exactly do you mean by an internal lawsuit?"

"Fenrir intercedes for and receives people from your family and from Cabo. As your lawyer I will come with you and will be at your side constantly. Witnesses will be called, and you can be sure that the lawyers from Atlanta will not deal gently with you. A real jury will not be impaneled, but when all the hearings are behind you, the delegations of the three enterprises will gather. We still cannot be certain of your fate."

"But if I'm no longer considered a suspect," said Oscar in astonishment, "I can come and go as I please—there is no law that says I have to go to Nevada if I choose not to do so."

"That is true," said Katja. "I can pull over right here and let you go, if that is what you wish, but I'm sure you know as well as I do that the conglomerates have stood miles above the law for many years now. You are still a member of the Man family, even if you are the bastard son without any business skills, and you'll have to justify your reasons to the tycoons. You owe it to your family who wants to clear their family name of all blame and shame. So please, don't talk to me about the laws that exist to protect ordinary people, Oscar, for you are not an ordinary person!"

The cars all came to a halt at the station where the Dragon stood ready along a platform. Along with Katja, Oscar stepped into a luxurious coach.

Once in the palace, after having thanked Katja for all her help, he walked to an elevator and indicated that he wanted to go to the chambers of his sister Johanna. He expected to arrive in one of her waiting rooms where he was about to tell the servants to announce him, but when the doors opened after the rapid trip, he saw before him the hall that led to his own chambers. He knew immediately that parts of the palace had been made unavailable to him. His chambers were deserted. So this was his welcome after his long, lonely time of imprisonment!

There had not even been a helicopter sent for him to fly him to the palace. Katja had brought him to the trains in her car, and on the platform and in the palace, he had not been -welcomed by anyone. Oscar wandered through different chambers, thinking. He wanted to contact Cathy Wheeler at his penthouse in Manhattan, to ask her to find out who Emlyn Gray was, but he was afraid that his conversations would be eavesdropped upon.

I won't be here for very long, he thought to himself. *In a little while, I shall go over to the side of the palace where the apartments and shops are, find a good restaurant and stay there for as long as possible. And only after I'm too full to take another bite or sip, will I come back here to sleep.*

He undressed, took a bath, selected a red velvet suit from the closet and found a new pair of boots. He stepped into the elevator, indicated where he wanted to go and after a trip of about two minutes, he stepped back in his own chamber! After further efforts to reach the other side of the palace failed, he attempted to return to the trains. He thought that if he could get out of the palace he could find the stationmaster Orville Hood and ask him a couple of questions about his daughter Angelina. But no matter what he did, he was returned to his own rooms. He was still a prisoner.

His cell in the prison along the Hudson in New Jersey had been exchanged for a deluxe cell in the chambers in the palace. Oscar went out into the hallway and began walking through the corridors. Maybe he could get somewhere where he could find food, drink and friendly companionship. He walked across the marble floors, past the clusters of bronze and iron sculptures and along the walls covered with surrealistic paintings, but there was no sign of any other living soul. The corridors all ended at big, wooden locked doors. Even the doors that led to the chambers where the other people in the family lived were closed to him, and kicking them fiercely brought no response.

Back in his apartment again, he rang for servants to bring him food and keep him company, but there was no answer to his repeated summons. Oscar entered his own gigantic kitchen where there was a marble chimney, and the ceiling was five yards high. There were cupboards and freezers full of food, and as he began to prepare a meal, he suddenly felt very tired and shaky, unsteady on his feet. Maybe if he ate something he would feel a little bit better.

The part of his chambers that was located on the fifth floor of the palace had no windows. Oscar went to a section of the suite from where a glass veranda looked out upon a square shaft. When he bent far enough forward and looked up with his cheek pressed against the glass, he could see high, barred windows behind which lights were shining. The roof of the veranda was made of colored glass, which he could not see through. Oscar opened a window and leaned out. Many stories above him, where the shaft opened out onto a flat roof, he saw a square piece of the starlit evening sky.

He realized that it was already very late. He also realized that it would be impossible to climb up or down the walls. When he looked up again, he saw a zeppelin float slowly through the sky, darkening the shaft even more. Dim light shined through the small windows of the blimp's cabin. A few moments later, the big airship had disappeared, and he was able to see the stars again.

Oscar stayed awake for as long as he could, drinking deep ruby Port wine. When he finally decided to go to bed, he fell asleep immediately. He began to dream about Emlyn Gray but was shocked out of sleep when he licked his lips and tasted blood. Sitting bolt upright, he began to cough. He wiped his mouth with the back of his hand and turned on the light to see if his fingers were red with blood. His dream—no, his nightmare—had been full of slaughter, but he could not remember if Emlyn Gray had been solely responsible for the bloodbaths or if he himself also had a hand in it.

Oscar could not shake the feeling that he had been drinking blood. He got out of his bed and poured himself another glass of Port. The same panic that had seized him in Elmore Farrell's prison had possession over him once again. He emptied the glass and for the second time that night roamed the hallways of the palace where the lights now burned day and night. He ran up and down the corridors, knocking over sculptures and kicking all the doors. He no longer cared whether or not anyone was watching him. He did not need a key to open his own door since the lock on his door was coded to the touch of his own hand. All of the other doors remained closed to him, just as his door remained locked if someone other than himself, except for properly appointed household staff or authorized palace occupants, touched it.

He sorely wanted to get in contact with Cathy, but instead he returned to his bed and tried to get some sleep. It took quite some time before he nodded off, but at least now the bad dreams let him be.

* * *

Fenrir City was located in the desert near Las Vegas in an area where, years ago, a great number of nuclear tests had been conducted. Fenrir International owned the largest number of airports out of all the multinationals, and to go hand in hand with that, they also owned most of the aircraft factories. They heavily invested in the aerospace industry in general and were extremely involved with the launching of satellites. Las Vegas business was also in the hands of the company as were most of the important gambling cities in other parts of the country and around the world. Fenrir held sway over a chain of hotels with establishments in all the important cities and tourist centers in North and South America, Canada, Australia, New Zealand, Europe and Asia. They specialized in communication systems, transportation, tourism, hotels and casinos. Fenrir was also involved in a number of other industries and was, along with Dis Pater and Man-Mandate, one of the three mightiest conglomerates after Cabo de Barra.

In the laboratories of Fenrir City, which were specially equipped for research in aerospace programs, a miraculous discovery had been made. During research into the composition of new materials that could be used to replace light metals such as aluminum, there had been a staggering development.

A chemical reaction had caused the inflation of highly compressed material from the size of a small shoebox to about one yard high. The resulting porous construction appeared to be as strong, if not stronger than a piece of steel.

They had succeeded in modeling a much larger amount of the primitive form of this new substance into a structure that was subdivided into various floors and rooms. Fenrir International had found a way to ensure that no one in the world need ever be homeless again. The corporation had gone on to convert slums into thriving, livable communities. This new, compressed element was delivered free of charge and inflated on location. Windows and doors were then installed, and the outside was covered with a thin protective coating. Interior staircases were constructed or ladders simply placed between floors. Small, comfortable bungalows could be inflated or three-story homes, depending on the need. In popular jargon, the structures became known as popcorn houses. They were a blessing for mankind, and the name Fenrir became synonymous with goodness and altruism.

Over the years, Las Vegas was further developed with the new material, and the well-known sea of neon had become an ocean. Fenrir City, the home town of this building revolution, however, remained a place of imposing simplicity.

All the homes there were built out of the new material, which was manufactured in laboratories on the north side of the city. Not a single structure was higher than three stories, and the offices and public buildings were made of modules that were linked together. The CEO of Fenrir International, the King of Nevada, Don Bradshaw lived here.

He extended great hospitality to the representatives of Cabo de Barra and Man-Mandate Enterprises and was spearheading the lawsuit against Oscar Man.

Oscar had arrived in a small family plane and was brought from the airport to the city by minivan. On the trip into town, he saw a giant zeppelin swinging softly to and fro above a field of grass, restrained by anchor cables. On the side of the cigar-shaped, uninflammable, helium-filled balloon stood the armored man who was the Man clan's logo. Oscar pointed at it and said, "I saw this same airship floating above the palace just a couple of days ago."

"That's very possible," said Katja, who sat next to him. "The witnesses in the lawsuit were brought to Fenrir in it."

They sat together in the middle of the van. In the front, next to the chauffeur, sat an armed security guard. Behind, in the back seat, sat two other armed men wearing the uniform of the Man palace guard.

Oscar wore a suit of emerald green and ruby red checks and boots of soft, light brown leather. He looked to all the world like a jester, but his face was not painted.

Katja had to sit slumped down in the seat to prevent her huge, bouffant hairdo from being flattened against the roof of the vehicle; each time she lifted her hands to check her hair, her heavy bracelets jingled. The stones in her rings were as green as her eyes. During the flight, she had instructed Oscar as to what his behavior ought to be, and he seemed to be complying, at least for the moment. Oscar, relieved to be among people again, but also nervous about the lawsuit, had listened to her with rapt attention. At her request, he appeared as the family had always known him—as a misfit, a jester but fresh-faced and clean cut. He wore no trinkets, and no jewels sparkled on his clothing.

The van sped through the sad, bare landscape of the Nevada desert. The sun blazed overhead, but inside it was cool. After his remarks about the zeppelin, and Katja's surprising reply, not another word was spoken. In the plane they had been able to sit a little further apart from one another, and conversation had been much easier.

"There is a game of intrigue being played by the superpowers of which I don't know the rules," Katja had told him during the flight. "No one really believes that you, of all people, are responsible for the death of Walter Krocht. What's really behind it is difficult to guess at, but it is very convenient for somebody that the murderers and pilots can say nothing about the events of that day. For your family, these problems come at a very bad time, if you can call any time someone is killed a *good time*. If everything goes well, we'll have a new president in the White House who is entirely on our side simply because the family has opened the door for him. The power of your half-brother Ferdinand is still growing, and now that Walter Krocht is no longer in the way, he may become the most powerful man yet. It is rumored that he got the greatest pleasure and benefit from the elimination of Walter Krocht. The police have heard only good things about you because we have instructed all the witnesses exactly what to say. In

Fenrir –City, though, things will be different. You cannot count on everyone taking your side."

"You're talking about witnesses," Oscar had said with indignation. "As if someone had seen the twins and me sit at a table and draw up a contract that obligated them to kill Walter Krocht!"

"They will offer evidence about your behavior, Oscar, that will be listened to carefully, and then judgment will be passed. They are looking for clues to any defects in your character, strange behavior or suspicious statements. No effort or expense has been spared in the search for another offender, do you understand? Anyone could be a suspect, from the tycoons at the top to some lunatic at the bottom who thinks he might have been wronged by Krocht, but let's face the facts. There are countless people who could have private reasons for murdering Walter Krocht. How many people are there who could have brought Jay Jay and Richard Wright so far along that they would draw their weapons at the cathedral on the coronation day of Ferdinand and shoot down the most powerful man in the world? Who could have persuaded them to carry out the execution with so many people and so many cameras around?"

"What can happen to me?"

"As long as there is no real proof against you, you will live."

"What a strange choice of words that is for a lawyer!"

"It's the truth, even if all this does not sound serious to you. I am but a cog in the machine, Oscar. I travel around and around in the big clockwork—to speak in figurative language. I can do nothing when the huge gearwheels suddenly go wild and crush someone like you."

"You mean there's a chance someone will be made a scapegoat, for lack of a better solution?"

"You've said it even better than I did myself."

"From the moment I was whisked away from the cathedral, I have not seen my family, Katja. Where was Johanna? Why didn't Ferdinand come to visit me? Didn't Jimmy or any of them realize that I wanted to—and needed to—talk to them?"

"It's no use to go into that. You have to prepare yourself now for what is coming, and we don't have much time to discuss all the different possibilities again."

They had come to a suburb of long, similar-looking bungalows that formed a boring, unimaginative district. The porous walls of the buildings were all painted in pastel colors, and as they got closer to the center of town, they saw more and more two and three-story houses.

Oscar Man was thinking about how he had always managed to lead his own life and keep to himself. He had always succeeded in suppressing any thoughts of personal accomplishment and had been able to awake from his nightmares with someone lying next to him in the bed who could take his mind off of his life. Without ever being truly satisfied or content with himself, he at least had always been able to feel that he had done the right thing. He avoided trouble and controversy, looked for and found the pleasure he needed and always kept his spirits up, but now he was receiving so much personal attention that he would have to re-evaluate the way he lived his life. It had become a matter of survival now. If he ever got the chance to leave this town after all this, he would do everything differently.

He had to figure out a lot of things, starting with the riddles of his own mind. He had to have private consultations with his own feelings and discover who he actually was and what the turbulent world around him was all about.

The van pulled up to a broad, low building and stopped. As a garage door slowly opened, they all got out, blinking their eyes in the bright desert sunlight. A second vehicle, with a security contingent in it, pulled up behind them.

That evening, Oscar had dinner alone in a deserted restaurant with guards at all the doors. He spent the night in a spacious apartment in the company of two very pretty women who did their best to please him. He only slept for a couple of hours, dreaming once again of blood and adversity. He got up once or twice during the night and tried to open the door; it came as no surprise to find it locked. His accommodations became more luxurious all the time, but still remained a prison. His feelings of claustrophobia made him shiver, and it seemed that his fearful thoughts would be locked in his head forever.

The next morning, he found himself walking beside Katja Donahue through long, low corridors whose ceilings, walls and floors were all made of the same material that Fenrir City was built of. There was no carpeting or floor covering of any kind, and Oscar put his feet down carefully on the thin synthetic fiber that reminded him of oversized cobwebs. He found it unbelievable that the fiber could bear his weight and not sag in the least. The corridor they were walking in widened; the walls here were wood paneled, the ceilings covered with paintings and ornaments and the floor carpeted. Everything Oscar saw radiated pureness and simplicity. They proceeded through numerous sparsely decorated halls. Here and there, carved wooden wolves clasped terracotta pots containing mint green ferns.

Oscar did not let himself be misled by the lack of pomp and circumstance.

Walter Krocht of Cabo de Barra may have been the most powerful man on earth, but Don Bradshaw of Fenrir was the richest. With the opulence of Las Vegas right around the corner, he had no difficulty giving his properties in Fenrir City an almost cheap look. The most expensive hotels in Las Vegas were built in the style of the nineteenth century, and the furnishings were ornate, with excessive use of gold, ivory and ebony.

A double door opened for Oscar and his lawyer and they entered a spacious hall, the walls of which were lined with long wooden benches. Oscar was led to the middle of the hall by a uniformed man where he was made to sit on a small stool. Behind him he heard the doors close.

He looked to the left and saw Katja Donahue walk over to the benches where Jimmy and Johanna Man and Hugh Willis, the primary stockholder, were all sitting. Other members of the Man clan with whom Oscar had never had much contact were present, both male and female.

He wondered if the face of Jimmy Man was painted or powdered or if he looked so white because he was scared. Oscar looked over to the benches on the right and saw the delegation from Cabo de Barra sitting there. Of all the stiff, silent faces that he saw there, he recognized only that of Isodore Clement, whom he had met once in the palace. The men all wore black clothing piped with gold that reminded him of old-time naval officers' uniforms. The two women in the company also wore black clothing.

Directly in front of him, about fifteen yards away, stood several chairs. Don Bradshaw entered, followed by a few people, and they all took their places on these chairs. Bradshaw was big and broad and wore a long, royal-looking robe with wide flaring sleeves. He leaned forward, his arms stretched out in front of him, grasping an ebony cane with a silver handle. His forehead was high and narrow, and he had long sideburns, while the rest of his face was clean-shaven. His eyes were steel gray, but there was a certain warmth about them as he looked round.

Along all four walls armed guards had been posted.

In a loud, deep voice, Don Bradshaw welcomed everyone and then asked for a moment of silence in memory of Walter Krocht.

As uncomfortable as a man could be, Oscar sat on his stool and waited. The soles of his boots slid quietly back and forth across the smooth floor as he sat with his arms folded and tried to remain calm.

After a couple of minutes, Bradshaw broke the silence and made a short speech about the friendly relations between the enterprises. He held out to those present the prospect of a perfect lunch and a fabulous dinner and invited everyone to join him in Las Vegas that night. Then he gestured to the representatives of Cabo de Barra and leaned forward in silence, his hands on the silver grip of his cane.

One of the women in black rose to her feet. She spoke in a soft voice, but the acoustic qualities of the hall were surprisingly good and no one had any trouble hearing her. She introduced herself as Kim La Croix, and with her hands behind her back, began to walk around Oscar in wide circles, immediately taking the verbal offensive.

"Oscar Man—the illegitimate son. We have come together today to judge him, which is something quite different than condemning him. We have to see if we can come to some kind of a conclusion in this affair. On behalf of all the people of Cabo de Barra that are present here today, I want to thank our host Don Bradshaw for his request for a moment of silence. It shows great sympathy. Our loss has been almost insufferable, for the family as well as all the others who are concerned with and in the company that bears the proud name Cabo de Barra.

"For many years I have been the minion of Sascha Krocht sister of the late Walter Krocht. I have always been very close to the family. Now I can finally prove my love for them by rising to the task that has been set before me in this room. And that is to try and find the truth concerning the brutal, pointless murder of Walter Krocht."

Oscar felt that all eyes were focused on him. He looked first into the eyes of Johanna and Jimmy then turned to the other side and saw the people of Cabo de Barra. A man with short hair and a stubbly beard caught his attention; his piercing stare filled Oscar with fear. The man looked much like Walter Krocht. Oscar would later learn that he had been Krocht's longtime minion, and his name was Faron Hayes.

He was paying close attention to La Croix, who was circling him, and jumped when she suddenly stopped, pointed at him and called his name.

"Oscar Man—the jester. What are we supposed to think of a man who has no specific talents and does nothing more than hand out his family's money all across Europe?"

"That is far from the truth!" came Katja Donahue's voice, sharp and shrill.

She had stood up and made a questioning gesture to Don Bradshaw.

He tapped his cane on the floor and said, "You will be given the opportunity to express your opinion soon enough, Ms. Donahue; but for now, we shall listen to what Ms. la Croix has to tell us, and I earnestly request that you do not interrupt her again."

Katja sat down.

"He owes his position in life to his half-sister Johanna Man, who provided him with an education at the court. It goes without saying that everyone had hoped he would inherit some of his father's talents, and that hope was based on the fact that Ferdinand, Jimmy and Johanna Man had developed considerable business skills under their father's tutelage.

"But were he still alive, Otto Man would have been bitterly disappointed with his illegitimate son. Johanna had been his protector and had spoiled him, just as all big sisters spoil their younger brothers. She had, unfortunately and misguidedly, given him too much freedom, and he had developed into a young man who appeared to be unfit for a post at the top of Man-Mandate Enterprises. It truly seemed that it would be better for all parties involved to send him back to where he had come from, so Oscar left quietly and headed back to Europe where he was given the chance to play with the big money! The influence of the Man-Manward Bank opened many doors for him and financed his most insane and harebrained ventures. Half the city of Paris was renovated at the expense of the Man family, and I can name more than twenty other cities that eventually would be restored to all their former glory, thanks to the generous gifts of Man-Mandate Enterprises. Now, I don't want to deny or belittle the benefits of fostering goodwill among the less fortunate people of the world; as far as that is concerned, Cabo de Barra certainly holds its own with Man. I simply want to point out that Oscar was allowed to play the role of philanthropist time and time again. He played with money that was not his own. I don't think that Oscar Man has ever earned a single cent on his own. Why, just look at him, my respected friends; look at the way he sits there so smugly."

La Croix stopped speaking, raised her arm and motioned toward Oscar, who tried not to squirm as everyone stared at him in his green and red fool's suit.

"I hope that what I think is not true!" cried Kim La Croix. "I fervently hope, with all my heart, that Walter Krocht did not fall victim to a frustrated bastard!"

A disapproving murmur rose from the Man side of the room while the people from Cabo nodded solemnly.

"He came back to New York to be present at the coronation of his half-brother Ferdinand. Did he decide to try and finally prove himself by showing the world that he was capable of carrying off something that anyone else would burn their fingers attempting? The most important man in our lives, our leader, was shot and killed on Man-Mandate territory. We demand satisfaction. And here, on neutral territory, under the watchful and just eye of Don Bradshaw, the price will be set—and paid!"

As La Croix continued speaking, Oscar hardly listened to her words; he was lost in thought. It was clear that there was a game of bargaining for power going on here and that Cabo wanted to have their cake and eat it too. It was basically a business meeting and Don Bradshaw provided the perfect setting for it, from extravagant meals to an unforgettable night in his new and improved Vegas. Johanna and Jimmy were here more to negotiate their own positions than to save his neck.

He listened carefully as the hellish accusations against him continued. When Kim La Croix had finally exhausted her fury and venom, Don Bradshaw gave Katja Donahue permission to begin.

After some polite opening remarks about Fenrir's hospitality, she began her defense of Oscar.

"If Oscar is really as vile a person as Ms. La Croix has made him out to be, even his loving sister Johanna would have washed her hands of him long ago. As she already indicated, the liberal generosity of the big enterprises has become a fact of life. The very best example I can offer is the free global renovation of shanty towns by Fenrir International. Well, the man who maintains the name of Man-Mandate in Europe is Oscar Man. As his popularity increases, the prestige of the enterprise strengthens. But, in fact, Oscar Man is more than a man who deals out money and shows his face at parties. He manages an extremely interesting and vital part of Man-Mandate out of his company in Switzerland. This bastard, this jester, is the savior of our literary inheritance!

"He renews old, moldy manuscripts, rescues the knowledge of centuries past and allows the contents of unknown works to be made available to everyone. Yes, his name is known throughout Europe, and it is just because he is so well known that the most important books and manuscripts find their way to him.

"The written words of the ancients find immortality, thanks to Oscar Man. One of the world's most important treasures is Johanna Man's library, which has been filled through the efforts of her half-brother Oscar. When I speak to you of Oscar Man, I sketch the portrait of an intellectual pioneer, not a dissolute psychopath with a lust for blood!"

Oscar relaxed a little on his uncomfortable, backless stool.

He was able to take some comfort from her words as she continued praising him to the heavens, and he noticed that everyone listened just as attentively to her words as they had to those of Kim La Croix.

Later on in the proceedings the two lawyers argued and debated with each other about Oscar, and after Katja had returned to her seat, Kim began to question him. He gave his answers in a loud, clear voice and hoped that his voice would not tremble. When she was done with him, Don Bradshaw tapped his cane on the floor, stood up and left the room.

The entire assembly followed him into another great hall, with Oscar trailing behind. To his surprise, the entire company who just a short while ago had been arguing vehemently over him sat down together at a long wooden table, while he was seated by himself at small table on the other side of the room. Great amounts of food were brought in; wine was served, and Oscar was all but ignored, except by a single guard assigned to keep an eye on him.

Every now and then he was able to catch bits and pieces of the conversations going on, and it was clear to him that everyone was talking business. There sat the new royalty accompanied by their minions, the living status symbols of this new time. The minions were all dressed exactly as their masters were and shared many a secret with them. What these men and women of lofty position would not dare to tell even members of their own clans was easily and comfortably entrusted to their minions. Don Bradshaw naturally had a minion, as did they all, and he too was dressed like his master in a long robe with wide, flaring sleeves. From a distance, it seemed to Oscar, as he looked at all these people, as if he were looking at so many sets of twins. The only one without his twin was the minion of Walter Krocht, now a sad, lonely figure. The lord he had served was dead and buried, brutally murdered, and this thought brought Oscar back to reality.

As he ate and indulged in a few glasses of wine, he could not prevent a smile from creeping across his face, which he carefully hid behind his hand. He thought about the possibility that he could be condemned by this group of tycoons and their stockholders who were already drinking such large amounts of wine at lunch. He let his imagination play freely and wondered how many innocent people throughout history had been treated too harshly—or guilty people too mildly—because kings, queens, emperors, dukes, counts, emirs and judges administered justice after they had too much to drink. Under the circumstances, it seemed like a wise thing to do to drink at least as much as his judges, so he refilled his glass one more time and just as quickly emptied it.

Back in the hall, after lunch, the two groups sat apart once again with Oscar on his little stool in the middle. The witnesses were now called.

The first one called was Samuel Higgins one of the many members of the board of Man-Mandate Enterprises. He was escorted in by guards and then led by Kim La Croix to the middle of the room to stand directly in front of Oscar. Short and corpulent as he was, he seemed to be a dwarf in this large space. Not once did he look in Oscar's direction, except when he was asked to identify him. His answers to the lawyer's questions were short and right to the point.

"Oscar Man visited me a few days before the coronation."

"How did he seem to you?"

"Slightly nervous. He seemed to have had a few glasses of whisky."

"Was there anything else that struck you about him at the time?"

"You mean besides the fact that he was nervous?"

"Yes."

"Not really. Oscar's moods are always hard to gauge, which makes it even more remarkable that I noticed he was nervous."

Oscar would have liked to stand up and give the man a slap in the face, but he knew he must control himself. He wasn't even allowed to interrupt him as he stood there telling his lies.

"Hard to gauge?" asked La Croix, her eyebrows raised.

"The jester knows how to act, as does any jester."

"What else can you tell us about his visit?"

"Nothing really, except that his departure was even more striking. He requested a helicopter from Man-Mandate. There are always several choppers ready for takeoff on the roof of our office building. I did not go up with him, having said good-bye to him in my office. Later on, I heard which chopper he had left in and who the pilots were."

La Croix gave Oscar a sly, suspicious look.

"It was the lizard," Sam Higgins hurried to say. "And it was flown by Stan Woodring and Francis Finnigan."

La Croix nodded, held her head to the side and looking at the man said, "The chopper that was used to whisk Jay Jay and Richard Wright away from the cathedral after they had riddled Mr. Walter Krocht full of lead, with Stan Woodring and Francis Finnigan at the controls."

"You may go," she said and subtly smiled.

Samuel Higgins heaved a sigh of relief and toddled away.

The next witness was Orville Hood, the stationmaster. He was wearing his white uniform and his cylindrical hat with the tassel that swayed back and forth. He, unlike Higgins, looked at Oscar and his glance conveyed a feeling of sorrow and pity.

He had made the trip along with the others in the zeppelin but had taken no time to sightsee. Instead, he had sat quietly by himself and thought of the questions that he might be asked and the answers he would give. He was scared and nervous now, and it showed. His chubby cheeks were a flaming scarlet while the rest of his face was pale. Kim La Croix circled around him like a wasp searching for the right spot to stick its sharp, poisonous stinger.

"Mr. Orville Hood, stationmaster at the palace of the Man family," she said, her voice loud and clear.

Orville hunched his shoulders up and lowered his head.

"All visitors to the palace arrive at the station and proceed up by train, whether they arrive by auto or helicopter, is that correct?"

Orville nodded, but after the lawyer had stared silently at him for some time, he realized that he was going to have to speak.

"Yes," he said. "That is correct."

"Prince Oscar had been flown from New York City to the station by helicopter. You saw it land. What struck you about the arrival?"

"Helicopters come and go and—"

"What struck you about the arrival?"

"The chopper, the lizard, did not land right away," Orville said with a long, drawn-out sigh. "It struck me that it kept circling the palace and then hovered over the park."

"As if the pilots were carefully checking the area out just in case they had to get away quickly, right?"

Orville Hood shook his head so fiercely that his double chin swung obscenely under his jaw and the tassel on his hat danced crazily.

"It's impossible to draw that conclusion," he objected. "How can you presume to know what a pilot is thinking by the movements of a chopper?"

Oscar closed his eyes for a moment. The stationmaster was doing his best to exonerate him, and he was grateful for it, for he knew how scared he was. La Croix kept on walking around him and continued.

"Understand me well, Mr. Hood. The men who would eventually murder Walter Krocht were on board that helicopter, and it was flown by the same men who would try assist in their escape after their ultimate act of cowardice. And, of course, the prince was also on board! Oscar Man was their important passenger!"

"I remember it all very well; I even discussed it with the prince," said Orville, sitting up straight and trying to resist La Croix's stinging look. "I even mentioned the fact that I noticed the chopper had circled the palace for so long before landing. The prince told me that he had fallen asleep and that the pilots did not want to wake him. He even joked about it saying that he was getting old and needed his naps, and I replied to him that he was still a young man."

"One would, at the very least, call this a bit odd, don't you think?" said La Croix. "Down on the ground, everyone had to put up with the noise of the helicopter because the prince was taking a nap! And besides, I cannot imagine that a mere stationmaster is on such familiar terms with a prince from the Royal House that they share a joke. Quite the contrary, I would think that the prince would not even notice you at all. That, Mr. Hood, is why I think that you are lying!"

"Prince Oscar is different!" Hood said.

La Croix's response came just as quickly.

"He is indeed, Mr. Hood. The prince is very different, and that is why we are all here, because this brutal bastard *is* so different from the rest of us! You may go."

Cathy Wheeler, Margaret Sharpe and Hugh Willis were the next witnesses, in that order. They were followed by a procession of men and women who had come along to have their say. Oscar's back was beginning to ache from sitting on the backless stool, but he was determined to maintain his dignity and not squirm.

Slowly but surely, they were painting a picture that portrayed him as the brains behind the murder. Who could think differently, having heard the testimonies? No one would believe that he had nothing to do with this crime. Even if they could not establish conclusive proof and were forced to give him the benefit of the doubt, he would be stigmatized for the rest of his life while the real offender would be free and clear. Oscar knew that the only reason he was sitting here was to keep someone else out of harm's way.

He listened to Cathy Wheeler, dear sweet Cathy, who referred to him as an intellectual and admitted to all present that she and Oscar had had an affair and that she was still in love with him. Margaret Sharpe suggested the possibility of the existence of a split personality in Oscar and asked who would ever stake his life on the reliability of a jester. Yes, she was fond of Oscar Man but honestly didn't know him well enough to pass judgment on his character.

"It comes down to guessing about his possible motives," she said. "He attends every party, laughs and drinks with everyone and still remains mysteriously withdrawn. When Oscar Man comes to mind, I see a contradiction—an open smile and a closed character."

Oscar had never had any kind of a special bond with Hugh Willis, Man-Mandate's major stockholder. He got up from his seat between Jimmy and Johanna and made a brief statement, ignoring the questions of the lawyer. He stated what he thought of Oscar, and Kim La Croix smiled, content with what he said.

"He is of no importance to his family or the company," Willis said. "Therefore it was wise to send him to Europe, and in light of the shame he has brought upon us, I would have liked to see him stay there—permanently! But he returns every now and then, and his sarcastic attitude is like a mosquito's sting: he leaves people uncomfortable and itchy long after he's gone. I think he dislikes everything and anything that has to do with the success of the various royal families, and Walter Krocht was the epitome of that royalty above all others. He was the imperator! We are all eager to know what goes on in the mind of someone like Oscar Man, but I doubt we ever will."

Oscar stared at the ground.

It is very well possible that there is something wrong or missing in my head, he thought to himself cynically.

Even the presidential candidate Angus Sebastian was present. He depicted Oscar as a quiet, nervous man who, on the day of the murder, had sat next to him in the car during the parade through New York City with his eyes hidden behind dark sunglasses.

Jimmy Man was called to testify and was surprisingly mild in his statements about Oscar. His sister Johanna wept, big tears flowing from her eyes as she talked about Oscar; her words quickly became completely unintelligible. Her minion had to console her and help her back to her seat. Katja Donahue called a few of the earlier witnesses back to the floor and then became embroiled in another argument with Kim La Croix.

Don Bradshaw once again tapped his cane on the floor. Many hours had passed, and it was time for dinner.

There were already several guests present in the dining hall, important guests who had arrived earlier. Carl Holdorf of the European concern Dis Pater was present with a delegation, and there was a group of people who all bore an emblem that depicted naked nymphs, the symbol of Richthausen Gold Ltd, on their right sleeve. Food and drink were again served in copious amounts, and again Oscar Man sat forgotten, feeling like a fool.

Not one person from the Man clan, not even Katja, took the time or trouble to join him or even speak to him. Perhaps there was some unwritten protocol that forbade them from doing so. Finishing his meal quickly this time, Oscar stood up and walked to the door through which he had entered. Two large guards came up, escorted him to the room where he had spent the night before and locked the door behind him. There were four beautiful girls present in the sparsely furnished suite, who, like Oscar, were doomed to remain there until someone from outside was ordered to fetch Oscar. The two women from the night before were not there.

"No doubt we shall all get along very well together," said Oscar. He asked them their names.

At the time, there was no way he could possibly have known that he was destined to spend the next week locked in that little apartment. Katja Donahue came to visit him after a couple of days and stayed a short time, telling him that the witnesses had been brought back to the airport immediately after their testimony and had gone back to New York in the zeppelin.

More guests had arrived, among them important representatives of Fortuna Fund, Syrinx Colorado and Hygnos Hybrid Corporation.

"I have absolutely nothing to do," complained Katja. "I'm bored stiff in this dull town. Only the members of the royal houses and the most important of the tycoons have been invited to accompany Don Bradshaw to Las Vegas. I know that Johanna has been staying in the most beautiful Fenrir hotel and that there are meetings, alternating with fantastic parties. I would do anything to be invited."

"Is this all because of me, Katja?" he asked in surprise.

"Honestly, I don't think so," she answered. "Appointments are made and contracts drawn up, but my information is too thin to know what's going on."

He understood that Katja could not tell him everything she knew because a representative of Fenrir was present during their conversation. Meanwhile, it became harder and harder for him to suppress his bizarre thoughts, and his dreams were dominated more and more by the presence of the phantomlike Emlyn Gray. His appearance made Oscar's dreams and visions bloody and made him wake up in the middle of the night in a cold sweat, his eyes bulging with fear. Over and over again he repeated to himself what he had thought as he had listened to the witnesses' testimony: There is something in my head that no one else here would wish for himself.

Chapter Four

Lonely

Oscar Man was close to panic by the time he was finally allowed to leave his apartment and was brought, by armed escort, to the big hall. His nightmares were dominating his waking life also now, and he could no longer bear being locked in. He had smashed four chairs against the walls of his prison, and the parlormaids had retired to a side room where they crouched in fear until his fury had spent itself. He had only calmed down after slamming his fists so hard against the locked door that they had begun to bleed. He had even battered the door with his forehead and kicked it violently, all to no avail. He still had the bruises on his knuckles and forehead to show for all his futile efforts.

The benches had been rearranged and were now all pushed together. All parties concerned sat side by side as if to present a unified front. Johanna sat next to her minion and looked at him blankly with absolutely no trace of emotion on her face. Katja Donahue deliberately looked away from him when he once again took his place on his humiliating little stool. Kim La Croix came and stood beside him, holding a large sheaf of papers dramatically above her head

"The decisions made here are irrevocable," she announced to the assemblage. "Before Prince Oscar came in, I reviewed all the decisions with you, and I trust that everyone is satisfied."

She fell silent for a moment and looked around at the people on the benches. Today she was dressed in red as was Sascha Krocht, the sister of Walter, which made perfect sense since Kim La Croix had previously introduced herself as Sascha's minion.

"All that remains is for us to listen to the verdict, which, as we have agreed, will be announced by a representative of Man-Mandate Enterprises. Therefore, I yield the floor to the Man family lawyer, the honorable Lady Donahue."

Fanning herself with the sheaf of papers, she walked over to the bench and sat beside the other woman in red as Katja, also clutching a pile of papers in her hands, approached Oscar. Her bracelets jingled in the silence of the cavernous hall.

"Cabo de Barra demands satisfaction and will get it, both in compensation and rehabilitation. The arrangements that have been made and the contracts that have been signed are exceedingly favorable to Cabo de Barra. We all know that nothing can bring back Walter Krocht, the great imperator, to our midst. The fact that we were able to come to an agreement is owed exclusively to the very kind authorities of Cabo de Barra. One more time, we would like to express our thanks to these noble ladies and gentlemen. Now then, it is time to tell you all what will happen in the matter of Oscar Man. We will not speak in terms of guilt, proof and innocence, but as has been already said, we will talk about satisfaction."

Oscar sighed softly. He was the scapegoat and had been from the beginning. He was going to suffer for something he had not done. This was how the jurisprudence of the royalty worked, and it was of no concern to them at all what he thought.

Katja Donahue began to read out loud from one of the many papers she held:

Oscar Man shall be stripped of the title of prince and with it every claim he may have had to the family fortune, along with any rights of succession. He shall be relieved of all his functions and properties, except for his penthouse in Manhattan. The funds to which he had the right of disbursement in Europe, are all now secured by his family.

Only his personal finances at the Man-Manward Bank in Manhattan shall remain his, but must be duly transferred within a period of two months to a bank of his choice that is not in the possession of the Man family. All family ties shall be cut, and admittance to the palace is forever refused to him. This has all been clearly put on paper, and all parties concerned will receive a copy signed by Ferdinand, Jimmy and Johanna Man. As of yesterday, the papers were delivered to New York and signed by His Royal Highness Ferdinand Man and then countersigned by Jimmy and Johanna. This verdict is now binding and irrevocable.

There was complete silence except for a short gasp from Johanna. Oscar was tapped on the shoulder by a guard, whom he had not heard approach. He rose and followed him through the double doors, which were then slammed closed behind him. As they walked in silence through a series of long, gloomy, dark corridors, Oscar felt like a dog that had been renounced by its master. The events of the morning had caused a strange pressure behind his eyes that resulted in a morbid, melancholy mood. He was in such a detached state of mind that it seemed as if it were somebody else who, dressed like a fool, trudged along behind the armed guard.

Oscar was led into a small office where a uniformed man sat behind a narrow desk. Without preamble, the official said, "You will leave Fenrir City. It is the explicit wish of Mr. Don Bradshaw that this happen in a proper and timely manner. Tell me where you want to go and how you wish to get there, and I will see what I can do for you."

"And if I say Switzerland, what then?" asked Oscar.

The man placed his fingers on the desktop with his thumbs underneath and leaned backward until the front legs of his chair were off the floor.

"Is that your decision? If so, you will be driven to the airport, and you can take the first flight to Basel, Bern, Zurich or anywhere else in the country you wish."

"No, no, never mind—have someone take me to Las Vegas. I would like a reasonable hotel room there."

The man put his chair back down, opened a desk drawer, took out a pile of folding money and pushed it Oscar's direction.

"Is this your final decision?"

"The final one," Oscar affirmed.

"You will be taken, then, to the Fenrir Grand Hotel. You may stay there for up to two months. All room charges and meals during that time period will be free of charge, courtesy of Fenrir. The Fenrir Grand is the best and most stylish hotel in Vegas. This money is yours. It is a gift, not a loan. When you arrive at your hotel, everything will have already been arranged. Good-bye."

Oscar took the wad of cash and put it in his pocket. Outside the door the guard stood waiting for him, and together they went into the garage where Oscar had arrived a week earlier. A few minutes later, he was sitting in a copper and silver colored automobile driven by a uniformed chauffeur. No guard had come with him this time, and Oscar was alone in the back seat. The characterless town of simple, rectangular buildings receded behind them as they drove through the sun-drenched desert on a divided blacktop road. On the horizon low ranges of hills loomed up, and a single, elongated cloud floated high above in the steel blue sky making Oscar think of the zeppelin that was making its way back to New York. Johanna and Jimmy Man had perhaps wanted to show their appreciation to the witnesses for their participation, and that was probably their reason for making the luxurious airship with its gourmet restaurants and palatial sleeping quarters available. He had been fortunate enough once before, prior to this last trip as an accused murderer, to have been a passenger upon it himself, and he recalled looking out of the window while sitting in a big bathtub in one of the elegant cabins. There was also a large chamber within the ship with a glass floor that imparted the feeling of floating as free as a bird as one walked across it and looked down.

He could not help but smile when he pictured the treacherous Higgins and the faithful, honest Cathy Wheeler in his mind's eye, fellow passengers avoiding each other like the plague. Cathy could be very fierce at times, and she would probably abuse Samuel soundly should a chance meeting occur.

"So the apartment in Manhattan is still mine," he said aloud. "All my books are safe, and Cathy will be there waiting for me."

"Excuse me?" said the chauffeur.

Oscar paid no attention to him.

"I should be running to Cathy with all due haste," he continued, still thinking out loud, "but first I have to clean up my affairs and try to get my mind back on the right track. Only then will I return to New York City to arrange my financial affairs and see my Cathy."

The chauffeur looked straight ahead and sped up as if he desired to get this unwanted passenger to his final destination as quickly as possible.

Oscar had been disowned and disenfranchised by his own family and was on his own now. There had been extensive deals and trades made between the conglomerates about which he knew nothing at all. He had been a pawn in a game that they were playing, and there was nothing he could do about it. Walter Krocht had been murdered—that was a fact. Oscar had not been indicted, but he had been made to stand trial just the same. Everything had been taken from him, and with that, the affair seemed closed as far as Cabo de Barra was concerned. But he still could not help but wonder who the culprit or culprits actually were, and he imagined that there were others who entertained the same thought. It was painfully obvious that this diabolical plan could not have been hatched by Jay Jay and Richard Wright, and there was no way that they could have enlisted the aid of Stan Woodring and Francis Finnigan. Four such sensible men would not let themselves become the victims of a firing squad of their own free will.

I wonder what the reaction of the people will be when I walk the streets of New York City again, he thought. *In the eyes of the law I am innocent and was made to sit in one of Elmore Farrell's cells for no reason. But people may want to molest me, and a walk in Atlanta, the home base of Cabo de Barra, could be like crossing a minefield.*

Protected in his air-conditioned limo against the rising heat of the desert, and listening to the hum of the motor and the whizzing of the tires on the road, Oscar relaxed. Finally, he fell into a deep sleep. The chauffeur had to shake him awake when the automobile arrived in front of the Fenrir Grand Hotel.

After checking into his suite, Oscar visited a barber and a clothing store and then took a stroll, visiting all the biggest and best casinos in Las Vegas. He was far less conspicuous now without his trademark head of hair and ridiculous clothing. He saw how all the casinos treated their guests with bored nonchalance and how the players' faces and eyes burned with greed. They crowded around the slot machines and gaming tables hoping to somehow strike it rich. He, on the other hand, had no fascination with gambling, for he had never really had an interest or need for money.

Everyone was so preoccupied with the myriad temptations of this town, this modern day Sodom, that no one paid any special attention to him. Every now and then it seemed as if a passer-by looked at him a bit more closely, but not once was he approached by anyone wanting to know if he was Oscar Man, the accused murderer and bastard son of one of the wealthiest men in the world. Las Vegas was still the clamorous, kitschy town that became a nightmare of multicolored artificial lights as soon as the sun had been devoured by the desert, but now it had a nineteenth century flavor to it. Fenrir's architects who did so many spectacular things with their prefab popcorn houses had really outdone themselves with the rebuilding of this Mecca of sin and gambling. Everything was such a grotesque caricature of bygone hedonistic days that visitors to the city felt as if they were looking at the past through a magnifying glass. The immense marble staircases at the entrances could not have been higher or wider; the basaltic columns that adorned the facades could not have been higher. Colossal bronze statues gazed down at the people; buildings rose from the middle of man-made ponds as big as mountain lakes and could only be reached via stone bridges full of sculptures and cast iron lanterns.

His meanderings through the streets had tired Oscar, and when he arrived back at the Fenrir Grand Hotel, he bypassed the casino on the ground floor and took the old-fashioned looking elevator up to the ninth floor where the most luxurious suites were located. As the elevator doors opened, Oscar was struck by the profound silence that permeated the entire floor. He stepped out into the middle of a corridor that was one hundred and fifty yards long and twenty-five wide. Along both sides were double rows of black marble columns, inlaid with golden flowers, curled branches and leaves. The floor was covered with deep-pile, black carpeting with dark red designs woven into it. Three yards above the ground the columns were spanned by luminous circles that shone like halos. The suites were situated along the colonnades, and at either end of the hallway windows afforded one a spectacular view of the city. There were smaller windows beneath them, but the small panes were opaque.

With his hands behind his back, Oscar walked along between the columns. All the doors on the floor were closed, and Oscar had noticed when he was first shown to his room by the bellboy that there was not another living soul around.

It was here, in the serene silence of this cavernous hallway that evoked the feeling of an ancient temple, that Oscar suddenly began to stagger.

He leaned against a column with one hand while he covered his eyes with the other.

He slowly sank to the floor until he was sitting on the soft black carpet with his back against one of the columns. He felt totally exhausted, very cold and was having trouble breathing. Countless thoughts whirled through his head, not one of which could he catch long enough to distinguish from another. They were fragments, transient and elusive, making him dizzy and creating in him a physical feeling not unlike seasickness. All that had happened to him since the Wright brothers had emptied their guns into Walter Krocht had slowly undermined his self-confidence and changed a world he had always been able to depend on into an existence filled with uncertainties and unpleasant surprises.

The red flowers and abstract forms in the black carpet seemed to shine in the dim light of the hallway and now appeared to be liquid rather than solid. What Oscar saw in his befuddled state, and much to his consternation, was blood--thick, red blood, flowing sluggishly across the floor. Here and there, air bubbles escaped from this crimson river with a short muffled sound as if the blood were coming to a boil. He heard footsteps coming down the hall that sounded as if someone was walking through thick mud, splashing down and then being noisily sucked back up. He looked up, and there before him was his nightmare—Emlyn Gray.

Oscar reached out with his fingers spread wide. He opened his mouth and attempted to speak but could not form any words; the only sound that escaped him was a soft, gurgling sound from deep within his throat. The bearded face of Emlyn Gray bent down close to Oscar's and nodded at him as if to acknowledge a certain shared, unspoken understanding. He then gave Oscar a wink and a smile. Panting with fear, Oscar managed to get back on his feet, still leaning against the smooth surface of the column.

Oscar heard the sound of voices approaching. A small group of people came into view, all dressed festively and obviously in a merry mood. They gathered around Oscar, looking him up and down. It wasn't until then that Oscar realized he was gesturing wildly and making strange guttural sounds.

"Is everything all right with you, young man?" asked a short woman, peering up at him. Her tall, swirling hairdo formed a blond cone that jiggled to and fro like Jell-O as she spoke. "Do you need help?"

The face of Emlyn Gray had disappeared and was replaced by a man who stood so close to him that Oscar could almost taste the alcohol on his breath.

"I have seen you somewhere before," said the man. He put his hands on Oscar's face and rubbed his thumbs over his cheeks.

"Of course!" he said. "You are the prince; you're from New York! Prince Oscar Man! Under suspicion of having murdered Walter Krocht. Good heavens, man, how you've kept everyone in suspense." He stroked Oscar's face as if trying to convince himself that he was not seeing a ghostly apparition. "They set you free. They had to, you had nothing to do with it. Now you're here to relax! You, of course, could not know this, Prince, but thanks to you, my fortunes have grown considerably as of late."

Oscar had not the slightest idea what the fellow was talking about.

Then the man let go of him, and laughing cheerfully, the little group of people continued on their way, each one stopping to have a closer look at him. Oscar moved to the other side of the corridor, shuffling his feet but not daring to look down at them. He feared his boots would be red with the blood that flowed in the hallway.

Once in his suite, he searched the drawers of a writing table that stood near a window. The nostalgic atmosphere of the hotel was evident not only in the style of the construction but also in the furnishings and fixtures. He finally came upon a drawer that contained old-fashioned stationery. Oscar sat down at the table, placed a sheet of paper on the desk in front of him and stared, pen in the hand, at the blue and gold letterhead of the Fenrir Grand Hotel. As he focused his attention on the image of Emlyn Gray, he shivered and gasped for breath. With his eyes closed, he waited for the hand that held the pen to move of its own volition.

He woke up ten hours later and slowly sat up. He had fallen asleep, bent over the desk, but the paper was empty. His stiff muscles protested when he stood up and moved over to the bed where he slept uninterrupted for another six hours. He had originally sat down at the table at three o'clock in the morning. He had slept through the entire day, and it was now almost seven o'clock in the evening. He showered and dressed and went down to the restaurant for a big, long-overdue fancy dinner. While dining, he was approached by a man he vaguely remembered from the previous evening. He recalled that the man had touched his face and told him something, though he could not remember what it was.

"Would you care to come along with us, young prince?" the man asked. "First, enjoy your meal quietly, and then afterward we are going to have our own Las Vegas style celebration and see just how long we can go on. There are some ladies in our band of revelers who would be very honored to have the attention of a real prince."

He was a tall, slender, handsome man with a proud attitude and impeccable manners. Leaning on Oscar's table, he continued, "Everything on me, of course, Prince. The business world was in quite a turmoil for a while; prices of almost everything went up and down like a tiny sloop caught on a wild sea. No one knew what was going to happen with Cabo de Barra and Man-Mandate Enterprises, and naturally all the other multinationals took advantage of the situation. Syrinx Colorado did especially well and I, by chance, happened to have quite a bit invested in it. Without even being aware of it, Prince Oscar, you have made me far richer in a short time than I already was. By the way, my name is Dave Paddock."

After Oscar had promised to join him and his small company, Paddock jovially gave him a slap on the shoulder and then left him to enjoy the rest of his dinner in peace.

The meal, the wine and the many hours of sleep had made a new man out of Oscar. He could not recall any of his dreams from the night before, and although Emlyn Gray continued to play about the edges of his consciousness, he was no longer nervous or afraid. He joined Paddock and his followers and allowed himself to be dragged along to all the festivities Las Vegas had to offer.

Oscar soon felt as if the United States were his new playground. He resumed the old ways that he had enjoyed in Europe, and after a few days of celebrating he was once again wearing the fool's cap. Those people who wanted to be and needed to be in the company of a prince swarmed around him. The attention was helping him become himself again. His self-confidence got stronger by the day, and one morning he decided that he had hung around here quite long enough. He left Las Vegas with all the money he had received from the man in Fenrir City since his stay in the hotel hadn't cost him anything and Dave Paddock had paid for everything else they did. He left a beautiful woman named Antoinette Nikolow, who was part of Paddock's company, asleep in his hotel bed. She would undoubtedly wonder where he had gone when she woke up alone. But he would not be back.

* * *

Orville Hood and his wife Phoebe lived in one of the twenty towers that ringed the station building. The high, narrow windows of the living room looked out on the park and the palace of the Man family.

It was late and dark outside, and they sat at their dinner table by the light of a single lamp. Orville wore his white uniform, minus his hat with the tassel. Phoebe, smaller than Orville but just as fat, wore a long skirt and a blouse with puffed sleeves; her cheeks were as red and chubby as those of her husband. She was just about to clear away the dishes and the remains of their meal when she heard a tapping sound.

Orville heard it too, and together they looked with surprise toward the narrow doors that opened onto the balcony. It was almost impossible that there could be someone outside them: the balcony was over thirty yards from the ground. Again came the tapping, and now the couple could clearly distinguish the silhouette of a man through the colored glass. Orville got up. As he passed the table, he picked up a copper candlestick, removing the candle and placing it quietly on a dinner plate. He held the candlestick and tested the weight of it like a hammer to determine its effectiveness as a weapon. He was not afraid, nor did he have any reason to be, for nothing had ever happened here to be afraid of. His improvised club was merely a precaution. With his free hand he opened the narrow doors.

"Prince Oscar!" he gasped in a soft voice and immediately stepped aside to allow his guest to enter.

Oscar wore dark brown boots, tight black trousers and a brown leather jerkin. He nodded to the amazed Phoebe and sat down, silent and uninvited, at the table while Orville closed the balcony doors behind him. Orville returned to the table and not quite ready to inquire about Oscar's mysterious and dramatic entrance began to replace the candle in the candlestick.

Oscar had never before been here and had had to make careful discreet inquiries to find the Hoods. He had always thought that they lived in a house somewhere outside the station building until someone had drawn his attention to one of the twenty towers.

"I will understand if you are angry," said Orville in a soft voice. "I apologize to you, Prince, and fervently hope that you have not come here to tell me that I'm fired. We have lived here so for long, and there is nowhere else that we could be as happy as right here."

"Angry?" asked Oscar. He grinned and slowly shook his head. His grin widened when it dawned upon him that although Orville Hood had been called as a witness in Fenrir City, he had never heard the verdict in this strange lawsuit. No doubt he was apologizing for his performance there, feeling that he had not defended Oscar as well as he might have.

"You stood up like a man in that big hall, Orville, and you stood up to their lawyer, La Croix. Don't you worry anymore about that."

"I should have stuck up for you, Prince Oscar, and cut her down to size," Orville fretted.

"Orville, I am no longer a prince, and I have lost almost all of my possessions. Entry to the palace is forbidden to me, and it is better for you that no one knows I'm here, which explains my dark clothes and dangerous climb up the walls. There were a couple of moments when I thought I wouldn't make it and was going to fall to my death."

He had given Orville too much information to digest in such a short time, and the man remained silent. Phoebe heaved a deep sigh, pulled up a chair next to her husband and sat down as quietly as possible as if afraid that the slightest sound would disturb them. She was the first one to speak after the uncomfortable silence.

"I am so very sorry for you, my prince."

"What can I do for you?" asked Orville, and he patted tapped Oscar's hands in an almost fatherly way.

"There are things I must know," said Oscar. "Things I never thought about before, or maybe my subconscious simply repressed them. I lived day by day, sometimes looking toward the future but never to the past."

Orville raised his eyebrows, and Oscar realized that he was speaking in riddles. Now he came straight to the point.

"You are not the biological parents of Angelina, are you? I remember her as Rosanne Vesper, daughter of Herbert and Anne Vesper from Switzerland."

Orville Hood's cheeks turned a dark red; Phoebe sprang up, snatched a cup from the table, turned around and walked away with it.

"I'll clean the table," she hurried to say, "and then I will pour us something to drink."

Orville turned halfway around on his chair, looked at Oscar and said with a sigh, "It looks like this is going to be a serious, man-to-man talk, Pr—Oscar. Damn, but it's strange to call you by your name only. And I am truly just as sorry as my wife is that such horrible things have happened to you. No longer a prince, lost all your possessions. And now you want to talk with us about our Angelina—Angelina Hood!"

"I saw her right before the coronation of Ferdinand. She has grown into a beautiful woman. That long, red hair full of curls and a quick and ready tongue, too! I recognized her as Rosanne Vesper, and there is no one that can ever make me believe that I am wrong, Orville, including yourselves."

"I will not deny it at all," said Orville. "You are searching for information, and I will tell everything I know. I will do so for the sake of our friendship, my boy."

"Is this something that you should be silent about?"

Phoebe returned to the table and put down two glasses of red wine. "These are yours. I'll have a glass myself when I can sit with you."

"I have promised not to discuss this with anyone, no matter what the case. It was not in the plan that you two would ever see each other again, here in America or anywhere else, even when you didn't live that far from each other. That is why I have never talked to you about her."

"To whom did you make that promise?"

Orville took a sip from his glass, and Oscar followed suit.

"To Princess Johanna, your half-sister. Angelina is her true name, not Rosanne Vesper. Just as your name is not really Oscar Vesper. Your last name is Man, same as Angelina's. You see, Oscar, you are half brother and sister."

Oscar was momentarily shocked beyond words. He saw her before him, sitting provocatively on the shoulders of a young man, her round naked breasts, her long legs, her long hair and her pretty face—his sister! Orville gave him a moment's time to reflect on what he had just told him and then continued.

"As you know, Otto and Veronica Man had three children: Ferdinand, Jimmy and Johanna. Do you know the name of your birth mother?"

"Hildegard Floyd," Oscar answered immediately. "I only know her name because Johanna has mentioned it a few times, but I hardly know anything about her."

He looked up, his eyes wide and mouth open, amazed at his own remark. It only now dawned on him how strange it was that he had never wanted to know more. Recent events in his life, though, had transformed him into another man. The new Oscar Man was in search of his past, going on the assumption that that was where the key would be found that could open the door to the secrets of his present.

"You know how important minions are to the nobles. In the highest circles," said Orville, "they have reached a noble status of their own. Hildegard Floyd was the minion of Veronica Man. We can presume that these women shared everything, as most important people do with their minions. There are certain things in everybody's life that should never be shared with anyone else, but even these things are shared with one's minion. How great was the shame then when it became known that Veronica Man and Hildegard Floyd had shared more than secrets; they had shared the same man! Hildegard was pregnant with you, and she was sent to Switzerland. There was also another woman whose name will not sound familiar to you. Her name was Jolene Harvey, and she too had a child with Otto Man."

"Angelina," said Oscar.

"Yes, Angelina. But Jolene Harvey was a nobody in your father's eyes, a commoner. He forgot about her, and he forgot about their daughter—Angelina. I can even tell you that Otto Man never saw his son Oscar or his daughter Angelina! The two mothers lived together while in Switzerland, although you were both too young to remember that now. Then the women took a trip to England together, and in a raging storm the small airplane they were traveling in developed engine problems and crashed into the icy cold water of the North Sea. Neither one of them survived the disaster. You and your half-sister Angelina were placed with foster parents."

"Herbert and Anne Vesper."

"That's correct. Later, you, being the child of a minion, were taken to the palace and received with all due respect and regards. Johanna came to talk with us. We were a young married couple without any kids and faithful to the Man family. I was offered a worry-free, lifetime job at the station, a nice amount of money deposited in the bank and a terrific pension for my old age, and of course, this comfortable apartment in the tower. We took Angelina under our wings and into our hearts as our own child. Phoebe and I knew immediately that we would gladly have kept her by our sides forever, even without all those promises and privileges."

"She's our daughter, and that's final!" Phoebe declared as she sat down next to her husband.

"So much has become clear to me," said Oscar.

He did not tell them how he had used Angelina as a model for himself and imitated her every nuance of behavior. He also did not tell them about his strange experience with Laura Langen the strange blond woman who had pinched his arm in the churchyard.

"Our mothers died in a plane crash," said Oscar more to himself than to Orville and Phoebe Hood.

"I would occasionally ask Johanna about my real mother when we were alone, but I came away none the wiser, except for that fatal trip to England. Don't worry, my friends, I can talk about this without becoming too emotional, for I never knew her, did I? The situation is quite different with Anne and Herbert Vesper. All I have to do is close my eyes to see them right in front of me."

"You were always an extraordinary child, Oscar, and now you have grown to become an extraordinary man," said Orville. "Angelina hardly remembers anything about Anne and Herbert Vesper. Only a few special events left a lasting impression on her, and those were very few and very far between."

Oscar told them about his youth, and it was very strange for Orville and Phoebe to learn so much about Angelina that was so new to them. Oscar finally related the story about her fiery performance in the park near the palace when he had immediately recognized her.

"Yes, she's a young women from a new age," remarked Phoebe. "She wants to experience every hour of every day as intensely as possible."

"Do you see now what makes you so extraordinary?" said Orville. "It speaks for itself that Angela could not possibly have recognized you, a prince of the Man family, as her brother."

"My face was painted, and as was usual in the not so distant past, I was dressed like a fool."

"That does not matter at all," said Orville waving his hand through the air to reinforce his words.

"With or without makeup, it would have never occurred to her that she had spent the first years of her life with you in Switzerland. My wife and I never met Mr. and Mrs. Vesper. We have never even seen pictures of them."

Oscar thought how strange it was that, considering all the years he had spent in Switzerland, he had never searched for them. He had simply never taken the time, and now it was painfully clear to him that anything that reminded him of the past he had kept locked away in a dark corner of his memory.

Phoebe left the room giving Oscar and Orville a chance to have a long overdue talk. As they talked, now and again refilling their glasses, it became obvious how much Orville had always liked the young prince and how those short rides they had taken together on the big trains, from the station to the palace and back again, were now recalled as long journeys during which the bond of friendship between them had continued to grow. Through Oscar's young eyes, they had been long, comfortable voyages of adventure. He had always felt right at home as he walked through the luxury compartments with Orville or just simply sat and gazed out the windows with him. And through all those wonderful days, Oscar realized now, Orville had known that the little girl he and Phoebe were raising was his half-sister. If Oscar had not decided to pay this unusual visit and have this talk with him, Orville would have maintained his silence about it forever.

Phoebe now returned, accompanied by her daughter. Angelina lived elsewhere in the enormous building. Phoebe had gone to get her and on the way back had informed her about Oscar's surprise visit.

"Oscar Vesper is Oscar Man!" Angelina cried out, laughing, and before Oscar could even stand up, she fell into his arms causing Oscar to stagger as she squeezed him tight.

They sat around the table, the four of them, while Oscar told them again about the things he remembered from their early years in Switzerland. Angelina played with her long, curly hair and tried to form pictures in her mind's eye to illustrate Oscar's words. She imagined the furnishings in the house, the garden, the wide-open spaces and the towering Swiss mountains. She could remember the gentle eyes of Anne Vesper but shrugged her shoulders in blank despair when Oscar told her that Herbert Vesper had a moustache and a beard. Cautiously, Oscar asked her about the day they went to a funeral and stood in the open air listening to the words of a priest.

"I really don't know what on earth you're talking about now," she said looking at him with admiration.

"How is it possible that you remember so much and I almost nothing?"

Angelina Hood was not married and worked a few days per week as an architect at an office where the ideas of Ferdinand Man were developed. She had been instrumental in the building of the cathedral and was now working on the design of a museum that would eventually be built in the park not far from the palace. Oscar vividly recalled what she had said to the man in black while sitting on the shoulders of the boy in that very same park.

"We are from the intervening period. In front of us lies the period and promise of eternal life. Beyond the horizon lies a time in which no one has to close his eyes forever. It is hard to accept that we were all born too early to lay claim to eternity. That is why it is wise to continue celebrating and keeping a smile on your face for as long as possible."

She had many, many questions about their time in Switzerland, and while Oscar told her what he knew, he realized that he was talking about these things for the very first time in his life. His memories were becoming clearer all the time, and he was just as surprised as the others at the flood of details that poured out of him. All this, and still he kept so much to himself.

He did not mention how he had imitated her behavior, but it dawned on him that he had, without her knowledge, learned how to behave like a child and fit in with his surroundings.

Then Oscar thanked the family for their hospitality and apologized for his strange, unannounced entrance. Angelina wanted him to spend the night with her or her parents, but Oscar said, "There is a very real chance that I will endanger you all if I do that. The palace and its environs are forbidden to me. Who knows what questions will be asked of you if someone were to find me here? It is best if I slip away unseen while it is still dark."

He was already standing at the narrow balcony doors when she walked up to him and gave him a big hug.

"If I had only known earlier who you were," she said, "before you were treated so unfairly. We will see each other again, won't we? I have time enough to travel, and I could come to New York."

"Later," he decided. "First I need time to work out a lot of things."

Phoebe embraced him, and Orville was also determined not to be left out of this emotional scene.

"Take good care of yourself, boy," he said with tears in his eyes.

Oscar went out onto the balcony. He felt a sudden terrible loneliness when the doors closed behind him. Through the tinted windows, he saw three motionless shapes, like unreachable figures in a dream. He began his descent.

Panting and sweating, he finally reached the ground, stepping quickly out of the glow of a high, cast iron lantern. He stood on a pitch-black street corner and gazed at the lights of the palace off in the distance. There were his own chambers, the personal sanctuary he could never resort to again. Within those walls were the closets filled with his clothes and the bed on which he had so often lain looking at the frescos on the ceiling. There were memories of his youth locked within those walls: the elevators that had carried him all over the palace, the corridors, offices, apartments, shops, restaurants, royal halls and chambers—all out of his reach now. He knew the stables, the country palaces, the views from the towers, the kitchens, the garages, the terraces and the gardens. He was no longer welcomed here. There was no longer a place for him in any of the cars of the great black trains.

He had no idea how his family would react if someone informed them of his visit to Orville Hood. As he thought back on his warm, heartfelt meeting with Angelina, Phoebe and Orville, he was moved to tears and a lump rose in his throat. He went quickly to the side of the station where the copper colored taxis always stood waiting.

   * * *

It was a bright, sunlit morning when he walked into the head office of the Man-Manward Bank in New York and asked for a financial statement of his accounts. He had already roughly calculated the figures in his head and knew approximately how much money he should have. It was not a great deal of money since he hadn't often put money aside, but it would do for a while if he was careful not to squander it on useless things.

His face remained stoic and unimpressed when the exact amount was given to him.

The amount he had saved himself, combined with his salary from his work in Switzerland, plus the special advances from the court, enabled him to pay off the expenses of all his houses and servants. A new account had been opened for him a few days ago with a formidable initial deposit. The money had been transferred by Man-Mandate Enterprises; on the deposit slip was his sister Johanna's signature.

All his privileges were revoked and his holdings repossessed; he was no longer a prince and his family shunned him, but he was an extremely wealthy man now thanks to Johanna, and that confused him greatly. This act of kindness and charity simply did not fit in with everything that had happened recently.

He immediately transferred all of this new-found money to an account he had opened less than a quarter of an hour earlier at the head office of the Hydra Bank, a subsidiary of the mighty Hygnos Hybrid Corporation. The family had wanted it this way. He had been ordered to put his money in a bank in no way affiliated with Man-Manward. Now that this was done, he no longer had anything to do with Johanna, Jimmy and Ferdinand.

Oscar left the bank and headed over to his penthouse, the only residence that he had been allowed to keep. There was no need to take a cab to get there; if he walked at a brisk enough pace, he could be there in forty-five minutes, and he was in the mood for a morning walk.

As he left the bank and descended the broad, marble stairs, he was immediately surrounded by an impudent, crushing mob of journalists, photographers and television crews. Most of the men were dressed like old-fashioned musketeers with high boots, capes and broad-rimmed hats, while the women looked like countesses and princesses also from days gone by. Oscar himself was wearing knickers, a jerkin of dark green damask and light brown boots.

Everyone was speaking at the same time, and Oscar looked nervously from one to the other not knowing which question to answer first. There was no escape route; the flight of steps had been entirely closed off by the press. Oscar's option was to retreat back into the bank and ask the guards to close the doors, but he did not do that. Instead, he held his ground and crossed his arms.

"How do you feel, Prince, now that you have lost everything?"

"Are you going to remain in New York now that your family has publicly turned against you?"

One of the journalists then said something that made Oscar's situation painfully clear to him.

"Yesterday the public relations department of Man-Mandate Enterprises," the reporter shouted, "stated that there had been a meeting at which the leaders of Cabo de Barra were present, and it was decided that the Man family would completely wash their hands of you. Where was this meeting held, Oscar? In the palace of the Man family, Atlanta, or somewhere else?"

Oscar raised his hands to quiet the crowd and said, "The meeting was held in the Nevada desert—in Fenrir City," he said. "Sponsored by Don Bradshaw. I personally would not call it a meeting as much as a mockery. I have been severely punished without having been found guilty: a contradiction of law and good sense that would never have been tolerated in the common courts. I was condemned based on the reading of a lawsuit at which indeed a delegation of Cabo de Barra was present."

"Based upon civil law, you are exonerated from all blame," yelled a man standing beside the journalist. "But there will be people who will only seem to give you the benefit of the doubt while in their thoughts they will always see you as the brains behind the murder."

Oscar looked at him with burning anger in his eyes but did not answer.

"No longer a prince," cried the woman reporter, "no possessions, no tasks or royal responsibilities to accomplish. How do you see your future?"

"The sun will rise again tomorrow," said Oscar. "At least that much is for certain. Now, if you will excuse me—"

He wanted to leave, to work his way out of this crowd and be free of them, but they all remained standing shoulder to shoulder, boxing him in. Oscar looked behind him and saw that the big metal doors of the bank were slightly ajar. Behind them a guard was posted, but it was obvious that he was no longer welcome in the Man-Manward Bank.

"What is your opinion about what has happened?" he heard someone call out. "Was it someone's intention from the start to let you take the rap for this disaster?"

A cameraman stepped to the side to get a better picture, and Oscar saw his chance at escape. He slipped past the cameraman and another man, pushing some other people out of his way. With bounding jumps, he ran down the marble steps and sprinted off.

The street was lined with office buildings whose ground-floor walls had been remodeled in the architectural style of the eighteenth century. Modern automobiles, which had been manufactured to look like steam vehicles, stood bumper to bumper along with copper colored taxis in a droning, smoking traffic jam. They had all come to a halt to allow a long procession of brightly dressed, cheering, singing people cross the street. The parades went on day and night here, and there were never-ending parties in bars and restaurants that never closed. With the press close upon his heels, Oscar ran along the path of the procession trying desperately to elude them. He reached the head of the procession where men in high hats and women in long shiny dresses danced to the music of a brass band. Loud drumbeats echoed off the walls of the skyscrapers, and the blaring of trumpets seemed to come from everywhere at once. A group of royally dressed, masked men, whirling and spinning wildly, noticed Oscar and insisted that he dance along with them.

"It is Prince Oscar Man!" a loud voice boomed above the noise. "The bastard! We have the jester in our midst!"

The crowed shouted with joy. The throng continued onward through the streets and over the sidewalks, ignoring traffic lights and crossings. The blaring music drowned out the sound of the slow-moving automobiles behind them whose constant blowing of horns only added to the pandemonium. The press had not given up their pursuit, and as they attempted to push forward into the dancing crowd, the cameramen had to lift their expensive equipment high above their heads.

Oscar did what the crowd expected of him: he jumped, tumbled and even walked on his hands, his spectacular somersaults eliciting shouts of encouragement and applause.

Office employees on their way to work stopped to watch the spectacle.

"Oscar! Oscar Man!" came the shouts from all sides.

Then came the cry "Murderer!" It seemed to Oscar that the horns had fallen silent and the parade had come to a halt. The entire world stopped turning. Then, just as suddenly, all the noise came rushing back to his ears, and wildly moving people surrounded him.

As he was about to give a mighty leap, he was hit in the stomach with an elbow. He moved aside and received a kick against his left shin. Oscar was knocked to the sidewalk and although most of the people walked around his fallen figure, some of them stepped on his legs and back. With great difficulty, he got to his feet again. His hands were bruised and bleeding and he was closed in by whirling dancers who pummeled him with punches.

"It's the bastard!" one shouted. "A murder for a murder! Don't let him escape!"

If he stood still, he was pushed; if he danced, he was tripped. He had first thought that if he didn't resist, the kicking and beating would soon stop, but it did not. He attempted to defend himself now, warding off the blows and dealing out several of his own, but this only made his aggressors angrier and more violent, and they continued their beating with even more precision. The skin under his eyes split open; his chin was hit hard by flying fists, and a painful ringing in his ears drowned out all other noise. He was lost in the wild horde, and no one was there to help him. There was not even a cameraman present to record the event.

When the crowd of people on foot had finished with him and the last man in line had walked over his outstretched body, the cars were forced to stop to avoid crushing the fallen jester who had so recently performed his dance macabre.

"The cowardly bastard is in our midst!" shouted someone.

Oscar had managed to get back on his feet once again when a kick on his side made him stagger. Stumbling on, the crowd continued to abuse him. A man in a gray suit came up to Oscar carrying a wooden cane in his hand. He danced around, spinning and jumping, and then, with one leg up and balancing on the heel of his other, he brought the metal knob of the cane down.

But Oscar Man refused to die on this sunny morning in the bombastic hell that was modern New York, and he evaded the stick that was aimed at his head, dragging two men along with him when he fell yet again. The crowd stopped and fell silent, like extras in a play waiting for new instructions from the director. Oscar scrambled to his feet quickly as the sirens of police cars became audible. The musicians and their entourage came to such an abrupt halt that they almost bumped into each other. With the music stopped, the partygoers seemed to become frightened about what they had done to Oscar.

Oscar, bleeding profusely but unaware of the pain, broke away from the group and began to run. Behind him the road was filled with people from sidewalk to sidewalk, and the police were doing everything in their power to clear the way. It was not for Oscar's benefit, however; they were trying to clear a path for an ambulance on its way to the scene of an accident, not to rescue the bastard prince! The siren of the ambulance mixed with those of the police cars and the horns of taxis and other vehicles, and the band began to play once more, setting the wild mob in motion once more. This time, however, the crowd was staying more to one side of the street so as to allow traffic to get by.

Oscar had the entire road in front of him to himself now. As the police cars raced past him, they did not even look in his direction. With his torn clothes flapping all around him, he simply looked like one of the more oddly dressed members of the parade. After the sound of the sirens had faded into the distance, Oscar heard someone shouting his name, and he looked back. He had left the procession of thugs more than a hundred yards behind him, but there was one man standing on the sidewalk with a camera on his shoulder. The cameraman shouted at Oscar, "Please wait here until the rest of my crew catches up. You need help and we—uh—we need—"

Oscar stopped and turned.

"Of course! You need a story," he shouted at the man. "They have done my makeup, and now I'm all ready for an in-depth interview!"

He ran on.

Glancing at his hands, he discovered that his nails were split and broken, and blood trickled down his fingers. His entire body was battered and bruised, and he suddenly felt pain all over but primarily under his chin and around his eyes. There was blood dripping down his face from along his eyebrows; he wiped it away with what remained of his left sleeve. It began to get more crowded again, and he came upon another parade. He heard the people singing, but it did not register what their song was about. He began to have trouble breathing; each time he sucked air into his lungs, the pain in his chest became more unbearable.

For a moment he was sure that he could not go on and was going to collapse right there. He felt himself blacking out.

When he had gathered his equilibrium a bit, he was surprised to find that he was walking at a decent pace and was being supported by a man in a purple velvet suit while he himself had a long coat of the same material around his shoulders.

"Did you say something?" Oscar asked.

"We'll be right there," said the man. "Stick it out! There is a doctor's office not far from here."

A few hundred steps further on, and he was steered through a set of glass doors that opened into a mall with shops on both sides and a roof constructed of metal and stained glass. They went through another door, and Oscar stumbled into a waiting room. A few moments later, he was sitting on a chair in an examination room. Gallantly, the man who had brought him in retrieved his coat from Oscar's shoulders, threw it around his own, bowed and said, "I must go now; I am in a hurry. If you are Prince Oscar Man, which I firmly believe you are, I have done more today than simply scrape an injured drunk off the street. I leave you to the good care of the doctor."

Oscar nodded gratefully at the man.

"You recognized me," he said managing a weak smile. "How clever of you to see through this mask of blood I wear. What do I owe you?"

But the man had already gone.

"It seems we have quite an important guest," commented the doctor. He was a middle-aged man with a narrow face and a tall, thin body dressed in a tight white lab coat. "I guess the other patients will just have to wait a while. Can you stand up? If so, let's get you out of these clothes and see what has happened to you. No doubt, I will hear later how it all happened."

The man worked on Oscar for an hour. There were deep cuts above the left eyebrow and under both eyes that had to be stitched up. Oscar's smaller cuts and bruises were disinfected, and the larger wounds on his arms, chest and legs were bandaged.

When the doctor was finished, Oscar redonned his torn clothes. He offered to pay the doctor, but the man shook his head decidedly no.

"Just like the man who brought you here, Prince, I will not ask for or accept compensation. I am quite impressed by everything you told me as I took care of you. I wish you strength and good health!"

Oscar could not even shake the doctor's hand due to the pain in his hands and fingers. He nodded politely and stumbled into the waiting room where he was busy outstaring the curious looks he received from the people sitting there when a chauffeur in a copper colored uniform entered and asked who had called for a taxi.

Chapter Five

Double Resistance

Oscar headed for the front passenger door, but the driver jumped in front of him and opened the rear door for him. He sat down on the cracked leather seat in the back and waited for the driver to slide in behind the wheel before giving him the address of his destination. The tinted windows of the cab gave Oscar a view of the street that was much like looking through a pair of dark sunglasses. He was grateful for the anonymity that the windows provided; they did not permit anyone on the outside to see who was on the inside. Looking past the driver through the windshield, he could see the copper colored hood, trimmed with steel bands and adorned by an angel with her wings spread wide, as if she were about to take flight. Beyond that he saw an endless sea of people and vehicles, all bathed in bright sunlight.

"My God, what have they done to you?" asked the chauffeur turning his head to the right and peering at Oscar between the two headrests. Without waiting for an answer, he continued, "It makes no sense to take you home. There is an army of press people waiting for you at your building and an even larger group of people just hanging around and sightseeing, trying to catch a glimpse of the fallen prince. It's almost impossible to get through, and even if we did, you would never get inside without being seen."

Oscar had long ago gotten used to the fact that most people on the street recognized him, but he wanted to see for himself if the man was telling the truth. He could not help but be suspicious since the taxi had started moving before he had even told the driver where he wanted to go. He wondered, somewhat nervously, where he was being taken.

"Let's go by there first anyway and have a look."

"As you wish," said the chauffeur. "But I wouldn't advise getting out when we get there. You aren't in any condition to beat off a second attack. You look like you wouldn't survive it. There are many people who are angry with you; they have condemned you for something you obviously haven't done. But even if no one were to molest you, it doesn't seem to me that you should be talking to the press in your present condition. The way you look now is—"

"I was in far worse shape a little while ago, with blood running down my face and into my eyes, and I allowed myself be filmed then," Oscar remarked.

The cab was moving so slowly that Oscar could probably have walked faster to where he was going, and it finally had to stop completely to let yet another parade of people pass. This group was all worked up and extolling the virtues of none other than Angus Sebastian, the Man family candidate for president. The crowd had but one voice, and that voice was insisting that Sebastian should become the new chief executive of the United States. A group of beautiful, exotic women danced on top of one of the floats to the music of Jamaican musicians, undoubtedly hired because some of Sebastian's ancestors had come from that tropical island. They played, sang and danced so entrancingly that more and more people fell in behind them and joined the long procession. Suddenly, a cheering arose that drowned out the music. Oscar suspected that Angus Sebastian had showed his face from one of the floats, though from his sunken, secure position in the back seat, he could not be sure.

Although the doctor had sedated him, he still felt broken and sad as he recalled how he used to watch the long ponytails of Jay Jay and Richard Wright swing back and forth whenever he rode in the back seat of a car and they were sitting up front.

"You seem to be unusually sympathetic toward me," said Oscar. "Tell me, do you have a particular destination in mind?"

"Yes," said the chauffeur. "There is someone who would love to have a talk with you."

Oscar sat up straight and leaned forward.

"And what's your opinion? Is this person someone I would want to meet, or am I going to regret it later?"

"Please trust me," replied the chauffeur. "You will also be able to change your clothes there. You will be given new clothes of the best quality. And nothing bad will happen to you, I promise."

He raised his right hand, forefinger up, made a few circles in the air and said, "This automobile is completely secure against bugging. We can talk freely in here."

Oscar sank back against the cushions again and muttered, " We'll talk later. First, I want to see if I can go home."

The chauffeur nodded, looked straight ahead and smoothly maneuvered the vehicle through the busy Manhattan streets.

Oscar knew better than anyone that everywhere he went, the walls had ears. It was for that reason that he rarely used normal means of communication to contact his confidants about anything not meant for others' ears. He desperately wanted to talk to Cathy Wheeler and see what she could come up with when he told her the name Emlyn Gray, but he knew he could only discuss it with her in the security of his own penthouse. That was the one place that he could be sure all precautionary measures had been taken to make any eavesdropping completely impossible.

The chauffeur spoke and snapped Oscar out of his reverie.

"Your building, Prince. The building, the press, the crowd: You see what I mean?"

Oscar looked out through the darkened side window and immediately saw that the chauffeur had been right; it was impossible to get through. The steps to the entrance were full of news hawks and their equipment, and they were further surrounded by gawkers. It was impossible to say how many people had gathered there to try and catch a look at Oscar. Leaning forward, Oscar craned his neck and tried to to see the top of the skyscraper. His efforts were in vain, though, and he leaned back in his seat again. These movements, in his battered condition, made him dizzy, and he was suddenly beginning to feel terribly exhausted, both physically and emotionally. He fought as hard as his poor, tired mind would allow against feelings of self-pity and over-emotional, irrational thoughts.

"I've never had a sound thrashing like this before," he said honestly to the chauffeur. "The sedatives the doctor gave me are helping somewhat, but still I feel weak. Weak and defeated. If I didn't trust you, though, if I thought you were trying to kidnap me or something, I would give you an enormous blow to the head and jump out of here before you knew what had hit you! Drive on; take me to this person you're talking about."

The car immediately sped up.

"All right, Prince," the driver said. "It might be simpler if you just call me Eddie from now on, Eddie Brooks."

He held his hand out behind him with his thumb down and his arm bent, elbow up. Oscar grasped it with powerless fingers and said, "And you please call me Oscar. I am, as you undoubtedly know, no longer a prince. Tell me, Eddie, how long has the press been hanging around on the steps of my building?"

"A couple of days now, right from the moment it was made public that you had been brushed aside by your family, Oscar. They take turns. Someone's there day and night. Like everything else in this city that never sleeps, the press has people permanently posted in spots where something important might happen.

Oscar nodded when he saw Eddie look at him in the rearview mirror.

He thought about how it was no longer only New York that never stopped in this world. Over the past few decades everything seemed to be in perpetual motion. It was one of the ways developed to ease the pressure caused by overpopulation; employees shared their work spots in offices and worked short shifts. To millions of people, a working day of two or three hours was normal, and those who didn't work at all tried to get through life constantly celebrating. There were people who seldom saw the light of day and like nocturnal animals only left their houses after the sun had gone down. People had learned to deal with each other as little as possible. He had only to look outside to see examples of this callous new world.

He saw people working in office buildings, behind high windows, completely oblivious to the laborers working outside replacing the brick walls with an impressive colonnade and marble roof. Out on the streets, partygoers cavorted together, singing and laughing, on their way to a park, a show or a banquet being given by one of the multinationals. Men and women who were headed to work, attaché cases under their arms or in their hands, had to fight their way upstream like dying salmon, and when it all became too crowded, they stepped out into the street where angry chauffeurs blew their horns and swerved around them with screeching brakes.

"I suggest that you lie down," said Eddie looking in the mirror and noticing that Oscar was beginning to look worse. "Lie down and close your eyes. Not only will you get some rest, but that way you won't be able to see where I'm taking you, either. You can't reveal what you don't know."

Oscar's face disappeared from the mirror, and when Eddie turned his head, he saw that he had followed his advice.

Oscar slept. And dreamed. In a short but intense dream, the masses of people became armies of ants that ran crisscross through the streets, all looking for their nests, which they could not seem to find. The town swarmed with ants, which he expected to begin battling each other at any moment, tearing each other to pieces with their razor-sharp jaws. Before it came to that violent end, though, exhaustion blurred the dream, and he slept peacefully on the leather cushions of the back seat, swaying softly to and fro with the motion of the vehicle.

Suddenly, he sat up and opened his eyes.

He found himself sitting in a strange bed in a half-dark room. Behind ragged curtains a glaring sun was shining. Oscar pulled back the cover and saw that he was still wearing his torn clothes. It was only then that he became conscious again of what had happened to him on the streets of Manhattan, and the pain returned to his body. The stitches above his eyebrows and under his eyes felt weird. With trembling fingers, he stroked his swollen face. Everywhere he touched, the skin and the underlying flesh felt like a rotten, overripe fruit. It was impossible for him to take a big enough breath to fill his lungs entirely with air. Besides the pain, and the fact that he didn't knew where he was, he was also aware of an enormous hunger and thirst.

Other than the bed, there was only a low, wooden cupboard in the room. He stood up with great difficulty, staggered over to the window and opened the curtains. The copper rings from which they were hung made a scraping sound over the iron rod, and even that seemed to make his headache worse. The sudden, glaring sunlight that poured in was translated by his eyes into pain, and he had to hold on tightly to the curtains with both hands to prevent himself from falling. After a few moments, he was able to lean with outspread fingers on the windowsill. He looked down into a street filled with old houses and saw the inevitable stream of people and vehicles. He saw that he was on the third story of the building, but it was impossible to tell if he was still in New York or, if so, in what neighborhood.

He heard a door open behind him, but he did not turn around. Someone spoke, and he immediately recognized the voice of Eddie Brooks.

"The sun will disappear behind the houses soon, Oscar, and it will be evening. You have slept for a couple of hours; follow me, and I'll show you to the bathroom where clothes have been laid out for you. I heard you get up and open the curtains; I was waiting in the adjacent room."

Now Oscar turned around and looked at Eddie.

"Are you going to tell me where I am?"

"This place is nothing special, that's for sure, but no doubt you've already seen that for yourself. You're in a hotel in the Bronx. After you have cleaned yourself up and gotten dressed, I'll take you to a bar where there is someone waiting for you. I'm going to introduce you to Tony Falcon."

Oscar shrugged his shoulders, and his face twisted with the pain this simple motion caused.

"The name means nothing to me."

Eddie helped him across the room and down a corridor to a bathroom where he left him alone. Slowly, Oscar removed his tattered clothes and flung them into the tub. Standing in front of the sink, he inspected his bruised face in the mirror. He looked as if he was made up for his role as the jester again, ready to go out into the streets, with red, purple and blue as his dominant colors. He leaned forward, turned on the cold water and drank greedily. He held his wrists under the jet of water and then washed himself as well as he could. He was beginning to feel a little better.

A jacket and trousers were laid out for him, woven of simple linen with abstract embroidery. Pulling on his own brown boots again and leaving the bathroom, he found Eddie waiting for him in the hallway. They went down to the crowded, noisy bar on the ground floor. Three merchants in wide knickers and coats with high collars, all with the naked nymph emblem of Richthausen Gold Ltd on their sleeves, were passing out glasses of wine and beer to the motley crew of pub-crawlers. A man in a long coat and conical hat was asking loudly if anyone was willing to take him on their shoulders so that he could deliver a tirade, but there were no takers. Eddie and Oscar went to the back of the big bar where semiprivate rooms lay behind walls of opaque glass. Eddie opened a door and indicated to Oscar that he should enter alone.

"I'll see you around," he said. "I'm jumping into the cab and hitting the road again."

He closed the door softly behind him and was gone.

In the small room there stood a couple of chairs and a bench around a wooden table. On one of these chairs sat one of the strangest-looking men Oscar had ever seen. He was slender and dressed all in black. His hair was also black, and it had the effect of outlining his white face. What made his appearance even more peculiar, though, were his eyes. They were a pale gray in color, and although he was looking directly at Oscar, it seemed as if he didn't see him at all. It was if he were concentrating on a point visible only to himself and looking straight through Oscar. He wore a huge tie of black velvet and no jewelry of any kind, which lent an even more somber feeling to his dark attire.

Unasked, Oscar sat down opposite him.

When the man closed his eyes for a moment, his imposing demeanor was immediately lessened, although he retained a powerful presence.

"I am Tony Falcon," he said when he opened his eyes again, "and I have the power to knead and mold people in a fashion so that they will conform to a predefined model, so that they are able to function in a manner that they have always wanted to. I am sure that you do not understand what I'm talking about right now, but you shall."

It was difficult for Oscar to resist the man's stare because it was still as if he were looking right through him and seeing things visible only to himself. For a moment Oscar had the suspicion that the man could be blind, but that thought disappeared when the man remarked on his looks.

"It's horrible what they have done to you. Who knows how long it will be before your face is as it was before you were beaten so badly. Is it okay with you if I call you Oscar?"

Oscar nodded.

"I will shake your hand some other time, Oscar, for I'm afraid that if I did so now, I would further damage your already bruised fingers. I assumed that you would be hungry and thirsty; both needs will soon be taken care of. How is your voice? They haven't taken that away from you, have they?"

"No," Oscar replied.

Falcon opened his black jacket and revealed an emblem embroidered on the inside. Inside a golden square, two artists were carving each other out of a rock with hammer and chisel. From the waist down, they were still locked in stone.

"You've never seen this before?"

"No," said Oscar. A slight smile illuminated his face at the sight of the clever symbol.

"Each one is helping the other," said Falcon nodding with satisfaction at Oscar's smile. "This image will allow you to recognize people associated with the resistance movement."

A waiter entered silently with a tray, placed it on the table and left immediately. As soon as the man had disappeared, Falcon took two glasses and a carafe of wine from the tray and said, "Serve yourself while I pour. The food is all yours, and everything looks and smells delicious."

While Oscar was eating, Tony took small sips of wine and began to speak.

"As an individual, you can't possibly have an effect on the major events in life. There is nothing you can do when the world around you changes, no matter how badly you may want to. You may think that you are conquering the sea by sailing across it with a ship, but you still don't have the least bit of influence on its ebb and flow, and you will always be at the mercy of its storms and calms. I never asked to live in a world such as this, Oscar. Did you?"

Oscar kept his head down as he chewed his food. He raised his eyebrows to look up and was punished by a stabbing pain behind his eyes. He took another bite, swallowed, emptied his glass and gestured to Falcon to pour some more wine.

"I have never asked for anything," he replied, "especially not for the recent events in my life."

Falcon laughed, and as much as Oscar wanted to laugh along with him, his entire body hurt with the effort. Even moving his jaws to eat caused him a good deal of pain, but his hunger was too great to allow this tasty meal to go untouched. Falcon was about to say something, but Oscar spoke first.

"A resistance movement: what exactly do you mean by that? I was certainly grateful earlier tonight to be able to wash and put on clean clothing, but it remains to be seen if I will find everything else presented to me as pleasant."

"A large and still growing number of people are rebelling against the renaissance of the last few decades. It hasn't done many of us much good, has it? The new democracy has thrown decorum to the wind, and in its place has come an oligarchy. The people no longer have a say in the important matters. The most important decisions are made for us by the tycoons who run the big corporations. You have experienced that reality firsthand; Ferdinand Man is an extremely powerful person. So was Walter Krocht."

Oscar had raised his glass halfway to his lips, but he now cautiously put it back down on the table, looking Falcon right in his mystical eyes.

"Am I to understand from this that I should be taking your talk of a resistance literally? Am I now speaking to someone who belongs to a group of rebels who are willing to take strong action? Was it you who inspired my bodyguards to murder Walter Krocht?"

He suddenly had a bizarre thought and saw Jay Jay and Richard standing in front of him, their coats open, the emblem of the two sculptors freeing each other from the rock emblazoned on the inside fabric.

"I'm glad that you brought that up," said Falcon. "I can assure you, once and for all, that we had nothing to do with that. And furthermore, your quick response and anger on the subject proves that your hands are also clean of this heinous crime. I had my doubts about that, Oscar, but I am satisfied now that you are innocent. I am extremely happy that one of our men found you and was able to persuade you to go with him, although I would have much preferred it if he had done so before you were so barbarically beaten."

"I still don't know who you really are."

"We are a group of intellectuals, Oscar. A group of people with common sense. The time has long since passed when it is acceptable for the nations of the world to make war when they do not agree on current political conditions. We are a tightly knit group of people working together to break the powerful control of the tycoons by installing men of our own in important positions within the cartels. We attempt to sway the media to our way of thinking, and toward this end, we have managed to gain some powerful, if not controlling, interests in several radio and television stations and also a few publishing firms. I will tell you more about all this later, though, if you haven't stood up and walked out on me yet! At the moment the world is a complete madhouse, and if someone doesn't do something about it soon, the whole thing is going to spin out of control."

Falcon got up and began pacing up and down, wineglass still in hand. Oscar saw that his hair was long and tied in a ponytail, just as Jay Jay's and Richard's had always been.

"A very select group of men runs things in this world today, and free men everywhere have been turned into puppets who are encouraged to drink to excess and party night and day. The streets are filled with pompous asses in their fancy clothes on constant parade. A second, new, renaissance is upon us, and everyone seems to enjoy being a part of the show. They love the decadence and the mindless waste while I, on the other hand, am someone who must have an explanation for everything; but I only seem to be able to fathom the truth to a certain depth. It seems there is always a mist hanging over us that covers the whole truth. Do you follow me? Or am I talking to the wrong man after all? I would be surprised at that, though, for I have personally chosen you, and my intuition rarely fails me."

"You have chosen me," Oscar muttered. He pushed his empty plate to the middle of the table and leaned backward on his chair. "I don't quite get that, but as for the rest of what you have been saying, I follow you quite well. I am very knowledgeable about all aspects of world history; I have studied in depth the adventure of mankind from his origins right up to the present. The time we live in now is unique, and I must admit that there are many things that we cannot explain. From democracy to oligarchy, as you said—that should have never happened. It was not supposed to be able to happen. The fact was it could not happen! There were laws passed that forbade the creation of a monopoly in every way; formation of trusts should always have been prevented by the laws we made to protect ourselves. In the end, however, their loot, our world, was divided between themselves anyway, and they gulped down everything that was left like matter disappears into a black hole."

Tony heaved a deep sigh. His pacing brought him directly in front of Oscar. He leaned on the table and said, "You must become one of us." His strange gray eyes seemed to be seeing visions again. "You need us just as much as we need you. Yes, yes, of course, you demand an explanation to that statement. I can tell you right away, but first I must apologize in advance for what I am about to say, Oscar Man: Perhaps it was not such a bad thing that they beat the crap out of you on the streets of Manhattan. You have now experienced the fury of the crowd, and if we don't do something about it real soon, a large part of the population will probably continue to hate you irrationally, and you will never again be able to simply walk through the streets of the city. In this world of manipulative people like Walter Krocht, the instigator of all this chaos, there are also the misguided heroes who squander their money trying to make life more pleasant with their feasts and orgies.

"The great Roman emperors knew how to keep the mob in check and the lions fed, if you catch my drift! Now then, Oscar, as I told you earlier, I have the ability to form and mold people. We need a hero, a shining example to everyone who desires to see things changed. Let me lay out the course for you, allow me to work with you on your behavior, your charisma and your personality. Let me handle the media; let me be the manipulator. And you can be the one to go down in history as the man who saved the world!"

"I believe you really are serious about all this!" Oscar said.

Tony sat down and poured the balance of the wine into the two glasses. "Of course I mean it! The way the world is now, even the greatest minds will not achieve their goals alone. They will be passed over and pushed aside by far less talented people who are connected to and supervised by the right masters. I can turn a simple soul into a television personality, and I can turn a successful businessman into someone who cannot even count to ten. With you, the talent and personality are already there. The success of the plan depends on how you are introduced back into society and with whom you will have contact. Understand me well, Oscar. You must know that it's all just a game. You will be seen as a charismatic leader while in actuality you are a puppet, and those behind the scenes pull your strings. Let me put it in a different way. Philosophically speaking, I want you to view our dangerous undertaking as a ship. The assigned crew is already on board and in place. From the captain to the cook's boy, from the officers to the sailors, all are ready. The only thing still missing is our figurehead, and that, Oscar, is where you come in."

"The jester, I suppose? One more time?" asked Oscar.

Tony Falcon banged the table with his fist and startled Oscar.

"Yes! Yes, indeed," he said, his voice much louder now, and his gray eyes flashing fire. "Everyone has his own part to play. And to you, Prince, goes the part of the jester. After all, is the part not made especially for you? Once I have transformed you into the favorite, the sweetheart of the public, you will be able to say things in public forums that would cost another his head if he dared to say what you said! Are there any ancient jesters who became world famous personalities? Do we even remember their names? Not at all! We know only the lords whom they served, those foolish kings who had disputes with each other and had the power to back it up, sacrificing the lives of their soldiers for it. Oscar Man, the bastard, the disowned prince, will be the first jester who will be remembered forever!"

Oscar had always taken things and life in general, just the way they came. He had merely accepted the circumstances as they were. But he was different now; he had reached a point in his life where he felt the need to take control of some things for himself. Everything this man Falcon had told him began to amuse him more and more, but he still had no intention of promising anything to anybody yet. Oscar was not sure if Tony Falcon fit into his own plans; so, for the time being, he was not going to make himself available as some kind of folk hero.

As if Falcon had read Oscar's thoughts, he said, "We have lots of time. Believe me, I'm happy that you are here at all and willing to hear me out."

"Can you tell me, short and to the point, what it is you wish to achieve in the end?"

"First, and most important, a free world for all people who must be able to decide their own fates once again. Primarily, I am thinking about others. Let's get them functioning as free-minded and strong-willed individuals again. As for myself, what I need to achieve as a personal goal is to find out what the hell is really going on in this world! There is more going on here than meets the eye, and I would like to make it visible to everyone. Something has a stranglehold on all of us. And I do mean all of us; I mean the tycoons, the men and women who call themselves princes, princesses, kings and queens. They too are being repressed. I want to find out what it is that is strong enough and intelligent enough to influence world events this way."

Oscar had to admit to himself that this way of thinking actually fit in pretty well with his own, but Oscar was already a step ahead of Falcon. He knew the proper way to proceed was to trace his life back to his own youth. Once there, perhaps he would be able to uncover the secrets that had caused the present world circumstances. Oscar could not even put these thoughts into words for himself, so it seemed like a wise idea to remain silent about it with Falcon.

"I want to start with getting your wonderful personality to beam," said Falcon. "Look at me. I am not tall or handsome, but I know that I strike many people as a man with an overwhelming personality. I've always had these special, mysterious, enchanting eyes, and they have been a major factor in the image I project. As for the rest of the show, I had to learn everything myself: attitude, clothing, speech, movements—everything! My magical aura and my bottomless well of self-confidence make me a man one cannot ignore. I don't even need an entourage to appear imposing, as so many of our 'beloved royals' must have. Here, in the sparsely furnished back room of a small, rundown bar, I am not any less impressive than if we were meeting in Ferdinand's palace. Don't you think you can agree with that?"

The light gray eyes stared deep into an unknown dimension somewhere behind Oscar Man's head.

"Yes, I agree with that. I think I know what you mean."

"You are blessed with more charisma than I, Oscar. From you, on this canvas, I can create someone who is head and shoulders above all others. I wanted to meet you here, Oscar, because I was sure that we both could have our own way once I had told you of my plans. I already trusted you, and now I know that we can go very far together. You know what? I want you to come with me outside. A couple of streets down from here I have my own company!"

Before he opened the door of the small room, he said, "Nothing will happen to you; there are people around who will protect you."

Together, they walked through the noisy bar and went outside. It was evening now. Oscar was tired and ached all over, but he was not sleepy, and in an odd way he found it therapeutic to talk with this man and be in his company.

Falcon lead the way and pushed through the crowd while Oscar took care that no one bumped against him, afraid he would be hurt again. Soon they stood on the corner of a broad street, facing a huge, square building with no visible embellishments. It was completely out of tune with all the other styles of architecture in the area, which showed the hand of modern masters using old techniques.

On top of the building burned the emblem of the two sculptors, formed by thousands of small lights. Under it, bright neon letters formed the words *Mason Media*.

This symbol, which Falcon had been so mysterious about, now appeared as a giant, illuminated advertisement. Through groups of lamps that alternately blinked and caused the sign to appear to have motion, the illusion was created of the two sculptors cutting each other out of the rock with their hammers and chisels.

Oscar pointed up at the sign. "With this you will be able to recognize the people of the resistance movement," he said repeating Falcon's earlier words.

"You bet," said Falcon with a smile. "No one will ever suspect it means anything while we so prominently display it in public."

Approaching the entry, he placed his hand in front of a small glass eye in the wall. With a subtle click, the large metal door opened. Oscar followed him into a central hall, which led off to different corridors. Toward the back of the hall, staircases built along either wall mirrored each other. In the middle of the hall was a stone fountain with a mosaic floor.

"Welcome to Mason Media, Oscar. A free enterprise that has managed to keep itself from being absorbed by the big multinationals. There are other companies in the United States and Europe just like Mason Media, and together we have formed a strong alliance. In principle, everyone can reach out to us, and we, in turn, can reach everyone."

As they walked and talked, they quickly ascended the staircase on the left side of the room, taking the steps two at a time. Oscar, who was having trouble following Falcon's swaying ponytail up the stairs, looked up and said, "Mason Media. Are you Freemasons?"

Falcon stopped, looked back and said, "While it is true that the Freemasons stand for freedom, fraternity, raising the intellect and much, much more, we are far more pragmatic."

He waited until Oscar had almost caught up with him and then said, in a softer voice, "You have no idea of the people I have had under my care—those whom I have trained and taught and then managed to place in important positions within international corporations. They are infiltrators, spies and informants who have all of our resources at their disposal to assure their popularity with the public. It is our task to stay alert as long as we are ruled over by leaders who don't see us as human beings, nor even as individuals, but as a collective—a collective to be gagged and made to serve the royals in their dream world of majestic beauty."

Oscar wanted to continue going up, but Falcon remained glued to the spot.

"What keeps our society in balance? Why is it that none of the conglomerates ever hint that society, as a whole, cannot possibly go on this way? We feast until we are ready to drop; we live our lives on a day-to-day basis. We serve people who have proclaimed themselves kings. All in all, one would have to agree that this is all just a ridiculous charade!" He turned around, and with a shrug of his shoulders, continued upstairs.

Falcon led Oscar through the building, showing him studios equipped with the most modern equipment, editorial offices and meeting rooms. Oscar had been a visitor before to radio and television stations, publishing companies and other multimedia establishments, and he noticed that the people working here were dressed much more casually than their colleagues who worked at Man-Mandate Enterprises, Syrinx Colorado or Fenrir International.

Falcon's office was on the top floor and was furnished with an imposing desk of black hardwood, a couple of leather easy chairs and several bookcases. Carefully, Oscar sat down on one of the chairs as Tony slid open a big panel revealing a large screen in the wall. He then sat down at a keyboard on his desk and said, "We bring you the news, like any other station."

The screen revealed a holographic image of a small figure on a busy street. To his horror, Oscar recognized himself. His clothes were torn, and blood dripped down his face and hands. A clear voice in the background was saying, "Please wait here until the rest of my crew catches up. You need help and we—uh—we need—"

Oscar watched himself turn around and shout, "Of course! You need a story. They have done my makeup, and now I'm all ready for an in-depth interview!"

The background faded away, and—battered, bruised and provoked—Oscar stood there, a lone, rebellious figure. Then, on his left, several other Oscars appeared, quickly succeeded by a cascade of figures to his right. One of them wore a fool's costume; another was clothed in a dress uniform with a wide cape over his shoulders. Oscar saw himself standing there in decuple. The most shocking image of Oscar stood rooted to the ground, staring in front of him with nothing but fear in his eyes. Had Falcon restored the original background to the picture, one would have seen that Oscar was watching the attack on Walter Krocht in the park near the metal cathedral.

The three-dimensional figures now walked slowly along with each other in front of the large screen.

"You see, I have done all my homework where you are concerned," said Falcon. "I can reinvent you in many different forms, and I can even control your actions. Here you see yourself in several different moods, all caught by the camera. You are a handsome man, Oscar, and you are intelligent. It is rumored that you even have a talent for writing wonderful poetry and giving stirring recitations of it. Raised in a modern-day royal house, endowed with the wit and irony of the jester, the eternal misfit and the illegitimate son, you have all the qualities and idiosyncrasies needed to fulfill the hero's part. Let us agree on something, you and I. And then you must go home, for you need rest."

The Oscars on the wall disappeared, and the panel slid closed silently over the screen.

"Home? That's impossible!"

"You just leave that up to me." Falcon came and sat across from him. "I'm going to begin work on a new Oscar Man. I know exactly how to go about it while you remain in the background. I'm going to make you so famous that you won't ever again have to fear attempts on your life by those who think you had anything to do with the murder of Walter Krocht. We will meet again later. I hope you feel inclined to cooperate with me because you'll end up a freer man than you are right now, and a beloved personality as well. As so many people in Europe see you as the generous philanthropist, the merry partygoer, the jester, so everyone here will see you too. And a true hero, with the right people behind him, has the power to shake even the most dictatorial regime."

Oscar reacted laconically, slowly rising to his feet and saying, "As soon as I get a chance, I'm off to Europe. I want to hide out in Switzerland for a while. What you do with my image in the meantime is entirely up to you."

"I will not only take you home," said Falcon with renewed enthusiasm, "I will also see to it that you arrive safe and sound in Switzerland, but please stay just a bit longer so that we may continue our conversation."

Falcon again did most of the speaking.

He fired countless questions at Oscar and seemed to stare through him as he listened to his answers, paying full attention to everything he said. Oscar found him extremely intriguing but still made no promises. He remained suspicious of the whole situation; maybe this man was using him simply for personal gain, or perhaps he was just as mad as so many other people Oscar had come to know.

"They may even beg you to return to the court," predicted Falcon. "How do you feel about your family? Do you bear much hatred toward them?"

"Their power is so great these days that they seem to have lost all sense of reality," said Oscar. "No, I bear no malice. We all have our own path to follow."

It was just about midnight when a mobile Mason Media TV crew pulled up in front of Oscar's apartment building. A young woman with long, jet-black hair got out and walked toward the steps where a large group of people from the press still hung about. She was followed by a cameraman and a sound technician who were in turn closely followed by two armed and uniformed members of Man Security Service wearing full-faced white helmets with the family insignia emblazoned on the front.

All the multinational corporations had their own private security forces whose power and authority was far-reaching. Several members of the NYPD, who were permanently stationed in front of the building, had established a fraternal bond with Man Security and could be counted on to cooperate.

"You would have been better off staying at home," someone from one of the other stations said to the woman with the black hair. "There's no way Oscar Man will show up here. No doubt he's gone deep underground after that dreadful beating he got. All the entrances are being watched. So many people went in and out of here today that it made my head spin! There are a ton of offices in the building with an army of personnel working here at all hours. You can only get inside if your fingerprint is in the system—or of course, if someone lets you in. I'll be glad when my relief gets here!"

One of the security guards took off his glove and placed his index finger on a glass eye in the wall. The door immediately opened. He stepped quickly inside, and the door closed just as quickly behind him.

"What's going on?" asked the man who had just been speaking.

"Just a routine inspection of the Man apartment," one of the guards replied.

Inside, Oscar had pulled the helmet off his battered head and now heaved a sigh of relief as he walked toward the elevator, helmet in hand. He paid no attention to the people in the hall who were looking him up and down. He no longer cared if he was recognized. Hell, for all he did care, they could go tell the press that he had managed to get past them and was inside now.

He took the elevator up to his penthouse and stepped inside. A smile spread across his face now that he was finally home again. He saw that his personal possessions from the palace, including his clothes, had all been shipped here. It had to be Johanna who had arranged this for him, the same way she had arranged the generous deposit to his bank account. With slow, cautious movements he removed the uniform and put on his own trousers and a silk shirt. He went to look for Cathy Wheeler, and as he walked through the apartment filled with his books, New Art posters and paintings, he noticed most of all the beautiful ferns that stood in the tall, red pots, evidence of Cathy's green thumb. He entered the round, central chamber of his apartment, which had a high, glass dome-shaped roof. This was his private sanctuary. Here he kept his most important books, and he could sit, reading for hours, in one of the comfortable armchairs. This had always been his favorite apartment, and he was happy that Johanna had let him keep it.

He suddenly noticed a man sitting in one of his easy chairs whom he immediately recognized as Algernon Sparks, the homicide detective from the New York City Police Department. Startled and embarrassed at having been caught red-handed, Sparks put a half-full wineglass on an end table, jumped to his feet and buttoned up the jacket of his gray linen suit. He ran his hand nervously through his short, bristly hair.

"Hello," he said. "You definitely don't look like someone willing to receive an uninvited guest with open arms. Good gracious, your body must hurt all over!"

The sum total of all the misery Oscar had recently been through— seeing someone he knew murdered, the accusations, the solitary confinement, his disownment and the attempt on his life—would normally have resulted in an act of extreme aggression, but he had managed thus far to keep himself in control. Now, however, when he saw Algernon Sparks getting up from his chair in the room, he considered his absolute private territory, something snapped. Later he would explain what happened as a break in the mental barrier he had put up to protect himself from bad influences seeping in from the outside, a crack in the wall he had built in his youth. But the evil he had always been afraid of committing did not manifest itself now in this quiet room. Instead, something horrible sprang forth from his mind.

Algernon Sparks grew stiff as he felt an irritating heat under the top of his skull as if his brains had begun to boil. He wanted to open his jacket and reach for his weapon, but all he could do was cover his face with his outspread fingers and simply stand there, silent and unmoving, until Oscar had regained his composure. Once Oscar was back in control of himself, Algernon was able to move again, and the terrifying feeling in his head disappeared.

"What was that?" Algernon asked. "What happened?"

Oscar didn't respond to his question but answered with one of his own.

"What are you doing here?"

"Please, allow me to sit down again."

"Certainly not," Oscar said sharply. He motioned around the room, pointing at the bookcases and the high domed ceiling above them. "Everything I owned has been taken away form me except for this apartment. I want to be alone. But before I throw you out, tell me how you got in here."

Algernon Sparks stood there trembling.

"I just thought I was going to die," he said. "Give me a moment to pull myself together."

Oscar walked up to him, grabbed him by the shoulders and began to push him toward the door. As if he no longer possessed the physical energy to resist, the detective allowed himself to be herded through the rooms of the penthouse to the outer door. Oscar opened the doors of the elevator and pushed him inside. Sparks, a dazed look in his eyes, descended to the ground floor, holding his hands against his head as he mistook the feeling of dizziness caused by the speed of the elevator for a renewed attack upon his mind. Meanwhile, Oscar had returned to his domed sanctuary.

There he found Cathy Wheeler waiting for him. She had heard the two men's voices and had come to have a look. The sight of her warm, familiar face, framed by long curls, gave Oscar an immediate peaceful feeling in his soul. They fell into each other's embrace and exchanged a long-delayed kiss. Oscar was grateful that she didn't make any remarks about his battered appearance.

Her pale, gray eyes were similar to those of Tony Falcon, but while his were ominously mystical and disturbing, Cathy's were penetrating in a pleasant way. Oscar sat down, pointed at the wineglass that Sparks had left behind, and said, "I have so much to tell you, Cathy, but first I want to know why that man was here."

She didn't bother him with any of her own questions but immediately sat down and answered him. She was overjoyed to see Oscar again and could not hide the tears of happiness that glistened in her eyes.

"The police were here earlier and turned everything upside down. Oscar, not a book remained untouched on the shelves. After you were released from prison, Algernon Sparks came here regularly to see if you had arrived. I could have refused him admittance, but he told me that he would just come back with a search warrant. But when he finally gets to see you, he leaves again immediately. Did he say anything to you?"

Oscar shook his head. He did not mention the psychic attack he had unleashed on Sparks, since he really didn't even understand himself what he had done.

Cathy continued, "He has an office somewhere in this building and has been staying there. He really wants to talk to you; he told me that a contingent from the army was awaiting your arrival."

"The army and the police," said Oscar, more to himself than to Cathy. "Everyone seems to need me. Regardless, I'm much too tired to talk to anyone besides you."

"I understand; it's already very late."

He noticed now that she was dressed in a long, black nightgown.

"Were you already sleeping?"

"Yes."

"While the detective was sitting in my chair, drinking my wine," he muttered. He felt himself becoming angry again. "But I'll worry about that tomorrow," he decided and tried to smile while he slowly stood up. "I'm going to sleep."

"Come to my room," said Cathy. "At least then you won't be alone."

She wanted to ask him a thousand questions, but more importantly, she wanted him to know just how happy she was that he was home again. She decided to wait until the morning to ask her questions. Supporting him, she led him to her room.

Late the next morning, Oscar and Cathy sat on the terrace under a cloudless sky. They were happy to be together again, and this time they didn't lean over the railing just to look at the city and test each other's knowledge of the past.

Oscar felt well rested, and as long as he didn't make any sudden movements, his body didn't hurt too much. Likewise, if he didn't smile too broadly, which was difficult now that he was home with Cathy, he had little problem from the stitches under his eyes. Countless thoughts occupied his mind, but the most prevalent was what had happened last night between he and Sparks.

He gave Cathy the chance to unburden her soul and listened attentively to her. She had worried about him constantly and was especially shocked when she had heard on a news flash that he had almost been trampled to death by a wild mob. She handed him a set of papers that had been delivered by an officer of the palace guard and that described exactly what the condemnation by his family meant. She was worried about the status of her work and lodging.

"This house is as much yours as it is mine, Cathy," Oscar told her. "I need your help; your clear mind is essential to me. And thanks to a considerable donation by Johanna, I have no financial problems, so everything here can remain as it always was. At least that will remain status quo—that and the fact that you must never, ever forget that I love you dearly."

This last sentence was spoken in a soft voice as Oscar stared off into the blue sky.

"I almost went crazy when I didn't hear anything from you," she said. He thought to himself that her voice sounded strange. "I knew you were in prison, and then I heard about your release and about Katja Donahue, your lawyer. What happened afterward remained totally unknown, until I received these papers."

He looked at her from the corner of his eye and saw the tears running down her cheeks.

"I know how you hate conventional communication systems, because you are afraid of spies and eavesdroppers, but I never heard from you. No one would have been suspicious of anything if you were only letting me know where you were."

"You're right," he said. "I will try and mend my ways."

Oscar rose to his feet, went over to her, sank on his knees and wiped away her tears with his bruised fingers. They continued their conversation as they went inside to get something to eat and then returned to the terrace.

Cathy felt that Oscar was truly home when he had related all the events that had occurred between his release from prison and his arrival back at the penthouse. He now stood with both feet planted firmly in the present again, and she felt more involved with his life than ever before.

"So you want to go to Switzerland," she said. "But not today, nor tomorrow, right? You will stay here a bit longer with me, won't you?"

"Yes. Besides, it seems that I will not be able to avoid a meeting with Sparks, and I have not the faintest idea what he and the army want to talk about. There is something else of great importance on my mind also now, Cathy, but you must not ask me what it means because I couldn't give you a sensible answer. I need you to find out for me if there was ever, anywhere in the world, a man by the name of Emlyn Gray. It seems to me that if he ever existed all, he is no longer alive. I don't know in what time period you should begin your search, or even if he lived in America or Europe. As an older man, he had a moustache and a beard, thick curls, small lips and restless eyes. But please, you must not discuss this with anyone!"

"Do you think he might have been an important historical figure?" asked Cathy.

"Possibly, but he might as well be a chimera. I cannot give you any further clues."

"That makes the challenge so much more interesting," she mused aloud. "Of course, I'll do my very best. As far as secrecy is concerned, I won't repeat his name, and I'll leave no traces during my investigation."

* * *

Oscar wore knickers and a shirt made of brocaded fabric. He had found them among the clothes that had been brought from the palace, and he recalled wearing them at a reception for an important delegation of the Hygnos Hybrid Corporation. He had recited a poem he had written, which had moved Johanna and her minion to tears. A tycoon from Hygnos Hybrid had invited him to a party to recite his most beautiful poems, but he had preferred not to. Silken, gold and silver fox heads adorned the clothing. The ears of the animals were touching and formed staggered rows, the eyes of one row of foxes above the ears of the foxes in the next row. His boots were made of diamond-shaped pieces of red and green leather, a clear indication of his jester past.

Cathy had managed to cover the bruises on his face with makeup, but the stitches were still clearly visible. Still, Oscar was looking very much the prince when he stepped onto the elevator with Algernon Sparks.

Sparks had come for him in the afternoon, and Oscar had kept him waiting in the hall, among all the unsorted things from the palace, until he had changed his clothes. Algernon made no protests about not being allowed to come any further. He had even been somewhat relieved when Oscar disappeared into his chambers. Now, alone with Oscar in the elevator, he looked around nervously and kept close to the wall so as to be as far away as possible from Oscar.

Sparks started the elevator; Oscar assumed that he had entrance to all the floors in the building. The elevator stopped on the twentieth floor; the doors opened and the two men stepped out.

They were in a square hallway with a floor constructed of red stones. There were no plants or statues, but directly in the center stood a round wooden bench. Along the hallway, Oscar noticed a number of doors without windows.

"Before we go any further," said Algernon, "I want to know something. What happened to me last night, right before I left your house?"

"What do you mean?" asked Oscar, his tone of voice nonchalant.

"Come on now! I told you that I felt like I was going to die, and that's the truth! I let myself be turned out by you like I was a common drunk. It was as if my skull had become a pressure cooker, the contents of which were brought to a boil rather quickly."

"This seems like an exaggerated way of telling me that you felt very stressed," said Oscar. "But of course, I'm no doctor. I do not see a clinical picture before me when I listen to someone listing his physical complaints. Now then, let's meet these people who anticipate my arrival so anxiously."

Algernon Sparks bit on his lower lip and walked with long strides to one of the doors. He held it open, and Oscar entered a corridor lined with glass walls, behind which were offices. Here and there, men and women sat and worked at their desks, but it was unclear to him what kind of work they were doing. Algernon caught up with him, and together they walked to the end of the corridor.

"Different businesses have space here," Algernon volunteered. "It was pure coincidence that we established an office in the same building where you happen to live, although it suits us splendidly now. This is one of the places where various services can consult with one another. The army and the police, for example."

"Police, army, different secret services," said Oscar.

"A complex society automatically creates a complex system of authorities that must watch over the security of all concerned," stated the detective.

Oscar Man could not count the hours that he had been forced to listen to Algernon Sparks during the time he had been in prison. From their first meeting, they had found themselves less than sympathetic toward each other, and neither had yet to find a reason to change his feelings.

Sparks opened a second door, and they entered a spacious meeting room that was dominated by an oval table made of metal with a gray material top. In high-backed leather armchairs sat men and women who all now looked at Oscar. Some wore simple clothing, but there were also three men present in army uniforms. Algernon offered Oscar a seat, and as he sat down, wondering how long all these people had been sitting there waiting for him, the men and women in plain clothes stood up and left the room giving Oscar the impression that he had disturbed a meeting. When the door had closed behind the last of those leaving, the men in uniform got up, and one after another, shook Oscar's hand, introduced themselves and then resumed their seats. They were all generals and appeared to be between fifty and fifty-five years old. Dean Howe, who had been the second one to greet Oscar, was apparently the eldest, and after observing Oscar for a moment, was the first to say something; he was immediately misunderstood.

"We live in a strange world, Mr. Man."

Oscar studied the general. He had white, thinning hair and long, white, neatly trimmed sideburns. The jacket of his uniform made him look very broad-shouldered and was adorned with epaulets, braided gold, silver buttons and an imposing row of multicolored decorations. On the table in front of him was a commander's cap with a silver emblem on the front.

"I think we both look rather ridiculous to each other," Oscar said with a smile.

The general raised both hands, palms out.

"I'm sorry if you misunderstood me, Mr. Man. I in no way intended to hurt your feelings, and I certainly find no fault with your clothing," he hastened to say. "I was alluding to the stitches in your face. What I meant was that we live in a strange world when we can no longer guarantee the safety of our citizens."

An uncomfortable silence ensued, which seemed to last forever. Finally, the officer sitting to the left of General Howe said, "Welcome, Mr. Man. We all thank you for coming. Many is the time we have sent Detective Sparks to your apartment to try and make an appointment with you. We were, of course, willing to visit you ourselves, but this room, we can be sure, is free from any bugging devices."

Oscar understood this only too well; no one was as vigilant as he was when it came to protecting himself from the prying eyes and ears of others. It was for that reason that when he had spoken to Cathy about the mysterious Emlyn Gray, he did so only outside on the terrace. He had taken all possible precautions to make any kind of bugging impossible, but still he stayed on the alert.

"Do you have the time to hear us out and tell us what you think afterward?" asked Dean Howe.

"Since I'm already here, I would like to know why Algernon Sparks went through so much trouble to get me here."

Sparks had come into the room with a big pot of coffee and a stack of plastic cups.

"We need you, Mr. Man, and we are prepared to offer you a great deal if you decide to help us. Your information can be of great importance. I imagine that you have mixed feelings about your family now that you have been cast aside. They have taken your title and possessions from you, and you now stand apart from the mighty Man family and all their fabulous riches. It would not strike me at all sound strange if you said that you hate them all. Them, and the whole system that allows a handful of people to rule, control, and—yes— even own the world."

Oscar smiled as he compared them to the charismatic Tony Falcon.

"Are you thinking about resistance?" he asked.

The men sitting opposite him all slowly nodded in unison without verbally answering the question.

Double resistance, thought Oscar. *It comes from two sides, from the U.S. Army and from the media, and both camps have obviously chosen me to polish off the job.*

He took a cup of coffee from Algernon Sparks, along with sugar and a couple of packets of powdered milk.

"It seems that this would all be easier if we could drop some of the formalities," he said. "Since I'm no longer a prince, and the entire world seems to know that, I would prefer it if we call each other by our first names."

The gathering of generals seemed to relax.

"You should all be aware of the fact," continued Oscar, "that I am about to go to Europe for an extended and long-overdue vacation and that I have absolutely no intention of changing my plans."

"No problem, Oscar," said Dean. "No problem at all."

Chapter Six

Mason Media

Dean Howe continued speaking for quite some time with no interruptions from his peers, Sparks, or for that matter, Oscar. He began with an overview of the current world situation, the international corporations being the mighty powers and the tycoons their undisputed rulers. He stuck strictly to the facts leaving the philosophy and speculation as to how and why it could have come this far for later.

Howe stood up and walked around the table a few times, putting his hands on Oscar's shoulders whenever he neared him.

Oscar listened intently but heard nothing new. Only when the general sat down again did his monologue begin to get more interesting.

"If we forget about the how and why for a moment and just face facts, we come to some staggering conclusions. Our government, and the governments in Europe, is still performing its duties; all official departments function the same as always. Legislation still proceeds smoothly—until something is done that goes against the interests of one of the conglomerations. Then a fight ensues, which the government will lose every time! The tycoons know that everything and everyone is for sale. The internationals have made their own laws. Look at your own situation, Oscar. According to American law, you were innocent, for nobody could prove that you had anything to do with the death of Krocht. In Fenrir City, though, you lost everything you had."

He paused and then went on speaking when he saw that Oscar had no intention of responding to his words.

"Slowly but surely, everything was duplicated on both sides. Opposite our own police force stand the security forces of the big enterprises. The guards of the Fortuna Fund, Syrinx Colorado, Hygnos Hybrid, Richthausen, Fenrir, Man-Mandate and Dis Pater, if combined, form a highly trained and extremely well equipped militia that almost outnumbers the U.S. Army.

"Were the banks affiliated with the big corporations to cut off funds, they would be capable of shutting down the nation. The issue is no longer about whether or not we should have seen this coming, but what should be done about it. Besides, our problems may escalate the moment Angus Sebastian is elected president.

"All the rules and traditions concerning the elections have been simply abolished. The new law states that a president can rule for six years and that the election campaign does not have to travel from state to state any longer, but may make use of modern media applications to appeal loudly to the people at home. The mystical center of this new world is right here in New York City where parades for the presidential candidates are so numerous that they sometimes bump into each other. The streets are full of mad, feasting masses of people who wander through the city like migratory ants leaving everything empty in their wake.

"Other cities are also honored with a lightning visit from a candidate, but the most important speeches are given here; strategies are thought out here, and campaign organizers have their offices here. And New York City, my friends, is the hometown of Angus Sebastian. He became governor of the state and was worshipped by the people. Hell, the entire country loves the self-confidence he radiates! With his straightforward mind and powerful rhetoric, he is like the fighter who will reach the top no matter what. We all know the prediction: Sebastian will be the new president, and we will lose anything we may still have had, for he is owned by Man-Mandate Enterprises and everything he says will be dictated to him by Ferdinand Man. It won't be long after he is elected that I, and people like me, will be given a warm handshake and a couple of pretty medals and asked to step down to make room for a general of the Man guards."

Howe fell silent for a moment but only because his mouth had run dry. His eyes sparkled, and he had become red in the face. He took a sip of his coffee, which had long since become cold, and then poured himself a fresh cup. He looked at Oscar and pointed to Algernon.

"Before I forget," he said to Oscar, "you must not think that Sparks is just a detective who had nothing better to do than make life difficult for you with his relentless questioning. He is one of the most important people in our organization and fulfills many different functions both with the police and the army."

Oscar nodded.

"We would have preferred it if Algernon had a position within the palace of Ferdinand Man, as close as possible to the family and their inner circle of tycoons and stockholders. You are the one who is best informed about the rules that apply in the palace, Oscar: you grew up there, and you were the protégé of your half-sister Johanna."

"This is all true," acknowledged Oscar.

"That is why it is so important for us to work together with you. If you only knew what great trouble we have gone through to get our people inside the multinationals. All the infiltrators, without exception, were fired and sent away after a very short time. No one ever mentioned the fact that they weren't trusted, even after they were discovered and unmasked. There was always a plausible reason given for the discharge.

"Let us take the palace of your family, the stronghold of Man-Mandate Enterprises, as an example. You cannot enter it unnoticed. You must arrive by train, and before you are in, you are thoroughly checked out. The ingenious system of elevators sees to it that visitors only have access to the chambers in which they are expected. Freedom of movement inside the palace depends on your status or on the sympathy extended to you by the family.

"People who leave the palace, for whatever reason, are approached by us and pumped for details. And still we are no wiser. There is no way for us to gain any kind of clear insight into the things that happen behind closed doors. What genius is capable of making things run this smoothly? Our infiltrators were discovered almost effortlessly, and Man-Mandate Enterprises continues to grow.

"The company is getting bigger and bigger, like an overinflated balloon. And we are the pin that will pop it. I have only used Man as an example; I could mean Fenrir, Cabo, Fortuna and all the others. Oscar, if you have feelings of hatred, or if you would like to have some revenge and make a nice little fortune as well, let Sparks pump you for more details. This time it can take place in a friendly atmosphere, and of course, it will not be limited to what you know about the murder of Krocht. He will want to know everything you know, everything you can remember, about the inner workings of Ferdinand, Jimmy and Johanna Man and their most important staff members. What do you say?"

The corners of his mouth drooping, Oscar hung his head. Howe banged the tabletop with the palm of his hand.

"Please, Oscar, be honest. Is it not simply too ridiculous for words that someone can actually have a crown placed on his head and play the king? You're no longer a prince yourself, but should we ever have had to take that title seriously? Or am I offending you now?"

"Not at all," replied Oscar. "But the fact remains that millions of people always considered Ferdinand a prince, and now he is truly a king in their eyes. You all know this just as well as I do, and if you can see it from that angle, you will take it just as seriously too! My half-brother Ferdinand is now a king. Throughout history you either had to be born into the title or else conquer a country and take it. Today all you have to do is run a good business. *King* is merely a word, but it is a word that stimulates all kinds of favorable associations. All the pomp and circumstance surrounding the royalty, the crown, the scepter, the cloak, the palace, the royal household—all seem to be very well thought out. Perhaps it is because when we think of a king, we think about warmth and security, and when we think of a CEO it brings to mind a man who is tough, with a cool matter-of-factness, who is used to making hard decisions."

"What you say is so horribly true," sighed Scott James one of the other two generals. "Everything seems to be perfectly thought out beforehand. Joseph Krocht, Walter's father, was one of the most important architects of the new society. Unfortunately, he died in the arms of a whore a very long time ago, and we cannot ask him about his 'blueprint' for this new world, and now we can't question the son either."

"Did the army have anything to do with the murder of Walter Krocht?" Oscar asked bluntly. "Did you have my faithful companions Jay Jay and Richard Wright conspire to—"

"No!" Dean Howe said emphatically. "But it is good that you brought that up. You cannot walk around believing that; it is absolutely not true. We also are very well aware of the fact that you really were completely out of the picture. The lie detector does not mean as much to me as do the words of our friend Sparks on this matter. Algernon is a professional detective and an expert at finding out the truth. Believe me, Oscar, if you had anything at all to do with the murder, he would have found out.

"So, the most important question still remains: who is responsible for this bloody crime? Once again I must reiterate, it is impossible for us to get inside where the answer most probably lies. Everyone agrees that it might possibly have been a loose cannon act of the twins, with no one else involved. The police have talked to all of the guests who were present at the coronation of Ferdinand. So many reports were written that anyone who lives long enough to read them all will come to the same conclusion as the police: everyone is a suspect, but no one is more suspect than anyone else; therefore, there can be no arrest. We must do something quickly. That is why we ask you, with all urgency, to stand with us. Please. Have a long talk with Sparks, and give us permission to return you to your family any way we can so that you can be our most important informant."

Before Oscar had a chance to respond to any of this, the third and final general picked up the verbal gauntlet. General Alvin Hodgkinson was a wafer-thin man. His skinny neck emerged snakelike from his wide collar, and it seemed as if he were imprisoned in his stiff uniform like a tortoise in its shell. His field of expertise was economics. He was the man best suited to throw some light on the complicated realms of autocratic monopolies, formation of cartels, majority interest and unfair competition. But when he finished his arguments and explanations of world finances, he was a military commander again.

"When we cannot assault the fortresses of the tycoons from the outside, we must weaken their power from within. But it is so very difficult! While they know how to influence judges and senators, we can't get a foot in the door. We have to get men positioned at the highest levels. Once the power is subdivided again between new, smaller enterprises, perhaps the real government will get a say. Then everything can get back to a normal status quo: free enterprise thriving in a healthy democracy.

"If, by chance, we do not succeed despite the help and efforts of people like Oscar Man, then we have to take more drastic action. The presidential election especially worries me and is a thorn in my side. With Angus Sebastian in the White House, our chances are as good as gone."

The five men adjourned to another room where a cold lunch had been laid out for them. There was no time to be wasted on small talk.

The generals stuck to their subject; Algernon Sparks kept silent, and Oscar listened intently.

Oscar's thoughts, however, were somewhere else at the moment. He knew now that Algernon Sparks was a man to be reckoned with, someone who was much more important and powerful than he let himself appear. But he had not discovered everything during his investigation and this subsequent hearing. Oscar still had certain things that he kept to himself, and he was proud of the fact that he could once again hide his deepest feelings.

"We don't know exactly how you fit into our plans yet, Oscar," he heard Dean Howe say, startling him out of his reverie. "As soon as we are sure of your cooperation, we can work that out together."

The room fell silent, and the four men looked at him questioningly.

"I will be here in New York for a while longer," he said. "I can make time to exchange thoughts with Sparks for a few days. Then I'm leaving for Europe. As soon as I come back, we can pick up the thread again."

After lunch, back at the negotiating table, Howe, James and Hodgkinson said good-bye to Oscar and thanked him asking him to please keep everything that had been discussed a secret. They then went to another room to change so that they could leave the building inconspicuously in plain clothes. Algernon Sparks remained to begin further questioning.

"I really hope that you won't keep comparing me to the man who put such pressure on you during the hearings when we were trying to find out if you were involved in the murder of Walter Krocht," said Sparks when he felt he had received enough information for one day. "I hope you and I can start anew." He held out his hand across the table. "Can we be friends?"

"Friends," said Oscar, and he got up and shook hands with him.

For the next week, Oscar was picked up every morning by Sparks, and together they went to the offices on the twentieth floor.

Sometimes the military officers were present as well to ask Oscar questions about the life he had led at the court of Ferdinand. At times, various men and women whom he had never seen before came in to ask him specific questions.

Oscar remembered much of his youth. He amused himself during the hearings by delving into his past and recalling things that were influential during his formative years. He was actually telling them less than they already knew. Algernon pressed to get even the most unimportant things explained in complete detail, and Oscar was beginning to think that Sparks was planning to go undercover himself.

"Are you trying to get a permanent appointment at the palace? In as high a post as possible? Is that what you want?"

"You are much too intelligent a man for me to attempt to lie to you," Sparks said. "You would have figured it out for yourself sooner or later. Yes, Oscar, I will try to get the attention of Jimmy, Johanna, or perhaps even Ferdinand himself, and obtain a high post from one of them. I have taken several training sessions and won't make too bad a showing as a businessman."

"And I'm sure there is no shortage of documents that fully emphasize your numerous business achievements."

They both laughed.

"When I'm inside, Oscar," Algernon said quietly, "I might need some support. If we can get your family to take you in again, we can work together. Imagine having all your privileges back! And we could get around easily with your extensive knowledge of the elevator system."

"I wouldn't count on it," said Oscar. "In the first place, I cannot imagine that my family will take me back. Johanna perhaps, but to my half-brothers, I don't even exist any more. In the second place, I can't take you with me in the elevators. Each elevator carries only one person at a time and records who used it and what route was taken. And in the third place, do you really think that you can fool them?"

Algernon Sparks sighed and pulled at the short hair on his head.

"I've got to try. When they do their background check on me, they will hear the same things that I told them. The remarkable record of my achievements you mentioned does exist, of course, and all my success in business will help to make the right impression. I have covered every angle, and everyone in our organization has been instructed to help me. What can go wrong? And if I am discovered and kicked out of the palace, all our hopes will be resting on you. Even if you can just tell us how we can penetrate all the way into the center of the building undetected, then you've been a great help to us."

I've been a great help to do what? thought Oscar. *To bring down the Man family*? *To eliminate everyone*? *To paralyze the entire system*?

He did not ask these questions, but remained, as always, on the alert. It was interesting to have talked to Tony Falcon and find out about the existence of Mason Media, and it was just as interesting to hear what the army, police and secret service were planning. For now he felt no tie to either one of these parties, and certainly no one could blame him if he broke contact and locked himself in his penthouse or simply went abroad for good. For whatever reason, it didn't frighten him that he was slowly beginning to play a central part in all these plans.

He supplied them with fairly innocent and innocuous information and in the meantime learned enough to know what was currently happening and what they hoped would come to pass.

* * *

Oscar returned to his apartment just past noon hoping that Cathy would have some information about Emlyn Gray, but she unfortunately had to disappoint him. She had searched, and his name was nowhere to be found. She had examined every possible file, from the Central Register of Population to lists of names that she had found in books that Oscar himself had restored, copied and saved in artificial memories.

Falcon sent news with a journalist of Mason Media, who, along with a full camera crew, was received in the domed chamber. As soon as the reporter walked in, he showed Oscar the inside of his jacket on which the logo of Mason Media was embroidered in gold. Oscar understood that although the emblem was well-known, only initiates recognized each other by wearing it and showing it this special way.

While outside the building, people from the various press services still waited hoping to catch a glimpse of him; he gave an exclusive interview to Falcon's people.

Sitting in his armchair surrounded by his collection of valuable books, Oscar told about his life. He talked of his early youth in Switzerland, about the strong bond between him and his half sister Johanna, who had originally brought him to the palace, about his work in Europe, and, of course, about the recent dramatic changes in his life. He discussed the fact that he had never been officially charged or indicted for murder of Walter Krocht and about the decision that had been made in Fenrir City. He radiated with the glow of a well-rested man and was looking good in his new clothing adorned with fox heads. He had had the stitches removed from his face earlier that day by a doctor Falcon had sent.

The interview was to be part of a documentary of Oscar's life. The documentary also would show Oscar as the jester, always present at festivities in Europe throwing money about. The murder of Walter Krocht at the hands of Oscar's bodyguards would be included as well.

"It is my task to make a martyr out of the fallen prince," said the journalist. "With Tony Falcon's help, I will combine the interview and the pieces about your life in such way that the end product is an almost magical program to which everyone will be susceptible."

Before he and his crew left, the journalist told Oscar that a plane had been arranged for Oscar, which he could take to Switzerland undisturbed. He would be picked up by someone from Mason Media and would be brought safely to the airport. The day and date set for this presented no complications in Oscar's schedule, so he readily agreed.

Algernon also dropped by to talk with him later that afternoon, but this time the topic of conversation was the night that Oscar came home and found Sparks in the apartment.

"What happened that night still haunts me. I have never felt like that before, nor ever since then. You really can't explain what happened to me?"

Oscar stuck to his guns. "I still don't understand what you're talking about."

"Hmmm," said Algernon. "I'll have to take that to be the truth then, won't I? I must trust you. You realize that we may have to work closely together down the road when we are firmly entrenched in the palace?"

"Yes," said Oscar. "Then we'll have to rely on each other. Are you guys trying to penetrate all the headquarters of the multinationals?"

"Without exception."

"And what happens when you all come to the conclusion that it is quite impossible to launch a revolution from the inside, that everyone is keeping a level head and not responding to the call for reform? When all of your people have been kicked out with nothing gained, are the bombs still going to fall then?"

"If that turns out to be the case, then there will be war. We can no longer let this state of affairs remain unchanged."

Oscar had fully recovered from his wounds and was feeling fit and strong again. He was beginning to feel cooped up in his penthouse despite all the space it afforded. At night he slept with Cathy, and so far he had not been haunted by his night terrors, but he knew that they would return. He had decided to get Cathy much more involved in his life—and problems. He needed a confidant, someone he could talk to, and Cathy seemed perfect for the job. He always could talk to her. And besides, he was in love with her. When he had filled her in on the recent events in his life, he decided to enlist her help in an experiment using his newfound power. He was going to make another attempt at automatic writing and try to find out more about the mysterious Emlyn Gray. He felt his last attempt at the hotel in Las Vegas had failed due to his exhausted state of mind, but quite honestly, he was afraid to try it alone a second time.

One warm afternoon, they leaned over the railing on the terrace and watched the city go by. In two days, Oscar would be boarding a plane for Switzerland. Oscar's thoughts turned to Rosanne Vesper, and he found himself telling Cathy about the girl in the park who had debated the black-dressed, venom-spitting orator right before Ferdinand's coronation. He repeated what they had said and imitated their wild gyrations. Cathy was carried away by his enthusiasm, happy that he was beginning to act like his old self again.

"It was different in the old days!" she said. "At the end of the fifteenth century, those who preached penitence condemned the people who were wallowing in wealth, and their words were quite inflammatory. There were monks who managed to recruit small armies of volunteers to break into the homes of wealthy, decadent people and drag all their fabulous belongings outside. From pants to pornography, everything was thrown into a bonfire and destroyed. At some town squares, the fires burned like hell itself, especially in the rich cities of Italy. It seems to have solved the problem for a while; people decided to live a more simple life. They put an end to their extravagance and to their ostentatious behavior, right up until those preaching eternal damnation died at the stake themselves. Then the party really began with everybody trying to go just a bit further than their peers."

Cathy began to pace and with her fists clenched, imitated one of the preachers of penitence.

"Do not forget: you will have to account for your behavior when you stand before the throne of the Creator after you have choked to death on your food and drink. You will no longer be wearing your fine clothes to emphasize your social status or jewels to show your wealth. Judgment will be passed on your lawlessness, your immodest behavior and your unabashed selfishness. The gates of hell are already wide open and waiting to receive you, and it will be too late for apologies or forgiveness when you behold the torches burning forever to light the unholy face of your tormentor, Satan!"

Oscar threw himself at her feet and raised his hands up to her.

"Have mercy on me! I let myself be dragged along with all that surrounded me! What must I do to escape from the devil's claws?"

She remained standing in front of him, her hands on her hips. Her long curls bounced alongside her pretty face.

"Tell me about your riches, sinner!" she hissed.

"I am a wealthy merchant; my house in Milan is a palace of incalculable value. I wallow in an excess of sexual abuses with my mistresses, who all live like queens. If someone took an ax and smashed all the wine casks in my cellar, my town would surely be flooded, and of course there is my gold, which is worth just as much as the jewels I have decorated my clothing with, not to mention that of my women."

Cathy, the hellfire preacher, looked at him and proclaimed, "Since your wealth has become such a burden and a damnation to you, I will help you as I help all sinners who are sincere in their quest for forgiveness. From the moment all your possessions become mine, your soul will be as clear again as on the day you were born. Come, let us go and draw up the papers and celebrate this joyous occasion with enough wine to save your town from that flood you were talking about."

She kneeled down beside him, embraced him and gave him a kiss. Her lips were warm, and the skin of her cheeks felt cool to his touch. They sat there and gazed at each other for quite some time, her pale gray eyes soft and wise. Her eyes moved searchingly as if she could read different things in his left eye than in his right. It was Oscar who finally broke the enchantment of the moment when he rose to his feet with a heavy sigh.

"There is something I want to tell you, Cathy. Well, more than something--quite a lot, actually. I will give you the wine you asked for because I am also thirsty myself, and maybe it will give me the courage that I need."

"I am here for you, Oscar, and I will gladly listen to you," said Cathy.

He knew he could share his secrets with her, and the knowledge that she truly cared for him was worth more to him at that moment than he could ever have imagined. So he told her his tale about his youth, about Anne and Herbert Vesper and Rosanne Vesper, whom he now knew as Angelina Hood. He told her about the nightmares in which Emlyn Gray played such an important role. He revealed his connection with Falcon and told her what Sparks and the generals wanted from him. The bottle of wine was empty by the time he had finished his story, and he had drunk most of it.

Now that he had told her everything he was relieved. He had more love for her than ever. He had once heard that a burden fell off your shoulders after you divulged your secrets to someone else, and now he knew it was true. His mind was finally at rest, and with it came physical relaxation.

Cathy wiped tears from her eyes and walked to the railing. She leaned forward and looked into the depths at a miniature world of slow-moving automobiles and swarming masses of people. Some wore such ridiculously large hats whose colors she could discern even from this height. She turned and Oscar sat up, curious about what she was going to say.

"Don't you feel that it is a betrayal to tell Sparks about your family?"

This question surprised him. He had expected her to ask questions about his youth and his dreams. He shook his head negatively and firmly.

"Not one bit! I have been kept out of everything my entire life. Yes, I lived in the palace; I ate there, slept there, even studied there. But I had nothing to do with family business. I share no secrets with Ferdinand or Jimmy nor even with Johanna. Anyone who really wants to know how Man-Mandate Enterprises operates, without bothering my brothers or sister, should approach the tycoons for information or the stockholders. Hugh Willis for instance. But they are tightlipped, and Sparks knows that. No one will quote chapter and verse to an outsider. Perhaps Algernon Sparks should throw all his charms into the fray and invite Margaret Sharpe around for a dinner. Seriously though, Cathy, until I have found answers to some important questions for myself, I will betray no one--not even the people who have put me down. And besides, I cannot imagine what I could tell the generals that would be of any great importance to them. So the word betrayal is, in relation to my family, not exactly appropriate here."

He put his arm around her, and she began to ask question after question; Oscar answered her as quickly and as briefly as possible.

Half an hour later he was sitting at the little table on the terrace with a writing pad in front of him and a pen in his right hand. Cathy sat next to him, her hands folded in her lap and her eyes focused on the trembling point of the pen. Oscar had put on dark sunglasses. He stared at the tabletop. He broke out in sweat when he concentrated on Emlyn Gray. He felt himself getting lighter both mentally and physically, and after a while, he felt as if he were floating. He was not aware when his mouth dropped open and the pen began to move across the paper in front of him. He was aware of nothing at all, not of his breathing nor of the pounding of his heart.

He no longer had any conception of time or place; the perimeters of his world were no longer restricted by the dilated eyes behind the dark sunglasses.

"Oscar! Oscar! Stop!"

Cathy Wheeler's voice hurt as if a horn had been blown directly into his ears. With his left hand, he pushed up his sunglasses. When he looked down, he saw that the pen had slid onto the tabletop and scratched it.

He sucked air into his lungs and exhaled slowly. He repeated this over and over until he had regained his composure. He took the sunglasses off and wiped the stinging sweat from his eyes with his sleeve.

"Can you talk to me, Oscar?" asked Cathy. "You were far away, so far away—"

"Everything is under control," he said in a shaky voice.

At that moment, he couldn't explain exactly how he felt; he only knew that he was glad to be in a safe surrounding with Cathy close to him.

Oscar didn't recognize the handwriting on the paper. It was written in a sloping hand in big letters with elegant curls on the capitals.

In a poem consisting of twelve stanzas, the duration of a human life was weighed against the vast infinity of the universe. It was flawlessly written using modern spelling. Cathy stood reading over his shoulder. They were both moved by the poem and recognized a master's hand in it. By the time she got to the sixth verse, Cathy felt as if she were slowly losing her balance, and she held on tightly to Oscar. After reading the last lines, she found herself momentarily in the dark, endless depths of the universe feeling diminutive and unique all at once. With a shock, she suddenly snapped back into reality.

"I did not write this," she heard Oscar say.

Cathy's response was immediate as if she hoped that speaking would help her get more of a grip on herself.

"You've always been a poet, a troubadour. Your poems always could bring people to ecstasy. Perhaps the text is straight out of your subconsciousness, without your senses putting it into perspective. You were calm at the beginning, and then you began to write faster and faster until suddenly you were scrawling across the tabletop—"

"No, it is not of myself," Oscar said decidedly. "I would feel it, somewhere deep inside me. I wish I had written it—it's so beautiful! Wait a minute, Cathy, let's try something else."

He tore the paper off, put his sunglasses back on and held the pen above the fresh paper.

Immediately his hand began to tremble. With sharp, twisting, scraping motions he allowed the pen to go over the paper. Cathy watched and got the feeling that Oscar was busy trying to fill up the paper with a layer of ink in no particular fashion. Oscar raised his head up to the sun; the sweat on his cheeks felt cool in the soft breeze. He suddenly threw the pen and rubbed his hands across his face in such a way that the sunglasses also went flying.

Cathy picked up the notepad and held it in front of her so that the sun was blocked and she could look at the pattern of ink without blinking her eyes.

"Is that Emlyn Gray?" she asked shocked.

Alarmed by the fear evident in her voice, Oscar picked up the pen and sunglasses before looking at the drawing. At first all he saw was a complicated pattern of lines covering most of the white of the paper; then slowly but surely he began to discover its depth and structure. The face from his dream began to take shape. The thin lips laughed cruelly between the moustache and beard, and above the high forehead there was a shock of short, thick curls.

"Yes, yes," he said nervously. "That is Emlyn Gray!"

He took the drawing away from her and walked with it to the railing. For the next five minutes, he tore it into tiny pieces of paper, letting each scrap drift down on the breeze.

* * *

Oscar was beginning to regret that he had entrusted his secrets to Cathy. Now he sat with her in the middle of the night because she was too upset to sleep. She was sitting in one of the big armchairs, her feet up, contemplating in silence the answers she had gotten to her questions. The poem and the drawing had made a definite impression on her perhaps because she had seen them come into existence before her very eyes. She knew that Oscar was a poet who could thrill and fascinate, but he had never attempted anything in this style. He had never had a talent for painting or drawing, but she had often heard him play the piano; when she would ask him the name of the composer, he could never answer her and would simply shrug his shoulders.

"It's just in my head," he once told her. "But I have never heard anyone else play it, and I certainly didn't compose it myself."

Cathy Wheeler had studied history and specialized in the Middle Ages. She had published articles in scientific magazines ranging on topics from the growth of the European cities to the exploratory zest of the early navigators; she had expounded on theories about life, death, heaven and hell, the flourishing of art and the fast growth of international trade. The money she earned from her writing she had spent on a short trip through Europe to see with her own eyes what was left from the centuries of history she admired so much. She had traveled to England and France and had seen part of Italy. Back in America she was approached by someone from Ferdinand Man's royal household through the university she worked for. She worked for a short time in one of Johanna's libraries in Atlantic City until she was asked to bring some order to the chaos of Oscar's collection of manuscripts and books. That was how she had ended up at the penthouse. She had neatly arranged the entire historical treasure and had gladly accepted Oscar's offer for her to stay on. Oscar sent containers full of books from Europe to the palace. The most interesting works he had copied twice so that he could also send them to Cathy. Being a wealthy prince, he could afford to build up his own impressive library and keep Cathy Wheeler employed as a well-paid archivist.

Because Oscar stayed mainly in Europe, Cathy had the big apartment to herself most of the year. She loved to spend long stretches of time with her work and then walk out the door and plunge into the bustling party life of Manhattan.

As a historian, she was more aware than most of how different movements had changed the world. More than once, she had tried to put all these developments down on paper in a logical order, but like everyone else who had tried, she could not do it either. When the changes become fact, they fit easily into an understandable whole, yet the sources remain elusive. She understood that Oscar, in his own way, was also searching for that source, as were Tony Falcon of Mason Media, Algernon Sparks and the American generals.

Oscar had a strong feeling that he personally had something to do with it and that he must bring out the truth. That very night he spoke of it to her as they sat in the domed chamber:

"If we think of the world as a stampeding horse, we must find out who whipped it up. Once the horse behaved to everyone's satisfaction, but it broke loose and nobody seems to be able to get it back in check. Something of that shit-stirrer, the bogeyman, lives in me! It has to do with my origins, I'm sure of that. And to make matters even more complicated, Emlyn Gray, or at least his appearance in my dreams, is evidently involved too. In a mysterious sort of way, I am aware that I belong to something that is really disgusting, and I am determined to explore this down to the last detail. That's why I keep men like Falcon and Sparks on a string. They claim that they need me, but perhaps I need them more and might have to count on their help before too long."

That was all Oscar had said. As Cathy sat quietly in her chair, he now paced along the length of the bookcases. Every so often, he picked up a book and quickly leafed through it.

The domed ceiling was dark; beyond the glass, the stars sparkled in a cloudless sky.

Here, rest and silence now ruled; here, all that Cathy found interesting and important was gathered; and here, she had been happy for a long time. She was not looking forward to Oscar vanishing again and leaving her behind alone. Finally, she broke silence.

"Will you be gone long?"

He closed the book he was holding and put it back on the shelf running his hand down its leather spine.

"That is so difficult to say, Cathy. Listen, I did not burden you with my problems just to leave you behind so you could worry about them afterward. What would you think about coming with me? You have never been in Switzerland before."

It did not take her long to decide.

"I'd like nothing better! And I'd like it even better tomorrow than the day after tomorrow!"

"That suits me fine," laughed Oscar. "We leave tomorrow then! Falcon has arranged the entire journey and guarantees my safety. If I really wanted to, I could get an army plane through Algernon Sparks and Dean Howe. What luxurious treatment for a fallen prince! It's very possible that no one is out there anymore who would like to see me dead. We might as well have taken an ocean liner."

Cathy didn't seem to hear him any more. She was on her feet and running across the room toward a door.

"I'm going to pack right now," she cried, "and after that, I'm going to make a serious effort to get some sleep."

Oscar sat down in one of the big armchairs and stared through the dome at the starlit sky. He had intended to follow Cathy, but he fell asleep in his chair. She came to look for him after a while and finding him sound asleep turned off the lights and closed the doors. His mind seemed empty after writing the poem and drawing the portrait. There were no dreams tonight to upset him.

He slept with a smile on his face.

* * *

No longer having any possessions in Europe, Oscar had to take quite a lot of baggage with him. Six men, all dressed like laborers, brought down his trunks. They were employees of Mason Media, and one of them was Tony Falcon himself. Dark sunglasses hid his mystical eyes, and his ponytail disappeared into the collar of his livery coat. On his head he wore a hat with an upturned brim.

He had already made one trip down and ran into Oscar in the hallway on his way back up. Oscar wore a long coat of gold brocade and under it a suit of black velvet, the pants legs of which were tucked into knee-high leather boots. Today he looked like a prince, not a jester.

"That documentary about you was disseminated quickly over different stations in many states," said Falcon. "Wherever you were seen, people were impressed by your story. As a result, the papers hooked up on it and wrote extensively about you. Even the press that has no connection to us joined in. This is the beginning; I have more strings on my bow. You shall become the symbol of all freedom fighters."

"I am certainly not important enough for that, am I?" remarked Oscar.

"Not yet, you're right about that. But give me time: I will succeed. You must not forget, Oscar, that the smallest birds are usually the best singers."

His men carried the last of the baggage out as Cathy entered the hall and closed the door behind her.

"I hope we haven't forgotten anything," she sighed. "As far as I'm concerned, we can leave right now; I'm ready."

If Oscar was a prince, Cathy was surely a princess today. She was also wearing black velvet, decorated with precious stones. She had her long curls piled atop her head. Around her neck was a string of big pearls, which fell across the top of her high collar. Her makeup concealed the fact that she had only slept for a few hours the night before.

"She's the perfect woman to be at your side," remarked Falcon. "Listen to me for a moment, Oscar. You must not be frightened when you step outside. I have everything arranged for a perfect public relations coup. Instead of fearing an attempt to kill you, you should be on the look out for overzealous admirers. Be princely, but not pompous. Your behavior in public is always instinctively perfect. You had your ways, but you never came off as someone who feels superior to other people." He studied Oscar, smiled and said: "But this combination of simplicity and royal birth, this contradiction of prince and jester makes it even easier for me to place you on the shoulders of the people. Come, let's go down."

Oscar closed the door of his penthouse and locked the elevator using a code known only to him and Cathy. A few moments later, he was walking through the hall on the ground floor, Cathy at his side. He was surrounded by Falcon's men, all in livery garb, who accompanied him outside. A huge crowd had gathered there that almost outnumbered the press corps. A detachment of guards from Man-Mandate stepped in to clear the way for Oscar and to allow the press room enough to obtain good film footage of him.

Oscar stood on the top step for a while with Cathy right beside him and the footmen lined up behind him. Cameras were pointed at him from all sides. Several reporters pushed forward and began to shout questions, but before he could answer any of them, a number of people, both men and women, broke through the cordon of guards and scrambled through the press people. Kneeling on the step below Oscar, they leaned toward him with outstretched arms, reaching out and attempting to touch his boots. Cameramen all over sank to their knees to film the event. Other people stood, their hands raised up in adoration to him.

"Prince Oscar Man!" shouted one of them. "Our savior!"

Not another word was spoken; none had to be. Oscar understood very well how an outburst, even as short as this, could be viewed in many different ways. This was all part of Falcon's plan, carefully arranged to be presented to the public and to lead them in the direction in which Falcon wanted them to interpret it.

The worshippers bowed and backed down the stairs. The entire crowd, including the bodyguards, suddenly parted and made a path on the stairs. Oscar looked over the mass of people, and with a determined look on his face, leaped high in the air, his jacket flapping around him, circled once and landed flat on his feet at the foot of the stairs. He shook hands with several people and patted them on the back. Falcon's men had made their way to him, bringing Cathy with them. The security detail moved the crowd back even further as Tony Falcon himself held the door of a big automobile open for them.

"Well done," he said softly as Oscar passed him. "Prince and jester, the ideal combination! Have a safe and happy journey, my friend, and come back soon!"

As Oscar looked back toward Cathy, he saw Algernon Sparks sandwiched between men from Mandate and people from the press. Oscar waved slightly at him, and Algernon carefully raised his hand just to shoulder height and quickly put it down again, neither one of them wanting to acknowledge their relationship in public.

Sparks watched in amazement as Oscar and Cathy drove away slowly through a sea of people who absolutely idolized them. How fortunes change!

Oscar had not given any indication or hint to the press as to his destination. His whereabouts would be a mystery to all, and that also fit Falcon's plan very well.

To Oscar's surprise, Eddie Brooks, who had first brought him to Falcon, was sitting behind the wheel.

"Hiya, Prince," said Eddie looking at Oscar in the rearview mirror. "Yeah, yeah, I know—you'd rather I call you Oscar, but you really are looking like a prince! This car is going to be a bit slow due to the fact that it is heavily armored. Many celebrities have ridden in it to the Mason Media studios, but this is the first time I get to drive it. I'm pretty much married to my taxi. But Tony Falcon thought it would be nice if I took you to the airport."

Oscar turned around and looked into the glaring headlights of the car behind them.

"Your baggage," explained Eddie. "I have an idea that Falcon likes to show you just how much he likes you. There's even a private jet ready for you."

Brooks drove the armored monster quickly to Kennedy Airport where Oscar and Cathy waited in a comfortably furnished lounge until their baggage was loaded onto the plane.

They left the United States on a plane rented from Fenrir International. It was a new type of aircraft that had left the Fenrir factory less than a year ago. It was used mostly for business trips and sat fifty, including pilot and crew. Oscar and Cathy were the only passengers. They allowed themselves to be spoiled by the Fenrir stewardesses, who served them a royal dinner accompanied by the finest wine. By the time they were halfway to Europe, Oscar was completely relaxed. All he could think about were all the nice things he would do with Cathy before he went out to search for the path to his past. Cathy had never been on skis before and wanted terribly to know what the world looked like at the top of the Swiss Alps.

He watched one of the stewardesses come toward them; she wore a brilliant red uniform with a silver wolf on either sleeve. Her gloominess struck him: She was very pale, and it seemed as if she might burst out in tears at any moment. Cathy noticed her as well and instinctively put her hand on Oscar's arm as if to better prepare herself for bad news. Before she even reached them, the stewardess stopped, and with tears running down her cheeks and her hands raised, she said in a choked up voice, "It's terrible! The captain has just received a message from Fenrir City. Don Bradshaw is dead."

Oscar sat up straight with his mouth open.

His mind flashed, and he saw Don Bradshaw sitting in front of him in the hall where the delegates from Man-Mandate and Cabo de Barra had come to express their opinions of him. The imposing, broad-shouldered Bradshaw in his long robes with wide sleeves and his ebony cane with the silver knob: the undisputed leader of the mighty Fenrir International!

Cathy rose from her chair and went to comfort the stewardess. With her arms wrapped around her, she rocked her softly back and forth. "You just cry for a while," Oscar heard her say, "and after the tears have stopped you must sit down quietly. You can tell us more later. Just cry."

A second stewardess, who had managed to get herself under better control, asked Oscar if he would like her to pull down the television screen for him so that he could watch the latest news. That thought had not even crossed Oscar's mind, but as it did, he said, "I can do that myself, can't I? I just a push on a button—"

"Of course," she answered quietly with her face to the floor. Then, in a soft voice, she said, "This is an extra-large screen, and it is all so puzzling what has happened, and we would really like to watch along."

"Of course, of course, no problem at all," Oscar replied sympathetically.

Cathy sat down next to him, and both stewardesses sat on the other side of the aisle. A screen came down in front of the first row of seats. The plane they were traveling on was equipped with satellite dishes to receive stations from all over the world. Using code words in a random, nonsequential manner, Cathy was quickly able to find the breaking news about the supreme tycoon's death. She was so nervous that she could not remember the names of the usual stations and said, "Fenrir, news, Don Bradshaw."

The screen listed a wide variety of news programs covering the story, and Cathy picked one.

To the great surprise of all watching, pictures appeared of a slum in Buenos Aires, Argentina. Fenrir International had razed everything to the ground here and constructed sewers and sewage plants and provided water, power and the supplies needed to build the famous popcorn houses. The town planners had not shown much imagination: perfectly straight streets were set at perfect right angles to each other with block after block of square rows of houses. The people of the town had been busy with their trees and gardens trying to make the neighborhood look nicer, and Don Bradshaw himself had come to preside over the official opening of the district and the fabulous party that had been organized by Fenrir.

On the screen before them were three-dimensional images of Argentineans dressed in their finest holiday attire on their way home with heads hung low or standing on street corners in small groups. There were no parades, and there was no sound of music. A television journalist with a monotone voice was reporting the latest developments in the story.

"Don Bradshaw was stabbed to death by an assailant with a razor-sharp knife right before the stunned partygoers, all residents who had just moved into their new homes. The assassin was immediately apprehended by the outraged crowd. Bradshaw was worshipped here; he has banished poverty and given the people more than homes; he has given them hope. Fenrir has begun construction of aircraft and automotive parts factories that will provide work for everyone who wants it, and the local merchants are already contemplating huge profits. The killer was one of Bradshaw's closest business associates, a tycoon in his own right with a brilliant track record of his own. His name is Niels Hurt, sixty years old, also known as Whippet. He was given the nickname early in his career because of the way he handled his business: with the speed of a greyhound chasing a hare on the racecourse. He is also as thin and nervous as one of the racing canines and has a reputation for betting big stakes when gambling. Hurt was beaten to death by those who witnessed his abominable act and grabbed him. He did not get more than ten yards away from his victim, who had been his friend and partner for so long, before he also met his fate."

Images now appeared on the screen that forced Cathy and the stewardesses to close their eyes. A cameraman on the scene to film the party was present at the moment the murder was committed. With his camera on his shoulder, he managed to wriggle through the crowd and show the dying Don Bradshaw, bleeding profusely. As the screaming behind him got louder, the cameraman turned, and his camera zoomed in on the frenzied crowd standing over the second corpse.

Cathy desperately searched for other stations that would not bombard her delicate mind with the barbaric images that were flooding the airwaves. She came to herself a bit when she found a station that was offering children's cartoons filled with loveable creatures straight out of a child's fantasy.

She continued searching and did not stop until she saw Oscar and herself standing at the top of a flight of steps with people kneeling before them.

Suddenly, a loud voice was booming, "Prince Oscar Man! Our savior!"

The sea of people rose and parted as Oscar turned an aerial somersault, landed flat on his feet and began greeting and shaking the hands of several bystanders. The picture then cut to a young woman in the television studio sitting at a small desk. She was in such tight close-up that everyone watching felt as if they could reach out and touch her. In front of her was the silver and gold logo of Mason Media.

"That was New York City," she said. "At the very same moment Don Bradshaw of Fenrir International was stabbed to death by Niels 'Whippet' Hurt, Oscar Man was stepping into a taxi on his way to Kennedy Airport. He was given a hero's farewell and greeted by one and all as friends and admirers. Clearly, Oscar Man was undeservedly stripped of his title. He had absolutely nothing to do with the war that is raging between the multinational corporations at the highest levels. Now, new pictures of the situation in Buenos Aires—"

Cathy Wheeler searched the vast databanks for more background information. For the next hour, she and the other two women watched everything they could concerning Fenrir International, along with running commentary on recent events. Bewildered, Oscar leaned back in his chair. He had great difficulty stopping the dizzying waves of thought that raced through his head. The plane had hit an air pocket and bounced through the sky like a flat stone being skimmed across the water. He held on tightly to the armrests, not knowing if his head spun because of his running stream of thoughts or the turbulence of the flight. He realized that the death of Don Bradshaw would cause a shockwave every bit as big as the one caused by Krocht's murder, and there were certainly people who would search for a connection between the two events. Among the other kings and tycoons, the fear of more attacks upon themselves would begin to grow. Furthermore, he realized now that Falcon had at his disposal a powerful propaganda machine in place that could react with lightning speed to any situation. The images shot in front of the building in Manhattan had been put to immediate use in the program covering Bradshaw's death.

Oscar shivered at the thought that Falcon must have had to know about everything beforehand in order to arrange all this. He must have some kind of personal connection to the murder of the tycoon. Of course, Oscar had no proof of any of this, just as he had no evidence to show that Algernon Sparks and his triumvirate of generals had anything to do with it. It was also extremely difficult to understand how someone like Whippet, or anyone for that matter, could commit such a deed in front of a crowd of deliriously happy and loyal people, all there solely to honor Don Bradshaw. It was as illogical as the lunatic actions of Jay Jay and Richard Wright.

The plane glided over the ocean much more calmly now. Oscar looked at the screen along with the others. More and more stations were broadcasting the news about Bradshaw now, and some had already gone even further. A few directors were broadcasting archival film of events in the life of the big man of Fenrir International; anchormen provided improvised, but nonetheless professional, comment.

Suddenly the face of Oscar's half-brother popped onto the screen stretching his arms outward in despair as if to touch all his subjects and listeners with his royal, comforting hands.

Ferdinand expressed his sympathy and condolences and offered his help to Bradshaw's relatives should they need it. He made an impassioned speech in which he beseeched everyone to remain calm.

"For panic is a bad adviser," he said, deeply serious.

Isodore Clement of Cabo de Barra appeared briefly and announced the new leader and successor of Walter Krocht. It was to be Krocht's minion, Faron Hayes who Oscar had seen before during the so-called hearings in Fenrir City. The likeness to Krocht was striking, especially now that the big man wrapped himself in a black, hairy coat. He was fat and lumbering, and he had trimmed his beard even shorter than for the last crisis.

"The loss of a great leader under these circumstances means only one thing," Hayes intoned in a low voice. "Our undertaking is clear. We must do everything in our power, together, to dismantle the organization that is behind this."

In no uncertain terms, he expressed his rage over the entire situation. A short time later, over another station, Carl Holdorf the CEO of Dis Pater, who was entitled to call himself king, did the same.

"We shall not rest until we know exactly what happened here today. Don Bradshaw was a good friend of mine. He ruled gently with wisdom and had a long and happy life still stretching before him. No punishment is harsh enough for the people who are responsible for this. For I am sure that no one is willing to believe that this has been the work of one man—Niels Hurt."

People from Syrinx Colorado and Fortuna Fund appeared and spoke. Later, even presidential candidate Angus Sebastian was on camera. He was somewhere in a park and in short, strong sentences gave his opinion on the events. The wind blew through his clothes, and his unbuttoned jacket was blown aside. For the first time since the stewardess had brought the message about the death of Don Bradshaw, Oscar managed a smile. He saw the gold and silver emblem of Mason Media on the lining of the jacket and thought that Falcon really did everything to give publicity to his organization. Falcon had also been wearing a jacket with the logo on the lining just before his departure from Manhattan.

Cathy allowed the screen to disappear. The stewardesses stood up and walked away.

"Thank you very much," said the woman who had originally brought the bad news. "I will bring you some more wine."

Cathy leaned against Oscar and laid her head on his shoulder.

"If only I knew what to say," she sighed. "It's all so confusing."

Oscar was searching for words himself.

"I'm glad that I decided to leave Manhattan," he suddenly said. "I really prefer following these events from a distance; if I were at home, I would be disturbed by too many people."

They drank the wine that had been brought and didn't say much more to each other. It was the captain's voice that stirred them from their reverie. He had come in now to say good-bye to his two passengers as he was going to be busy with the landing. The plane would be on the ground in ten minutes at the airport in Bern.

"I had expected to land near Zurich," said Cathy.

"Bern," said Oscar. "From there we can reach Interlaken quickly, and from Interlaken, which will be our base for a while, we can visit the places that seem to be important to me. Besides, you can be in the snow in no time from there, at the top of the Swiss Alps."

"You're the guide," smiled Cathy. "I rely entirely on you."

"The end of summer is nearing," he said. "It can already get quite cool and very rainy. When you walk outside, you can suddenly feel a pleasant warmth stroking your face. That is the foehn, the dry mountain squall. It's a very special experience. I love Switzerland, Cathy. We have to stay long enough to see the snow fall. Getting snowed in somewhere with you seems like a terrific idea to me. We'll only come out to take the rack-and-pinion railway for a ski tour, and the rest of the time we'll hibernate like satisfied bears."

"You're the guide," Cathy repeated with a contented, faraway smile.

It was nighttime when they landed in Bern. There were no curious bystanders or members of the press waiting for them at the airport; no one knew about Oscar's arrival. After clearing customs, Oscar would take a couple of cabs to Interlaken as soon as possible.

"We'll leave Bern and return to enjoy its charms at a later date."

Just as he was about to leave Cathy with the trunks to arrange the cabs, he saw a customs officer approaching him.

"Prince Oscar Man!" the man shouted. "Wait a minute, please."

More customs officers were heading his way.

"My name is Lorenzen, Mr. Man. Will you please follow me? Don't be afraid; there's nothing the matter. That is, not here at least."

Oscar and Cathy went along with him as the other customs officers followed them with their trunks. They were ushered into a small waiting room where they were asked to have a seat on a bench.

"As a member of the Man family, you are naturally very closely connected to and familiar with Man-Mandate Enterprises and the other corporations," said Lorenzo.

Oscar was about to protest, but the man quickly raised his hand.

"Yes, yes. I know, they stripped you of your title, but that doesn't mean that you are not interested in the latest, dramatic news."

"The death of Don Bradshaw?" queried Oscar.

"You already heard all the details during your flight," said the customs officer. "I know, because I was in contact with the captain of your plane. As you were landing, more news came from the United States. Do you know the person who is the power behind Syrinx Colorado?"

"Sure," Oscar answered immediately. "I met her once when she was visiting my family in the palace. A pretty, distinguished-looking woman who could rightly call herself a queen, for she has such a royal charisma and charm about her. Roberta Rodriguez—"

"She's been murdered," interrupted the customs officer. "I'm sure you'll hear all the details soon enough in the news, but I thought it important to inform you quickly and personally."

"Thank you very much," was all Oscar could manage to say.

"I suppose you were about to take a taxi? To—"

Oscar was still too shocked to answer.

"Two, please," said Cathy. "To Interlaken."

"We'll be glad to help you with your baggage," said Lorenzen. "First, let me get you some coffee, and you can recover a bit from the shock."

Only when Oscar finally found himself in the back of a taxi was he able to speak again.

"Roberta Rodriguez of Syrinx Colorado. As soon as we have settled into our suite at the hotel, I want to know all the details. I must say, it was very attentive of the customs officer to inform me. Where will this end, Cathy? Who is next? Ferdinand, perhaps? Jimmy? Or Johanna?"

The cabs drove through the dark night. Oscar pulled Cathy close to him and closed his eyes.

Sleep would do him good, even if it was only a catnap. He sat there wide awake, however, a thousand things racing through his mind at the same time.

Chapter Seven

Black Metal Statues

Orville Hood walked across the platform to the luxury coaches hitched behind the Dragon. The shining black locomotive stood there, at full power and under steam, and let loose an impatient puff. Along the platform uniformed guards stood in line, looking straight ahead.

Orville led the way for a large group of army officers among whom were generals Dean Howe, Scott James and Alvin Hodgkinson. He opened the doors and stepped back, bowing as everyone filed inside. The officers settled down in the soft cushions of the benches; servants immediately rushed forward offering them sweet cakes and assorted teas. Orville smiled as he noticed how the officers did their very best to remain aloof to the old-fashioned beauty of the furnishings.

When they get into the palace, he thought, *their mouths will be agape in astonishment. No one remains untouched by the enchanting, old-world class of those halls and corridors.*

After he had closed the door behind the last officer, he approached two men who were still standing on the platform. He had been ordered not to place them among the military men.

A man of medium height stood waiting, arms crossed. He wore blue boots under silken knickers and had a purple cloak wrapped around himself. Rings adorned every finger, and above his cloak rose the golden collar of his tightly cut jacket. His hair was short and partially hidden by a tall purple hat of simulated fur. He wore earrings in both ears, and his face was white with makeup. He raised his blond eyebrows when Orville Hood bowed to him. The man standing behind him was smaller, but dressed identically. This was obviously his minion who remained in the background as he was expected to do in all circumstances.

"Mr. Algernon Sparks?" asked Orville.

The man nodded.

"Welcome, lord. This coach is at your disposal, and I'm sure you will agree that it is so beautiful, you'll probably regret that the trip to the palace will only last a few minutes."

Sparks said nothing and moved past him. Even after the two men had been seated in the coach, they remained silent.

The Dragon whistled, and its massive metal wheels began to turn. With a tremendous display of power, the locomotive began pulling the coaches forward. Panting and increasing in speed, the black metal Dragon's head pushed into the wind, a thick cloud of smoke and steam rising above it. Without slowing, it passed through the gates of the palace leaving the platform behind. Only after they had reached the other side of the immense building was the fury of the Dragon curbed. The metal wheels locked and screeched along the smooth rails, creaking and shooting out orange-red sparks, until the Dragon came to a complete halt.

Palace guards opened the coach doors as a brass band played a piece that had been written by one of the eighteenth-century composers. The musicians all wore fiery red uniforms adorned with golden epaulets while the conductor was dressed all in black. He wore a three-cornered hat that was so wide he had to hold his arms almost completely outstretched as he directed the orchestra.

The American generals, who were standing together, were approached by a delegation consisting of palace guards and a small group of businessmen under the leadership of Hugh Willis a major stockholder in Man-Mandate and a powerful tycoon in his own right. They all shook hands with one another, and then Willis made a motion with his hand that made it quite clear that he would lead the way. Ascending a marble staircase, they left the platform.

Willis, who was walking alongside General Howe, said, "Well, gentlemen, at least we can hear each other now. My voice certainly isn't powerful enough to be heard above the blaring of a brass band! Welcome, Dean."

The two men had met each other previously. On various occasions, ranking personnel from Man-Mandate Enterprises had found it necessary to confer with the military commanders. Once, they had met at a Man office in New York City, and the last time was at a retreat on the Massachusetts coast.

The military placed annual orders with the various conglomerates. The land, sea and air forces, in addition to the space program, which was also controlled by the military, were in constant need of new materials and products. It was a well-known fact that Fenrir International reaped the ripest fruits from these contracts, for they owned the biggest aircraft factories. They also developed, constructed and perfected new technological equipment, which the armed forces certainly always needed to be supplied with in order for them to properly ply their trade.

One of the main tools of the military is to divide and rule; therefore, they did business with everyone. Man-Mandate was about to land a big contract. The army needed new trucks; the equipment on almost all of the naval vessels was outdated, and the air force was considering replacing all of its helicopters. There were also new projects being planned for the further exploration of the cosmos. Vast sums of money were at stake. The generals and their staffs had visited the various Man factories throughout New York State from those in Albany and Syracuse, which specialized in building technical equipment, to the massive factories along Lake Ontario, which produced everything from automobiles to rockets.

It was almost guaranteed that the defense forces had come to do business.

General Howe said that he had hired an independent agency to act as a middleman between the army and Man to nip any problems that might arise in the bud and to see to it that each party stuck to its side of the agreement. This is where Algernon Sparks came into the picture. He had requested an office inside the palace. If this were granted the generals could be sure that all of their plans would materialize. Sparks would have free access to areas of the palace where, up until now, no outsider had ever been allowed to go. It had already been decided that Man-Mandate would be allowed to execute the bulk of the orders, and as the military commanders' plan began to evolve, they found that they could use it to bring Sparks in as a spy and have him securely placed inside the walls of the palace. If for some reason it all fell apart, though, General Howe had another plan up his sleeve. One way or another, he would get Oscar back inside the palace, regardless of the cost.

"Something is going on in there," Howe had said more than once. "There, in the palace of the Man family, and also in the headquarters of all the other conglomerations. A man cannot describe what he has never seen, so don't press me for details. Think about an entomologist sitting in a field studying a beehive. It is impossible for him to see from the outside that within that hive lives a queen bee, which may live up to forty times longer than her worker bees and give birth to an entire swarm!"

The Dragon had brought them to the side of the palace where the offices were situated. There were also apartments, shops, restaurants, gymnasiums and even hotels for visitors who chose to stay overnight. Orville Hood's prediction was coming true; the gathered guests' eyes were wide with astonishment as they walked through the broad corridors and lofty halls. The artistic treasures of Jimmy Man were displayed everywhere. There were original paintings from the eighteenth and nineteenth centuries, and there were newly composed groups of bronze, copper and steel sculptures, in addition to specially crafted ceiling and wall paintings. Behind high arched windows people worked in beautifully furnished offices. Palace guides, easily recognizable by their uniforms displaying the Man family emblem, lead businessmen from Europe and Japan to their destinations.

Chandeliers reflected their soft light on the smooth marble floors. The corridors gave way to circular, pillared halls, and some staircases reached so high that the lamps in the gigantic glass domes above them seemed to hang in the sky like unreachable stars.

The military officers understood that this trip, which could have been accomplished much more quickly by using the elevators, was arranged intentionally to impress everyone with the pomp and circumstance of the family. Long before any of them had a chance to tire of all the pageantry, the doors to a large meeting room swung open, and they were all invited to sit in oversized, comfortable armchairs.

Hugh Willis waited until everyone was seated around an oval hardwood table inlaid with ivory. Servants hurried in and put down a wide assortment of food and drink.

Hugh Willis answered to the most important members of the family and was duly authorized to speak for them. He welcomed everyone and spoke in measured, well thought-out sentences. The previous friendliness and flattery now changed into pure business and matter-of-factness, and before anyone realized it, they were involved in a formal business meeting that had not even been officially announced.

What Willis had to say boiled down to this: after all the visits and amenities, each one of them knew what the others wanted and what they would have to do to accomplish these ends. Now was the time to conclude the business transactions and sign the contracts, which had already been drawn up. From the army came questions that were answered by Willis and his men.

"You know Sparks very well by now, Hugh," said General Howe. "Keep your eye on him, for he feels like a fish out of water, stuck between the two parties, and he expects to be shamefully spoiled by both sides."

"Now you put me in an unfavorable light, Dean," said Algernon producing a thin smile. "I enjoy leading a life of luxury, but that is no reason for me not to take my work seriously."

"Relax, Sparks, it's just a joke," Dean Howe hurried to say. "We all know very well that you have been chosen by the Department of Defense to watch over the expenses and to see to it that we get what we have ordered. "

Hugh Willis shrugged his shoulders.

"You will get exactly what you ask for, let that be clear," he said. "With or without Sparks. He is impartial, but he will indeed be on our side when you unexpectedly come up with impossible demands. The contracts are good, and Sparks is mainly here to see to it that we all honor them. If everyone does what he is supposed to do, Sparks should feel as if he is on a holiday."

"Then I suggest," said the general, "that Algernon, his minion and a handful of his closest assistants should be assigned a place to live in the palace and should also have a decent office at his disposal."

"I will see what is the most suitable," replied Willis, as diplomatically as possible.

* * *

Two days later, Man-Mandate held an exhibition of all kinds of machinery, trucks, choppers and spacecraft while their technicians explained everything. In the park, not far from the Ferris wheel, prototypes of helicopters were demonstrated, and all sorts of new military vehicles were lined up.

The guests had all been given spacious rooms on the fifteenth floor of a luxurious hotel and were welcome to dine in any of the palace's gourmet restaurants. Everyone could move freely through the complex system of corridors, and there was always a uniformed guide on hand to answer their questions and show them the way. The contracts were signed, and then the visitors were taken once again by train back to the station where Orville Hood and the other stationmasters opened the doors of the coaches for them, escorted them out and wished them a pleasant journey home.

Only Algernon Sparks, his minion and the three generals stayed behind in the palace. They were all invited to a grand banquet where they would meet King Ferdinand Man, his brother Jimmy and his sister Johanna for the first time. The guests would no longer stay in hotel rooms but were to be assigned luxurious cabins on the Ferris wheel.

Now, for the first time, they traveled through the building by elevator. Stepping into an elevator, Algernon had expected to be transported to the hall where the sunroom led out to the garden in the heart of the palace. Oscar Man had told him that the family loved to gather and hold feasts there. He had given Sparks a detailed description of the gigantic hall with its walls that were thirty feet high and its blue ceiling full of angels.

But when the elevator stopped and the doors opened, he found himself in a room that seemed even larger than the room he was expecting to see.

The floor was made of shining, flaming red and white marble. The four walls were constructed with rows of arched windows containing stained glass images from Greek mythology. Algernon quickly calculated the size and spacing of each window and came to the conclusion that the ceiling had to be at least 120 feet high. In the middle of the room stood a stone tower that was built upon a base of four metal feet formed into lion's paws, the claws of which disappeared into the marble floor. Under this impressive arched vault sat the Man family accompanied by their minions, important stockholders and tycoons, all sitting at a round table. Outside the lion's claws, smaller tables had been placed where people of all nationalities sat dressed in extravagant clothing in any color imaginable.

Algernon and his minion were assigned a place at one of these smaller tables. Generals James and Hodgkinson were placed even further away from the family. Only General Howe had been given a seat of honor, between Jimmy Man and Hugh Willis. On the other side of Willis, dressed in a suit of ochre colored velour, sat the presidential candidate Angus Sebastian.

Sven Rimmer Algernon's minion, leaned with his elbows on the tabletop, his fingers along his nose and his thumbs under his chin. In a soft voice, so that only Algernon could hear him, he said, "This tactic I had not expected at all. They simply ignore you."

Algenon looked at him with a smile, as if something funny had been said, and cheerfully said, "I believe so, too. I absolutely don't count."

Sven Rimmer had worked for the Ministry of Defense for years and had a strong technical background. He was the ideal man to render assistance to Algernon when questions were asked about his role as intermediary. Both men had withstood hours of hearings and questioning by people who had been chosen by General Howe himself. Businessmen, technicians and politicians had all tried to draw them out and test them, but they had proven themselves to be prepared for any and all traps that anyone in the palace may have set for them. But Rimmer was right; for the time being, there was no indication forthcoming that Algernon would be getting an office or living accommodations within the palace walls.

"Any feeling for proportion becomes lost here," said Algernon as he leaned over to Rimmer. "We came here thinking that the Man family would be very happy with the orders the army has placed. In our eyes, fabulous capital and profit is involved while to them, it probably is no more than a sigh in a storm."

Rimmer waved his remark away.

"All the powers want to know what the army has in its house, and the best way to find that out is to make it yourself. As far as that is concerned, money is secondary."

That was all they dared discuss together. The first plates and dishes from what later turned out to be a twelve-course dinner were cleared by silent servants. At all the tables, all that could be heard was slight whispering. Algernon had no contact with his fellow guests, although he thought that they were probably from France and Portugal. When someone under the arched vault rose to say a few words, the room became as quiet as a tomb. No matter how Algernon tried, he could hardly understand a word of it. Everyone stopped eating and drinking when Jimmy Man finished speaking and sat down again.

Sven Rimmer nudged Algernon and whispered, "A moment of silence in memory of Roberta Rodriguez of Syrinx Colorado."

Algernon finally understood why there was such a melancholy atmosphere in the hall; the family was in mourning. Ferdinand had put his crown down on the floor beside his chair, and his face was painted black. High up in the tower, an orchestra played funeral music, complete with weeping violins and somber double basses. Larry d'Ariola, the actor, appeared and walked from lion's paw to lion's paw reciting a long poem that dealt with the end of time. His sonorous voice was carried along on the tones of the orchestra and echoed throughout the hall. Algernon clenched his fists under the heavy damask tablecloth when the poem was finished and Angus Sebastian stood up to continue the eulogy. He captured worlds of pity and comfort with his words, and Sparks watched as the big man stood there, head down and shoulders sagging, like a boxer after a losing fight.

He will have to bow deep and often to Ferdinand Man before he will ever be the new president, thought Algernon grimly.

He found it impossible to show a grain of sympathy for this man.

For the first time that evening, he was spoken to by a woman who sat at his right side. Blue precious stones sparkled in her towering hairdo, and the high collar of her dress hid the sides of her face up to her cheekbones. Her accent betrayed her Spanish origin.

"Of course, I know, just as everybody does, that Roberta Rodriguez was murdered. The how and why are not clear to me, however. Who was the offender?"

"The why is clear to no one," answered Algernon. "The offender was a parlor maid who hit her on the back of the head with a vase and then drowned her in her bath. A couple of minutes later, the maid lay on the stones of a courtyard of the palace in Colorado Springs herself. Maybe she committed suicide; maybe she was pushed out of the window. She fell from the eleventh story."

"Rodriguez," said the woman pursing her lips as if she could taste the name. "She must have had Spanish blood." Suddenly she looked at him with a sparkle in her dark brown eyes. "The murderers of Walter Krocht, the twins, were shot dead. The man who stabbed Don Bradshaw was beaten to death, and now the parlor maid is smashed. In retrospect, if everything turns out to be a conspiracy, I understand very well why the offenders were silenced immediately."

Algernon gave no indication of what he thought about all this.

"Bet on it that everything will be investigated thoroughly," he remarked.

At that moment he was glad that he was forced to lean aside to make way for a showily dressed waitress, who set silver drinking horns filled with wine on the table.

After a dessert of excessive proportions, the tables were cleared. Everyone got up and began to walk through the big hall, lost in conversation. Algernon did the same, making it his business to come as close to the Man family as possible. Seeing him approach, Hugh Willis drew him over and introduced him to Jimmy Man, who had his face painted black like his brother and wore clothes of dark green silk adorned with a huge red bow. Algernon praised the works of art he had seen so far in the palace and tried to make it obvious that he knew something about the various art forms exhibited there.

"I saw the sculptures by Max Klinger and paintings by Gustave Moreau. I was delighted when I discovered canvasses by Henry van de Velde among the multitude of art nouveau and masterpieces of Lechter and Hofmann."

Jimmy Man reacted ecstatically.

"What is brought about with paint, provided that a master hand is involved, is the most perfect form of expression of the mind. Then, and only then, can the limits of human ability be reached. Yes, I am talking about the hand and the mind set on one single purpose. For what would be the outcome of this noble art if a man had the presence of mind but had, instead of hands, let's say, the paws of a dog?"

He burst out in laughter, and while Algernon was laughing along with him, he could not help but wonder whether or not this man was raving mad. Everywhere around him the conversations had grown louder, and now laughter could be heard as well. Soft music descended from the tower that had been lit from all sides by torches. Algernon stood right in front of Jimmy and raised his hands with the palms up.

"Lord," he said, "I feel as if I am in paradise here where all ugliness is banished and beauty predominates. Now that I have settled my business and can make more time for the enjoyment of art, I look forward to becoming an inhabitant of the palace and adapting myself, along with my minion, to the noble, courtly companionship here. It would be the crowning glory of my work, and I am extremely happy that Mr. Hugh Willis will do his utmost to make this possible for me."

"I have sculptors working for me," said Jimmy. "I love to watch when an artist starts his work. I even have great respect for forgers who are able to copy the old masters perfectly. I look at how they progress all the time so that I may see beauty arise from stone and unreal fantasies take form on linen. Are you a painter yourself?"

"Unfortunately not," Algernon had to admit. "But I would eagerly watch with you when you honor a studio with your visits."

Without another word, Jimmy Man walked away from him and joined a small group of dancing people who moved rather stiffly over the marble floor to the beat of the music.

Algernon had reached one of the walls and noticed a door standing ajar. He looked around quickly to see if anyone was paying any attention to him; when he saw that he went unnoticed, he slipped outside.

He entered a broad corridor with a floor of black granite. Deep basins had been cut along the bases of the walls where water streamed that had been spit out by monster heads at both sides of the door he had entered through. Curious, he continued on to an arched bridge, crossed it and stood in front of an elevator door. It slid open when he raised his hand. He put one foot inside to study the control panel. The functioning of the elevator intrigued him; perhaps he could pry out a panel to see what was behind it. His ringed fingers slid over a field of square buttons and round glass bulges. He suddenly got the feeling that he was being watched and looked behind him, but the corridor was deserted, and all he heard was the murmuring water in the brook. He began to get that same, irritating feeling in his head as he had when he had stood opposite Oscar Man in Manhattan. It was as if his brains had become liquid and were slowly coming to a boil. He winced and removed his purple hat of simulated fur, laying it on the ground outside the elevator.

Algernon stepped into the elevator. The door closed, and with a little jolt, the cabin began to move. The pain in Algernon's head eased a bit, but now he began to feel dizziness and a disturbance of his equilibrium. By the time the door opened again, he was in a panic, fed by disorientation. He staggered outside and balanced on the upper step of a steep staircase that ended deep down at the edge of an oval space.

This oval space was bordered by a marble wall nine feet high and a foot and a half thick. Behind it were columns and windowed walls, while the ceiling was as high as that of a cathedral. On the marble wall stood black metal statues of artisans and farm workers from days long past.

Algernon stumbled back against the elevator door. Then he sank to his knees and leaned over the step. He tumbled down the staircase, bruising his body over and over. He managed to protect his head by pushing his face against the biceps of his upturned arms. He scrambled to his feet but still did not understand where he was. From here, the oval space looked more like an arena, and behind the wall, all the forms became blurred; he saw only somber colors with beams of light between them that seemed to come down from out of the narrow windows.

He had a strong feeling that everything he saw was more a vision than a tangible reality. He felt along his body with his bruised fingertips. His long purple cloak hindered his movements. He felt ridiculous in his silk knickers, tight jacket with golden collar, blue boots with curled up toes, white painted face and earrings. With both hands, he began to wipe his face. He threw away his earrings and let the cloak slide off his shoulders.

"All gods in heaven, stand by me," he whispered. "How did I come to be here?"

The figures of black metal tore their feet loose from the marble wall and jumped down. They held hammers, scythes, spades and chisels in their hands and came after him. With every heavy, pounding step, they crushed the upper layer of the stone floor. Their movements were so supple that they seemed more like people of flesh and blood immersed in tar than metal statues come to life. Besides the noise of their footsteps, the creaking of their hinged limbs could also be heard.

A metal fist smashed Algernon in the face, but he managed to evade an ax coming down at him and took to his heels. Behind him, some of his pursuers stumbled over his fallen cloak; their iron bodies knocked into each other with an ear-splitting noise. They made hissing, hoarse, guttural sounds and fiercely shook their heads. In a minute, they had surrounded Algernon. They threw away their tools, and forming a circle by taking each other's hands came closer and closer, lifting their knees up high as if doing some macabre dance of death.

Algernon's dizziness disappeared instantly. He ran up to one of the creatures and jumped on its left upper leg the moment it raised up, grabbed hold of the cold metal head and slid over the top. He floated over the shoulder and landed on his feet behind the ring of statues.

In front of him, he spotted an opening in the marble wall and ran toward it with the sound of metal on stone right behind him. A hard hand reached out for his neck and stroked along his bristly hair. Algernon ran as fast as he could through the complex of long corridors, the direction of which was arbitrarily determined by his panicked mind. He saw nothing in the tunnels he could use as a point of reference—all he could do was hope that he would escape from his pursuers through sheer luck and not exhaust himself by running in circles in idle flight. He still heard the metal feet close behind him as he came into a broader corridor hoping to see an elevator door. Running even faster now, it suddenly occurred to him that he had not seen another living soul this entire time. There weren't even any guards or guides visible. He ran up to a tall door and bumped hard against it. He was not able to open it, and the black metal living statues came crashing into him. He screamed with pain. Iron fingers closed round his neck. He had no strength left to turn around and undertake one final escape bid.

Metal nails sunk into his flesh, and he gasped for breath.

Then, all of a sudden, the door fell open. He stumbled forward but caught his balance and managed to stay on his feet. He shook his head wildly a couple of times and then looked up.

He found himself back in the hall with the tower. Two guards had him in their grip, holding him by his arms and under his armpits. Directly in front of him stood General Howe, staring at him. Beside the general stood Ferdinand Man, who had thrown on a long red cloak with snow white trim and was wearing a crown of shining gold on his head. He did not even deign to look at him and dragged the general along with him.

People were staring at him from all sides. A muttering sounded, and from above it came the clear voice of a lady who said, "At the end of every dinner, there are always so many people who have sat at the table and not touched their silver drinking horn filled with wine. and then there is the one person who empties them all."

Algernon Sparks wanted to call out to her that he had drunk only a little and hadn't even taken a single sip from his own drinking horn, but he was afraid to speak for fear that his throat would be crushed by metal fingers. His body felt heavy and his legs weak in the hands of the two strong guards. He was panting, and the sweat trickled down from his forehead and stung his eyes.

"Take Mr. Sparks to his cabin," someone said as he tried to get his thoughts in order.

He recognized the voice of Jimmy Man, not far away from him. When he mustered the courage to look up, he saw that Jimmy held his purple hat out to him. He took it from him and let himself be dragged along through the door to the hall where the water streamed through the basins.

He was lead across the arched bridge and pushed into the elevator. Afraid that everything would happen all over again when the elevator had brought him to the staircase of the arena, he sank down against the wall and began to sob, determined to remain sitting there after the door had opened again.

But this time the car stopped somewhere else. Two men he had never seen before pulled him on his feet and took him through a straight line of columns upon which heavy cross vaults rested. Two doors opened, and fresh air mingled with a penetrating smell reached his nostrils. In a dimly lit stable, he saw mustangs and pintos, giant Clydesdales, black Frisians and Arabian thoroughbreds. A horse-drawn tram stood ready, drawn by Frisian horses covered with long red cloaks. A coachman sat on the box and tipped his gray hat to Algernon. The two men lifted him into the tram and climbed in behind him. The coachman clacked his tongue; the horses began to walk, and the tramway rolled outside over the narrow gauge into the dark park.

"Where is my minion?" asked Algernon. "I think that Sven is still in the palace. Someone must go and get him. There are urgent things that I must discuss with him."

"Sometimes, a gentleman prefers to be alone for a while," he was told. "In your case, this is certain."

"We will show you to your cabin," the other guard informed him.

Behind him Algernon saw the thousands of lights from the palace. He was able to think more clearly now. He suddenly recalled a crèche from his youth, an heirloom from his father that had been in the family for several generations. The figures were of artisans and farm workers, cut from soft wood. They were hand painted, and over the course of years, the colors had faded and had even disappeared here and there. Algernon realized that the metal men who had ushered him through the palace were greatly enlarged terrors of these figures, which had always lived in his memory. He explained their black color as an expression of fright; he had created the images himself, but not without the help of a source that was alien to his being and which he could not sanely explain. An iron fist had hit him, but his face was not bruised. His hands were white from the paint he had wiped from his undamaged skin.

The horse tramway traversed a dark part of the park. Algernon could see only the candles burning in the lanterns at the sides of the carriage. It began to get lighter as they neared the Ferris wheel. A long procession of stooped figures walked in a circle around the Ferris wheel, each individual carrying two flickering torches. He could hear them singing through the thin glass windows of the tram. One of Algernon's escorts explained:

When the court has not arranged for any special festivities, the park is officially closed to the public. Only pilgrims who come to honor the work of King Ferdinand are admitted, and then only under the most rigid of conditions. They must stay together and follow the orders of the guards who are present. The wheel has a great power of attraction; the steam engines bring a complex mechanism into motion and to many people the turning Ferris wheel is a model of the universe. It makes difficult concepts visible and tangible.

The tram stopped. For a few moments Algernon toyed with the idea of taking to his heels and disappearing into the darkness behind the circle of pilgrims. How could he ever look Dean Howe and the other generals in the face again? He stood between the two men at the foot of the slowly and seemingly eternally turning wheel and looked up. Most of the cabins were lit, and the singing of the pilgrims was louder in his ears now.

"It will take too long for your cabin to come down, so we'll send you up through the system of tubes by an elevator," a voice to his left informed him. "May I wish you a pleasant night's rest?"

A small door in the heavy foundation was opened for him, and with a heavy sigh, he stepped inside. A short time later he stepped into a cabin high above the ground. Algernon turned and slid his hands over the panel that had closed softly behind him. There was no way to open it. This deluxe cabin was his prison until the Man family was willing to let him out.

He gave a start as he saw two copper images, a naked woman and a hairy, goat-footed satyr with a curly tail and horns who pressed their fingers together with raised arms to form an archway opening to the staircase leading to the glass-covered upper deck. The ceiling and parts of the walls were also made of copper. There were big easy chairs, benches, low tables, a bar, thick carpet and heavy curtains. Everything created a pompous, decadent atmosphere in which he felt not at all at home.

Opposite him, on the other side of the cabin, there was a tub-sized basin with a copper fountain in the center in the form of a laughing satyr that looked exactly like the one near the staircase. With his hands on his hips and uplifted head, he spit a stream of water into the basin. Two young, naked women rose up from the basin. Smiling, they allowed themselves to be admired by him and invited him to join them.

Algernon Sparks was trained to cope with serious predicaments, but what had happened to him this evening had completely taken him aback. His resilient mind, however, was recovering from the fright. What did remain, though, was the inexplicability and the mysteriousness of the whole situation. He decided that this was neither the time nor the place to rack his brains about it.

Removing his clothing and stepping into the basin, he waded in the direction of the two naked beauties. They did not even ask his name as they found one erotic way after another to chase his thoughts and woes from his mind.

Algernon had not even been in the basin for ten minutes when the loud sound of metal on metal penetrated the splashing of the spitting satyr. Frightened, he pushed both his lovers away and listened. His heart began to beat faster, and he saw visions of black metal statues coming alive.

"It is nothing," he heard one of the women say. "Nothing for you to pay any attention to."

The sound came closer. Something or someone was climbing up the outside of the wheel. He jumped to his feet, stepped out of the basin and rushed upstairs to look around. The cabin had almost reached the apex of the wheel. He saw the lights of the palace in the distance, and in the depths below him, the large circle of torchlight from the pilgrims. He could see lights burning in other cabins but was not able to see what was going on inside them. The sound had become louder, and a giant metal hand appeared along the wheel's framework. The hand grasped with crooked fingers a protruding bracket. A metal head popped up, and Algernon saw a robot twelve feet tall disappear onto the roof of the cabin above his. He reeled back and almost fell when the robot flung itself down.

Holding on to the railing, he looked down and saw the body burst into flames. The fire crept along the robot's limbs and then it exploded, lighting the foundation with a vivid display of multicolored fireworks. The pilgrims extinguished their torches, and it quickly became dark down below. Naked and wet, Algernon sank down on the floor and remained there, staring at the lights of the Man family's palace. His breath came fast, and his head began to hammer.

He succeeded in forcing himself to calm down only after one of the women, following him to the upper deck, explained to him that the robot climbed up several times each day and night to entertain the visitors.

It was almost noon the next day when the door of the cabin opened, and he saw that he was on ground level. There were guards from the palace present, and generals Howe, James and Hodgkinson stood together, looking at him blankly. Algernon wondered if they too had just stepped out of cabins.

"The horse tramway is ready," said a guard. "Will you please follow me, gentlemen?"

In the tram, they all sank down into soft cushions. Howe was sitting opposite Sparks and took a bundle of papers from a leather suitcase he carried with him. Without wasting any words over the strange behavior of Algernon the night before, he began shuffling through the papers one by one until he had found the passage in the text he wished to discuss.

"We have presented a petition, as you know, to accommodate you in the palace. We figured that you would be able to communicate easily with both parties from there. Mr. Hugh Willis gave the matter due consideration and feels he has come up with a far better solution."

Algernon pressed his lips together, heaved a deep sigh and stared outside. It was quiet and empty in the park. A couple of crows swarmed around the cabins of the wheel. The horses that pulled the tram had settled into a steady rhythm.

"In stead of giving you permanent quarters in the palace, Willis is offering you a deluxe accommodation in Albany, on the property of a Man factory. In Syracuse, you will be given a large apartment between the office buildings and near the factory buildings, along Lake Ontario, where most of the products we've ordered will be manufactured or completed. You will also get a bungalow with a jetty at the waterline. You will even be provided with a speedboat so that you can work off your frustrations when things are not going exactly to your liking. There is also a rowboat you can use if you feel like fishing. Isn't that wonderful, Sparks? A bungalow at the lake!"

He held up the papers.

"It's all here, in more formal language. A house, an apartment and a bungalow. What more could you want?"

With an angry motion, he put the papers away again in his briefcase and stared out of the window sullenly. James and Hodgkinson had sat down far enough away from them to make it clear that they did not feel like interfering.

From the stables, they were brought to the platform, one by one, by elevator. There, Sven Rimmer stood waiting with a number if suitcases surrounding him.

With much bravura, a black locomotive appeared, the Elephant this time. It came grinding to a halt and stood impatiently blowing smoke and steam before it was allowed to go on. Hugh Willis waved good-bye to the five men.

They all kept silent until they were off the train and sitting in the back seat of an army vehicle. Only then did Dean Howe lean sideward to Algernon Sparks and say, "You have a lot to explain. And I suggest that you start right now."

* * *

Oscar and Cathy stood on the balcony of their suite in the Dis Pater Europe Hotel and looked out on the splendid town of Interlaken and the mighty mountaintops of the Jungfrau, the Mönch and the Eiger. It was a clear day, and the snow-covered peaks of the mountains stood out starkly against the cobalt blue sky. From their aerie, they could see the lakes that held the town pressed in their grip, the Lakes of Thun and Brienz where small ships and cruise boats glided across the smooth water.

Interlaken was already a tourist attraction in the eighteenth century, with deluxe accommodations for the rich. What Oscar and Cathy saw now was the magnificence of the past at its perfection. The Second Renaissance had its influence on Switzerland, but while elsewhere excess and extravagance ran riot, the Swiss towns were bastions of rest, style and class. The brilliant architects of Dis Pater had given Interlaken a classic, majestic look.

The heart of the town was formed by the Höhematte a meadow of thirty-five acres that had remained undeveloped for more than a hundred years. In the middle now, a labyrinth of hedges was laid out around an outcropping of rock upon which Dis Pater god of the underworld and fortune was standing. He was a giant who stood ten yards high, dressed in simple clothing, cut from the stone in such lifelike form that it seemed as if he had climbed on top of the rock himself in order to get a better view of the majestic north face of the Jungfrau.

All the big corporations had built hotels here and had done their utmost to outdo each other. They had all worked together, however, to take care that the historic, monumental buildings, churches, stations and restaurants were all restored to their former glory.

Along the seven hundred mile long stretch of the Höheweg, the most beautiful buildings had sprung up, including the Dis Pater Europe Hotel. Coaches passed by, drawn by plumed horses, and men in suits with long coats tipped their high hats to ladies in long dresses. Here the richest of the rich came to relax. Here sojourned a select public that was willing to pay staggering prices for accommodations. The flashy atmosphere that characterized so many cities was far from here, where style and grandeur ruled. From Interlaken, the river valleys of the Bernese Alps were within easy reach. Oscar knew that somewhere out there in the distance stood a house where he and Angelina Hood, as children, had lived with Anne and Herbert Vesper.

"The first tourists who came here in days long past were mainly the well-to-do," he told Cathy. "There were many Englishmen among them. They were prepared to make a long journey. They crossed the channel by boat, and then they traveled on by train and coach. Adventurous freebooters also arrived, attracted by the grand nature of the Alps. Everything was pure then and filled with an unspoiled beauty."

"What I see now is not bad either," said Cathy, who pressed against him and made a horizontal line through the air with her forefinger.

"Oh yes," he said. "The mountains have remained the same eternally. It is the human race that constantly changes. The way we are standing here together, enjoying the beauty of this city, could almost make us believe in the kindness of man. But don't be mistaken.

Behind the walls of these buildings, sordid plots and schemes take place among the tycoons. In their free time, they are the most dangerous creatures on the planet. They come looking for each other in the expensive restaurants and receive each other in their luxurious suites. The plans hatched here have an immediate effect on the rest of the world. Hide Interlaken somewhere in New York City and you will only find it again with great difficulty, but sometimes what is decided here turns out to be of more importance than all the business done in the offices of Manhattan."

Cathy didn't let herself be discouraged by what he said. Talking and staring together on this balcony gave her that special feeling she'd always had when Oscar would come back from Europe once again, and they would find themselves on the terrace of the penthouse. Here she felt at ease, and she had noticed that Oscar had also calmed down.

In the morning he brought a newspaper to the breakfast table and read it at his leisure. He smiled as he read an article about himself that was reprinted from the *New York Massif,* a daily periodical from Mason Media. He was described as a freethinker and the intellectual outsider of the Man family. He was almost filled with self-pity by the time he had finished reading it. It was predicted that the stigmatized Oscar Man would rise, like a phoenix from the ashes, to show the way to a new world as a worshipped leader.

It was still before noon when he took a stroll with Cathy along the Höheweg and through the shopping districts in the neighborhood. One afternoon they took a boat trip on the Lake of Brienz, and that night they had dinner in the restaurant of the hotel. He had bought himself a dark suit with a matching hat, and Cathy wore a long dress. During their evening stroll, she wrapped a warm stole around her shoulders.

There was a small office in their suite, and Cathy often opened a panel in the wall to make a screen appear. She used the equipment to inquire about Hildegard Floyd, who had been Veronica Man's minion,

Otto Man's mistress and Oscar Man's mother, and about Jolene Harvey the mother of Angelina Hood. She found documentation of their accident in a small airplane that had belonged to them in Europe, part of the fleet of Man-Mandate Enterprises. The twin-engine plane had taken off from the airport at Zurich, bound for London. An unprecedented storm and a failure of one of the engines proved fatal to the passengers and crew. Man-Mandate did its utmost later to raise the wreckage from the bottom of the North Sea. A Dutch salvage company had finally managed to do so, but it came up in two parts and the bodies were never found. Oscar tried not to think about what happened to bodies lying unprotected in the depths of the cold sea.

When Cathy had given him all the information, he said to her, "Then we must concentrate on Anne and Herbert Vesper. We will rent an automobile and go out investigating. From the moment I got so angry about Algernon Sparks, I have been feeling big changes taking place inside of me. My memories seem to be even stronger now. If I rely on my intuition during the drive, I think I will automatically arrive on familiar ground. The company I led, Cathy, lies not far from here. Along the Lake of Brienz, closer to Sarnen. The equipment for revising old books is stored in a small, rebuilt castle where I also had my own apartment. I have traveled so often from there to Interlaken. Strangely, though, something has always held me back from going further from Interlaken in the direction of Lauterbrunnen and Grindelwald. Now I know I have to go and search there."

They were in the small working room when he said this. Cathy sat at the table, and he stood about four feet away from her. Looking up at him, she said, "If someone suddenly can know something like that, something must have changed inside of him indeed. It seems strange to me, even eerie."

"It's nothing special," he said. "I have always known much about my early youth. My dreams are beginning to contain more actual memories too—and they are beginning to scare me more and more. I hope I won't wake you up in the middle of the night doing battle with Emlyn Gray."

She said nothing, but from the look in her eyes, he could tell that she had awakened with a start more than once when he thrashed about in his sleep.

"Well," he said raising his hands, "that is not all, Cathy, not by far. Let me show you, just for a moment, what I mean."

He lowered his hands and concentrated. Cathy was just about to tell him that she didn't understand what he meant when she noticed an odd pressure growing quickly behind her eyes. It seemed as if the blood in her brains was coming to a boil. She let out a hoarse cry and slapped the sides of her head with the palms of her hands. Oscar stopped the experiment immediately and said in an apologetic tone, "I hope the pain wasn't too violent."

She looked at him, terrified.

"Are you trying to tell me that you did that to me?"

He grimaced and shrugged his shoulders.

"I obviously do not have it completely under control, for it has left me with a splitting headache. Let's go outside. I need some fresh air."

Arm in arm they left the hotel and walked to the Höhematte to take a look at the statue of Dis Pater.

"Are you afraid to find out who you really are?" asked Cathy. "What you did with me is—not human!"

In the hotel, she had known how to conduct herself, or perhaps she had just been too dazed to show her emotions, but now she pressed her head against his shoulder and let her tears flow. In the meantime they went on. Oscar tipped his hat to another couple they passed, also walking arm in arm; the other man returned the greeting likewise. At the labyrinth, they found a little bench and Cathy sat down. Oscar was still standing and noticed a young woman looking at him. She smiled and motioned to him with her hand.

"It seems someone would like to have a talk with me," he said to Cathy. "I'm going to go up there for a bit. You just stay here."

The woman was wearing a long skirt and blouse and had wrapped a cloak around her shoulders. Although she was smiling at him in a friendly way, he observed that she had a hard face and cold eyes.

"Lord," she said when he stood in front of her, "I bring you a message in the name of General Dean Howe, whom I believe is well-known by you."

"I am listening," said Oscar, his hands behind his back and his gaze fixed upon her.

"It is wise that you seldom make use of the regular means of communication," she said. "The general advises you not to do so in the future either. I am Lieutenant Ruth Lancaster. Shall we go for a short walk? Say, around the labyrinth?"

Oscar nodded. He saw that Cathy had risen to her feet and begun to follow them from a distance.

"You know about the plan to place Algernon Sparks in the palace of the Man family. What you don't know is that these plans have already begun to take shape. No one informed you about that. The army had a big, very interesting and very profitable order for Man-Mandate, and Sparks was to act as an intermediary. A large delegation went to the palace. Finally, only Generals Howe, James and Hodgkinson remained with Algernon Sparks and Sven Rimmer, who passed as his minion. Everything seemed to succeed, and it appeared certain that Sparks and Rimmer, together with a number of assistants, would be approved to live and work in the palace. Things turned disastrous, however. There was a dinner, and near the end of it, Sparks suddenly vanished. After some time, he returned, acting like a perfect fool. He was carried off to the Ferris wheel. The next day he left, together with his minion and the three generals. With absolutely nothing accomplished! I'm not telling you this simply to keep you posted, but to make you understand that the generals have placed their hopes on you now.

General Howe is eager to know when you will be back in your apartment in Manhattan. Everyone is anxiously waiting for you, and they are all working on a plan to make it possible for you to return to the palace."

Oscar stood still. He stared at a terrace on the other side of the meadow where people sat in the sun eating and drinking. He saw black hats close together, moving when the owners nodded, reciprocating when they shook their heads. Ladies leaned forward and risked their hair springing loose from the complex pattern of slides and little combs to be able to hear each other's whispering better. It was an innocent scene of people making conversation, but Oscar knew that secrets were being shared and business was being done at every table.

"Lord?" sounded the voice of Lieutenant Lancaster.

"Tell me about Sparks. You said he was behaving like a fool. Was he drunk?"

"That is what everyone thought at first. It made General Howe furious! But Sparks himself tells a quite different story, although it doesn't sound very plausible. He said he had slipped away unseen in order to look in the corridors. He stepped into an elevator and from that moment on, fantasy began to mix with reality, as he describes it. His head felt like a pressure cooker. He perceived large metal figures who wanted to kill him close upon his heels. He asserts that he fought with them and that an iron hand almost crushed his neck. But General Howe had him examined by an army doctor, and no signs of violence were found on his body. His neck was perfectly smooth, without even the smallest extravasation of blood.

"When he came staggering back into the dining hall, he had wiped off the white makeup on his face and was perspiring heavily. Jimmy Man returned his hat to him, which he had lost in the corridor. Ferdinand Man also saw him in this state of confusion, and we have no idea what he must have thought of all this. Sparks is telling us now that he got that same strange feeling in his head he once had when he was alone with you, before you met with the generals."

"Tell General Howe that I will be back as soon as possible," said Oscar ignoring her last remark.

"Can you be a bit more precise? Can you send me home with a date?"

"No. I first must arrange some personal business, and it is impossible to say how much time that is going to take. The general can count on it that I won't let him down. At any rate, it will be less than a month."

Ruth Lancaster nodded, pulled her cloak tightly around her shoulders and turned up the collar so that her face could hardly be seen.

"Then I shall move on, lord. General Howe wishes you a pleasant time in Switzerland and sends you his warmest regards. Good-bye."

"Wait a minute," said Oscar as the lieutenant turned to walk away. "Tell the general that the story Sparks told him is true. I know it might sound strange, but that's the way it is. He didn't lie about a single word."

The lieutenant looked at him with astonishment. Then she nodded and quickly walked away.

Cathy came up to him, wrapped her arm around his waist and asked, "May I inquire who she is and what she was doing here?"

They went back to the bench in the labyrinth, and Oscar told her everything. Afterward, he asked her to look at him.

"I can very well imagine that you are beginning to become afraid of me, Cathy," he said. "If you want to, you can go back home. I would understand it if you never wanted to se me again. I will give you the apartment in Manhattan and a generous yearly allowance so that you can live quite nicely."

"You have told me all your secrets," she replied while she continued looking directly into his eyes. "And you've indicated to me how much you care about me and how much you trust me. I know that you love me. I am not afraid of you, Oscar, but I am afraid of everything that is happening and what is going to happen. Let's try to get through this together."

Suddenly she began to laugh.

"I have studied history; you know that my knowledge of the past is great. But the things I'm experiencing are so interesting that I will pounce on the opportunity to write about it all later. I want to be the chronicler who sits closest to the source. Don't even consider sending me away!"

Oscar laughed too, and for a couple of hours, they remained sitting there as the big statue of Dis Pater threw his shadow over them. Cathy shivered, and she and Oscar stood up and walked along together again. It was still busy out on the terrace that he had looked at when he was listening to Lieutenant Ruth Lancaster.

He dragged Cathy along between the occupied seats and found two free chairs in the sun. People were looking at him from all sides as they watched him when they entered the restaurant of the hotel. The soft, murmuring voices now fell silent. Oscar ordered something from a waitress who rushed right over to him, and he nodded here and there to those who stared at him for what he considered a rude amount of time.

"You are recognized everywhere," whispered Cathy. "Falcon uses the mass media to give you an image that the tycoons who choose Interlaken as their holiday destination do not consider exactly respectable. You are portrayed as someone who stands diametrically opposed to them. In the mornings, they read the local papers, and over and over again, they have articles about you to digest."

Their drinks were served; normal conversation around them resumed, and the sun changed from yellow to orange. Oscar emptied his glass, got up and began to walk among the little tables. The gravel creaked under his soles, and as everyone fell silent again, it was the only sound to be heard. Cathy wondered what he was up to.

Slowly, Oscar moved his hands to and fro, fastened his eyes upon the alpine peaks and started to recite a poem in a loud voice.

He spoke four lines in German and then translated them into English making the words rhyme and then proceeded again in the same tight rhythm. At first everyone looked up in surprise, but after the words sank in, they listened, full of attention. Slowly but surely, everyone turned his face to the snow white tops of the Jungfrau, the Mönch and the Eiger. Oscar Man told about the eternal majesty of the mountains and the blindness of stone. He talked about the silence of the rocks, which perhaps could feel the footsteps of the walker, but could not see the passing of the generations in the valleys. Spared the knowledge of hate and war, they kept their white radiation forever, for snow was nothing less than a reference to the pure soul hidden deep in the stone. The words Oscar Man said sounded across the terrace, over the road, over the large meadow, to the buildings on the other side and to the mountains he praised.

At the moment the poem ended, he was standing next to Cathy. He took her hand. With a flamboyant gesture, he took off his hat and bowed to the left and then to the right and then walked with her across the terrace out to the broad boulevard. They were about twenty yards away when loud applause broke from the terrace. His name was shouted; everyone wanted him to come back and shake hands and drink together with his enthusiastic audience, but Oscar and Cathy walked along into the direction of the Dis Pater Europe Hotel.

"I saw tears in the eyes of men and women," said Cathy, who noticed how her own voice trembled with emotion. "When did you write this brilliant poem?"

"I never wrote it," said Oscar. "It came to my mind as a memory." Grinning he added, "But don't underestimate my talent. The English translation was perfect, even though I did it on the spot."

Chapter Eight

Revelation

A coach with two horses brought them to an area on the south side of Interlaken. There they rented a car. It was a fast, two-seater convertible with a powerful motor suitable for mountain driving. The car rental agency was owned by Dis Pater, and the bearded head of the god was emblazoned on the copper hubcaps.

Oscar felt awkward as he sat behind the steering wheel. He was used to the Wright brothers driving him everywhere, and besides, this was not a pleasure trip. He took the road that led from the valley up to the high mountains, into the direction of Grindelwald and Lauterbrunnen. Cathy had put on sunglasses, not so much to protect her eyes from the bright mountain sun as to prevent her eyes from watering in the wind since they were driving with the top down.

It was still early in the morning. A veil of mist hung above the brooks that ran at the side of the road. He saw cows standing in the meadows with their legs fading away in the dew. Small villages loomed up and then vanished again, and all along there was the supreme beauty of the gigantic mountains.

Oscar spoke every now and then, but for the moment he was silent, looking straight ahead of him. He and Cathy went the same way, saw the same things, felt the same tingling of the morning cold on their faces, and still their world of experience was so different that they could not have possibly made their feelings recognizable to each other. Oscar wasn't even listening to her as she told him about the excitement she felt at all the sights she was seeing.

He had withdrawn into himself and was traveling on the vague indications of his instincts. Memories invaded, bringing him back to his early youth, and it seemed as if he was slowly tearing himself loose from the present and becoming the boy once again.

He stepped on the brakes brusquely and turned the wheel sharply. Cathy looked to the left with a start but could not read a single emotion on Oscar's face. His skin was pale; his thick, straight hair blew in his eyes, but it didn't seem to bother him. He was speeding up the mountain roads and on more than one occasion took a bend in the road much too sharply. The road was very steep and winding, and Cathy hardly dared to look into the depths at her side. She was beginning to feel sick. As they came around one of the hairpin turns, she suddenly saw a sloping meadow with a forest of pine trees behind it. With a deep sigh, she relaxed and began to feel a bit more at ease. Not much later, the little vehicle turned to the right and jolted over an unpaved road. Oscar brought the car to a stop in front of a wooden picket fence, opened the door and stepped out. With the stiff movements of a sleepwalker, he approached the fence. Cathy hurried to follow him.

They faced a grassy, gentle slope bordered in the back by trees. In front of them stood a square house with a stone foundation and a wooden upper structure. It was three stories high with a slanting roof of irregularly shaped pieces of mountain slate. In front, there was a wooden porch and a covered staircase that led to the upper stories. A part of the meadow was fenced off, and an old donkey grazed there. In the wet grass, in front of the porch, lay a gray dog gazing at them and softly wagging his hairy tail.

Cathy touched Oscar. He reacted with such shock that it made the dog jump up. The animal began to bark, and an old lady appeared on the porch. She wore faded clothes, and her white hair was pulled back tightly and bound in a braid.

"Who is she?" whispered Cathy.

Oscar spoke for the first time in a while. "I have no idea, but I have lived here, that's for sure."

Carefully this time, she took his hand.

"Isn't it possible that you are mistaken? Are you telling me that you have found your way back to the house where you lived up till you were seven years old?"

"Beyond the shadow of a doubt," he said. "But much has changed. Only the stone foundation is the same. Everything above it has been rebuilt. I don't remember a porch or a staircase: neither was there. The roof was made of reddish brown stone. I can still see it now. It consisted of little, flat pieces that were round at the bottom edge and overlapped like . . . scales."

He pronounced the last word slowly.

"Yes," he continued as he nodded enthusiastically. "Scales. Father Vesper called the roof the back of a dragon, and we both laughed about it, Angelina and I. She was still called Rosanne then. It is unbelievable that I never searched for this house before. I was in Interlaken so often, but something always held me back. Something that obviously is no longer there."

The old woman was standing in front of them now, on the other side of the low fence. Next to her stood the dog, growling and wagging its tail at the same time.

"You are Prince Oscar Man," said the woman.

Oscar stared at her friendly eyes in amazement. More wrinkles appeared on the face of the old woman as she smiled shyly. She didn't know quite what to do, so she made a short, stiff bow from the waist and then held her hands behind her back, shifting her weight from the one leg to the other.

"You know who I am?" asked Oscar awkwardly.

His thoughts were still in the past, and he didn't realize that she knew him the way everybody else in the world knew him.

"My husband bought this house from your family," said the woman and reached out to him over the fence. Her grip was firm when they shook hands. "That is to say, he didn't do business directly with your family, but with a representative. It is already a long time ago, and now I live here by myself."

"Much has been rebuilt. Everything looks so fine and new."

"Thank you, Prince. You're right." She introduced herself to him. "I am Heike Wellmann."

She nodded warmly at Cathy and then resolutely opened the fence.

"I rent the upper story out to tourists," she said. "The separate entrance at the top of the staircase is especially made for that. There are people who prefer to be on their own, and then there are others who like to come into my kitchen for a meal and a talk. Are you intending to stay here? Come then, I'll show you around the house."

Cathy stepped onto the porch and followed the old woman through an open door into the spacious kitchen. Oscar slowly followed, his hands deep in his pockets, searching for memories. By the time he was inside, he had decided to spend the night here. The women talked about the house, and Heike led the way to another room. Oscar instinctively knew that they had gone into the living room. He sat down at the kitchen table, so awash with feelings that he was glad to be alone for a while. Later it dawned on him that Cathy had perfectly understood his mood and arranged to allow him that moment of rest. When she came back with the lively, little woman, the dog between them wagging its tail, he asked the question that burned on his lips.

"Mr. and Mrs. Vesper. Anne and Herbert. Did you know them?"

Heike opened a cupboard above the sink and had to stand on her toes to get a bottle of liquor. The thin braid dangled to and fro along her back. She took three small glasses from a lower shelf and filled them to the brim. She picked one up with the intention of bringing it to Oscar but realized that her hands were shaking too much. Cathy noticed it and took the glass from her. Impatiently, Oscar waited for an answer.

"The names do ring a bell, Prince. Anne and Herbert Vesper. Yes, I have heard them before, but at this moment I cannot place them."

"They were the former owners of this house. I believe my family may have bought it from them and resold it immediately to you and your man."

"Of course," she said. "Now I remember. Well, to your good health!"

She lifted up the small glass and emptied it quickly with a slurping sound. Cathy did the same and made a wry face. She was not used to hard liquor. Oscar only sipped at it.

"Do you know what happened to them?"

Heike Wellmann stared at the stone floor.

"Certain things you do know," she said, "but they are of so little use to you that you don't store them in your memory as ready knowledge. Do you understand? There are things that you know and actually never seem to need anymore. And the older you get, believe me, more disappears to that place from where you almost can't get it out again."

Cathy began to laugh, and Heike herself laughed out loud too. Then the old woman snapped her fingers and said, "Wait—I think I know. The Vespers. There was something about children they had sheltered. Maybe they were orphans. They went off to America, those children, and that had something to do with your family. My husband did know the Vespers, I am sure of that. You see? One memory recalls the other. The children went away; the man and the woman stayed behind. Then they wanted to move, and I remember how my husband found it strange that they didn't say where they would go to. I thought to myself that they would go far. To Australia or New Zealand. They wanted to build a new life. I also remember how my husband told me that he thought they both looked so sad, and he knew for sure that the woman had often cried. I never saw them myself. They were the former owners indeed. Wait!"

She opened a door to a small room that was fitted as a pantry. Stepping in and bending down, she rummaged among boxes and wooden crates. She muttered something, straightened herself again and emerged, turning to Cathy with a triumphant look, her left hand raised. Between thumb and forefinger she held a rag doll around the neck so that the little fabric body moved to all sides. The doll's head was of synthetic material. Vivid blue eyes stared ahead from under a wreath of black stripes that were supposed to be the eyelashes. Cathy took the doll from her and Heike said, "One of those children must have been a girl."

Oscar even knew the name of the doll: Nina. He was sure that his half-sister would like to have it back.

"I will give you a good price for the doll," he said. "I don't think you care a bit about it. My family will do the utmost to find out who the girl was that played with it. Furthermore, I would like to make use of the upper story. If possible, I would like to go there immediately to take a rest."

"With pleasure," Heike hurried to say. "Such an important guest in my house! The doll is yours, of course, and I hope it will end up with the owner. Let me show you the way."

She touched the doll resting in Cathy's hands and then walked outside. Oscar had noticed that the sink was made from the same granite as in former days. The pantry had been used as storage for clothing and shoes back then, and in the center had been a wooden hat rack. On one of the shelves Anne and Herbert Vesper had kept their books, thick novels they read and re-read during the long winter nights.

Heike Wellman was surprised that her visitors had brought no luggage with them. With Cathy at her side, she went up the steep, outer staircase while Oscar went to put the automobile around back. The dog followed him, and he stroked its head. It was a wire-haired mongrel with a merry character. Before he opened the door of the vehicle, he looked around and took a deep breath. The cool mountain air filled his lungs with oxygen and his head with memories. Behind the pines rose the mighty head of the Eiger, its snow-covered top reaching thirteen thousand feet into the hard blue sky.

Just as Cathy was about to enter the door that the old woman held open for her, he put his hands along his mouth and shouted, "Cathy! I'm going to go a bit further on. I'll be back soon."

He brought the dog back behind the fence, got in the vehicle and started the motor. He turned off the property and drove along the unpaved path and out onto the road. There was no mist at this height, but his eyes focused on little of the sun-drenched surroundings.

A mind-narrowing process had taken over him. Intuitively he knew where to turn, and he groped his way down into a long valley and then up again. It was becoming a long drive. He passed through villages, driving through the main streets without noticing the houses, the stores or the hotels and then went up so steeply that the motor had to strain. He parked on a horizontal part of the road not far from a chapel, got out and went up three stone steps and through a small gate to enter the churchyard where he had stood as a child, hand in hand with the blond woman with the veil, Laura Langen. With long, self-assured strides he went over a path along the tombstones and arrived at the other side of a small, white-plastered church.

"He was a good man," he remembered the priest saying. "And he was not afraid of meeting his creator."

Just as on that day long ago, he was aware of a world which wasn't his but whose existence he recognized nonetheless. He could look over the imaginary brim and gaze at something that remained hidden to others. As a child this special feeling had scared him. Now he was back as a grown man and dared to open himself to the unknown.

"All wisdom a man has gathered during his earthly existence, he will take with him on his final journey," the voice sounded in his head.

"Everybody who is born has to learn everything from the start. One cannot ask questions of a dead person."

Laura Langen tightened her grip around the boy's hand. Little Oscar sweated in the hot sun.

Now Oscar bent his head and read the text that was ground into the marble tombstone in big letters.

EMLYN GRAY

MINION

Reading the name did not frighten him nor did it surprise him that no dates or place of birth were mentioned. To minions that was not important, for they could bridge time by passing on a spiritual inheritance to each other.

His mind was filled with a grand knowledge that was not descended from the grave, but had been inside of him all the time and only now had been revealed. Tears welled up in his eyes when he realized that little Oscar Man, standing on the same spot, had saved his life by not reacting to Laura Langen's pinches. He was not a real minion himself. But those who were, and had challenged him to commit himself, would have killed him had they learned that he possessed special qualities. In the eyes of the minions, too, he was a bastard.

For half an hour, he remained standing there in silence, head down, digesting all the knowledge that had come flooding back to him so suddenly. Then, all at once, he looked up as if awakened from a dream and forced himself to close that part of his mind again that could give himself away to the minions. He had no difficulty with that at all, for as a child he had taught himself to keep his inner life hidden and to always be on the alert.

He had been the princely jester who removed all problems by dancing and writing poetry. And a jester he would be. But now he knew what was happening in the world, and he also understood how important he was to people like General Howe and resistance leaders like Tony Falcon. Filled as he was with everything he had retrieved from his subconsciousness, he felt the strong need to share this fearsome knowledge with someone. This urge made him turn and go back to his automobile. He got in, started the motor and drove away.

He was thinking about so many things at the same time that he hardly paid attention to where he was driving. On the way to the churchyard he had been able to rely on his impulses, but now the automatic pilot in his head let him down, and when he pulled over after a short drive and looked around, he no longer knew where he was. Spotting the top of the Eiger, he drove along and tried to come nearer to it. He had to stop several times and ask people along the way how he could reach the house of Mrs. Heike Wellmann. It was to be expected that everyone shrugged their shoulders at hearing that name, but fortunately there was a woman who happened to know her; she was a veterinarian who had treated the wire-haired dog a couple of times.

He followed the route she described and finally reached the unpaved path and drove up to the low fence. Apparently Cathy had been watching for him, for she was waiting outside and opened the fence. She looked at him searchingly. His eyes were wet with the wind from his fast driving; his hair was all tangled, and his face looked bloodless.

Not knowing if he was willing to tell her where he had been, she said, "It is marvelous upstairs. We have a great number of rooms all to ourselves. Are you coming to take a look? You will probably find nothing there any more that reminds you of your youth."

Heike Wellmann had come out of the house and taken up an ax to cut wood for the fireplace. Big logs of wood lay in the grass.

"Just a moment, Cathy," said Oscar.

He went up to the old woman and took the ax from her.

"Let me do that for you. A bit of physical exertion will do me good. After that, I will go out for a mountain walk with my girlfriend. We will be back before dinner."

Heike smiled and pointed at some paving stones alongside the house. There was a shelter above it and some wood chips lying about.

"My husband used to pile everything up there. He only was satisfied when the wood touched the underside of the shelter. Now I only cut what I think I will need. If you do this for me, Prince, I will pack a lunch for the both of you. I will put it in a rucksack with a bottle of wine. A stiff climb makes one hungry and thirsty."

Cathy opened the door of the car and sat down with her feet outside on the ground. Oscar put a number of logs in a row and began chopping. He had to work hard to make small pieces because the wood had become moist. It should have been piled up under the shelter to dry for a long time already, and he knew it would bring a lot of smoke when it was finally burned in the fireplace.

With all his strength he hacked at the wood, and all the while he was thinking about what had become clear to him in the churchyard. He thought about how he should explain all this to Cathy.

"You help Heike, I help you," he suddenly heard her say.

He hadn't heard her close the car door again, but that was undoubtedly because he made so much noise with the ax. She smiled at him and began to pile up the wood on the paving stones. He noticed that she looked at him every time she came back to pick up more.

When the last log was cut, he wiped the sweat from his face and saw that Heike already had the promised rucksack ready. He put the ax against the wall and took the bag from her. She showed him a path behind the fence and told him how he could reach the most beautiful viewpoints quickly.

As soon as they were on their way, he began to talk.

"I've been to a place where I had made a crucial decision in my youth, Cathy. I was in the churchyard I mentioned to you when I told you my story back in New York. I can conclude with hindsight that I made the right decision then. I'm going to explain to you why a big part of the history books must be rewritten."

"You are making me very curious," she said. "And I'll do the rewriting myself, if possible."

"You know much better than I how drastically people can differ from each other. Just place a number of historical figures opposite each other, and you will understand what I mean."

"These are the games I like to play," laughed Cathy.

She loved walking here, together with him. The old Europe appealed to her so very much, and this was a sunny day in a splendid environment. She knew in her heart that he was going to tell her things that would bare a horrible truth, so she took the chance of putting it off for a while.

"Mozart and Napoleon," she said. "Roosevelt and Picasso. The time they lived in is of no importance, is it?"

"Oh, no. The longer the difference in time, perhaps the bigger the contrasts are. So if you could lock Socrates in the same room with Billy the Kid, you would get a nice picture of how the playfulness of the human mind can develop itself in all possible directions."

Cathy came up with several other names and coupled them to sinister mates in history. In the meantime, they had left the unpaved path and gone up a small road along the pines.

"Still, all the people you mentioned possess the same possibilities," Oscar explained. "There is a difference in talent, intelligence, skillfulness, comprehension and so on. Characters vary, the influence of their surroundings is of great importance, but in principle, their brains are as good as identical, and of course, we can only do things that are within the capacity of our brains.

"In and of itself, that is already an unbelievable amount to deal with. You must not think in differences between people, but in extremes, where their behavior is concerned. Someone can play music that brings tears to your eyes, and someone else can commit a brutal murder. How big is the difference between moving someone and killing someone! But there will always be limits. Regardless of how eagerly we might want it and in how many myths and legends it is described, we will never be able to practice witchcraft. Maybe we could do that if we were built otherwise under here." He knocked with the knuckles of his left hand on his head. "About many a thing we can only dream and fantasize. No matter how hard we try, we cannot move objects without touching them and how eagerly we would grasp the power of mind to make it possible. We cannot neutralize gravitation so that we might fly through the air, and we cannot predict the future."

"What you are trying to tell me, Oscar?" Cathy interrupted. "Does this have something to do with yourself? With that strange feeling you are able to cause inside my head? I called that inhuman—"

"Yes, it has to do with me. But even more so with others. It has to do with the people who have created this insane world around their own ideas. It is not the tycoons of the big enterprises who pull the strings, Cathy. They are all manipulated, and those who do not let themselves be controlled are killed. It is their confidants who divide the power between them. It is the minions of whom I speak!"

Cathy's mouth fell open, but she said nothing. She held on to his arm tightly and let herself be dragged along the stone path, which was becoming very steep. The sun was hot now. Their walk had only just begun, and they could already look out on a green valley dotted here and there with a little village or farm.

"It has become the fashion to keep a minion when you have reached a certain status. In most cases, it is an innocent imitation of what the tycoons and royal families do. A wealthy man allows his fellow companions or best friend to wear the same clothes as himself and takes him along to every occasion; a rich lady grants her bosom friend a life of luxury and sees to it that they look as like each other as two peas in a pod and that they will be seen everywhere together. In those cases it is only a game, the elite adapting to the habits of the noble of the earth. It only gets serious at the top of the internationals. The power of the minions there increases by the day, and there is no one who can stop them. They are not like other human beings, Cathy. Not like you, and—" he hesitated and then muttered, "a little bit like me." He continued walking on, with Cathy still holding his arm. "They have at their disposal a multitude of talents that make them superior. Let me give you a horrible example: When my half-brother Ferdinand had himself crowned and left the cathedral with his most important guests, Jay Jay and Richard Wright did not realize that they would riddle someone with bullets a minute later. They were prompted to that by an incredibly forceful power that they could not resist. Walter Krocht died right before my eyes, and my own bodyguards were driven to their own deaths. Stan Woodring and Francis Finnigan, the pilots of the chopper, also could not resist the impulse to respond, and came to rescue Jay Jay and Richard. The new leader of Cabo de Barra is Faron Hayes. And Faron Hayes—"

"Was the minion of Walter Krocht," Cathy supplied. "Please, Oscar, let's sit down somewhere for a while!"

They quickened their pace, walking along a sheer cliff. The path widened, and they found a place at the edge of a pine wood where pieces of rock rose above the fern and moss-covered ground.

"Don Bradshaw was killed, just like Roberta Rodriguez," sighed Cathy. "You must suspect that soon minions will be the heads of Fenrir International and Syrinx Colorado."

"It's not a suspicion; I know it for sure."

"Tell me more about the minions. All I know is that they crop up in the Renaissance of the fifteenth and sixteenth centuries. The king has a minion, a favorite who goes where his monarch goes. The queen has her confidante, her minion. It is, so I have understood from the books, a caprice, one more extravagant joke from the ages of waste and excess. It is simply too bizarre to have a person dress the same as you, be your mirror image and be completely dependent on your favors at the same time. All this fits exactly into the picture I have of that gilded age!"

"And that's the same way parasites are tolerated," said Oscar. "For their true nature was not recognized. How did a king find his minion? Did he choose him by himself from his circle of friends? Or was the minion the stray cat that came along and picked out, self-willingly and mysteriously, his master? The latter was the case. The minion was ensconced in the highest circles. The special relationship in the noble classes was so imitated by the lower classes and wealthy businessmen that no one ever would be able to tell the true minion from the innocent imitator. There have been countless remarkable relationships between men and women and their appointed minions, but they are all much different from the group I'm talking about now.

"I don't know where and how it ever got started, Cathy, but it must have been long ago. Anyhow, there were people who were different from their contemporaries, and they recognized that. They found each other, and after generations their special gifts had been passed on in such a way that it was as if a new species of man had evolved. The main quality they discovered within themselves was the possibility to provide each other with genetic information."

"What do you mean?"

"Listen, Cathy. I have been away alone in the car, right? I drove to the churchyard where I had been once before as a child. Emlyn Gray is buried there—"

"The man from your dreams—your nightmares!"

"He was my grandfather. My mother Hildegard Floyd was obviously married to a certain Floyd once. Her maiden name was Gray. Now, pay attention. If I had been a minion, like my mother was a real minion, I would have had so much of my ancestors inside of me that I would have been able to reproduce a great deal of their behavior, qualities, views and knowledge. I would have been able to walk and speak like Grandfather Gray. I could have acted like my great-grandfather because I would have known how my ancestors would have acted in certain situations. A genuine minion carries a whole lot of his ancestor's knowledge in his genes and is actually able to make use of it. With normal mortals everything stops after death. Dear Cathy, everything you have studied, all that knowledge about the history of man, will disappear forever with you. Whoever wants to know as much as you shall have to travel the same long road you have."

She looked at him, fascinated.

"It sounds so logical and so very beautiful and honest to pass all your feelings and knowledge to your children so that you may live on in them when you're no longer here."

"It would have been beautiful and honest if the matter had rested there," said Oscar. "But the minion has more qualities. He is also terribly mean and attaches no value to another's life!"

He jumped to his feet and walked to the other side of the road, stared into the valley and continued.

"We are dealing with a successful human mutation that not only has at their disposal special gifts but has also thrown several important human values to the wind. Regret and remorse do not hinder them. They are a viperous brood!"

He stood there talking into the depths, knowing that the woman who sat behind him on the rock was listening to him.

"They are parasites who have everything their own way. They create their world at the cost of others. They survive best when chaos rules. Don't get me wrong, I don't know all the rules that govern them because I wasn't born a genuine minion myself. I am a bastard in the Man family and a bastard among the minions! They manipulate and scheme; they kill and seize power. They can make people sick or crazy and make them do things against their will!"

He turned around again and looked at her.

"Fortunately, they don't have such a major influence on everybody. There are people who remain insensible to their telepathic powers. I believe that the great Walter Krocht was one who remained elusive to them where that is concerned. That is why he had to die. Preferably in front of the whole world so that no one would get the idea that the real offenders had to be searched for inside his own small circle of confidants. My bodyguards had to take the rap, and then it was all laid at my door."

"What you are telling me is terrible," sighed Cathy.

The hot sun shone in her face, but she shivered with the chill of her newfound knowledge.

He sat down beside her on his knees and took both her hands in his.

"They were emphatically present during the First Renaissance. It is impossible for us to find out now who was a genuine minion then and who wasn't. They have given themselves that name and have always been proud of it. But one who had taken the position of his patron or patroness never used the word *minion*. You know all the kings and noblemen of that age by heart; you know in what time to place them and who their successors were. But you couldn't name whether a single high-placed person of theirs had been a minion or not. I can, though, Cathy, where my contemporaries are concerned! I only realize that now—now that I have allowed myself to open up to all the feelings that live inside of me. I am a great danger to all minions."

He sat down next to her again, picked up some little stones and rolled them around in his hand.

"There was one who hoped that I would be an important minion. Just imagine, the son of the great and powerful Otto Man—a bastard, true enough, but what kind of a bastard! With a minion as a mother! I was predestined to succeed my father, to outstrip Ferdinand and Jimmy Man and deliver Man-Mandate into the hands of the minions.

But things went quite differently. I didn't appear to have at my disposal some of the specific minion qualities. I was always on the alert. Something inside of me worked as a warning bell, and I succeeded in misleading everyone. The funeral of Emlyn Gray was the occasion for the minions to subject me to the final test. I don't know how Anne and Herbert Vesper fit in. They didn't tell me where we were going, and at the churchyard no one mentioned the name of the dead man. I didn't know who Laura Langen was, who held me by the hand. I had never seen the priest. Now I know I did the right thing. I was an innocent child in the eyes of the minions, and I could go safely to America where Johanna wanted me at her side. But the minions remained distrustful, and I received a special charge."

Cathy looked into his bright blue eyes.

"I studied at the palace and had no idea what I was meant to do after that. Then I was sent to Switzerland to set up a business that would provide the library of Johanna Man with the most special books. So I traveled all over Europe, gave orders to have books copied and was allowed to hand out money all over the continent in order to make Man-Mandate popular. I lived like an open-handed jester, going from one place to another. In the meantime, the minions constantly checked to make sure I wasn't searching for something in all those old books—because they were searching themselves. I did very important work! There was a big chance that I would dig up something they were anxiously waiting for, and if I recognized the importance of it myself, I would betray myself as a connoisseur of their special way of life, and that would have rung my death knell!"

"Oscar, what are you talking about? What were they looking for?"

"It is something all minions know and have passed on to each other. I, as a bastard, know it too, without anyone ever having to explain it to me. Long ago, I suspect it was at the end of the First Renaissance, a document or book was written in which it is told in great detail who the minions are and how they can be fought and ultimately destroyed. The company I led was looking for that text, and I honestly don't know whether or not it has been found yet. It is worth everything to them to get hold of that manuscript. I must find out, but I cannot simply step into the offices and ask. I am no longer a prince, and my family has relieved me of all functions. They will not even let me in the door of the offices I used to live above!"

They rose to their feet. Oscar took the rucksack, and they slowly walked farther up.

"There could be even more books and documents," suggested Cathy. "A considerable number of copies may have been printed. You think that the work was written at the end of the First Renaissance. Let's, for convenience's sake, say at the end of the sixteenth century. If we go back in time one hundred years more, at the cusp of the fifteenth and sixteenth centuries, we see that books were already being printed in a couple of hundred European cities, by more than a thousand different publishers."

When Oscar showed no reaction whatsoever, Cathy was puzzled. Not daring to look over the edge of the precipice into the depths, she stared straight ahead at the path on which they walked, watching her feet move in a calm, steady rhythm. She let herself be carried along by her fantasy and saw only libraries, wooden printing presses and book burnings. She thought of Johannes Guttenberg the German goldsmith, the inventor of the cherished art of printing.

"The exuberance, the craziness, the extravagance: they all disappeared the way they had come," she suddenly said. "New times came, different times. Maybe the minions were chased away or conquered. And it all has to do with the text of that book."

"That is very well possible," Oscar said. "And do you realize, Cathy, how our own world has been turned upside down? How democracy has decayed into oligarchy? While the masses are entertained with huge parties, with pomp and circumstance, with wealth and excess, with dissipation. The minions have taken over command from the tycoons. They prosper in chaos like pigs in the mud. I believe that I am the only one who knows with what kind of an enemy we are dealing. I know what I must do. The power of the minions has to be broken before it is too late."

Suddenly he stood still and put his hands on her shoulders.

"I have told you everything now, and I realize that it makes you vulnerable."

Bravely, she looked him in the eye.

"Everyone needs someone to tell their story to. I want to be your biographer and will follow you everywhere. What's more, I will help you with everything you must do, to the best of my ability. You are probably the only one who knows what is happening in all those palaces of the conglomerations. But do you know what you want to do now? Do you have a plan?"

"We will stay here a bit longer, so I may think. Here, in the mountains, I feel at ease. I want to sleep in the house where I slept in my youth. Then we will go back to our hotel in Interlaken, and from there we will travel by automobile to the firm to which I once devoted myself so fanatically. Perhaps I can contact one of my old, loyal employees. I know who I can trust and who is best left unaddressed at all. I must use my time wisely and make my plans. Then I shall return to America. The army is behind me, and the generals will listen to me and believe me. No matter how fantastic it may sound, they will know that I am telling the truth. I can give them a logical explanation for everything that has changed in such a short time in the United States and Europe. And then, I can also knock at the door of Falcon, the freedom fighter. Come, let's go on."

They walked and talked until they reached a point where their path along the edge of the steep cliff narrowed. To go any further, they would have to walk behind each other. The path was not even half a yard wide.

"I'm not going there," said Cathy firmly. "If I look down, I may take a wrong step and fall. Is there no other way?"

"No, but it doesn't matter. We will go back at our leisure. You and I have traveled far enough today."

They turned around and found a decent spot to sit and see what Heike had packed for them. There was a bottle of wine and a bottle of mineral water. There was bread, cheese, a piece of hot sausage and some apples. When they were done, all that remained were two cores. Oscar had drunk most of the wine, for Cathy was afraid of losing her balance during the descent. She talked incessantly, for every time a silence fell, she began to feel afraid. She had understood very well all that Oscar had told her. What he had said about the generals was also true for her. It was a fantastic story, but she knew it was the truth. While they talked about things of less importance, Oscar's revelations remained on her mind, and this was an ideal method to slowly become used to it and learn how to deal with it.

It was already late in the afternoon when they returned to the house. After resting in their own rooms, they went down to the kitchen where Heike Wellmann surprised them with a sumptuous and extensive meal. While Cathy was quickly satisfied, Oscar ate like a ravenous wolf. Heike watched him throughout his meal, and with every bite he took, her smile grew bigger.

"My husband also enjoyed the things I prepared for him," she said in a confidential tone to Cathy. "I still miss him every day but mostly when I sit here at the table, alone. . . ."

That night Oscar was haunted by dreams in which Emlyn Gray waded up to him through a lake of blood. As soon as he awoke with a start, though, he realized it was all about memories that had been passed on genetically and that Gray was only the messenger of the evil caused by the minions. As soon as he had calmed down a bit, he tried to explain it to Cathy, who lay beside him, sleepless.

"People have always attached too much importance to the content of their dreams. They think that they bare someone's character, foretell things about the future or provide healing through the psychic digesting of sad experiences. What is shown to me in my dreams, however, are pictures from the past that are usually pretty unclear or just symbols that I don't understand. I don't know what the minions are dreaming of or how they think. I, being a bastard, am saddled with terrifying visions. I know I must look gruesome when I awake in a sweat with bulging eyes, but please don't pity me. I'm beginning to get used to it."

"But it is definitely troubling you more now than in Manhattan," pointed out Cathy. "And that seriously concerns me. There, you were also dreaming every night, and sometimes you were thrashing about with your eyes closed, as if you were fighting an invisible enemy. But you have already woken up from nightmares four times tonight."

"Perhaps you'd better sleep somewhere else—"

"Not a chance! I'll stay with you."

Oscar lay on his back and looked at the slanting ceiling and the heavy purlins and rafters. A smile crept across his face.

"Sometimes I do enjoy my dreams. I hear a beautiful melody that I can repeat the next day on the piano. It is very nice that something like that is possible. I cannot help but think about the priest at the grave of Emlyn Gray. All the knowledge a man has gathered during his life disappears when death occurs.

"Yes, that goes for most people on this earth. That is why I repeat: it is very nice that I am an exception to the rule. I wake up with a melody that has been in my head from the day I was born and has slipped into my consciousness unexpectedly. I didn't think that melody up by myself. Long, long ago, one of my ancestors heard it and remembered it, and that knowledge was passed on to me through our combined gene pool. It becomes really eerie, though, when we think of what the minions pass on to each other. They receive each other's feelings of hatred and—generation after generation—build up more and more rage and aggression. Their life-threatening powers increase, and they receive their lessons in cruelty and pitilessness during their sleep when their brains are most receptive to the memories that they have gotten from their ancestors. I think that minions must grin in their sleep and never wake up in a sweat! When they open their eyes in the morning, they are ready to execute the plans they have brooded on throughout the night. This system—the passing on of worldly wisdom and experiences to your descendants—remains fascinating to me. But it has turned the people who benefit from it into monsters. Do you understand me, Cathy? Minions are monsters!"

He got out of bed and walked to the bathroom to wash his face with cold water.

Nothing on the upper floor reminded him of his youth. Everything had been rebuilt, and the rooms were furnished to please spoiled tourists. What once had been an attic, used as a storeroom where he and his half sister had played, was now a comfortable apartment.

Back once more with Cathy, he said, "You have studied so much, your head is filled with dates, facts, anecdotes—you know everything about the history of the world. You know about cause and effect. Imagine if we had a child together, Cathy, and one day you heard that child, only ten years old, speak in an innocent tone of voice about things you once studied so hard. How wise can a child become when he has all your knowledge plus that of your ancestors already stored in his memory?"

"I don't know," said Cathy shrugging her shoulders as she sat up, her arms around her knees. "I find it a strange, scary thought. Maybe I can judge it better after I have played with the idea a bit. At the present, the whole thing is repugnant to me."

She let her chin rest on her knees and closed her eyes. Suddenly she looked up again and heaved a deep sigh. She asked, "I have to think about something else. You spontaneously play melodies composed by someone ages ago. You simply know things because they are warehoused in your head. One could say that you draw on a collective memory. Did you ever know your grandfather? Did you ever meet him?"

"No. No one even ever told me his name."

"The book or manuscript you were talking about, Oscar—"

"What about it?"

"Does it actually exist?"

"I suppose so, yes."

"Listen. I try to handle things in a logical way. If a text exists that describes how to fight minions, and that text—"

"Is read by the minions themselves," Oscar filled in guessing what she was pointing at, "then they should be able to pass on something of it to each other."

"Exactly! Do you remember anything about it? A word, a line, a paragraph?"

"Nothing. Absolutely nothing at all. Maybe the text is secret, and the book—if it is a book—should remain closed forever. But then it is of even more importance to the minions to get it safely into their possession. When they put it in safekeeping themselves, it will stay out of reach of the people who can use its contents against them. Suppose the book exists, and they are looking for it. What would they do with it when they found it?"

"Not put it away safely," said Cathy. "Destroy it. Book burning."

"That is very well possible," replied Oscar. "But curiosity is a human mainspring and not at all strange to the minions. Before I return to America, I must try to learn more about this. But for the present I need rest. I seldom have felt as tired as I do now."

He turned on his side and rested his head on his folded hands. Cathy planted a kiss on his cheek and turned out the light. He fell asleep before her and did not wake up until past nine the next morning.

Heike Wellmann had softly knocked on the door an hour before with breakfast. Cathy had placed everything on a table and had already poured coffee from a thermal carafe when he came into the living room. She asked him about his plans for the day.

"If it's up to me, we will go for another long walk," he said. "I want to be at peace and not make any hasty decisions. I have to be sure that I can close myself off to the minions again who would so eagerly fathom my thoughts and penetrate my mind. I have to succeed in that, Cathy. None of them must ever know my true feelings. Who knows how often they tried when I lived in the palace? They must have been among my teachers, and of course, they were constantly at the side of my half sister and half brothers. When they probed my mind, they found only the naivety and uncomplicated mirth of a jester. And that's what I will be one more time, a jester who goes through life with a smile and snaps his fingers at all the rules. In the meantime, I will keep my eyes wide open and make my plans."

He was silent as he drank his coffee.

"World problems are not to be underestimated," he said, more to himself than to Cathy. "I will probably not be able to save everyone from the mischief caused by the minions. That is why I will concentrate mainly on my half sister Johanna. I was with her in a cabin of Ferdinand's Ferris wheel where she began acting highly peculiar. She was without her minion, and every now and then she was even raving. Her mind is under a lot of pressure wherever she goes. Walter Krocht is dead, and his minion Faron Hayes has become the leader of Cabo de Barra. Don Bradshaw is dead, just like Roberta Rodriguez. It is obvious that pretty soon Fenrir International and Syrinx Colorado will also be run by minions. We've already discussed that. How long will it take before my family is murdered too? I've never been very fond of my brothers, but Johanna is near to my heart. I have to do something for her."

When Oscar showed up in the restaurant of the Dis Pater Europe Hotel, three days later, he wore his brocaded jerkin and knickers with the gold and silver fox heads and his checkered jester's boots. Cathy had woven pleated red threads throughout his beautiful, long, straight hair.

A new, extensive article about him had been published in the local paper, once again a reprint from the *New York Massif* of Falcon's Mason Media. This time, however, he was described as a popular hero and a rebel who resisted the present authorities and pleaded for the return of true democracy.

Cathy held his arm as they walked to their reserved table. She felt the eyes of all the guests upon her. There were many angry looks while other men and women demonstratively turned their heads. Oscar pushed her hand away, turned three forward somersaults in a row and danced over to a piano standing near a high wooden bar. Even before he sat down on the stool, his fingers were playing the first tones of a self-composed number.

He conjured up a spirit of feeling and emotion that moved invisibly but audibly through the room and took hold of everybody. His playing became wilder; the listeners became caught up in a whirlwind of tones that lashed them with fast-changing chords. They opened themselves up to him, and he transfixed them with sounds like spearheads into living flesh. Oscar Man could inflict wounds into those with sensitive natures and leave people in extreme confusion when he suddenly stopped playing. That was the case now as he calmly got up and with short, measured steps walked to the table where Cathy sat. Here now, in this restaurant, he was no longer the disowned bastard or the dangerous rebel who wanted to usurp the power of the tycoons. Here he was someone to fear because he had confused everyone with his virtuosity, with his devilish music. He was the jester who had the power to manipulate other peoples' emotions and allow someone a limited view into dimensions that usually remained hidden to normal mortals.

Oscar and Cathy enjoyed their dinner in silence and drank their wine from sparkling crystal glasses.

After his impromptu piano playing, it had remained quiet. No one dared to break the magical atmosphere he had created and that had remained stuck there among the whispers. Guests finished their meals and left the room walking on tiptoes past the table where Oscar and Cathy sat and silently bowing to them.

Cathy herself was impressed by the magical playing of her jester, and now she knew even better than before that he was indeed different from other people.

"That was so unbelievably beautiful," she said softly after not having said a word for a quarter of an hour.

"That's what you can do when you're a bastard," he whispered. "I've never seen a minion touch a musical instrument."

* * *

To his surprise, Oscar was more than welcome in the little castle in Sarnen where the company was headquartered that he had established and lead and where he had lived for so long. He and Cathy had driven up to it along the smooth water of the Lake of Brienz and through its long valleys. After he had parked the car, he got out and took a long look at the building. Man-Mandate Enterprises had made a glorious little castle out of a ruin, both inside and out. All around was a garden with hedges, arbors, ponds and statues. There were four towers with red steeples. Above the doors, the name of the company was carved in marble: Man-Manifest Books.

"Oscar! Oscar Man!"

A middle-aged man wrapped in a long red cloak, with red bows in his shining black shoes, had come along the side through the garden and looked up in surprise when he saw Oscar standing there. He raised both hands in a greeting and quickened his pace. A tight little red cap was pulled over his head, and as his cloak fell open, an imposing belly swung tremendously to and fro.

"That is Johann Helm," said Oscar. "A man who prefers to sit rather than stand and who prefers to read rather than anything else in the world. He was one of my closest contributors and kept things going when I was traveling out through Europe."

The man reached Oscar, grabbed him by the shoulders and drew him against his mighty belly. He then pushed him arm's length away and gave him a thorough shaking. His white face, which gave away the fact that he seldom sat in the sun, became red with excitement along his cheeks. His small eyes became watery, and his lips slid down in a frown as if he were about to cry.

"Oscar! I don't think you care much that you are no longer a prince. And you know how I feel about that! I honor the royal houses that color our history, but I don't give a damn about businessmen buying themselves crowns. I find it dreadful what has happened to Jay Jay and Richard. And I feel so sorry for you, too, for they were your friends!"

"Hello, Johann," said Oscar. "You know, I still think about them every day. It happened right before my very eyes. First Walter Krocht, then my bodyguards. I am so glad to see you again, Johann. Allow me to introduce you to my girlfriend Cathy Wheeler, historian. She knows only a bit less about world history than you, and that's only because she is so very much younger."

Cathy went to shake hands with him, but he gallantly gripped her fingers and bent forward to kiss them. After having straightened his back again, and having taken a good look at her, he judged, "You see? What does it matter that you are no longer a prince when you can go through life with a woman at your side who looks like a real princess? Very pleased to meet you, Ms. Wheeler."

Then he pointed with his thumb over his shoulder at the little castle.

"Your chambers have been emptied. There's really nothing there anymore. We have left it that way up till now. Come inside! Then we can talk in my office." With a sour smile he added, "I have become the boss here, more or less, because your office was unoccupied."

"It was always deserted anyway," grinned Oscar. "I was seldom here. But are you serious? Are you really willing to take us inside? Isn't that strictly forbidden by my family?"

Johann's breast swelled proudly, and as if by magic, the biggest part of his belly disappeared.

"This is Switzerland, my dear friend, or have you forgotten that? America is, as you may know, very far away from here. I would catch it properly from all the employees if I told them that I met you and let you go away again just like that. Come! Come!"

His belly had magically returned while he was talking. Johann put his arms around Oscar and Cathy's shoulders and pushed them along to the doors of the castle.

Inside the doorway stood life-sized images of the Man-Mandate symbol, the man in armor leaning on his sword with his head bent. Cathy counted twenty of them. Behind them old books were displayed in delicately lit glass showcases. Some of the books were displayed opened. When Johann closed the doors and the light fell down through stained glass windows, she had the feeling of entering a sanctuary. Before she had the chance to take a close look at the books, she felt Johann's arms around her shoulder again.

"Walk with me, if you don't mind. Oscar's old office is right here on the corner. I have left everything the way it was. Oscar is a man of taste—but that doesn't seem to apply only to his workspace. I have been able to establish that his girlfriend is also every inch a beauty."

A few moments later, Cathy found herself in a room as big as a banquet hall, furnished with desks of dark brown wood and bookcases adorned with sculptured lambs. The ceiling consisted of a mosaic made of different woods under which a number of winged dragons floated. There were at least as many books here as in the domed chamber in Manhattan, and the shining leather spines varied in color from light brown to black. The floor was covered with priceless carpets, and the pieces of furniture were made of mahogany.

Cathy sat down in an easy chair and listened to the conversation between the two men. She had a great admiration for Oscar Man, even as he sat there in his velvet fool's dress, baring his white teeth in a smile, his bright blue gaze cheerful and open. She made a quick mental summation of all his recent misfortunes, from the loss of his bodyguards and his confinement to his exile and disinheritance. He had made alarming discoveries about the minions and about himself, and he recognized the danger that threatened the world now as a strange, homicidal elite began to take over the leadership of all the big enterprises. And yet, here he was, sitting in the splendid office where everything he saw must recall old memories and where he had given a home to the books he cherished, all without showing any emotion whatsoever. She understood that his true feelings remained hidden behind the screen he had put up in his early youth.

Here, in this little castle, old books and manuscripts from all over Europe had been gathered, presumably because everyone was searching for one particular text. There must be people at work who kept an eye on everything that came and went and stayed in contact with the minions from the palace of the Man family. It was not even unimaginable that there was a genuine minion present here, and that could be Johann Helm just as well as anyone else. Cathy Wheeler could not help but love and admire the talent of her jester who despite everything conversed in merry banter and radiated an almost naive lightheartedness.

"Perhaps Cathy would like a tour of our little company?" Johann asked. "Shall we give her a guided tour together? That will give you the opportunity to shake hands with all your old friends."

Oscar pushed his hands off against the arms of his chair and landed on the soft soles of his boots.

"With the greatest pleasure," he said. "I wouldn't dream of missing a chance at that! I am so very happy with this warm reception."

Helm led the way. He walked through the hall with the life-sized armored figures and raised his hand as if he was greeting somebody.

"Welcome to Man-Manifest Books!" echoed his voice through the large space. "Where the ravages of time are brought to a halt and where decayed manuscripts are restored to all their old glory!"

Chapter Nine

Return

Oscar strolled around his old haunts—shaking hands, getting patted on the back and embracing his old friends and employees. Everywhere he turned, he was looked at with disbelieving but joyful eyes. He went from workroom to workroom and from office to office while Cathy, who followed him everywhere but remained a silent observer, began to develop an insight into how the company functioned. In one area was all the equipment necessary to transfer and store the text from the oldest and most fragile books without ever having to actually touch the pages; further on was a room where copies of those texts were produced on the finest quality paper, bound, following as closely as possible the design of the original publication, and then fitted with a beautiful leather cover.

"The material comes in from everywhere," one of the workers explained to her as they stopped in the binding room. "It is always interesting—not to mention extremely profitable—to be able to buy an original, antique manuscript at an equitable price and then totally restore it; if the demand for a particular edition is great enough, we can make as many splendid, exact replicas as need be. In this way, Man-Manifest gives the past a new breath of life and turns a nice profit at the same time! Those who are fortunate enough to have in their possession an old family collection are able to find us just as easily as the librarians at the Vatican. Major museums throughout Europe, large city archives, private collectors, antique book dealers, and even local bookstores, all are anxious to sell us their treasures for replication. We return to the world all the thoughts and ideas that were written down and then lost. We are the fountain of wisdom from which everyone may come to drink!"

He was a lean, pale man who wore a snowy white wig with a ponytail tied with a bow. He selected a book, removed it from the shelf and opened it carefully on a table.

He opened the book to a multicolored picture of a king sitting on a throne receiving his subjects who were kneeling before him. It was a very small work of art that must have taken an extreme amount of patience to create. On the same page was also an ingenious monogram made out of twisted branches adorned with leaves and flowers.

"This is from the middle of the fifteenth century," her guide said. "This book of illustrations is a perfect example of the kind of material we work with. This one happens to be exceptionally beautiful and well-preserved. They even used genuine gold leaf in the publication of this volume. This is the sort of material that is usually obtained from churches and monasteries."

He carefully closed the book and replaced it on the shelf.

"As far as the text and its translation are concerned," he said, "there are many different directions we can go. As soon as we have a book stored in the memory of our equipment, it is immediately retrievable in any language. It is possible to obtain any of our books in whatever language you desire, regardless of whether it was originally written in French, Russian or Japanese. You may also obtain an abridged version, if that is your wish. If you so desire, Ms. Wheeler, I can have someone else explain all this to you in greater detail. My area of expertise is the binding of the finished product, which is all done by hand."

"Trust me, sir, I am already pretty familiar with how it works," said Cathy. "I work in Oscar's library, and most, if not all, of his books come from right here. I sit bent over books, such as the one you just showed me, for endless days and nights, and I know how to obtain the English translation of any book I happen to be working on. It is certainly very interesting to finally see where all my work originates, for I have never had the opportunity to visit here before. Thank you very much indeed."

She had let the bookbinder tell his story without interruption but felt obliged to tell him that she was already familiar with everything that happened here. She also suddenly understood how important it was for Oscar to have someone close to him who could gain the confidence of someone on the inside, get access to the equipment and search for information about the minions, for he would undoubtedly give himself away immediately if he attempted it himself. She also understood why it had been necessary for him to construct a screen that blocked his deepest feelings, for all the while that he was working at Man-Manifest, he was surely under constant observation. If he had made his own inquiries about the how and why of minions, or about any of the books and manuscripts in which they were mentioned, he would probably have been murdered. Because, after all, he was not a genuine minion himself but merely a very talented bastard who should not, under any circumstances, be allowed to know anything about them. But he was back now and walking freely among the equipment that he so desperately needed to use.

Just as she was about to enter the office into which she had seen Oscar and Johann go, she heard someone call her name, and she realized just how vulnerable she was. This sudden awakening to her position caused her to become rigid with fear. Oscar had told her everything, and she knew that if enough pressure were put on her, she would reveal all his secrets.

"Ms. Wheeler," she heard again.

It was the skinny bookbinder; he came up to her and caught hold of her by the arm. She looked at him with fright as a combined surge of heat and cold washed over her.

"You know so much about the old books," he said, "and some of my colleagues have come across a book that they are not quite sure what to do with. Perhaps you would be kind enough to take a look at it. Do you think you could come with me for a moment?"

She heard her own voice tremble as she protested a bit and said, "But then—then I'll lose sight of Oscar."

His laughter sounded loud and shrill in her ears as he replied, "You don't really think that Oscar would leave without you, do you?"

She forced herself to calm down a little as she accompanied him down a long, cool, darkened corridor. He brought her into an office where a number of men and women were sitting at long tables on which were stacked many books. There were small screens flickering inside panels that had been opened in the walls around the room.

"Marcus," he said, and one of the men looked up. "This is Cathy Wheeler, who is visiting us as a guest of Mr. Man."

The man stood up, and Cathy saw that he was wearing a spotless jacket and snow white gloves. He had a broad black band around his balding head to which was attached a magnifying glass that sat in front of his right eye. He looked at her, his magnified eye as large as a saucer.

"Ms. Wheeler is Oscar's librarian. May she have a look at your mysterious discovery?"

"Aha!" said the man with the magnifying glass who reminded her of the legendary Cyclops. "Pleased to meet you, Ms. Wheeler. My name is Marcus Pike. I was born and bred in London, but could not resist the generous offer of Man-Mandate to come and work for them in Switzerland, and I have never regretted it for one second. All you have to do is sit here, and the past is paraded right before your very eyes! This is a historian's paradise, but as I am told, things are not going too badly for you either working in Mr. Man's library."

Cathy noticed that she was breathing much too fast. She became dizzy and looked past the men, searching for an empty chair. She made her way to the table on unsteady feet and sat down. She forced a smile she as looked up at Pike.

"Well, show me this mysterious book then, Mr. Pike. I only have a couple of minutes to spare."

The men exchanged a look of mutual understanding, and the bookbinder said good-bye to her. Pike went to a cupboard on the other side of the office as the other people in the room looked at her briefly and then continued with their work. Marcus, who was now wearing rubber surgical gloves, returned with a book in his hands and pulled a chair up alongside hers with his foot. He very carefully placed the book on the table and opened it up using only his gloved fingertips to handle the pages. Without speaking, he ran his index finger across the pages, pointing out the text and illustrations. The work had been written in French, and as Pike turned the pages, Cathy saw some of the most beautiful drawings she had ever seen. The people in the pictures were all richly, and excessively, overdressed. As Cathy gazed at them, something in her head kept screaming *Minions! Minions!* The dominant colors in all the pictures were red, green and blue and were all so shockingly bright that they looked as if they had been drawn quite recently, rather than hundreds of years ago.

"What are you thinking about?" Pike said so unexpectedly that he startled her.

He put his face uncomfortably close to hers and peered at her through the magnifying glass with his giant eye.

"Philip the Fair," replied Cathy. "He owned hundreds of books that he rewrote and illustrated. His collection contained books of all kinds. He was especially fond of romance and chivalry, such as this rhyme, which is probably a poem by some forgotten author that has been rewritten and changed over and over until it came to us in its present form. But then again, it may also very well be the original. It must have been written around the middle of the fifteenth century. Other noblemen besides Philip loved to show off with their valuable books, and this one could be a product of the hands of many different people."

"Right," Pike said with a sigh and then repeated what she had said. "It could a product of the hands of many different people. I was momentarily elated when you mentioned Philip the Fair so spontaneously. I would be so happy if I could find proof that this is a book from his personal library! The first few pages have been lost, and the ending has been rewritten several times. The origins of the story will always remain a mystery. I have been searching, unsuccessfully, for quite a long time for an expert who can tell me exactly from whom and where it has been handed down to us. Oh well, it's not all that important. It's a beautiful story, the date of which can be figured quite precisely, and the book itself is of incalculable value. Perhaps one day we'll find out who the author was."

Cathy slowly filled her lungs with air and then just as slowly exhaled again through her nostrils. She became deeply engrossed in an extremely interesting conversation with Pike about the book in front of them and about many other books from many different periods in time. Her initial nervousness had disappeared, and she had become talkative and comfortable. It was wonderful for her to talk to someone who studied the books with as much love and devotion as she did. She had forgotten all about the time and looked up in surprise when Johann Helm entered the room laughing and waving.

"There you are! Oscar is waiting for you in the garden by the inner court," he said.

Cathy said good-bye to the Englishman and went with Johann. He accompanied her to a courtyard in the middle of which was a pond that was surrounded by bushes and trees. Oscar stood there watching the big fish that swam back and forth in the crystal clear water. The only sound to be heard was the splashing of the water from a tall fountain in the center of the pond. The walls kept the wind out and the sun, sitting high in the afternoon sky over the castle, made it oppressively hot. Johann walked with Cathy to the pond and then excused himself. He told her he had work to do but would be most happy if they could all get together for a meal later. As soon as he had disappeared from sight, Oscar said softly, in a worried voice, "You should have stayed with me. Did anything happen?"

"Everything's fine," she said, "but for a moment there, I thought it was going to turn out differently. Never mind, I'll tell you about that later."

The door that Helm had just left through swung open again, and a woman somewhere about forty, wearing a long dress with a short throw around her shoulders, came into the court. As soon as she saw Oscar, she quickened her pace.

"Oscar!" she cried cheerfully. "I heard you had arrived, but I simply couldn't believe it!"

"That's Natasja Bruschlinski," Oscar told Cathy. "One of my secretaries. She is the very best at arranging and delegating. Without her, everything here would go haywire."

Cathy smiled as the woman hugged Oscar and rocked him to and fro as if he were a child. Her smile broadened into a big grin when the woman said, in a reprimanding voice, "That fool's dress is not good enough for you. And as for those red threads in your hair, I would just love to pull them all out by myself!"

"Maybe it would be better if I left again immediately," suggested Oscar.

But all his sarcasm managed to do was get him a playful, yet powerful enough, punch in the stomach.

"You can just forget all about that. But first, I want to take a good look at you. Once you do leave, who knows how long it will be before I see you again?" Her face fell, and she said, "It's too bad what happened to you, Oscar; I still weep for Richard and Jay Jay every day. Are you dealing with it well?"

"Don't you worry about me, Natasja. The harder I get knocked down, the faster I bounce up again."

She put her forefinger on her lips and opened her cape a little. Inside was the Mason Media emblem embroidered in gold and silver, the two sculptors eternally trying to free one another from the stone.

She put her hands down and said softly, "You just might be able to use some help."

"And what if I do?"

"Then wear what I wear, and we'll know for sure that we can trust each other."

He knew exactly what she meant.

She was one of Tony Falcon's freedom fighters and also knew that Oscar had met with him. When the time came that he could show her that he wore the same colors as she, Natasja would know that he had finally chosen sides. He had always believed that he could trust Natasja Bruschlinski, but suddenly he wasn't so sure any more. These days, Oscar trusted no one besides Cathy Wheeler.

"Suppose I did need some help," he tried again.

"I will be taking a short trip in two days," said Natasja. "It is beautiful this time of year in the high mountains around Grindelwald. At two o'clock in the afternoon on the day I arrive there, I am going up the mountain on the cable car to First Mountain and then walk to Bachalp Lake. The views are breathtaking, and you can talk freely."

Without saying another word, she turned and went back inside.

"Are you going to go?" Cathy wanted to know.

"Perhaps," he said. "She must have been very well briefed by Falcon. And the way she spoke, softly, but determined enough that I knew you heard over where you were standing—she would never have been so open if she wasn't aware of the fact that I have no secrets from you. Falcon knows that perfectly well."

"And he told her about that," she said filling in the blanks.

When they were sitting in the company cafeteria a little while later having lunch with Johann Helm, Natasja Bruschlinski was nowhere to be seen. People stopped by to chat with Oscar, some even sitting down and keeping them company for a few minutes. Marcus Pike came and sat down across from Cathy and started talking to her about gaps in history that were being filled in with information obtained from newly found books. The time was well spent and passed quickly, and then it was time for Oscar to say good-bye. Helm showed him and Cathy out and waved farewell to them as they drove off.

They came to a town along the shores of the Lake of Brienz, and Oscar found a restaurant with a terrace overlooking the water. They stayed until the sun had set and then drove back to the parking lot near Interlaken. From there, they took a carriage to their hotel. Oscar had no regrets about not going upstairs while he was at the little castle where he had spent so much of his life living and working. There was no need to see his little apartment again; he had no trouble seeing his sad little empty rooms clearly in his mind.

When they were back in the sitting room of their suite, they sat and watched a three-dimensional broadcast about the huge parties being held in New York City to celebrate the coming presidential elections. The Man family already controlled the city, and now they were doing their utmost to guarantee that Angus Sebastian, who thanks to the family was already governor of New York State, would emerge the victor in the contest for the presidency.

In an open limousine, Martha Manolow one of the most popular television personalities of the moment was chauffeured through the crowd interviewing well-planted celebrities who naturally were more than happy to be able to announce that their support and vote were gladly being given to Sebastian.

Singer and movie star Joey Nadi gave a spectacular concert in Central Park, and when Angus Sebastian unexpectedly appeared on the stage, he remained there, listening with amusement to the applause and cheering of a wild audience excited by the arrival of their next president. Angus had appointed Renzo Copeland the six and a half foot tall heavyweight boxing champion as his bodyguard. They played around a bit on stage and then sang a song with Joey Nadi, which was immediately followed by a short but concise *impromptu* speech by Angus. He let America know that his bed was already made in the White House, and that he had opened all the windows to let the fresh winds of change blow through and clear the air.

The Man helicopters provided spectacular views of all the festivities and the city in all its magnificence. No matter where they flew, whether it was over Manhattan, Brooklyn, Queens, the Bronx or Staten Island, the streets were full of happy celebrants proclaiming Angus Sebastian as the man of their choice. There were millions of people in the streets, and Martha Manolow reported with pride that this was now officially the biggest party in the world. There were many different parades, all containing dozens and dozens of floats. The people were all dressed in their showiest clothing and even had their cars decorated as if they were part of a royal procession. All regular police leaves had been cancelled, and the NYPD was being reinforced by the army. Along with the official security forces were another ten thousand private guards from Man-Mandate; yet, all this security combined would still be impotent should a major disaster occur. The streets were simply too crowded to be able to accomplish any quick movements of a sizeable force. But everything went smoothly and without incident; there was plenty of entertainment, and a feeling of togetherness had come over the people who realized that they were experiencing something unique.

Oscar and Cathy watched, becoming so spellbound by the spectacle that they actually felt that they were there in the crowded streets themselves. The mad swarming of the wild crowds had a hallucinatory effect on Oscar. He began seeing things isolated from, and outside of, the three-dimensional image they were viewing. Before he had time to register what he was actually seeing, Cathy switched off the television. Rubbing his eyes, Oscar sat up in his armchair as Cathy said, "You look so tired, Oscar. Why don't you try and get some sleep? You have seen your old house, and you have made some startling discoveries, and you got to see all those people again whom you worked so closely with. It seems like it's been a pretty busy day to me!"

He nodded, got up and walked to the bathroom to take a shower. A quarter of an hour later he was lying in bed.

The first dream brought him back to New York City. Before him, Angus Sebastian the President of the United States beat the air with both his hands to give emphasis to what he was saying.

Oscar sat up in his sleep, and with his eyes still closed, he remained sitting as the image of his dream quickly faded from his mind. Slowly he sank back upon his pillow and allowed a second dream to enter his relaxed and highly receptive mind.

It was Emlyn Gray who appeared to him now, behind whom stood a long line of their ancestors, who all looked so familiar to Oscar that he felt as if he had met them all personally. This was the first time he was not frightened by the appearance of Emlyn Gray; his breathing stayed calm, and he did not even begin to sweat profusely. For a change, the dream did not turn out to be his usual nightmare from which he would wake up screaming. It was also the first time that he heard a constant whispering that seemed to reach his ears from all around him. Gray's lips and those of all the people behind him were moving, forming words and transferring to Oscar knowledge that would have been impossible to obtain any other way than this.

Oscar dreamed—and smiled.

Cathy stood in the doorway of the bedroom and looked at his satisfied, sleeping face, which was dimly lit by the glow from the gas lamps in the room. She closed the door quietly, and not being particularly tired, decided to stay up a while longer.

There was so much to think about.

She went to the balcony and looked at the lights of Interlaken. The darkness away from the town was so complete that she could not even see the mighty mountains. She watched countless stars appear and disappear again behind thin patches of cloud. Despite the late hour, below her people still strolled along the town's lantern-lit main boulevard. She realized that she would have been much happier if Oscar had simply brought her here for a nice holiday.

Cathy was always busy studying the past. She knew more about the dead people she spent her time with than she did about herself. At least her heroes allowed her to admire them without rousing her jealousy.

The difference between them and me is that they're dead, and I'm alive and kicking, she often thought to herself. Since she had begun sharing her days with Oscar, she felt more alive then ever.

So here she was, standing alone in the middle of the night on a terrace in Switzerland, fantasizing about enjoying a vacation with Oscar, undisturbed by all the craziness in the world.

It began to get chilly, and Cathy went back inside. She sat down next to the bed and looked at Oscar's calm face. Sitting there now, she was immensely happy. With a little bit of imagination, she had no trouble believing that the smile on his sleeping face was caused by his dreams about her.

The truth was, however, that Oscar at that moment was in a world that was unreachable to her.

Two days later, just around noon, they left the large parking lot on the south side of Interlaken and drove to Grindelwald. From the center of the little village, they took the gondola up to the seventy-one hundred foot high First, and from there, they began to walk to Bachalp Lake, accompanied by several other hikers who on this warm sunny day had come to enjoy the views of the mighty Bernese Alps.

"From the lake you can still walk on for hours," said Oscar. "All the way up to the Faulhorn where the oldest and highest mountain hotel in the country is to be found. From there, you can see the deep valleys on the other side, and on a clear day like today, you can even see as far away as the German Black Forest."

Cathy had taken his hand and walked beside him in silence. During the ride up on the cable car, she had worn sunglasses, which she had since removed so she could see the true colors of the fantastic world around her. Along the path everything was green. The yellow of the flowers contrasted with the brown and gray of stone, and the high white peaks stood out sharply against the blue sky. When the path brought them close to the edge of the giddy depths, she squeezed his hand even tighter. Surprisingly, there were still many cows at this height. These alpine bovines walked slowly and indifferently, big, jingling bells around their necks, along the rim of the abyss. With their big sleepy eyes and their slowly, constantly chewing jowls, they seemed to tell the world that even if they missed a step, the cosmic magic of the mountains would allow them to transform themselves into eagles and fly away.

Oscar and Cathy looked inconspicuous enough. They both wore hooded jackets, long dark trousers and strong mountaineering boots. Cathy was so preoccupied with the beauty of the landscape that she had almost forgotten that she had come here to meet someone. When they reached the lake after an hour's walk, she saw standing on the other side someone whom she immediately recognized as Natasja Bruschlinski. Her cloak, which reached all the way to her toes but did nothing to conceal her big, bulky frame and her blond hair streaked with gray, made it easy to recognize her.

"She's standing right there," said Oscar. "Far enough away from the trail that passersby won't notice her, but still close enough that we could never have missed her."

They walked up to her, and as they got close, Natasja opened her cloak. Under it she was wearing the same cape she had been wearing when they met in the courtyard, and she discreetly flashed the secret symbol on the inside. Oscar, in turn, opened his jacket. He was wearing the jacket that Tony Falcon had put in his luggage right before his departure from the United States. He flashed the emblem of gold and silver and then closed his jacket again.

"Let's walk through the grass," suggested the woman. "Then we'll disappear from sight to the other walkers. We can enjoy the beauty of the panorama as we go. I come here every season. Come, we'll look at the tops—the Schreckhorn, the Eiger, the Mönch, the Jungfrau, all my lofty friends! The latter two are each higher than 13,000 feet!"

Her voice was full of excitement as if she were seeing all this for the first time, and Cathy understood how the woman could still be so enthusiastic about it. Together, in silence, they watched the timeless beauty of nature unfold before them.

Suddenly, there came a commotion behind them. An army of servants, all in livery uniforms, appeared on the path at the other side of the lake. Sedan chairs, both open and closed, carried men and women of great importance who reclined in luxury on soft cushions. As the entourage reached an open field, a group of female servants rushed forward carrying, in reed baskets, all the food necessary for a substantial picnic. Musicians began playing stringed instruments. Their notes, both high and low, swelled out across the field, returning as echoes from every different angle.

"You have joined Falcon's resistance," remarked Oscar paying no attention to what was happening on the other side of the water.

"Resistance leader or freedom fighter," said Natasja, "rebel or insurgent. He is a charismatic pioneer with a growing number of highly intellectual followers. I am one of them, just as you are now, Oscar. He is striving for a new world in which everyone's voice will be heard again, and to accomplish his aim, he will shrink from nothing, not even revolution. Oscar, I am so glad that you are on our side! The news about your being appointed to an important post has spread like wildfire all over Europe. Falcon is doing his utmost to advance you quickly in our ranks. I am very proud of you!"

Cathy had taken a step backward and looked all around her. She studied the mighty mountains in the distance, Oscar and Natasja, the people stepping out of the sedan chairs, the women on the field and then back again. But when she saw Oscar standing extremely close to Natasja, with both his hands raised, she concentrated on them alone.

It looked as if Oscar were using the power that flowed from his eyes and fingertips to bring the woman under his control. Cathy felt confident that his powerful mind had surprised and conquered Natasja's. Her physical reaction to Oscar's metaphysical manipulations was significant. Her chin sagged down to her chest; her arms hung limply at her sides, and her knees bent. Her eyes seemed transfixed, and her mouth gaped open.

"You are free to do as you please at Man-Manifest, are you not?" Oscar asked calmly. "You are qualified to use all the equipment on the premises. Has anyone ever forbidden you anything?"

Natasja continued staring at the ground with a glazed look in her eye.

"No," she said and swallowed with great difficulty as if her throat were parched.

"Is there anyone at Man-Manifest you distrust?"

"No," she said again.

"Johann Helm has taken my place. Can you trust him?"

"Johann is intelligent," she answered. "You can always count on him. He may not be a philosopher or a brilliant historian, but he sure knows how to organize. Since he replaced you, everything has been going much smoother."

"Have you ever heard anything about the minions?"

She seemed to take her time and think about the question a bit. "Of course . . ."

"Tell me about them."

"They are the confidants of kings, noblemen, dignitaries. They dress exactly the same as their protectors; they behave identically.

They are a prop, pleasant company and special friend to their masters. In the First Renaissance, of the fifteenth and sixteenth centuries, they appeared in all the highest circles. It is once again fashionable for the powerful and wealthy to keep minions, but nowadays it is an intentional, and often cheap, imitation of life among the noble classes during the First Renaissance."

"Are minions mentioned, or described, in any of the old books or manuscripts that have turned up at Man-Manifest?"

"Of course, they are mentioned every now and then."

"In what way?"

"They play no part in any matter of great importance and are usually mentioned in descriptions of situations. We have proof of their existence, but the authors who briefly talk about them never go deeper into the matter. You can read about a vassal, a duke, a merchant, a fisherman, a soldier, a tramp, a minion. A minion lends color to his time, which makes him different from, say for instance, the merchant and the soldier who have always been there and who will always remain. The minion lives in a specific period of time. Before that, no one had ever heard of them, and afterward, there's never any further mention of them—until they suddenly re-emerge in our times, that is."

"Is there anyone you know of doing any research at all about the minions?"

"No."

"How can you be so sure?"

"Well, at any rate, it's never come to my attention. And besides, why would anyone be specifically searching for information about minions in the new books?"

"What if I were to tell you that the minions once tried to rule the world, that they are a special breed of human and that they will most certainly try again to wrest the power for themselves? What would your reaction be then, Natasja?"

A slight smile appeared on her face.

"You have always had a wild imagination. How could they possibly accomplish something like that?"

He ignored her question and continued on with his own.

"So you're telling me that no one at Man-Manifest is searching for this information. Is the company controlled by outsiders now?"

Her reply was swift. "Yes, and for quite some time now, we have been in constant contact with Ferdinand's palace in New York State."

"Are you aware of when and what books arrive in Switzerland, and can you take note of their contents?"

"Of course."

"This is all very strange. I have always managed to obtain the most interesting books for my half-sister Johanna, and she always appeared to be seeing them for the first time. I can't believe that she was playing with me. Whatever I brought with me was new to her. Who is it that's watching you?"

"Kenneth Mayfield, Mike Farland and Tana Rowe, the minions of Ferdinand, Jimmy and Johanna Man, respectively."

Oscar and Cathy exchanged a look of mutual understanding. It immediately struck Cathy as odd that Natasja was not more surprised to suddenly hear herself discussing minions.

"This is the first I've heard of this," said Oscar. "Has this information been kept from me intentionally?"

"I don't think so. It just seems obvious that it was not interesting enough to bother telling you about."

"And how is it you know all this?"

"When I was given more important tasks to perform in my role as a secretary, one of them was to make sure that contact with the palace was never broken. I still check it every day. Your half brother Ferdinand came to Switzerland while you were traveling around Italy and France. He was accompanied by his minion Kenneth Mayfield, and he and I came to several important agreements."

"But no one ever asked you to withhold anything from a particular shipment or give them anything without telling anyone else at Man-Manifest? Anything concerning minions?"

"No. Never."

Oscar crossed his arms and closed his eyes. The spell broken, Natasja straightened her back and rubbed her fingers over her forehead.

"Falcon knows what he's doing, Oscar," she said. "Our democracy needs to be restored, and he needs men like you to propagate his ideas and help him reach a wider audience. But tell me, my dear friend, what can I do for you?"

Oscar grinned sheepishly.

"It's about Tony Falcon and his plans," Oscar lied. "He and I have exchanged views extensively, but I still don't know where I stand with him; that's what I wanted to discuss with you. Do you think I made the right decision?"

She took him by the arm and walked with him along the lake praising Falcon and explaining his point of view. Cathy followed them enjoying the view and listening to Natasja's voice, which was full of emotion.

Gradually they returned to the path. Out on the field, the picnic was in full swing.

No one recognized Oscar, who had donned his hood to hide his long hair plaited with red threads. He wasn't in the mood to sing or recite poems or to stop and spend time with the people who had gathered here and who would undoubtedly have invited him to join them once they had discovered who he was.

Back at the gondola station, they stepped into a car and descended to Grindelwald in the valley. There they said good-bye to each other. Natasja Bruschlinksi was glad that she had had the chance to talk with Oscar for such a long time. She had told him that she would like to see him again soon. They drove in tandem up to Interlaken. There, Oscar turned onto the parking lot, while Natasja followed the road along the Lake of Brienz in the direction of Sarnen. Only when Cathy was once again sitting alone with Oscar in a carriage on their way to the Dis Pater Europe Hotel, did she began to talk about the way he had interrogated Natasja. In the automobile, they had spoken little, watching the scenery go by, each wrapped in their own thoughts.

"It looked like you had her completely under your spell," she said. "And afterward she didn't seem to remember anything she had told you and began talking about Falcon again."

She said this quietly, watching the coachman out of the corner of her eye. The tramping of the horse's hooves on the pavement made enough noise to guarantee that he couldn't hear her at all.

"I know that all this confuses you and that sometimes you have absolutely no idea where you stand with me," he said looking aside, and when he saw her startled eyes, he quickly added, "No, don't worry, I merely guessed your thoughts, I didn't actually see them."

"But could you actually do that, if you so desired?"

"Difficult to say. Anyway, I never really tried. Since the day I got so angry at Algernon Sparks in my home, so much has changed in me, and during my stay here in Switzerland, things have gained incredible momentum. What I did with Natasja Bruschlinski, I hadn't thought possible not long ago. As I have already said, I know all this confuses you. I assume that is why you said so little in the car."

"I didn't know how to broach the subject. But I'm happy to have a chance to discuss it with you. Oscar, are you afraid? I mean, does knowing that you have such power at your disposal scare you?"

"No. I can handle this. What really scared me was when I had those unexplainable, threatening dreams about Emlyn Gray. I have begun to calm down about it, though. How about you? Are you afraid?"

Cathy shrugged her shoulders slowly in noncommittal silence.

The horses broke into a trot. The carriage had passed through the Jungfraustrasse and its extension the Centralstrasse and had reached the Höhestrasse where their hotel stood. Staring at the crowded boulevard, the beautiful buildings and the statue of Dis Pater, she spoke in her normal voice.

"Yes, of course I'm afraid. But I'm not trying to suppress my fear. This is just the way things are, and I must learn to deal with them. As a historian, I am very well aware of the fact that I am experiencing extraordinary events, and as your biographer, I must keep my head cool and my eyes wide open."

She took his hand and pushed herself against him.

"Another good reason to stay as close as possible to you at all times," she said.

"We must go back to New York," said Oscar. "I'm very sorry that we cannot stay here longer. Some other time we will return and together ski these wonderful mountains. Perhaps we'll even get to stay here through the entire winter, but now I have to return. I know certain things, Cathy, without being able to explain even to myself how I know them. I suppose the best way to describe it is as if something is whispered in my ear while I sleep and when I awake, I react impulsively on it. Maybe it isn't such a good idea after all for you to stay so close to me. When we get back, perhaps it would be better if you did not leave the penthouse. I will tell Algernon Sparks that his security people on the twentieth floor must watch over you as well."

The coachman brought the horses to a stop, and the two stepped out.

"It's a pity that we must leave already," said Cathy. Before they entered the hotel, she looked once more at the buildings on the other side of the Höheweg and at the majestic mountaintops in the distance.

* * *

Large parts of New York City had become unreachable due to the swarming crowds in the streets. Governor Angus Sebastian had become the new president of the United States, and in his hometown, where the Man family ruled, there was a celebration going on for millions of inhabitants and visitors.

The best way to reach Manhattan from any of the area airports was by helicopter. Public transportation and private cars became hopelessly mired in the unyielding traffic. Choppers were scarce, however, and it was not even a matter of bargaining; only people of the highest standing had a chance at getting on one. The privileged few were escorted to elegant waiting rooms by employees of Man-Mandate Enterprises, and in order of their importance, were brought out to a heliport from where the mighty flying machines came and went.

Cathy Wheeler had taken off in a chopper along with about twenty other extravagantly dressed passengers, most of whom were officials from Syrinx Colorado and Fortuna Fund. The pilot intentionally flew low to give everyone on board the chance to see the chaos taking place in the streets below. Flying low over Queens Boulevard, the multicolored hats of the people below formed a constantly changing mosaic, punctuated every now and then by a face looking up from the crowd. From the side streets, large groups of partygoers pushed forward, often spearheaded by musicians, dancers, slow-moving cars and floats.

Cathy had landed at Kennedy Airport where Oscar had arranged a seat for her in the chopper. She was flying in the direction of the Queensborough Bridge when she saw two other helicopters approach that had taken off from La Guardia. The larger of the two machines looked like a tarantula with its legs dangling below it. The smaller one was lined with thin copper plates, which formed the scaly skin of a monitor lizard.

Someone was talking about the glorious victory of Angus Sebastian and how odd it was that even though he had strengthened the influence of Man-Mandate Enterprises greatly, it was not he, but

Ferdinand Man, who was considered the most powerful man on earth now.

"Ferdinand Man now outshines even Walter Krocht," commented someone.

A giant zeppelin glided majestically over the East River casting its great shadow on the masses that surged across the bridge into Manhattan. One of the passengers sitting not far from Cathy compared what he saw to a symbolic shadow that was throwing a pall over this festive day. "The news will not have reached everyone down there yet that Carl Holdorf the driving power behind Dis Pater can no longer see all this."

A lady clad in a golden dress looked up in surprise.

"Excuse me," she said, "I am on my way from Colorado to New York. I have been invited to the party that Syrinx has organized down on Wall Street, and I haven't heard any news the whole time that I have been traveling."

"McVee, Fortune Fund," said the man in introduction. He looked quite important, wearing a long coat equipped with grotesque shoulder pads. On his head stood a three-cornered hat with little silver tassels. "Let me fill you in quickly. Last evening Carl Holdorf was dining in a restaurant in Lisbon. He often did business in Portugal with people from Richthausen Gold. After dinner, he enjoyed a fine red wine which, as one inside source claims, contained enough poison to murder all the guests present." He looked at her intently and added, "And the restaurant was packed!"

A shiver ran through her. "Carl Holdorf. A man of etiquette and courtesy. A visionary, a builder, a genius! Say his name and you think of grandeur! So, he is dead."

"The philosopher was given the poisoned cup, just like Socrates," said McVee, "but in this case, it wasn't exactly of his own free will."

His remark was not intended to be a joke. His voice was filled with bitterness.

"And the culprits?" asked the woman.

"Vanished without a trace," was the answer. "No one paid any attention to the waiter who served the wine. Holdorf normally had his confidant the minion Albert Herr taste everything before he ate or drank it. Maybe he felt that surrounded by business associates from Richthausen, who were his hosts, it would be improper. His death came so quickly that his last words got stuck in his throat. No one could even understand what he was trying to say."

Cathy listened to this conversation without betraying any emotion whatsoever. Her face remained unchanged as the man spoke more about Haldorf's minion. Hearing the name Dis Pater, she thought about the hotel in Interlaken where she'd had such a good time with Oscar.

The chopper descended over Bowling Green the historic little park at the southernmost end of Manhattan Island, and Cathy gazed out at Broadway, crowded with pedestrians. Beautiful, smooth buildings with imposing flights of steps and colonnades in front reached high into the sky as the chopper swung around to one of their roofs and landed.

Cathy stepped out. All she had brought with her was a handbag. Her luggage had stayed behind with Oscar at the airport and would be delivered to her later. Along with the other passengers, she went down in the elevator. On the ground floor most of the people headed off toward Broadway while Cathy walked up to the other side making her way through the crowded streets and giving as good as she got when someone tried to grab her bag. There were several moments when she could do no more than let herself be carried along by the stream of partygoers, and at one point, she had to wait behind a black granite pillar until a parade of horse-drawn carriages had passed. She finally managed to reach the entrance of a subway station. The subways could hardly absorb the steady stream of passengers inundating them. Finally on a train, Cathy stood there flattened against a wall with her eyes closed to avoid seeing all those faces so close to hers. She thought about her days in Switzerland and dwelt upon all the beautiful memories.

Just before she had stepped into the helicopter, Oscar had stroked her head, and she had felt surprisingly calm. Much of what she had recently gone through had been forgotten instantly.

"Go to the twentieth floor as soon as you are in the building," Oscar had told her. "Make contact with Algernon Sparks, General Howe, James or Hodgkinson. Tell them, for me, that they must keep the president alive. Do you understand me? Angus Sebastian must not be murdered!"

With a heavy sigh, she entered the building and hurried to the elevator. On the twentieth floor, she got out and told a man in plainclothes who approached her that she needed to speak to Sparks or Howe. The man had recognized her and could tell by her serious expression that she had something important on her mind. He asked her to wait for a moment and disappeared. Two minutes later, he was back, accompanied by General Scott James, who showed her an identity card and shook her hand. He looked at her with raised eyebrows.

"You are Cathy Wheeler, Oscar Man's girlfriend? My man recognized you immediately, but can you please show me some ID anyway?"

They were in a hall with a floor made of red stone in the middle of which stood a round bench. Cathy opened her bag and began to search for her passport. She took out the worn rag doll that had belonged to Angelina Hood. She had kept it with her hand baggage on the flight over. The general looked at it but asked no questions, although he undoubtedly found it strange that a grown woman would carry such an old toy with her. She showed him her passport.

"You are lucky that I am here," said the general. " Sparks, Howe and Hodgkinson haven't been here for quite some time, and I am only here because I am in charge of the troops assigned to guard this part of town. May I ask you where Oscar Man is? Has he already gone to the penthouse?"

"No," answered Cathy. "He has sent me to you with a short, but very special message. May I talk with you in private?"

"Come with me," he said and led the way to a door. "I will tell them that I don't want to be bothered by anyone for a while."

At the end of the corridor, he opened another door. For a moment, Cathy shrank back when she saw a swarming mass of people. Men in uniform sat at small tables behind all kinds of equipment. In front of them, over the entire length of a wall, gigantic screens showed three-dimensional images of the streets of lower Manhattan, the locations of which changed with such speed that it made her dizzy.

"Am I crazy or has it become even more crowded?" shouted Scott James. "Don't these people ever get tired?"

Someone at a table turned toward him and said, "Yes, sir. It is indeed more crowded than it was earlier, General. And yes, they do eventually tire, but they are quickly replaced by new revelers."

"Take over; I will be back in a minute."

He beckoned to Cathy. A few moments later, they were sitting opposite to each other in a small room that was barren except for a locked steel cabinet and four chairs arranged around a long table.

"I have troops standing by everywhere," said James with a sigh. "With our cameras, we can keep an eye on the situation, and we are ready to take action immediately if someone sounds the alarm. Everyone knows, however, that it would be a hopeless task. We couldn't possibly get anywhere in this city quickly. We have at our disposal a few helicopters, and only with those could we get anywhere fast."

"I came in by chopper," Cathy told him. "Oscar and I just arrived from Switzerland, and he sent me immediately to you."

"How did you reach us? How did you get through the busy streets? Walking?"

"Partly. I managed to reach a subway station."

"But—" He tried to imagine how long her journey must have been and how much trouble she must have gone through to finally get there. "For someone who has just come so far, I would have expected you to be more or less exhausted. But from the way you are sitting here, it would be easier for me to believe that you just had taken the elevator down from the penthouse."

He pointed upward.

"My holiday in Switzerland was relaxing and wonderful," she said. "Maybe that is why I appear so rested." Suddenly her face took on a more serious demeanor. "Oscar has told me that you must keep the new president alive. His actual words were that Angus Sebastian must not be murdered."

The general's face lost its stony look. He was clearly shocked by her words.

"What the hell is that supposed to mean?" he shouted.

Cathy shrugged her shoulders.

"The message seems clear enough to me, and I have nothing to add."

The man jumped to his feet and stormed toward the door. He had put his hand on the doorknob when he changed his mind and returned to his chair, shaking his head. He sat down again, and as the chair creaked under his weight, he leaned forward and rested his elbows on his knees.

"Where is Oscar Man?"

"We went separate ways at Kennedy Airport where he arranged a seat in a chopper for me. I suppose he'll be along soon. Anyway, he did not tell me if he had anything else to do first."

"Don't you find that odd? You travel all the way from Switzerland together, and at the airport, he lets you go on by yourself."

"To bring you that message!"

"Couldn't he have done that better himself?"

Cathy showed no reaction to this. She remained sitting there calmly, staring at him with unblinking eyes, which confused the general even more. He got the unpleasant feeling that he and Cathy Wheeler were on two different worlds and that they just happened to be sitting next to each other at the moment.

"Tell me, short and to the point, what you were doing in Switzerland," he said, his voice sounding like he was giving an order.

Still relaxed, Cathy sprawled in her chair with her hands folded behind her head.

"Making love," she said. "That's two words. Is that short and to the point enough for you?"

"Oscar Man wanted to go to Switzerland because he had to arrange something there," said the general. "Whatever it was, it was so important that he let us down. Dean Howe told him loud and clear what would happen if Angus Sebastian got to the White House. Man-Mandate would rule the United States of America, and the madness would be complete. Let me ask you another question: why did Oscar Man have to go to Switzerland so suddenly?"

"All I know is that Oscar and I really got to know each other while we were there," said Cathy. "We took short day trips and stayed in a splendid suite at the Dis Pater Europe Hotel. But we are back now, and we know for certain that we love each other. It was important to Oscar to be able to be alone with me."

He gazed at her, admiring her beauty, and wondered if she was telling the truth. He simply couldn't understand how she could look so fresh. And when he thought about the old, worn-out rag doll she kept in her bag, he touched his head with both hands and rubbed his temples.

"While you were away, the media here have done their utmost to make a hero out of Oscar in the shortest possible time. Suddenly he seems to be very important to a lot of people."

Cathy stood up and offered him her hand.

"Well, he certainly is the most important person in the world to me," she said. "I have delivered my message, and now I want to go home."

He also stood and escorted her back out into the hall. As soon as she had stepped onto the elevator, he went back to the big room with the screens and ordered a few people to follow him to his room.

When one protested saying that he could not leave his post, the general began to swear. With no further protests, the man fell in behind the others who hastily followed General James. Back in the room where he had been sitting with Cathy, he said, "Oscar Man has just arrived from Switzerland, and he immediately sent his girlfriend up here to tell us that we must keep Angus Sebastian alive."

* * *

In the park surrounding the palace, between the Ferris wheel and the cathedral, a makeshift auditorium had been erected that was big enough to accommodate a couple thousand people. Angus Sebastian had been celebrated at countless places in New York City, and afterward he was flown to this forum to be honored by a more select company. Although those invited were not important enough to be received in the palace, they were being given a chance here to see the new president up close and personal. Many of them would actually get the opportunity to shake his hand and have a short chat with him. Representatives of all the big international companies and the press were present in great force. A stage, ten feet high, had been built on which a gilded throne had been placed for Sebastian. At both sides were staircases leading up to the stage. At the bottom of these stood palace guards in the employ of the Man family. The army and police were not present, and with the exception of the royal guards,

Sebastian trusted no one but his own bodyguard Renzo Copeland, the boxer, who had been appointed just recently and now never left his side.

In front of the stage stood silver shields, especially made for this occasion, emblazoned with the emblems of Man-Mandate, Fortune Fund, Syrinx Colorado, Hygnos Hybrid, Dis Pater, Richthausen Gold, Fenrir and other, lesser multinationals.

All the voices in the crowd fell silent as the president ascended one of the flights of stairs and stood in front of his throne. Then a loud voice came through the speaker system:

"Ladies and gentlemen, the President of the United States of America!"

Immediately there was a thunderous burst of applause. Sebastian remained calm and smiled but once when above the tumult of the crowd, came the high-pitched screams of an overly enthusiastic woman whose voice drowned out all the others. He waved at a few acquaintances and then raised his hands to indicate that the applause had gone on quite long enough. As soon as it became quiet, he began his speech. He thanked everyone who had made it possible for him to be where he was standing now and requested a moment of silence in memory of Carl Holdorf.

"How much I had wanted to meet him later this day in the palace and embrace him," sounded his deep voice.

After a minute of absolute silence, during which the thousands of guests remained standing motionless, he resumed his speech.

* * *

After putting Cathy on the helicopter, it had been time for Oscar to act on some knowledge that had been whispered to him. A chopper had been all set to leave for the festivities by the palace. All the seats were taken, but they made room for him nonetheless, and absolutely no one, not even members of the security service, asked him what business he had on the estate of the family that had disowned him.

Today Oscar could go where he pleased, for he had pulled up an aura around himself that made him unassailable. He was present, as everyone could see, but he was infinitely far away at the same time.

The chopper took off and flew low over Brooklyn, Jersey City and Newark to give everybody a view of the bustle below. It then picked up speed, turned and began to climb as it now made its way upstate.

After they landed, the passengers stepped out and one by one were frisked by the president's security guards and the palace guards. Oscar was wearing a tight suit that made it obvious he concealed no weapons. The man who searched him looked intensely at him for a moment, and Oscar gazed back. Then the man nodded, bowed slightly and gestured that he should follow the others down a flower-lined path leading to the forum.

Inside, he immediately noticed the absence of his half-brothers and half-sisters. They were to receive the new president later in the palace where various kings and queens had already gathered. Sebastian ended his speech. When the applause stopped, he walked back to the stairs on the right side of the stage and shook hands with those people deemed important enough to congratulate him personally. He gave a tycoon from Hygnos Hybrid Corporation a friendly pat on the back and then kissed a woman stockholder of Richthausen Gold for so long that the crowd began to cheer and applaud again. Sebastian had become so incredibly popular that all of the big corporations wished that they had supported him as Man-Mandate had. It was, as everyone knew, Ferdinand Man who had supported him in all possible ways to get him into the White House. Now he stood side by side with the most powerful people in the world, and everyone hoped to profit from his future decisions and new laws.

Oscar mingled with people at the foot of the stairs and then slowly went up the stairs, taking one step at a time. His eyes met those of the president, but it was if the man didn't recognize him—or perhaps he was so engrossed with other thoughts that it never dawned on him who he was looking at.

Oscar felt minions present. One was very close, and others were scattered among the crowd in the forum. There were no minions from the Man family there, but that didn't really matter. He remained unreachable to them, for he knew their tricks just as well, or maybe even better, than they did themselves.

Somewhere a band began to play; employees from the palace served food and drink. Sebastian walked back to the middle of the stage intending to rest on his throne for a while and look at all these people who had came here especially to see him. Twelve of the palace guards stepped aside to allow him to pass with his own protection. He remained standing in front of his throne for a moment and whispered something in the ear of the boxer. A smile appeared on Copeland's face, and he nodded. He was also of Jamaican heritage and was so relaxed in the company of Angus that they almost seemed to be brothers. Their height and physical build were so similar that if they were to wear the same clothing, as patron and minion often did, it would be hard to tell them apart.

But Renzo Copeland was no minion. His fists had made him world famous. Angus Sebastian, one of his biggest fans, had been present at all the bouts that Copeland had fought in New York City. In Copeland's presence, Angus imagined himself a tough fighter. A staunch friendship had developed between them.

Under the wooden stage lay seven men, four presidential bodyguards and three guards from the Man family, all dead on the ground. An eighth one had a knife at his throat and was being forced to stay in contact with his colleagues using his cell phone and making it sound as if everything was status quo. A group of men, clad entirely in black, stood ready to open a trapdoor through which Angus Sebastian would fall.

It had taken a considerable bribe to get a few of the construction workers to build the trapdoor into the stage, and since the stage had been built with canvas draped along the back, an escape route had not been all that difficult to plan. A car stood that everyone assumed would be used by the president if he unexpectedly decided to leave. His own chauffeur was sitting behind the wheel, never suspecting that this was the very last day of his life.

Oscar felt the atmosphere filled with a rustling and vibration of countless emotions and thoughts. And out of this, he filtered the mental impulses that came to him from under the stage.

At precisely the right moment, he climbed the stage.

From somewhere in the area someone sent a wireless message to the men in black, and with a sudden tug, the trapdoor fell open. Renzo Copeland disappeared from the stage and landed ten feet below. Before he had a chance to see anything or anyone, several knives had been driven deep into his chest and stomach. Sebastian also fell through, but Oscar had positioned himself close enough to grab him by the shoulders of his jacket. With his legs spread wide, he straddled the gaping hole in the floor, holding the president inches from death. Suddenly Angus's weight seemed to increase, and Oscar realized that whoever was below them had taken hold of Sebastian's legs and was trying to pull him down. Guards appeared from all sides now and rushed to the edge of the hole to try and assist Oscar.

Angus Sebastian was pulled back out of the hole screaming in pain. His shoes were gone, and the bottoms of his pants were torn. Blood flowed down his calves and over his socks. He was laid on the floor, and as the guards stood around him in a circle, Oscar snarled at them, "Get him the hell out of here as fast as you can! They still might shoot him from under the stage!"

Four men quickly lifted Sebastian, who was still writhing and screaming in pain. A few others cautiously knelt down at the trapdoor and shined flashlights underneath. They saw the dead bodies of the guards and the boxer. As they jumped down, several doors flew open at the sides, and more armed guards streamed inside. Below the stage, the canvas flapped in the breeze where a long tear had been made in it. The sound of a quickly accelerating automobile was heard.

It had since become dark outside, but the man behind the wheel who had taken the place of the murdered chauffeur knew exactly how to get out of the park as quickly as possible.

The president was whisked immediately to the palace where one of the best-equipped hospitals in the State of New York was staffed twenty-four hours a day with the best doctors and nurses money could buy. Meanwhile, back at the celebration, the guests were urged to remain calm. And the band played on.

Oscar now shut down his extended mental abilities and once again pulled around the safety net to protect himself from the probing of the minions. He became the jester again. All eyes and cameras were trained on him, and everybody wanted to talk to him. He kept his answers evasive and remained in constant motion. Meanwhile, more and more security personnel had entered the forum, and the ones who were already present called for reinforcements.

Oscar knew that the security arrangements had been as leaky as a wicker basket. A palace guard told him about the dead men found under the stage. How many people had been bribed? How many had been paid to look the other way when the canvas was sliced open?

"This should never have happened," someone said. "But it did happen, and thanks to your swift action, the president is still alive!"

It became very quiet in the forum and then exclamations of astonishment arose. Ear-splitting applause erupted as Angus Sebastian, supported by two bodyguards, stumbled inside.

He was wearing new trousers, and his injured feet had been bandaged. He held his head up proudly, and his eyes sparkled. The men assisted him up to the stage and carefully sat him down on his throne. Beside him was the yawning hole of the trapdoor. Someone rushed up to him and put a microphone in front of his face, but it was another five minutes before he could make himself heard over the ovation.

"Renzo Copeland was my friend," he said in a strong voice. "And I have lost that friend. Forever. He was stabbed to death by a cowardly enemy. Those very same knives were the weapons that sliced up my legs—and were intended to cut through my heart. No one has claimed responsibility for this attack, but I hope to learn soon just who my enemy is. Until recently, I didn't even realize that I had any enemies! My sincere and undying gratitude goes to the man who saved my life: Oscar Man! Your Highness, may I ask you to join me? I would gladly come to you if my legs would only carry me. You are truly a prince in my eyes, and I am forever in your debt."

With a grand gesture, he beckoned to Oscar, whom he had discovered in the crowd. As Oscar made his way to the stage, Sebastian reassured the people that his injuries were not life-threatening, and the certainty in his voice was proof enough of the strength of his character. He was a brave man who would cave in to no one, even though he had so recently escaped death. Oscar stood before the throne now and shook hands with his president.

His president gave him a quizzical look as Oscar leaned toward him to whisper in his ear.

"I was sitting on a plane on my way to Switzerland when Don Bradshaw was murdered. I saw it all on film, and I saw you, too, as your jacket blew open and revealed the emblem of Mason Media."

Then he embraced the president, who in turn wrapped both his arms around Oscar's shoulders.

When they broke their embrace, Oscar stepped to the side, and Sebastian spoke into the microphone.

"I want to express my wish that the Man family exonerate Oscar and restore him to his rightful place within the palace and royal family. I have already said that he is truly a prince, and I doubt anyone would argue with me. Thank you, Oscar, for what you have done for me. You risked your own life to save mine."

Oscar allowed the cheering and applause to wash over him, and he once again was embraced by Sebastian as the cameras recorded it for posterity. Then he ran up to the edge of the stage, turned a cartwheel and landed on his feet ten feet below, letting himself fall forward as he rolled through the laughing, roaring crowd.

Sebastian began his speech again as if nothing at all had happened. He laid out the plans for his administration. Afterward, under the watchful eye of a greatly increased number of security personnel, some members of the crowd were invited onto the stage to greet the new president and shake his hand. They were all newly arrived guests who were all active in politics: governors, senators, mayors and various civil servants who had all pledged their support to Sebastian.

Oscar had gone over to the far side of the forum, where a bar had been set up, to get himself a drink. He was now the center of attention with everyone clamoring to speak to him at the same time. They all wanted to shake his hand and pat him on the back, but he had asked two guards to please keep the people at a distance. He stood with his back against the bar with a wide grin on his face. He nodded to the people who stared at him, but all the while he was thinking about Tony Falcon, the charismatic man with the strange gray eyes. He must indeed be someone special to be able to coach a man like Angus Sebastian in such a way that he was now trusted implicitly not only by the Man family but also by so many other influential people. He had managed to get Sebastian regarded with such esteem that it gotten him into the White House.

Angus Sebastian, the big man with the mentality of a prizefighter, was a member of the resistance. Where the army had failed in placing a man like Algernon Sparks inside the palace, Falcon had succeeded in getting Sebastian a prominent role in the affairs of all the major corporations.

If Oscar had not intervened, the army would have let the man they needed the most be killed, and now it was of the utmost importance to bring the military and Falcon together.

Oscar thought only slightly about the fact that he had been able to change the course of history due to a whisper in the night. Just as minions were a human mutation, he was a mutation of the minions. He knew this as the truth and was reconciled to it.

The two guards whom he had asked to insure his few moments of privacy parted to allow entry to a man who had arrived in a splendid carriage. The man bowed deeply to Oscar and said, "Prince, a carriage awaits you out front. Your sister Johanna has sent me to you to ask you to return to the palace. Will you please follow me?"

The smile remained on Oscar's face.

"Of course, my dear man," he said. "But first I will finish my drink . . . at my leisure. Why don't you have something to drink yourself?"

Chapter Ten

Meeting

The three generals who gathered in the domed room at Oscar's penthouse felt very ill at ease when they were led in by Cathy Wheeler. Oscar had stayed for over two weeks in his family's palace without sending any news of himself, and after he had returned, he had declined an invitation to visit the offices on the twentieth floor.

And now, although he received them in the most beautiful room of his apartment, he did not rise when they entered. Oscar wore his crown studded with precious stones, a multicolored fool's dress and gray boots. Beside him sat a mysterious man dressed in black with pale gray eyes and an eerie white face. He had long hair pulled back in a ponytail.

Cathy left the room, closing the door behind her. General Howe spoke first as he walked up to Oscar with his hand out.

"Is it Your Royal Highness, since you are a prince once again, or may I still call you Oscar?"

"The latter, Dean," was the slightly sarcastic answer. "Take a seat, all of you. There's a lot to discuss."

"Why have you stayed away for so long?" queried the wafer-thin Alvin Hodgkinson.

The obvious irritation in his voice caused the other generals to cast warning looks at him.

General Howe, grinning idiotically, said, "So, now you are considered a celebrity, as if you weren't that already, Oscar. The president's savior, the prodigal son who has returned home to the palace, the prince who has more to offer than anyone ever dreamed possible. Of course, we are all overjoyed with your return to the family fold, which is exactly where we wanted you to be. How on earth, though, did you manage to be standing at exactly the right place, at exactly the right time, so as to be able to catch hold of Sebastian? If only you knew how we have racked our brains about that one!"

Scott James coughed intentionally to bring attention to himself and then remarked, nodding in the direction of the man in black, "We have not been introduced to this gentleman, although it is not really necessary. I immediately recognized him as Tony Falcon, the owner of Mason Media. He is someone whom I have admired for a long time for his ability to continue operating entirely independently as a free employer, but I cannot help but wonder if the things we have to discuss are meant for his ears as well."

"I will personally vouch for his integrity," said Oscar. "Later, you will understand that he belongs here just as well as I do. As for your question, Dean, I cannot answer that yet, but believe me when I tell you that I knew what I was doing and that it was of the greatest importance that I did it."

"How can I possibly be content with an answer as vague as that?" Dean blustered.

He was about to add something but remained silent when Oscar sprang up from his chair and came at him with long strides, his long hair swishing to and fro. He had trouble written all over his face as he stopped right in front of the general and poked the forefinger of his left hand almost into his chin.

"You'll just have to be, Howe. If I were to ask you, man-to-man, who had given the order to murder the president, you would not give me a satisfactory answer either, and I would have to live with it. But while you and your officers keep racking your brains about the question of my foreknowledge, as you call it, I tell you loud and clear that you, along with Hodgkinson and James, are directly responsible for the death of Renzo Copeland, four of Sebastian's bodyguards and three of my family's guards. Your hands are bloodstained, and I warn you: I will not accept any lies about this. So I think it's better to keep your mouth shut about it from now on."

He walked back to his chair and relaxed again as if he had already forgotten his anger.

"Let's talk for a while, and then I will get us something to drink."

"Everything that happened has been thoroughly reconstructed," said James. "This would never have happened anywhere else, but the president insisted on trusting only a small number of his own men, and the Man guards seemed to be thinking more about celebrating than about any possible danger."

"Hopefully the prince will let that one that pass, Scott," said Hodgkinson. "I think we better listen to what else he has to tell us."

"You tried so hard to get Sparks inside the palace, and it ended so badly. I think Tony Falcon did much better with his pupil."

The generals looked at Oscar in complete confusion.

"Perhaps it might be better if we let Falcon explain it himself," he said.

Falcon did not wait for permission from the generals and began to talk, looking at them one by one.

"Cooperation is the key, gentlemen. In fact, it is the magic word if we are to change anything about the insanity of existence. It's so damn stupid that only now are we finally meeting and concentrating on the same man, our prince."

Only Howe dared to defy Falcon's mystical look for a moment, and then he too lowered his eyes.

"You have all known for a long time that I am merely a small contractor who somehow has managed to hold his own cast among giants. You are all well informed about my network. I have a talent for making news, whether big or small, quickly known all over the world. I have behind me a constantly growing group of people who are after the same goal as you, a free world for everyone, as it should be and as it once was. We can no longer remain at cross-purposes and suspicious of each other."

He stood up and paced back and forth in front of them.

"You can get the hang of things, of a situation, sometimes, without someone explaining it to you. You have come here to exchange views with Oscar Man on things that are not meant for other men's ears. Which means that you, without Oscar being aware of it, have checked everything out here. There is no one eavesdropping here; no one is listening to us—except, of course, your men on the twentieth floor! If any one of you suspected for a moment that anyone was listening to us, you would keep your mouths shut."

He said nothing for a moment, and when there was no reply, he launched into a new topic.

"I had prepared everything so very well. My man was well trained, and I let him play his dangerous game. And I succeeded! Governor Sebastian had become so popular with the Man family and assorted tycoons that they wanted him in the White House at any price. My fighter, with the mind and fists of a boxer, had everything accomplished for him by the Man family. The campaign was one big party, which just goes to show how popular you can be if you throw a lot of money around. And thus Angus became president. My first hero was in exactly the place I wanted him to be while my second hero Oscar was steadily climbing the ladder of popularity. With Angus as president and Oscar a folk hero, I could now dare to fight the international cartels: changing laws, shaking people up, slowly breaking down the walls behind which the despots hide, basically giving democracy a new chance. Then the army interfered with a plan to murder the president, not knowing that he was one of the good guys. Oscar sprang into action and made everything even more beautiful than it already was. He averted a disaster and made himself and Angus Sebastian the most popular men in the world while doing it. I won't ask Oscar how he did this; I'm just extremely grateful that he did."

Knowing that the generals needed time to accept all that they had heard, Falcon sat down quietly again. Oscar said he was going to get some drinks and left the room. He went straight to Cathy, who was in one of her own chambers. He found her gazing at a TV screen on the wall.

"Look at that," she said. "All I did was mention your name, and the broadcasting equipment is continually showing programming in which you are featured."

He watched himself on the screen, coming and going in all kinds of clothing, in many different places. He was in crowds turning somersaults and giving interviews concerning his actions in thwarting the assassination attempt.

"This are only the recent transmissions from all over the world; later on I can show you what you were up to twenty-four hours ago. Damn, Oscar, you're more visible these days than the president himself!"

As he stood there, she came up to him and kissed him.

Nodding toward the screen, she said, "These Oscars are for everyone, but this Oscar, the one made of flesh and blood, is mine alone! What's the state of affairs in the other room?"

"Falcon is taking the generals thoroughly to task, but he has also offered them a tightly knit cooperative I'm sure they will eagerly take part in. I'm glad that he did not get so angry about what happened to Sebastian that he wanted to cancel the entire team."

He held her tight as they watched the last bits of the broadcast.

"Doesn't it frighten you that you have become so incredibly popular?"

"The only thing that really scares me right now is that a minion can have almost anyone in my family murdered at any moment. The fame leaves me cold. It means nothing."

"You foresaw what would happen to Sebastian," said Cathy. "Do you automatically get a warning when something so drastic is about to happen? Are you able to look into the future and see, for instance, if your sister is in danger?"

"No, no. It doesn't work that way. What does occur I have started to call my 'night whispers.' They seem to be related some special mental quirk of mine, something that has been passed on from generation to generation and perfects itself more and more. I seem to have many special gifts. I can manipulate memory, as you know, and I can protect myself from the minion's probing, but the future remains hidden from me until I all of a sudden foresee a certain event. I knew I had to go to the park, and I knew that I would be a factor in the events there."

"Night whispers?"

"Perhaps I can describe it another way. It is something that happens to all minions. The intellectual storehouse of countless ancestors is all contained in one person's genetic makeup. When all these ancestors concentrate on the same subject, there is a whispering—a whispering loud enough to bridge the gap from the unconscious to the conscious. You are suddenly aware of something. Some kind of information, a melody, a warning—or whatever. The medium in my mind is a man called Emlyn Gray. Behind him stands a large group of helpers without clear features or recognizable faces. That's the way it works with me. I suspect that the genuine minions have much better contact with their ancestors and are able to see them a lot more clearly and sharply in their dreams. That seems to be the difference with me, but then, there are many other differences between the genuine minions and me."

"You are not violent, for instance."

"No, not inherently," he replied. "And there are other differences. The minions can probe people who are within their sphere of influence. That is what they did with Algernon Sparks. His intentions became clear to them, and they started to toy with him. The generals understand nothing of this because they don't know what minions are. But not everyone allows himself to be probed. There are some people whose mental processes remain unreachable to minions."

"You're talking about Sebastian now."

"Yes. They obviously cannot get through to him or else they would have been able to keep him away from my family."

"Are you going to tell the generals about the minions?"

"I'm going to wait on that for a while. First I want to discuss this with Falcon. I don't want to say that the generals are rigid in their thought processes, but this may be a bit too unbelievable for them."

"You can easily make them believers, Oscar."

"How so?"

Freeing herself from his embrace, she looked at him with sparkling eyes and said, "By getting it through their heads using the power of your mind! And when they are able to think clearly again, they will be ready to listen to you."

He nodded and smiled.

"I have to get back. All this talking has made everybody thirsty, and I promised them something to drink. Algernon Sparks has told them about some of my talents. He seems to have trouble holding his tongue. I am still wondering what he told them about the events in the palace. Or maybe they didn't believe those stories either."

"You heard what Lieutenant Lancaster told you in Interlaken. They must have been completely bewildered when Algernon tried to explain everything to them. But the difference between hearing about something and experiencing it yourself is enormous, Oscar. If someone told me that there was a poisonous snake loose somewhere in this building, I would look under my bed before I went to sleep. The real fear, the agony of terror, would only come at the moment that I opened my eyes and saw the serpent a hand's width from my face, ready to strike."

As it turned out, Oscar didn't have to explain anything. When he returned to the room with a tray full of cups, bottles and coffee, he discovered that Falcon had already taken things in hand. He could not help but notice how the generals stared at him in fascination as Falcon told them, unaware that Oscar had re-entered the room, "It's difficult, perhaps even impossible, to know if you acted out of your own free will when you implicated Oscar in your plans or if it was Oscar himself who arranged it so that a cooperation would come into being between us. It's also impossible to know just how far his power reaches."

Falcon now noticed him but continued nonetheless.

"He doesn't realize it, but he is still in a maturation process. Since we have nothing to compare it to, we will have to wait and see what he develops into. At any rate, we know that he is much different from the genuine minions who have already begun their slaughter."

Oscar put the tray down and looked at Falcon, whose overwhelming charisma was like a constant pressure in the atmosphere. He was almost overcome by the strange emptiness in the man's eyes; a shiver ran down his spine. The three generals, however, were worse off than he. They were as white as Jimmy Man might have been after putting on his makeup. Sweat trickled down their faces.

Falcon waved a finger through the air as if wielding a magic wand.

"Do not take any more initiatives upon yourselves. Wait. Leave things to me, but stay on the alert. When I ask for help, that is when you should take action. We have all come far, in our own ways. Fortunately, the army remains strong despite all the changes in the world. I know through my own organization that there are many people who want to bring the breath of life back into our democracy. The heavy repairs and cleanup can only begin, however, when the main problems have been solved. The power and range of the minion's dominion is beyond belief."

Oscar had banished his feelings of fear and sat relaxed in his chair again. Falcon, who noticed how serene Oscar was, smiled at him and said, "You and I are not so different, are we? Were you searching for me, or was I searching for you?"

"It was a cab driver who brought us together," answered Oscar with a smile. "It was Eddie Brooks, a Mason Media freedom fighter."

"Do you have any idea, Oscar, who I really am?"

"You know so much, Falcon, you could be a minion, but I have my doubts about that. It seems to me that you don't differ all that much from me. Perhaps you are another child, born at the end of a chain of minions, who by some freak of nature did not respond to the laws by which his ancestors lived. Am I correct?"

"Yes. Our similarities are greater than our differences."

"In heaven's name," said Alvin Hodgkinson, "will somebody please tell me what the hell a minion is? You tried to explain it to me, Falcon, when Oscar left the room, but frankly I understood little or nothing of what you said."

"A minion is like a demon," said Falcon calmly. "Is that clear enough? You could call it a devil. An evil parasite that feeds on mankind."

"Would you call yourselves devils, then? Aren't the ones you call minions just ordinary people?"

"Let's say I gave you two spiders," said Falcon, "two spiders who look pretty much the same. You decide which one you will let walk across the palm of your hand as you slowly make a fist. If you're lucky, your hand simply becomes a bit dirty where the spider is crushed. If things do not go your way, though, you will die, just as Carl Holdorf did after he had enjoyed his last glass of wine. The poison will have ended your life. In the same fashion, you can only tell a minion from a normal human being when he unexpectedly shows his true nature. And beware, gentleman! *Minion* is but a name that indicates a species, just like the word *dog*. I don't have to explain to anyone that there are many kinds of dogs. The most dangerous devils or demons are found associating with the most prominent people. From there, they can pretty much do as they please. Minions are everywhere, though we usually only have to deal with the less talented members of the species."

He ran his fingers down his ponytail.

"I mentioned Holdorf and the fact that the minions have begun to take the offensive. One murder will follow another. All the army brass probably thought that it was best to let matters take their own course since it would not be that terrible if all the tycoons of the big corporations were suddenly gone. But every murdered tycoon is replaced by a hellish minion, and the situation gets worse daily. You ask, of course, where will this all lead? Where will it end? What is it that the minions want? Total chaos? Yes! But also the complete enslavement of mankind. Only when everyone is groveling at their feet will they be happy. Then will they have found their paradise."

Dean Howe shivered visibly and did nothing to conceal it.

He thought about the comparison he had made not so long ago between the Man palace and a beehive. But now he was not thinking about a queen bee and her worker bees slaving away; he saw a long, greasy larva that fed upon human beings. He saw an endless row of people who pushed slowly up through a dark tunnel and as they came into the light were sucked into a huge, toothless mouth, swallowed and slowly digested in the acidic fluids of the continually compressing bowels.

"Be open to me, Oscar," he heard Falcon say.

Oscar rubbed his arms with his hands as though he were trying to warm them up.

"Make yourself susceptible to my thoughts—it is time to lower your screen and let me in."

Oscar did as he was asked; his face became calm, and his blue eyes sparkled. A stinging pain seemed to drill a hole through his forehead and into his brain. His body twitched.

"Understand this," said Oscar. "I recognize this procedure, and I could do the same with you if I so desired, but I am sure that I don't have to convince you."

"What's happening here?" Scott James wanted to know. "What are you two doing?"

"That's not important for the moment," said Falcon bluntly. "For the time being, you are sufficiently informed. It is important for you to know where you stand with Sebastian, and that you be aware of where the danger is coming from, but the only one who actually has a chance of stopping what has begun is Oscar, and he needs my help with that. Because I know more than he does."

He turned to Oscar again.

"You have an appointment in the palace tomorrow. You have to go back."

"That's right," said Oscar. "It is not my sister who has invited me, but her minion Tana Rowe. I have been given back my chambers and can come and go as I please. My sister's minion and I have hardly ever spoken to each other, and she's the one who invited me for dinner. Is that not odd? Have you received anything about that? Have you seen anything?"

Staring at him, yet looking right through him at something only he was able to see, it was clear that Falcon was always receiving things and that he saw what was hidden in the future before anyone else.

"You won't be alone with her, I can assure you of that. You will all be together. You, your sister and brothers and their minions."

Oscar made a face that was filled with the knowledge of impending disaster.

"How great is the danger, Falcon? Can you also see if I am going to survive this?"

"You must prepare yourself for a complicated future, Oscar. But I will help you all that I can, be assured of that! You sped everything up when you saved my pupil, the president. It had always been my intention to turn you into a man for whom an entire nation would go through fire. You have already reached that status, and now other tasks await you. We will provoke the minions. Serious obstruction makes them furious and panicky all at the same time. Believe me, Oscar, I would prefer to stand on the front line in the battle against these demons myself, but I am too weak for that. You are our man."

"I am trying to follow everything that has been said here," commented Dean Howe, "but I don't understand a single word of what you two are talking about! Things are happening which I cannot get a grip on. Is this black magic? Is this superstition?"

Oscar laughed.

"No, General. We are dealing with reality here. Let me give you an example of superstition. In a very brief amount of time I have heard three remarks made about poison. I was with Cathy a little while ago, and she made a comparison in which a poisonous snake played a part. Falcon referred to a poisonous spider and then the poor poisoned Carl Holdorf. Now, if I were a superstitious person, I would be terrified of being poisoned while I was in the palace."

Howe nodded and turned to Falcon.

"Okay. So Oscar goes to the palace. Do we stay together? You are going to have to explain enough for us to understand what is happening and what it is we must do."

"That goes without saying," said Falcon.

The room became silent as everyone poured themselves something to drink, and then the conversation picked up right where it had left off. The generals left a few hours later, but Falcon remained behind to be alone with Oscar for a while.

They sat facing each other as Oscar told him about his life starting with his youth in Switzerland and ending with his bold act in the park. Tony Falcon listened intently without interrupting him.

"You are an even greater man than I had thought," he said. "It seems that you have always stood alone, and I admire you very much for that. Now, let me tell you my story."

"Could my girlfriend listen too?" asked Oscar. "She has set herself the task of being my biographer and wants to know about all that transpires. Although everything that happens frightens her on one side, it fascinates her on the other."

"I have no objections to that, and I know that I can trust her."

"Cathy and I always talk about our affairs outside, on the terrace. There we can be sure no one is listening."

"I prefer to stay here," said Falcon with a smile. "I know that it is safe here and that the only one who may be listening is sitting on the twentieth floor. That way I only have to tell my story once—as you have just done, by the way."

They both burst out laughing. It was good to relax for a while. They developed a feeling of true camaraderie now as they made fun of the big, clumsy, eavesdropping ears of the army.

While Falcon poured himself another coffee, Oscar went to get Cathy. As soon as they were all seated, Falcon leaned back and began his story.

"There was no castle for me, no princely crown set with precious stones. I was an abandoned, crying child in stinking clothes. No one could tell me who I was or where I came from. My greatest gift would be to discover just that. I saw more foster homes in my youth than I care to mention; there was an endless train of people who took pity on me and whom I called my parents until I was sent along again. I had gotten a name, though: my surname from the man who found me (and no doubt must have held me up in front of him with outstretched arms because I was such an evil-smelling baby) and my given name from the truck driver with whom he hitched a ride to bring me to the nearest town.

"So I became Tony Falcon, and I'm convinced that the trucker must have driven with the windows wide open.

"My ancestors had given me valuable baggage, intuition and knowledge, and at first I had no idea that not everyone received all kinds of information from the voices in their heads! Then warnings began to sound in my head that I could not misunderstand. I knew that I must learn to protect myself against great danger. My existence soon came to the attention of the minions who knew that there was someone of their species who, while very much like them, was also dangerously different from them and must be eliminated."

Oscar nodded silently.

"Fear got a relentless hold on me. I became a characterless young man. My only defense against the panic attacks and voices in my head was to lose myself in drink, and I drank all that I could get my hands on! I got drunk at night to celebrate the fact that I had stayed sober all day. At other times, I drank only in the morning so I could say that I didn't drink in the afternoon or evening. Whatever my excuse was, I was always drunk. I had also become a petty criminal.

"The states of Utah, Colorado, Nebraska and Kansas were my fields of operation. In the crowded cities, where the celebrations never stopped, it was not difficult for a pickpocket to strike. Maybe it was my fuddled mind that, without being aware of it, protected me against the minions who were constantly looking for outsiders like you and me.

"One day I found myself in a state of drunkenness in the center of Denver, watching a procession honoring the completion of a grand monument. It was a statue built to commemorate the copper miners, who by the way, are still to be found there. Sixty feet up the statue, steam-driven figures played a huge piano and beat drums as big as houses, and a glockenspiel produced the purest sounds. I was standing there staring and listening when a float pulled by twenty horses rolled passed me. On it stood the tycoons of Syrinx Colorado, who had footed the bill for the erection of the monument. I was suddenly struck by a flash of pain so violent that I thought the part of my skull just above my eyes had been separated from the rest of my head by a razor-sharp sword. I got sick on the spot, lost my balance and fainted onto the ground, lying stretched out in my own vomit. I came to my senses again when the square was almost deserted and two street guards yanked me to my feet and began beating and kicking me to force me to move on. That day was the last time I was ever drunk!

"That huge statue was the witness of my good intentions, which I shouted out above the last strains of the celebratory music. Much had suddenly become clear to me. The awesome power that a minion of Syrinx had managed to hit me with in the deepest part of my being had torn open my spirit and allowed the truth to enter.

"Lying on the street unconscious and drunk, I had remained safe from the passing minion who must have briefly felt my presence.

"The guards beat the sickness out of my body. As I ran away from them gasping for breath, I sobered up quickly. I understood then that the insanity of existence found its origins with the minions who clamped to the mighty tycoons like leeches. It was an understanding that only men like you and I can experience, Oscar."

"I know that feeling."

Falcon was staring up at the sky through the dome, but he knew that Oscar and Cathy were listening to him intently.

"After this drastic reversal in my life, I became a diligent student. I began to search recent history for clues but found nothing that led to minions. I then looked inside myself and learned how to mellow out and get information out of my subconscious. That method yielded considerably better results. I came to the conclusion that I was a bastard—a human being, yet somehow related to minions. I began to understand the power of the genuine minions and determined to work against them, and if possible destroy them.

"On my journeys through the United States and Europe, I met people who also wanted to change the world. They wanted to do so out of an idealistic belief, and I wanted it because I was able to foresee the time when the minions would finally wrest control of the world from the tycoons. I was adventurous enough to get busy at my task, and along with a few trusted friends set up a private media company. I was clever enough to make it grow into a viable enterprise. Mason Media became a fact, and the stream of partisans to my door grew daily. We were an organization committed to freedom, and we were becoming stronger and stronger. All we were missing was a hero whom we could follow. Missing, that is, until a certain Oscar Man appeared on the scene."

"Did you know before I was brought to you that my mother was a minion?" Oscar asked.

"No," said Falcon. "I had no knowledge of that, but I saw great possibilities to mold you, the same way I had molded Angus Sebastian, into someone who could pave the way for us. When I met you, I suddenly began to get hope. Something in your phenomenal radiation told me that you were more than the illegitimate son of Otto Man. But it was only when you saved Sebastian from death that I knew you must be something like me: neither a genuine minion nor a genuine human being. That is why I asked myself out loud today if it really could be a coincidence that you are now in touch with both the army and me. You are still in the maturation process I mentioned. You, without being aware of it, are busy creating your own future and that of many others. A great task has been handed to you, Oscar, and I am the one who will guide you and help you. With any luck, the generals will be there to give you the necessary military backing. You must put an end to the power of the minions."

"And if I don't succeed, the minions will put an end to me."

"So it is, and we both know it. Tomorrow is your first test, in the palace. You must try not to reveal yourself. The minions are very adept at deduction. No one should have been standing at that trapdoor at just the right moment to save the president from death—except for a man with prior knowledge, obtained through some psychic medium."

Oscar stood up and began to pace nervously.

"Good heavens, Falcon! So they finally know that I have the powers of a minion. I suppose I couldn't keep them in the dark forever."

"They refer to men like you as false minions. They would have called me a counterfeit also had they been able to probe me. Some false minions pose no danger to them at all and are left in peace. They may simply be eccentric magicians, charlatans, phony spiritualists and so on. But your powers are greater than those of a minion. Hopefully, you are the unexpected variant against whom they cannot defend themselves."

"Like a resistant parasite that cannot be destroyed," Oscar quipped sarcastically.

Falcon continued as if he had not heard the last remark.

"It may have been imprudent of me, but I told the generals about minions and about us when you left the room earlier. When you came back and I was still talking about it, there already was no way back. Would you have preferred we had planned our strategy together first?"

"It doesn't matter, Falcon. Now we all know who we all are and where we stand, although I really think the generals will have trouble dealing with the truth. It's all so unreal to them. But once they have accepted the facts, they will understand that the world is even more insane than they thought before. Listen here, Falcon. You want to push me into action because you claim that you cannot do it yourself. Are you really so much weaker than me?"

Falcon put a finger across his lips to indicate that talking now might not be such a good idea.

"I told you that as a young man, I sold my life to the bottle. Well, in later years I had to pay the price for my drinking. Physically, I am much weaker than you would think. I am still able to fend off a few mental blows, but a good combination of the physical and mental hits might be too much."

As he spoke he stood, and with his finger still across his lips, pointed at the door and beckoned to Oscar and Cathy.

"Come," said Oscar. "Enough talking for now. Let's go outside and enjoy the view."

They left the domed room and went down the corridor out to the terrace.

"I am sound enough in mind and body, and you would be hard-pressed to find anyone who would question my intellectual powers," said Falcon. He leaned over the railing and turned his eyes upon the stone complacency of Manhattan where most of the rooftops were even higher than where he was standing.

"Come stand a bit closer to me, Oscar."

They followed the flight of a crow that skimmed along the buildings with a loud cawing.

"Do you have any idea why Man-Manifest Books in Switzerland was created, and why it is that you were made the chief officer?"

"To provide my sister Johanna with reading material," replied Oscar, and for the second time that day both men burst out laughing.

Cathy, who stood behind them listening, laughed along.

"We have saved some very important works from ruin," said Oscar, his tone taking a more serious note. "We have even managed to save manuscripts that had almost crumbled to dust. But more to the point, a search has begun for a manuscript that reveals the true nature of the minions. I have heard this in my vague night whisperings, and I suspect there must be a grain of truth to it. While in Switzerland, I interrogated a member of the staff while I held her mind under my control. It turned out that she knew nothing at all about this, but what she was able to tell me was that the minions of my family know exactly what is delivered to us and what the contents are."

"Do I know her?" asked Falcon.

"I believe so. She called you a charismatic pioneer and praised your work."

"Ah, Natasja Bruschlinski." When he saw Oscar nod, Falcon added, "She is one of us. A valuable woman in the organization who dreams of a normal world in which the people have regained their senses. I have talked with her also—about you, for one thing. It is indeed true that the company was set up to search for certain texts. It is also a fact that nothing of great import has been found. Which is no proof, by any means at all, that the text does not exist."

"Will we ever find it?"

Falcon stood up straight and stared at Oscar, beaming with such self-confidence that the latter guessed, "Is it in your possession?"

Tony Falcon took off his jacket, and Oscar saw the Mason Media emblem. Inside the jacket, on the back, there appeared to be a zipper. Falcon opened it and took out a thick file covered with transparent plastic. Oscar and Cathy saw a number of brown pages with torn margins. On the upper page something was handwritten in ink. He handed the file to Cathy.

"I suppose you have the equipment in the house to determine whether or not this is authentic. Would it take very long for you to find out when this was written? It is not a print, it is the original handwriting."

"The equipment is fast and accurate," said Cathy. "I can be finished with it, if everything goes smoothly, in a few minutes."

"Please get on it right away then."

Cathy went inside, and Falcon said to Oscar, "This all came about because of some knowledge that found its way to me through my psychic abilities. I was in Europe searching for clues everywhere, but that led nowhere, and I began to quietly make inquiries. I talked with collectors and librarians, again with no results. Then I gathered all my mental powers and used all the talents I had at my disposal through my ancestors, and based on the knowledge I obtained that way, I traveled to Italy and landed in the beautiful old city of Naples. I made my way deep into the slums where a little church stood. Stone for stone, it was an exact duplicate of the place of worship I constantly saw in my mind.

"I was hospitably welcomed by the sexton, and unfortunately had to say no to a glass of excellent old wine, since I am no longer a drinker. In an annex was an impressive library where I was allowed to search through the rare books while the venerable old sexton looked over my shoulder. They were later brought to Man-Manifest in Switzerland, and fine copies of them are now standing on the shelves in Johanna's library. I opened a book that contained the dispensation of a country estate from the seventeenth century, and between the pages I found the sheets of paper I just gave to Cathy. I immediately recognized it as an old text that contained no modern printing and that someone must have put there deliberately for some reason. It appeared to be an original manuscript, handwritten in French. Not the Old French from before 1500, as was explained to me later, but written by a scientist in the eighteenth century."

He ran his fingers through his ponytail, giving Oscar time to absorb what he had told him so far, so that he could continue with his narrative uninterrupted.

"It's possible that the author was an heir to the estate the older text came from. Now, I neither read nor write French, but I did understand one word that made me realize that I had made an important discovery."

"*Minion,*" Oscar said completing the sentence for him.

"Exactly. The sexton thought that it was about alchemy and gave them to me as a present with the condition that I had to be honest and share with him any gold I succeeded in creating. When I got back to the States, I had a translation done and found I was dealing with a very incomplete manuscript, which was not the original. It must have been copied from a work done at the end of the Renaissance. I had never seen anything like it before, and probably never will again, and I know that no one in your Swiss company has either. I believe my discovery is unique in the world of books and research.

"I researched the history of the estate in Burgundy, and the author—or perhaps it would be better to call him the copier—was probably one Jean Galliou a man of learning who owned the estate around the middle of the eighteenth century. He seems to have been a philosopher and an artist as well as an inventor who built unusual machines. One of those extraordinary people who lend color to their time—"

"The contents, Falcon," insisted Oscar impatiently. "What's in it?"

"I hoped to learn more about the Renaissance minions, but nothing was to be found. Too much of the manuscript has been lost. Ah, if only I had found it intact, we would have gotten an entirely different view of our foe; but what I did find is interesting enough—the largest surviving part of the text contains a prophecy!

"To summarize, Oscar, it comes down to this: in a future era, the minions will rise to power again. I don't have to tell you that we are living in that era! All their power will be utilized to alter the world situation so that it meets the necessities of life as prescribed by the minions. Chaos will rule, and mankind shall be oppressed. There is a warning, though—a threat if you will—of an incredible danger to them. An unruly young prince will rise like a phoenix from the ashes and claim a position of great importance. He will manifest himself as the guardian angel of a powerful person and be the leader of many people. There will be a great battle, the victor of which the author does not know.

"It looks like the complete manuscript is the distillation of all the minion wisdom put together. There are many hints within it; allusions are made and conclusions drawn. It is offered up as a comparison to the most enigmatic alchemistic formulas; it is quite understandable how that nice sexton thought it was about that archaic science. The incompleteness of the text makes it all even harder to understand, but we really don't have to think too long, or too hard, to know who the young prince risen from his ashes is, do we? The savior of the powerful man with a great many followers. We know who that is, don't we? Now you know why I am not the man who is feared enough by the minions to make me too frightened to come out in the open."

"Well—" was all Oscar could manage to say.

"I have known for a long time that I have a relationship to the minions," said Falcon. "It became clear to me in Denver, at the monument. I made my plans and have come far. Using the media, I brought together from all over the world people who realized that changes had to be made. At the right time, I would have contacted the army myself and explained to them we must take action. How that would have turned out will always remain a mystery. The rift between the generals and I could not have been repaired if they had killed the president! But you appeared on that stage, and that changed everything. You will change the course of history: by your hand things will get better—or worse."

"Can I make the chaos even greater then?"

"We must take that possibility into account. The manuscript tells us more, though. When the minions are forced to suffer one setback after another, they will panic, they will weaken. It is the general's job to constantly harass them. The president will rob them of their privileges; he will make laws that work against them, and he will be unreachable to them when they want to negotiate. Using the media, I will silence the fact that a growing number of people are fed up with the oligarchy. The army has to take over the security precautions for the international corporations as soon as possible. Policemen appointed by the government must take the place of private security.

We have to fight the minions on all fronts, and hopefully we are still in a position to save many of the tycoons from their murdering hands. In the meantime, we'll have to see how you make out. What's written in the text, Oscar, is not just a prophecy. It is universal knowledge handed down from generations of minions. Fragments of the text have survived time, and maybe it's not a coincidence at all that I found the papers and have been able to share them with you. I refuse to believe that you crossed my path purely by accident."

"Do you believe that the future is predestined, Falcon?"

The man had the eyes of a prophet when he looked at Oscar.

"The future only allows itself to be seen when it has already become part of the past, and by then, nothing can change it any more. When time has outdistanced the future, there is talk of established facts."

Oscar made a gesture of hopelessness with his hands.

"Don't rack your brains about it," said Falcon. "Just make sure that you are sharp for tomorrow's meeting."

"After I pulled Angus out of the trapdoor, I received an invitation to return to the palace, as you know. While I was there, a reconciliation took place first with Johanna and the next day with Ferdinand and Jimmy. I remained there for many days, and there was nothing to indicate that the minions suspected me of anything, nor were they hostile toward me. I was on constant alert, as I'm sure you can imagine. Now I must return again, and you're telling me that this time there will be a confrontation."

"Whisperings that came down a mystical road," said Falcon as he slowly nodded. "That's the best way to describe the knowledge we have, isn't it?"

Cathy Wheeler reappeared on the terrace, and the men turned to look at her.

"Oscar's equipment is perfect," she said. "Everything I have ever asked for, he had installed immediately. A translation of the texts is being made right now, and I have read the first lines. I have examined them, and I can say with certainty that the paper and ink come from the middle of the eighteenth century. We are dealing with fragments of a manuscript about minions, copied by hand. There is mention of a much older version, though, from the end of the Renaissance."

Falcon looked up in surprise. "That slipped my attention!"

"It's actually written there," said Cathy.

"I had it translated by a man and not by a machine," Falcon remarked pensively. "Perhaps he left out things he thought were of no importance. That's how it goes sometimes."

"The copyist ploughed the sands," commented Cathy. "That is very remarkable."

"He was supposedly a man of learning from Burgundy, Jean Galliou," said Oscar. "What is so remarkable about the work he did?"

"An important piece of work like this would have appeared in print halfway through the eighteenth century," said Cathy. "It was obviously not the intention that the text be reproduced. The contents were supposed to remain secret."

"That's what I think too," remarked Falcon. "Can I trust that we continue this tradition, Cathy? Do you have a steel box to store it in safely?"

"Of course! After we have read the translation we'll destroy it, and the original text will be put in safekeeping."

"Good," said Falcon. "Then I'll be off now, too. I have much to arrange at my office; I have to prepare for my visit to Howe, James and Hodgkinson. And of course, I must stay in contact with my pupil in the White House. Do you have any questions, Oscar? Do you think you'll be able to manage in the palace?"

Oscar reached his hand out, and Falcon closed his fingers strongly around it.

"We will see, Falcon. We will know the future when it has become the past."

Again there was laughter caused by a feeling of togetherness. Oscar walked inside with him and escorted him to the elevator. Before Falcon got in, he turned around, searching in vain for words.

"I will come back unscathed. So long, Falcon!"

The man nodded as he stepped into the elevator, and the doors closed.

Oscar returned to the terrace and saw Cathy standing there, looking out on the world of humans below her like a goddess on Olympus, and he knew why he would return unhurt. He stood beside with his arm around her and said, "Ask me one of your special questions again, about the New York of long ago, about all those events you know so much about—"

He abruptly stopped talking when he saw the tears running down her cheeks.

At that moment, the jester did not have the talent to put the smile back on her face.

Chapter Eleven

Show of Strength

As the helicopter that had brought him here took off again from behind the station, Oscar walked across the platform. He nodded to guards who bowed to him and saw that the stationmasters remained standing at a distance to give Orville Hood the chance to accompany him to a train that had a full head of steam up. Everyone knew that the prince was fond of the corpulent master. Hood ran up to him, hands outstretched to greet him and take his small traveling bag. When he stood before Oscar, he looked around nervously and bowed deeply, the tassel on his hat dancing up and down.

"Prince Oscar, welcome to the station of King Ferdinand. Your visit has been announced, and the Lion is ready. The most beautiful carriage is all yours."

"Hello, Orville," said Oscar. "Come and walk with me so that we may talk quietly for a bit. You could, of course, ride along to the palace with me, but we really cannot be sure that a conversation on the train will not be eavesdropped upon."

They hadn't seen each other since Oscar had entered Orville's house that night through the balcony. The night Oscar had left the palace to go to the penthouse, Orville hadn't been on duty.

"There are changes in the wind," said the prince. "But it is all too complicated to explain quickly."

"Are you in trouble again?"

"You could say so, yes," laughed Oscar.

"You must know that we are proud of you, my wife Phoebe and I. And with all her heart, Angelina would love to shout it from the rooftops that she's your sister. But what is happening? You were so very much in the dumps, and now you are world-famous again. There cannot be any problems, can there?"

The Bull came to a standstill on an opposite platform; guards and a stationmaster dressed in white hurried to the doors of the carriages and helped the passengers out. They were all young people in colorful clothes. They saw Oscar and began to yell and wave at him. Somewhat surprised, Oscar waved back.

"Who might they be?" he wanted to know.

"I'm not sure, but I think that they must be people who were invited to one of Margaret Sharpe's parties. She organizes nights that are a cross between an orgy and a bacchanal and invites hordes of people from the outside. Besides, everyone recognizes you immediately."

Oscar remained standing and opened the small bag he carried. He removed two packages and the Swiss doll.

"Here," he said. "Trinkets for Phoebe and Angelina. And as for you, I haven't forgotten my promise. One day we will take a ride in the Ferris wheel together and drink cognac, remember? At first I was planning on telling you only about Europe, but the things I have to tell you now will take up so much time that it will have to wait."

"Until when?"

"Soon, Orville, soon."

"Oscar, about the problems—do they have anything to do with the murders of the tycoons? This place is buzzing with rumors, and we are afraid that something will happen to King Ferdinand. And then all those things in the news about changes—"

"They all fit together, Orville. Many people think that the world has been turned upside down for too long. When I tell you about it, you will hardly believe your ears. Look, would you be so kind as to give this doll to Angelina?"

With raised eyebrows, the man in the snow white uniform looked at the rag doll with the synthetic head that was pushed into his big hands.

"This is Nina," said Oscar with a grin. "Angelina always played with it as a child. No doubt she will be very happy to see it. It is her only tangible memory of Switzerland."

Still talking, they walked on until they had reached the Lion, who impatiently hissed out a mist of steam. Oscar patted Orville on his shoulders and opened the door of the carriage that was reserved for him.

"No matter what happens, Oscar, you must always know that we think about you constantly and will always stand behind you."

"I know that, Orville, and I am grateful for it. Say hello to Phoebe and Angelina from me. See you soon!"

Oscar closed the door and sat down by the window to be able to wave to Hood.

The Lion came alive. A bang sounded as the carriages began to be dragged along the tracks. With a shock, the wheels under Oscar began to move, and he felt the enormous strength of the locomotive. He could not help but laugh when he saw Hood standing on the platform with a dumbfounded face, waving the rag doll. Orville's lips moved in an inaudible farewell as the train whistle sounded a shrill blast.

As soon as he knew that Orville could no longer see him, the smile disappeared from his face. He looked around at the exquisitely decorated interior. Above the windows were hung copper heads of lions and lionesses, and all the legs of the seats ended in claws. The ceiling was covered with black velvet on which was depicted a pack of golden lionesses cornering a fleeing impala on their wild hunt. There were mirrors and lamps decorated with sparkling jewels, and handwoven carpets depicted various hunting scenes. Walnut walls, panels and posts were polished to a brilliant shine.

Looking outside, Oscar was struck first by the Ferris wheel. He saw the long country lanes lined with majestic oak trees, the sculpture gardens, the high lookouts of the smaller outlying castles and the vast lakes where white and black swans swam. The Lion went into a gentle curve, and the palace came into sight. He looked at the countless towers and domes, the colonnades, the white marble frames, the gates that appeared as gaping mouths that could easily swallow the incoming trains, the corners and arches, the shadows, the intriguing lines of the patterns on the walls, the little castles and country houses in the foreground, the balconies and flights of steps, the roofs, the bow windows.

For the first time, it dawned on him that all this immense building, just as the Ferris wheel and the metal cathedral, was not only the realization of the dreams of Ferdinand Man and his architects. Now he knew that the grotesqueness, theatricality and excessiveness visible everywhere had much to do with the influence of the minions. What he saw was beauty that made him shiver. He felt more fear than awe, for the minions had used their talent to invoke their love of death by giving all the buildings a radiation of unbridled cruelty.

The Lion went straight up to the palace, and it became dark for a moment when the carriages entered through the gate. It would not have surprised Oscar if the mouth had slammed closed and mighty teeth had begun to crush the black locomotive. Grinding in protest, as if to complain about all the energy it still wanted to expend, the train came to a standstill. Oscar stood up, opened the door and jumped down onto the platform. Visitors stepped out of the other carriages as guardsmen and palace personnel in extravagant clothing came to meet their guests. They brought them either to the big arrival hall to chat awhile or straight to the elevators that would carry them to other parts of the building.

There was no one to welcome Oscar. He would go to his own chambers to change his clothes and wait for the messenger to tell him he was expected for dinner.

Instead of using an elevator, he decided to use the corridors and staircases until he was lost or exhausted. He was still always impressed by the marvelous interior that was built in the shape of a cathedral, by the covered squares where black and white marble shone in the light of lamps, by the spiral staircases, the silent chapels with golden statues, the towers, the wings and the halls. And, more than anything, he loved the works of art that his brother Jimmy had placed everywhere.

He had lived here for many years and knew his way around quite well. He had always preferred walking. Never before, however, had it struck him how everything was too grotesque and excessive; it all was too decadent and too chaotic to be beautiful. Because he was able to think like a minion, though, he saw unexpected lines in illogical constructions every now and then, and he could imagine that visitors here were caught up by a feeling of disorientation when confronted by all those styles randomly thrown together.

The French Palace of Versailles, where at least thirty thousand people had worked over fifty years, could dance in this gigantic building! The absurd fantasies of a minion had influenced the mind of Ferdinand Man's architects, and Ferdinand himself had worked so long and hard on this project that he did not realize that it was not only for himself.

This was the chaotic atmosphere minions needed to flourish and hatch their plans against humanity.

Silently going further, Oscar was absorbed by the multitude of impressions and felt himself become one with his surroundings as he passed strangely dressed people without greeting them. In general, the people who crisscrossed the palace kept silent to each other. They didn't do so because of impoliteness, but because they were entirely taken up in their own experience of the mighty building.

Only groups of people who belonged with each other were talking together, but they did so in soft, subdued voices. There were halls where even a little sigh caused an echo. There were galleries where the sheer impression of the weight that the columns bore seemed to be imbued upon the walkers who bent low and hastened their pace in order to get out of their way as soon as possible.

Outside at the train station, the noise of the engines and the musical fanfare that greeted guests belied the oppressive silence of the forbidding interior.

At the other side of the palace, where the offices, shops and restaurants were located, the streets bustled like the streets of any big city. Where Oscar was walking now was reserved for important people of the palace, and if a commoner had dared to walk there, he would been immediately stopped by a palace guard.

He—a bastard, a jester, but a prince as well—enjoyed many powers, although even to him large parts of the building were forbidden territory.

He smiled when it suddenly dawned on him that most rooms in the palace were of no use at all. It was not only that there was no logic in the variation of form and style; the building of countless galleries, domed squares and empty halls was simply and solely a morbid expression of waste.

And beauty for nothing in such proportions rose above human comprehension and was a manifestation of minion culture.

But even though so many chambers and halls remained closed to Oscar, this was still the building where he had spent an important part of his life. As a child, he had loved the sound that glass marbles made as they bounced across the smooth stone floors. He had studied in one of the west wings along with the children of the people who worked in the offices and factories. He had roamed through the chambers of his half-sister Johanna and knew the chambers of Jimmy and the halls of Ferdinand. Horrible minion statues didn't scare him, and he had no fear of the monster heads hanging above doors. He knew the art of the minions just as well as the New Art paintings and decorations that Jimmy collected. Once he had felt really at home here when he had been brought here from Switzerland by Johanna. This was his home just as well as it was the minions', and he looked forward to the confrontation that Falcon had predicted. He was on his own ground as much as they were.

Feeling reassured by his walk through the building and ready for his battle with the minions, he went to the nearest elevator and made his way to his old rooms.

He was greeted by two maids who asked him what they could do for him, but he sent them away with a simple wave of his right hand. He began to search for suitable clothes to wear to dinner that night. The clothes Johanna had sent had not yet been brought here, so someone was sent up to him to make him a brand-new wardrobe. He was pleasantly surprised by the choices he was given. He selected a pair of tight trousers with a jacket to match made of fine, soft fabric with a design that was typically minion. Just as fox heads had formed long rows on some of his other clothes, with the snouts of the upper ones touching the lower, these new garments were adorned with gold, silver and red lizards that bit each other's tails and formed a slanted, winding string. He wanted to wear a pair of gray boots and found several pairs that fit him at the bottom of one of the closets. He did not wear his crown, however. After having combed his long, thick hair, he sat down in an easy chair and relaxed.

He was startled by the messenger who appeared shortly after and said, "Prince Oscar, I bid you a good evening. Your sister Johanna has sent me to operate your elevator. Will you be so kind as to follow me?"

He sprang to his feet and went along with the man. The only thing the messenger had to do was enter a code, which was unknown to Oscar. The man stepped out of the elevator to make room for Oscar.

"I wish you a marvelous night, Prince," said the man who stayed behind in Oscar's chambers. Oscar nodded to him, and the door closed silently. The elevator began its assigned route, and moments later the doors slid silently open again. Oscar found himself in a circular reception hall with narrow windows that were each more than sixty feet high. A guard greeted him and escorted him to a wooden door, which he opened.

Oscar was welcomed by his sister Johanna, who embraced him and pressed him tightly against her.

"There been mistakes in calculation," she said. "After we have checked everything, it will fit. We don't put our reputation on the line for a little share of the profits."

Oscar looked at her. Her misty eyes swam in a white-painted face. Untidy spikes came out of her towering hairdo. Oscar didn't react to her words knowing that she had to be just as confused now as she had been on the Ferris wheel. She led him a table, where Ferdinand and Jimmy Man were sitting, and offered him a seat near hers.

Ferdinand and Jimmy had also painted their faces white and wore clothes of gold brocade. The company was also composed of the minions of the family, Kenneth Mayfield, Mike Farland and Tana Rowe, all three of them dressed and made up exactly like his brothers and sister.

On the table were seven sterling silver drinking horns. Oscar took the seat that remained after Johanna had taken hers. No one greeted him, and there was no talking going on amongst themselves, so Oscar leaned back and looked around this great hall, which he had never before been in.

He knew immediately that he was in a part of the palace now where the minions felt most at home, for the hall was decorated with their striking art. They had a definite preference for the dome shape, which was found all over the world now. They also loved interlocking symbols or figures, and in this hall they had combined these styles.

The room was circular, and along the walls, from the ground up, a gigantic work of art was erected, the highest point of which was a good thirty yards above the floor. Creatures with horrible faces stood in a circle with their legs spread wide apart and held other creatures at their cloven feet. In this repetitive fashion, hundreds of monstrous figures and devils, all holding on to one another, formed a great cast iron dome. The bearded, horned faces stared down with sinister gazes. They were hairy creatures, their skin scaly. Turning his gaze slowly upward, Oscar noticed that it became darker and darker behind the images until he saw six creatures at the top who held each other's hands and formed an opening through which a beam of greenish light shone down. He could easily imagine how a great number of people would feel fear upon seeing this particularly bizarre piece of art, for the figures were so lifelike that it seemed as if they were about to climb down from their acrobatic stance and slither across the table.

Oscar looked at those around the table again. Ferdinand wore a golden crown and rings on all his fingers. He lifted his drinking horn almost imperceptibly and looked straight ahead. Jimmy leaned to one side and held his head obliquely as if he sat listening to music, which only he could hear, with rapt attention. Johanna was counting on her fingers and moved her lips without saying anything.

The minions looked at each other with bright eyes, and every now and then they looked at Oscar. Of them all, he knew only Tana Rowe, whom he had met in the company of Johanna so often. He had learned to know her as a quiet, dignified woman who played her role perfectly, as one would expect from a minion. She dressed like Johanna, moved the same way, ate and drank the same and discussed literature with Johanna. He only knew the minions of his half-brothers by sight. He could not recall ever having spoken to them.

Kenneth Mayfield the minion of the king also wore a golden crown and ten rings.

Oscar was not intending to be the first one to break the silence but did not want to simply sit there any longer. He pushed his chair back, stood up and began to walk through the hall past the row of statues.

Looking at the various heads, he could not help but admire the artist who had been able to give every single creature, which were sometimes more beast than human, its own, frightening character. He began to feel a strange pressure in his head, and in his ears there was a soft buzzing sound. He got the impression that the dome of iron creatures above his head was radiating some kind of energy.

"We will eat and drink together," came a voice. Turning, Oscar saw that it was Mike Farland the minion of Jimmy Man who had spoken. "Will you return to your seat, Prince?"

"I'll gladly sit down again," he said, "but if I do, I expect that there will be some kind of conversation. If I am going to have to sit here in silence, I may as well just take a walk around the park."

Above his head was a crackling sound, and he thought that he saw a short flash of light. Behind the cast iron construction, everything had become white now, except where the top figures held each other's hands. The beam of light had turned dark red. Jimmy Man now shook his head and waved with one hand. Johanna moved her hands back and forth in front of her face. The king leaned forward on the table with his head resting on his hands.

The minions began to talk amongst themselves.

"Hygnos Hybrid Corporation has met with disaster," said Mike Farland. "Will Hugenholtz one of their most important men had gone fishing far out on Lake Michigan. There was no storm; there wasn't even a breath of air stirring, but still he was swept overboard and drowned. No one has an explanation for it. He was known to be a good swimmer. But no matter how we speculate, Will is dead and gone. Fate strikes hard. Death lies in wait everywhere."

He raised his drinking horn, and all the others at the table did the same.

"What shall we drink to?" asked Farland. "Oscar, do you have an idea?"

"To what can we drink better than death?" suggested Oscar. "You are so right; it lies in wait everywhere—death. But tonight it has passed us by, and to me that calls for a drink."

The minions nodded, and when they looked at Oscar, they bared their white teeth in cruel smiles.

"To death, Oscar Man!" they said and then emptied their drinking horns with greedy gulps.

Oscar gave them a meaningful nod, carefully tasted his wine and then also took some healthy swigs.

His brothers and sister brought their horns to their lips with stiff movements. It flashed through Oscar's mind that he probably had been invited here to watch one of his family members get poisoned, and he thought back to the remarks that were made about poison the other day. When he had lifted his own horn and taken a sip, he had known that at least his wine was pure. He had no logical explanation for that because the worst poisons were odorless and tasteless, but he could not deny that the knowledge was there. Today his instincts were unprecedentedly sharp, and he was aware of the presence of Emlyn Gray in his realm of thought. Behind Emlyn Gray were the generations who could have called themselves minions and who had passed on their knowledge through mystical ways, knowledge that reached Oscar, although he received and interpreted it in a different way.

Servants appeared to refill the drinking horns and put food on the table. The king gave a sign that everyone could start as his plate was filled.

"You have come alone, Oscar," said Johanna as she poked her fork reprimandingly in his direction and then rolled it around between her thumb and forefinger. "Why didn't you bring Cathy Wheeler with you?

She is your girlfriend, isn't she? When you decide to marry her, we'll organize a huge party here in the palace—"

"She wasn't invited," he answered.

"You must move your library to the palace," she said. "No doubt you have some interesting works that are still missing from my collection."

"I possess not a single book that you don't have," he said. "You know that, don't you?"

She did not react to that and continued enthusiastically, "If she comes to live here, you'll have more rooms at your disposal, and when you marry Cathy, she'll be a princess automatically. Isn't that so, Freddy? When Oscar marries Cathy, she becomes a princess, doesn't she?"

"Yes," said her eldest brother. "And if there happen to be laws that say otherwise, we'll change them immediately."

Jimmy Man said that he wanted Oscar to move to another part of the palace.

"What do you think of twelve rooms, Oscar, that have an oval hall with a marble floor and six rooms that overlook the park? You can see the Ferris wheel, and because you'll be on the top floor, you can even see the cathedral! And the roof will provide you with at least twenty times more space than the terrace of your penthouse in New York City. You belong here with us in the palace, and we will be delighted when Cathy and you have children."

Oscar was amazed at all this kindness spewing forth from his family. He had never wondered if his siblings had children of their own. The fact that they were not married didn't preclude, of course, that they might have some offspring somewhere. As far as that was concerned, he also didn't know anything about the minions. Maybe there were chambers in the palace where he was not allowed to go, where children of the minions were being raised.

During the meal, they kept on talking with each other. Servants came to remove the plates, dishes and cutlery and left again, closing the doors behind them. The moment the last one had disappeared, Jimmy returned to his listening of the music only he could hear, and Johanna sat looking at her hand as if it were a mirror. The king hat taken off his crown and began to polish it with a napkin.

High above the table, the crackling sound began again. Oscar saw lightning flash between the cast iron images. Flames began to leak along the arms and legs. At the top, a fire had sprung up that flickered audibly. Here and there it began to spark as if the metal were being struck with sledgehammers. Except for the crackling flashes, however, nothing was to be heard, until a slowly growing buzzing sound rose. The cast iron began to glow, and it became hot in the hall. Ferdinand, Jimmy and Johanna began to perspire so profusely that the white paint dripped down their cheeks. It didn't seem to bother them, for they continued listening, looking and polishing.

To Oscar it was obvious that the iron colossus was more than just a piece of art. Energy was building up in the hall, inside the dome, that caused a drumming in his head. The buzzing penetrated under his skull where a pressure arose that became more and more unpleasant. The three minions looked at him with wan smiles as if they were waiting for something to happen. Meanwhile, Emlyn Gray, who had stood, as so to speak, with one foot in Oscar's subconsciousness, became busy attempting to manifest himself entirely into Oscar's thoughts, followed by a train of other familiars who were still vague of form but obviously present all the same.

The blazing fire above him shot down from almost a hundred feet up as if a fabulous dragon has put his head inside to spit his hot breath. The flames scorched along his cheeks, but he wasn't surprised when his hair didn't catch fire. He remained unafraid. This was a game he wanted to join in, even if the rules and the meaning of it were not clear to him. He kept his mind closed, which was no trouble for him, for he had done so during his entire life. Now he realized that the flames were nothing less then the challenging, searching power of thought from the minions who were attempting to enter his mind. There were flashes of lightning around him, and now the rolling of thunder sounded along the figures of glowing iron.

The table and all six people disappeared from sight as if by magic.

He was alone now. The hammering and buzzing in his head had reached a frequency that caused a stinging pain. It was as if someone were trying to saw his skull open and search with their fingers for the secrets of his being. The dome was now entirely comprised of red-hot iron. The hearth of hell had closed in on him, and he no longer even knew if he was sitting or standing. The voices of the minions reached his ears as a whispering.

"Tell us who you are; tell us what you feel; tell us what you know; tell us what you want; tell us everything. Bare your soul, and wait to see if we shall cherish or roast it. Admit us to your heart, and we shall see if it gets to go on beating or if it must be torn to pieces. Give us answers to all our questions. If you remain silent, the heat will only become more intense. The scorpion, closed in by fire, kills itself with a sting of its own tail. You, however, cannot take your fate into your own hands and will have to wait until the flames take hold of you and you burn slowly. The pain will be unbearable as you burn as slowly as a candle. Tell us what you feel; tell us everything about your deepest feelings."

The images were shapes of white-hot metal, and Oscar suspected that the work of art could collapse at any second.

He was not in despair, though. The hot air burned his lungs as he breathed it in. His eyelids moved rapidly up and down to keep his eyes moist. His fingertips were so hot that he could burn the tabletop in two with them. He could feel his fingers without seeing them. He saw the hellish dome more clearly. The scorching heat made the metal sing. Blood red lava streamed from the open mouths and dripped onto the floor, forming a smoky pool and spreading a terrible smell of sulfur.

At the top of the work of art, a figure came loose from the grip of the others and dove downward. It was a horned satyr with a burning beard who came down into the pool and dissolved with a hissing sigh.

"Tell us where you stand; tell us what you want. Save yourself the tortures; let us lead you, and you will enjoy yourself for the rest of your life."

Oscar felt that he could no longer blink his eyes and stared straight ahead in amazement. Different figures melted together, and in the fire, he saw things that should have been held back from him. He looked into the mind of the minions and knew they were not aware. It didn't last long, but it was enough to give him sufficient understanding.

In high-speed succession, he had seen the generations pass by, popping up and falling away again in the roaring fire. He saw people who kept a secret and then passed it on to others, improving their talents and extending their power. He saw how minions formed their thoughts and prepared to carry their ideas into execution. Their secret associations could prosper in western culture, but they needed to satisfy their parasitical thirst in the highest circles of society. They played with their hosts like puppeteers, and their power grew in the chaos they created. Now the boiling point had been reached, and it was time to show themselves in their true colors. Like hungry ticks, they had sucked their hosts dry, and now they would kill them one after the other and take their places. And that would only be the beginning of the slaughter. They would rule over an enslaved humanity until the sea of chaos had become so big that everyone would drown in it.

Oscar blinked his eyes again. He had seen enough. He raised his hands and saw his fingers move in front of him now. The fire withdrew upward along the images until it disappeared into the center of a flash of lightning.

Oscar Man sat at the table and reached for the silver drinking horn that stood in front of him. He was very thirsty. He controlled himself and drank with calm draughts.

His brothers and sister looked at him searchingly. The minions sat down at their places with petrified faces.

"Now I have entirely lost the thread," he heard Johanna say. "Someone was saying something to me, I mean."

Tana Rowe made a gesture with her hand, and Johanna fell silent, marching her fingers across the table like a guard on duty. Ferdinand and Jimmy sat quietly with their eyes closed, sprawled in their chairs.

Kenneth Mayfield, the king's minion, stood up and walked over to Oscar. He offered his hand to Oscar, who took it. The man's flesh was icy-cold.

"We thank you for your coming, Prince Oscar," he said. "It has been an instructive evening for all of us. I am sure we will meet again soon. You must know that we have an enormous respect for you."

He was about to say something more, but Johanna Man pushed him aside and embraced her half-brother.

"I have the feeling that I haven't been as pleasant company as I should have been, Oscar. I'm sorry for that. We must spend some more time together. I don't have to tell you that I have always appreciated your presence here. If you only knew how delighted I was when you were brought here from Switzerland and finally saw you standing in front of me."

"I know, Johanna," he said. "See you soon."

He shook hands with the other minions and his half-brothers and then left the round hall. In the elevator, he entered his code wondering if it would still work and was immediately transported to his chambers where three sweet, sleepy-eyed maids were waiting for him. He sent them away, stretched out on his bed and stared at the paintings on the ceiling as he considered the events of the evening. It was already almost morning. The long mental battle in the hall had taken longer than he realized.

Oscar did not fear an attempt on the lives of Ferdinand, Jimmy or Johanna, who were like wax in the hands of the minions. It was the tycoons who appeared to be in danger of the minions' mental influence—they would be the ones who would pay with their lives!

Walter Krocht, the emperor of Georgia, head of the mighty Cabo de Barra, had been such a strong personality: his mind had remained unreachable to intruders. In the same way, Angus Sebastian was also untouchable, so Tony Falcon had been able to insert him into the highest circles. However, men like Walter Krocht and his father Joseph had let themselves be so influenced by their minions that they had, without realizing it, created the world their parasitic wards had planned all along. Now the parasites had made the most of it and finally could dismiss their exploited hosts. More and more tycoons were meeting with death, Hygnos Hybrid and Fortune Fund, according to the minions of the Man family, being the most recent victims to have fallen.

The death of a powerful man like Walter Krocht and the taking of his place by his minion Faron Hayes certainly didn't guarantee a maintaining of the status quo.

It rang in chaos!

Oscar also knew, after this tiring night, that he was proof that there could be a defense against the mental offense of the minions. Three of them had tried in unison to force him into submission by torturing him with the terrible powers of their mind. He had not been able to repulse their attack, for nature had not endowed him with a brain like that of Krocht, which prevented itself from being infiltrated, so he had had to defend himself. He had appeared to be the stronger, and that gave him courage for the future.

If they had managed to get him on his knees, he would have become a defenseless creature that crawled when it was told to do so. He had looked into the depths of their being and probed them, and he had perceived, despite their efforts to hide it, their fear.

Walter Krocht was not murdered in an inconspicuous place where all traces could be covered up. The minions had used their mental powers to make Jay Jay and Richard draw their weapons. So it had looked as if he, Oscar Man, were the brains behind the attempt. He didn't bother much about that last. But he would never forgive them for having killed the twins.

He only slept for two hours. Then he got up and went to the covered train platform of the palace. Even at this early hour, trains were running. He could get no rest in the palace and wanted to return to his penthouse in New York City as soon as possible.

* * *

The new president showed everyone right from the beginning that he knew how to set about his work. He was open and aboveboard in his dealings and gave the media full access. He had considerably enlarged the police force and at the same time forbade all multinationals from using private guards in public. In New York City the palace guard of the Man family had run the show, but now the armed and uniformed men of Ferdinand had retreated to their barracks, just as the guards of Cabo de Barra were no longer allowed to show themselves in the streets of Atlanta, and the security people of Fenrir International had to stay away from Fenrir City and Las Vegas. The strong-arm gangs of all the other large companies had to disband themselves entirely.

There had never been a law that justified their existence, and therefore, it was not hard for Angus to banish them altogether. In the meantime, his legal advisers worked on the possibility of bringing all the multinationals to court and trying them for committing a breach of the law that protected from the formation of cartels. He gave lectures at the universities about human rights and true democracy, two things that were at complete opposites to the limitations that the oligarchic Western world imposed on the population. The president encouraged small employers to help one another by making use of each other's services and buying each other's products. That way the power of the tycoons would be undermined, although the president did not rely on that alone to reintroduce a small middle class into society. The president felt that the middle classes had always been the backbone of any democratic economy.

Tony Falcon's men followed Sebastian everywhere, and all his plans received wide attention in the media. Where necessary, Oscar appeared in the media and supported the plans of Sebastian in his own, uncomplicated way. His immense popularity made it more and more comfortable for people to join the new movement and to begin working on making changes for their own good. All of a sudden there were people again who gave full scope to initiative and did not let their lives depend of the whims and caprices of the tycoons in their palaces who had themselves crowned and lived like kings, using the people as their private vassals and serfs.

But the power of the multinationals would not be broken by a few new laws.

The army was working on other plans. Under the leadership of General Howe, a plan was hatched to take a minion prisoner and force him to reveal everything and explain his miraculous methods of behavior. The plan also called for the hostage to divulge the truth about the power minions held over the tycoons.

It was Algernon Sparks who was asked to arrest a known minion. He organized a group of trained policemen and got cracking right away. But the minions of the most important tycoons refused to leave the palaces and would only consent to being questioned at home, in the presence of their lawyers. They naturally did not want to answer any queries regarding the murders of people like Don Bradshaw, Carl

Holdorf and Roberta Rodriguez, so Sparks concentrated on the favorites of less important people.

His hopes were misguided, however.

His special squad arrested three men who were the minions of respectively a manager of the Fenrir International Business Bank in Las Vegas, an enormously rich stockholder of Fortune Fund and a member of the board of Syrinx Colorado.

"The first one appears to be a talentless member of the family who is able to get his share of the unlimited luxury at Fenrir. He is a nephew who dresses and behaves just like his uncle. He is not allowed, under any circumstances, to open his mouth, for he knows as much about the banking business as a fish does about hurdle racing. The second one is thirty years younger than his retired patron, and his only task is to keep him warm in bed. Number three plays games with his protector because it is the fashion these days to service a minion. It is incredible to learn how many people who have reached an upper rung on the social ladder keep a man or woman around solely because it gives them more prestige."

One day, though, their luck changed.

Through General Howe it became known to Sparks that a delegation of Pilgrims Palladium one of the smallest multinationals was coming to New York City to negotiate with other enterprises. They wanted to buy several buildings on the southern end of Manhattan and establish offices and a bank there. The people of Pilgrims Palladium had booked hotels, and someone had found out where Gene Fletcher the minion of an important tycoon would be spending the night.

"He is the minion of Sven Enlart one of Pilgrims' most important men, and they have booked a suite in Greenwich Village while the rest of the group have opted for places downtown. When they leave their hotel and head for the Financial District, you must be ready to strike. We'll give you all the help you need, even if we have to block streets and divert traffic. You must try to separate Gene Fletcher and Sven Enlart. The minion has to be gotten out of town as quickly as possible. We will be all too happy to welcome him with all regard on our army base in Boston."

"It won't be a problem for the people I work with," said Algernon. "No one will ever suspect who is behind this. So many murders are committed among the wealthy that a simple disappearance will not cause any fuss at all. Give me all the details, and I'll get going as soon as possible."

"Time is getting short, Algernon. We must not miss this chance. Gene Fletcher will be turned inside out, and when we are finished with him, this minion will have no secrets from us, I can assure you that!"

    * * *

The morning was rainy. A copper-colored automobile drove along the Avenue of the Americas. The chauffeur and the man next to him wore the uniform of Pilgrims' guards. The traffic was jammed up, and they stood still more often than not. The man behind the wheel had never driven in New York City before and repeatedly asked the other guard to see if he had to turn yet. Rain ticked softly on the roof. The windshield wiper slowly moved back and forth.

In the back sat Sven Enlart, wrapped in a long coat, his hands in his pockets and his shoulders hunched. He was sick with the flu and felt weak. If possible, he would leave the negotiations that were planned for today up to his colleagues whom he was supposed to meet at their hotel before going down to the office.

Dressed in the same coat, but with straight shoulders and a lively look in his eyes, Sven's minion Gene Fletcher sat next to him.

"If I had known I was going to feel like this, I would have stayed at home," said Enlart. "But I didn't begin to feel sick until we were already on the plane."

Pilgrims Palladium had its headquarters in Portland, Oregon, in a gigantic pyramid.

"You will make the best of it, Sven," said his minion. "In fact, all you have to do is exchange compliments, for the buildings we want to buy have already been chosen, and the price has been negotiated. As soon as the documents are signed, Pilgrims has a place in New York City next to all the other big enterprises. We'll throw a party for everyone; the press will be there, and we'll let it be known worldwide that we count just as much as Man-Mandate or Fortune Fund. And no one will notice if you stay in the background a bit or even return to the hotel early. I will do the honors."

Sven Enlart sniffed clamorously.

"Thank you, Gene," he said. "It is good to have someone like you at my side constantly whom I can always count on."

The car was still on the Avenues of the Americas, just past King Street and nearing Charlton Street. In his mirror, the chauffeur saw that there was some room behind him. Two police cars with flashing lights were holding the traffic back by driving slowly. Suddenly an automobile that had been parked along the side accelerated, tires screaming. It was a black vehicle with a high bumper and dark windows.

"They've gone raving mad!" shouted the chauffeur. "Just a little while and then—"

Before he could finish his sentence, the nose of the black car rammed the trunk. At the same moment, someone in the car in front stepped on the brakes. The chauffeur couldn't avoid a second collision. The next moment, the vehicle sat jammed between the two. All four doors in the rear car opened, and four men in red overalls jumped out. They wore black balaclavas. Sven Enlart, hardly recovered from his fright, saw the men appear and cried, "What madness is this? Are the doors locked?"

Two of the men in red overalls pounded a metal battering ram through one of the windows. The glass splintered. Strong hands caught hold of the minion's coat, and Gene Fletcher was pulled outside. The man next to the chauffeur had drawn a revolver and was starting to get out. He had hardly opened the door when he was kicked back into the car with enormous power. The hand clutching the gun snapped audibly as his wrist was shattered, and his weapon clattered onto the street. The automobile in front sped off as the minion was dragged backward into the rear vehicle. The police arrived on the scene just as the vehicle sped off into the anonymous traffic of Manhattan. An officer stepped out and looked inside through the splintered window.

"Who are you?" he asked the man in the long coat.

Sven Enlart looked up, outraged. His chin and red nose stuck assertively forward out of the high collar.

"I am Sven Enlart of Pilgrims Palladium, Portland! My minion has been kidnapped. Don't lose the car that rammed us!"

Sirens sounded as more police cars rushed by. The chauffeur looked at the officer's face through the broken window and said, "You were behind us. Didn't you see this happening? Why didn't you come to us immediately?"

"We were about to arrest a suspect in a holdup, sir," said the police officer. "We had been searching for him for more than hour when we finally caught up to him, but there were still some vehicles between us. We considered stopping traffic and were about to get out when we saw what was happening here. We let the suspect go and gave priority to this brutal action."

"We are very grateful for that," Enlart hurried to say.

"I'll have someone drive along with you," said the officer. "He'll keep you posted on all developments as we do our utmost to find your minion. My colleague will get his name and description so that we can pass it along to other units on the road."

"Understood," said Enlart, who had great difficulty in suppressing a fit of coughing.

Pointing at the man next to the chauffeur, he continued, "Someone has to get him to a doctor. I think his wrist is crushed."

Meanwhile, the men in red and their hostage drove up Seventh Avenue toward Fourteenth Street trying to reach the Holland Tunnel as quickly as possible and get into New Jersey. The police cars had gone in another direction and given them a good head start.

The minion sat in the back, scared to death, between two armed men. The traffic was heavy, but thanks to the rain and the early hour, there were hardly any celebrating pedestrians blocking the roads.

After a while the automobile stopped. The men stepped out and dragged the minion out of the car and to a waiting truck. The rear door was opened and closed again immediately, and now seven men in red sat in the empty cargo space. In the cabin an eighth sat behind the wheel, and next to him sat Algernon Sparks.

"Drive!" said Sparks. "We've got him!"

They started the engine and took off. The kidnap vehicle remained behind. No one would ever find out who had driven it. Algernon Sparks was satisfied with the way things had gone. Sven Enlart would undoubtedly say that the police had been very helpful in searching for the minion. It would always remain a mystery who had kidnapped him.

Gene Fletcher was seated on the floor of the truck with his hands chained behind him. He was a lean man with an intelligent face and dark brown eyes that sparkled and now scrutinized the men in red one after the other.

While the truck drove on, he probed his kidnappers. He concluded that he could influence six of them. The seventh one was, exactly as Walter Krocht had been, totally insensible to impulses, invisible feints or brutal attacks from his side because he could not make contact with the instincts of this man.

He reached out his mental tentacles and began a battle only a minion was able to fight. A man rose to his feet and came staggering up to him over the shaking truck bed. He bent down behind him.

"There's nothing wrong with his handcuffs," said the man who was unreachable to the minion. "What are you doing?"

He could not see what was happening behind the back of the minion.

"Believe me, they are not too tight," he continued.

The locks of the handcuffs were opened. Fletcher brought his hands forward and began to rub his wrists. In the meantime, his murderous thoughts worked at full strength. The man behind him who had freed him took a revolver from his overall and aimed the weapon at the man who had spoken.

"What—" he managed to say before he was riddled with bullets right in front of the unconcerned eyes of the others. The bullets hit his chest one after another, and he fell against the side of the truck and slowly collapsed.

"Stop!" cried Algernon Sparks in the cabin. "Have they lost their minds? They are killing the minion! Don't they know the plan? Pull the truck over! Gene Fletcher is important to us only if he's alive."

The chauffeur drove the semi into the parking lot of a big supermarket and found a place where he could stop.

Meanwhile Gene Fletcher had collected all his mental powers. His face had grown pale and he looked frozen; only his eyes moved. He sat there silently while around his head a crackling halo of blue and orange light had appeared. Howling like banshees, the six men pressed their hands against their temples. They felt as if boiling oil raged inside their skulls. They began running around aimlessly, banging into each other and the sides of the truck. Algernon Sparks and the chauffeur stepped out and ran to the back of the truck where they pushed the button that brought down the door. Sparks had a revolver in his hand, and the driver had taken a rifle with him from the cabin.

A few people in the parking lot wandered over inquisitively.

The six men stumbled out of the trailer and fell to the ground, dying as they landed on top of each other. Behind them the minion was visible. The revolver and the rifle were aimed at him, but before Sparks and his man could fire, they also felt that unbearable pain in their heads. The rifle fell from the weakening hands of the man in the overalls, and he doubled up in pain, his palms clamped to his temples.

The mind of Algernon Sparks, now not much more than a spark of consciousness in a bubbling sea of boiling oil, fought an unfair battle against his rapidly approaching death.

"No!" he cried out.

He couldn't hear himself because the screaming pain in his head drowned everything. The revolver had already fallen to the ground. Something burst inside the brain of Algernon Sparks. For a brief moment, he stood bolt upright as the sweat ran through his short, bristly hair and down his forehead. Then his heart stopped beating; he collapsed dead on the ground.

The minion came out and jumped off the back of the truck. The bewildered bystanders didn't react at all as he strolled out of the parking lot toward the supermarket. It was as if he knew the art of making himself invisible, for when three police cars arrived a few minutes later and the officers began to ask questions, there was not one person who could give a good description of Gene Fletcher, and there was no one who could tell in what direction he had disappeared. The police sent for ambulances to transport the nine dead bodies.

Gene Fletcher appeared a few hours later than planned at the meeting in the Financial District and sat down in the empty chair next to Sven Enlart. He briefly apologized for his tardiness without mentioning what had happened to him. Sven Enlart was about to say something to him but suddenly felt an annoying pressure in his head. He took a handkerchief and after blowing his nose clamorously, he said, "I am very happy that my minion has shown up. The flu has got me so badly that I prefer to remain in the background. He can now speak for me."

For the generals, the news of the death of Sparks, along with his eight men, came as an incredible shock. Alvin Hodgkinson felt himself getting panicky. He raised his long, lean arms in the air, waving his bony fingers as he said, "This delivers us onto ground about which we know absolutely nothing. Algernon tried to arrest a minion, and now he is dead. We can establish the cause of death of the man who got shot. But what happened to poor Algernon and the seven others?"

He shook his head and closed his eyes, and in his ears resounded the voice of the coroner who had told the generals, "I have never seen anything like this before. All of the men we autopsied seem to have been fine. Algernon Sparks's heart was a powerful little motor that should have continued to pump the blood around in his perfectly healthy body for decades. He was physically fit and ate well—he had the body of an athlete! The other men were in no way inferior to him. They were all well trained, as you probably know even better than I do, and could handle any physical exertion. But they had the fear of death in their eyes, all of them. Yes, believe me: even in those dead eyes you can still see the fright. We took six bullets out of the body of the man who was shot. Bullets fired from a revolver of a teammate. They all landed in his chest, so his head remained undamaged. Examination proved that his brain was intact. That is only logical, you would say, for what would be the matter with his brain? But, gentlemen, how is it possible, how could it happen, that the brains of Algernon Sparks, the six other men from the cargo space and the chauffeur all are only the size of a walnut?"

The generals were in a big office on an army base in Boston where everything had been prepared to keep the minion prison and interrogate him. There were doctors and psychiatrists present, and it had been the intention that the experienced Sparks should lead the team of inquisitors.

Dean Howe urged Alvin Hodgkinson to remain calm.

"It's no use getting nervous, Alvin. We'd rather try to think clearly."

"Would Sparks have been able to think clearly with a brain the size of a walnut?"

"There must be an explanation for what has happened."

Scott James barged in on the discussion; he was just as panicky as Hodgkinson.

"An explanation? You want an explanation? The minion did it! He is the culprit—we just cannot prove it. And we can probably forget about ever getting a chance to get our hands on a second minion. They've had their warning. They'll all be on the alert now. Gene Fletcher has seen to that, I'm sure. If it's up to me, my friends, we will change our strategy instantly. There are still two men who, even though they are not genuine minions, might be useful in this. So what that they're a little different? I suggest we get Tony Falcon and Oscar Man here and lock them up behind a thick iron door. We'll do to them whatever it takes, starve or torture them, to get the information we need to defeat these damn parasites! Parasites!"

Dean Howe shook his head.

"That will not bring you one step closer to a solution. Of course, they have a lot in common with minions, but the differences are major. You can torture a saint as much as you like, but he will never be able to tell you how a murderer thinks."

"They are all the same kind of scum!" James yelled. "The minions who murder the tycoons; Falcon with his hollow, staring eyes; Man behaving like a damn jester—"

"We discuss everything openly and together, as much as possible," said Howe. "As far as I'm concerned, we form an almost ideal triumvirate. But in the end, I am the one who takes the final decisions when the opinions differ. We leave both Falcon and Man alone and go on with our strategy of pressing the big enterprises as hard as possible. The president is behind us, and the government agrees with us. We are strong enough to weather this storm and meet our objectives. Falcon has told us that the minions get very confused when things don't go the way they want them to. We must increase the pressure and wait to see what happens next. Let's hope that Falcon is right. Meanwhile, it can do no harm to make this crazy, sick world a little bit better."

"I suppose you're right," said Hodgkinson with a sigh. "Sure enough, we are more powerful than we had ever dared hope. More and more people are beginning to realize that the way life is dictated to them is, to put it mildly, improper. They feel the thumb of oppression on their necks and know, through Falcon's efforts in the media, that it was once different and can be again. He pushes Oscar forward as a great hero, fortifying and then making use of his incredible popularity. In fact, he has set Oscar up to be diametrically opposed to the minions. And when I think about that, I have my doubts about everything, Dean."

"What do you mean?"

"It's simply unbelievable. Yes. Oscar Man should be the minion's worst enemy; he is promoted to the world as the man who is going to change everything, who stands for a new society, who is willing to build up a new world--a world of freedom and democracy in which everybody has the same chances. Meanwhile, Oscar Man can come and go as he pleases and visits the palace regularly where his half-brothers and half-sister are under the influence of their minions. Why do the minions tolerate him? Why didn't Kenneth Mayfield, Mike Farland and Tana Rowe show him the door as they did when he was no longer a prince and all his possessions had been taken from him?"

"I know it. I know it all too well. Again, I must rely on what Tony Falcon has told me."

"And what is it he has told you?"

"That we will have to wait! Obviously, there is something brewing between the minions and Oscar Man. Something is going to happen.

Where, how and when no one can tell, but Falcon keeps on about the fact that we will have to be patient. I think it best to give him the benefit of the doubt, for he obviously knows more than we do. Our biggest mistake would be if we did what James just suggested. With Tony Falcon and Oscar Man behind bars, we would be standing alone. They are the only ones who at least understand something about the strange behavior of minions."

The two other generals nodded almost imperceptibly, agreeing—albeit subtly—that they thought Howe was right and that they would stand solidly behind him.

The death of Algernon Sparks and his team had been a staggering blow. With Sparks gone, they had lost an important partisan. The magical powers of the minions, which enabled them to shrivel human brains, indicated that they were dealing with an opponent that had at its disposal talents that could be stronger than the weapons the army could bring into action.

The idea was out there that they, when and if everything else had been tried and had failed, and if the power of the minions could not be broken, planned to kill every one of the minions. On paper the commandos who would carry it out were already selected. But it would remain a plan on paper. Howe, Hodgkinson and James knew that the minions were unreachable. They had hidden themselves like ground forces in their trenches. Sparks had already experienced this, long before he attempted his fatal assault on Gene Fletcher, when he tried to enter the palace of the Man family with its puzzling system of elevator shafts and the mental influences that were forced upon him, causing him to flee in panic like a fool.

The palace was impenetrable, and the situation was no different with the maze of low buildings that formed the palace of Fenrir International, the mighty pyramid of Pilgrims Palladium or the shelters of Cabo de Barra in Atlanta, which were hidden deep underground. The bunkers of Syrinx Colorado were just as impregnable as the carved halls where the tycoons and minions of Hygnos Hybrid Corporation lived. What was called the palace of Fortune Fund seemed more like a slum with hundreds of winding streets and alleys and thousands of buildings in which all who entered without a guide became hopelessly lost. If the army decided to harass the minions' luxury residences, they would unquestionably use their countless subordinates as human shields. The minions had made themselves invulnerable.

The only thing to do was undermine the power of the multinationals and change public opinion. Those were the two most important weapons, and the army, the police force and the government were working together where that was concerned to change the laws and see to it that everyone observed the regulations. The president showed the way and was already considered a traitor by the tycoons in general and the Man family in particular who had put him in power in the first place.

"Continue pressing the minions hard," was the advice that Falcon gave time after time. "When there are enough gadflies to sting the horse, sooner or later the animal will stampede."

And so, time passed by.

News of the horrible deaths of tycoons came more and more frequently, and not once did anyone succeed in apprehending the culprits. The government and the army no longer did business with the big corporations but rather with the new emerging enterprises. More and more media companies chose the side of Tony Falcon and rebelled outright against the mastery of the multinationals. The dissatisfaction increased, and people began to realize that the times needed some changing.

But the multinationals didn't bow, nor did they stagger.

The minions remained silent and did not show themselves.

"The calm before the storm," said Falcon, and President Sebastian and the generals fervently hoped that the charismatic man was right.

Chapter Twelve

The *Njord*

Cathy Wheeler had done exactly what Tony Falcon had asked of her. After reading it, she destroyed the translation of the manuscript attributed to Jean Galliou and put the original away in a steel box. It was indeed no more than fragments, but within those fragments were prophesies about a new era when minions would come to satisfy their hunger for power. She had read about the young prince who would save a prominent person and would fight an epic battle, the results of which were unknown. It was impossible to ascertain when the original text had been written that had been copied by Jean Galliou. Cathy understood, however, that the author not only had much knowledge of minions but also that he had been hostile to them. He described them as dangerous creatures who had to be defeated by any means.

What Falcon had already said, she had found in the text herself. Reversal of their plans would throw the minions into panic and weaken them. She suspected that the author had to be someone like Tony Falcon or Oscar Man, someone who was standing just as close to minions as to ordinary people, someone with special gifts who warned of new efforts by the parasites to gain control over the world.

About the nature of minions, not much was to be found. Presumably Galliou had copied all the available information, but parts of the manuscript had been destroyed or lay somewhere waiting to be discovered. The short comments she found about the way the minions thought conformed exactly with the things Oscar had told her about himself.

"Their knowledge is enormous," she remembered him saying, "for many things have been passed down from generation to generation. It is a slumbering wisdom, which can become ready knowledge in times of need."

The original author had personally been among minions, a fact that became clear in some of the different passages of the work.

"It is actually quite comical to watch a minion imitate an ancestor who lived a hundred years ago or more in attitude and gestures—yes, even in quirks of speech. Each generation lives on in its descendants, and it is impossible to predict what will take root and what will evaporate."

There were also notes about the mental powers of the parasites.

"They can think someone to death" was one of the things mentioned.

Those six little words had sent cold shivers down Cathy's spine. She had been indescribably happy when Oscar had suddenly returned to the penthouse. She had been afraid that she would never see him again when he left her to return to the Man palace.

For she and Oscar a period of rest had come. They lived high up in the sky and in luxury like gods while down below the government, the army and the media waged their war against the multinationals. Oscar was informed about everything that was happening when he would pay a visit to the twentieth floor where the generals still maintained an office. Falcon dragged him in front of the cameras several times to insure that his popularity was maintained.

"The minions have entrenched themselves in the palaces," Howe said to Oscar one day. "According to Falcon, this is the calm before the storm. He expects something to happen any day."

* * *

When Oscar came back from a walk, he'd been gone a long time. Cathy thought he seemed strange and nervous.

"Is anything wrong, Oscar?" she asked.

When she asked him if there was something the matter, he came up to her and took something out of his pocket, took her hand in his and slipped a golden ring on her finger. Then he knelt down and asked:

"Cathy Wheeler, after all misery is over--and if we have managed to survive--will you marry me?"

Cathy took his head in both her hands, bent forward and kissed him on the mouth. He rose to his feet and they kissed again.

"Yes. . . ," she stammered. "Yes, of course. I..., Oscar, if you only knew..."

She looked down at her ring. The tears in her eyes blurred it into a small golden sun.

"I have taken part in more than a thousand parties," said Oscar. "If you marry me, I will organize the biggest wedding party the world has ever seen. That's a promise. And for the rest..., I will remain faithful to you!"

He held her again, smiled at her and wiped the tears from her cheeks.

"I'd be happy with the second part of the promise."

"So it is yes?"

Cathy had pulled herself together and started to laugh.

"You just don't listen. Or do you want me to say it one more time?"

He nodded.

"Very well then. Yes. Yes, I will marry you. Yes, I want to marry you."

"Cathy Man," said Oscar. "Isn't that a sweet name?"

A name to be proud of, thought Cathy. She wanted to know how it sounded when she heard it from her own lips: "I'm Cathy Man. My name is Cathy Man."

"Don't forget that there is minion blood running through my veins."

"But you're different, Oscar, and unique. Never forget that. I love you the way you are!"

They made love passionately, intensely, that night as if each knew they were meant to be together for the ret of their lives.

* * *

Next morning, Oscar left early. He had an appointment with the generals and after that needed to see Falcon. Cathy's heart was filled with joy, and she was unable to concentrate on anything. Aimlessly, she walked through the rooms of the penthouse, with a teacup in her hand. She had decided to take a walk when an unexpected visitor announced herself. Cathy wondered who it was as she waited by the door of the elevator. When it finally opened, she saw Johanna Man! Johanna in a snowy dress of white tulle, her face painted a flaming scarlet. She looked, Cathy thought, like a bowl of whipped cream, crowned with a strawberry.

Cathy gave a deep curtsy and at the same time realized that this odd-looking woman would soon be her sister-in-law.

"Welcome. . . ," was all she managed to say.

Johanna said in a high-pitched voice,

"Well, here I am. Actually, I am not allowed to be here at all. We are forbidden to leave the palace. And that is exactly the reason why I have escaped."

Cathy was standing upright again and looked at Johanna. She noticed a gleam of madness in her eyes.

"What a pity; Oscar is not at home."

"That doesn't matter. It is so nice to see you again, Cathy." Suddenly she burst out laughing. "You know... when they discover that I went outside, they will kill my brother Ferdinand. Isn't that just ridiculous? Do they really think they can kill a king?"

Cathy grasped the seriousness of the situation. She took Johanna by the arm and led her into the apartment.

"Who wants to kill him?" she asked.

Johanna shrugged her shoulders.

"I... I don't know that exactly. But what I do know is that they actually will do it." Another trill of laughter erupted from her. "They know so much. Still they don't know everything. I can go to wherever I want, thanks to Freddy. He has taught me how to manipulate the elevators."

Cathy gently eased her into an armchair.

If only Oscar was here, thought Cathy.

The minions wanted everybody to stay inside the palace. Johanna, who was under their spell, had followed a call of her rebellious nature and had cleared off. She was too hysterical to realize that she actually risked the life of her brother. She made coffee for Johanna and tried to calm her down and elicit more information.

"Oscar proposed to me," she said while she put up her hand to show her the ring. "We are going to get married."

"Oscar..." said Johanna with a sigh while she closed her eyes and nodded her head softly. "I seldom paid him a visit here. Or perhaps not at all, I simply don't remember. If it was up to me, dear girl, I should choose white horses and a garden full of red roses."

"Are you talking about the wedding?" asked Cathy.

Johanna looked up in surprise.

"Fruit trees! It gives so much satisfaction when you gather the fruit by yourself. Baskets full of it. And if I was a child, I would play with dolls all day. Oh, I have always loved Oscar. He is my little brother."

By asking her question after question, Cathy was able to discover that Johanna had left the palace by train and then had come to New York by helicopter. The chopper stood ready for the flight back on the roof of a office building of Man-Mandate Enterprises.

She rose resolutely to her feet and took Johanna by the arm for the second time. Cathy had to try to avert a disaster; nothing should happen to Ferdinand Man! But first she must get Johanna back to the palace.

"Come with me; we'll go back to the palace together."

Johanna followed her docilely. Together they left the building and stepped into a cab that brought them to the Man-Mandate building. A copper-colored helicopter that looked like a gigantic horsefly took off almost at once. Johanna's voice chattered continuously in Cathy's headset. Cathy hardly listened but every now and then she reacted with a nod, a smile or an approving word or expression. At the station, the Elephant train stood there blowing steam and they quickly boarded. They were the only passengers. Cathy had been in the palace often to consult with Todd Dawson the archivist of the library. She remembered her excited, merry mood when she caught sight of the palace and saw the freakish forms grow bigger and bigger. Now there was no excitement, only a nameless fear.

"I'll leave you here, after I see you safely in the elevator. Then I'll go back."

Johanna shrugged her shoulders and started describing some fore edged paintings she'd just discovered.

Puffing and sighing, the train came to a standstill. The two women stepped out on to a deserted platform.

"Come," said Johanna taking Cathy's hand, "let me show you something."

She walked straight up to an elevator. The door slid open, and she dragged Cathy along with her.

"I really must get back. Oscar will be worried," stammered Cathy. "I have said that before, didn't I?"

"My dear child, my word is law here," Johanna bridled. "Now take a look at all those buttons. Let me tell you how Freddy, Jimmy and I are able to mislead everyone." She winked at Cathy. "All routes the elevators take get registered. All used codes will be saved. Ferdinand designed the elevators himself and saw to it that we can move around unnoticed. Sometimes you just don't want everyone to know where you're going. All you have to do is to keep the black button below pushed in with your thumb... like this... and then you key in the code with your fingers... Here we go. No one knows where to, besides you and I."

The door closed; the elevator set into movement.

"I don't know where we're going to at all!" cried Cathy. "Please, let me go! I must go back to Oscar!"

Johanna's shrill laugh echoed in the small chamber.

The elevator came to a standstill. The door slid open. Cathy was pushed outside. To her surprise, she knew immediately where she was: in a round room underground, the hall of the library. She'd been there many times.

"You are the girl of the books," said Johanna with a cracking voice. "Or were you thinking that I had forgotten that?" She embraced Cathy and kissed her on both cheeks. "I will retire to my own chambers now. You were very pleasant company."

A door opened. Todd Dawson stepped inside. He was a man with a crooked back and short legs. His face was deathly pale, as if he hadn't seen sunlight in years. His black suit of soft shining silk gave him the appearance of a giant mole. He made a deep bow to Johanna and turned to Cathy.

"Well, well, Cathy... What a pleasant surprise."

Johanna stepped back into the elevator. Cathy noticed how she already pushed the black button below with her thumb.

"Remember, the universe has no boundaries," she said. "But Jimmy says that there is a limit to everything." She looked at the archivist: "Cathy Wheeler has always served us well."

"That is a fact, madam, a true fact indeed," stammered Todd while he made another bow.

Johanna pushed in the code and waved with her free hand.

"Give her all she desires, for she has a good heart. And I have a generous heart!"

The door closed. Without a sound. But to Cathy is seemed as if a trap had slammed shut. Weak-kneed she stood there in the hall and it was as if she could feel the forcing powers of the minions down here. Todd rubbed his hands contentedly.

"What brings you here, Cathy? What can I do for you?"

She was seized by panic and wondered how she ever could have been so stupid to step inside the Elephant and go to the palace. Oscar would have torn his hair if he had known that she was here. She took a deep breath and mustered up her courage. With a few steps, she was back at the elevator. The door opened.

"Show me which code I have to use to return to the station."

The man came standing close to her and looked up to her in surprise.

"I can do that for you in a little while, can't I?"

"Show it to me, Todd."

"All right, all right. It is not a secret code at all." He stepped inside the elevator and pointed one by one at a number of buttons. "Is it clear to you?"

"Yes, it is. Thanks very much. I would like to go now."

He stepped into the hall again.

"You act so strange. If you want to leave, you just go. I hope you don't think I would try to stop you. . . , but I was hoping you'd look at some new items of particular interest."

"No. I'm sorry, Todd. I'm a little confused. Johanna had come to visit me, and I have accompanied her on her way back. She seemed unwell, and it upset me."

"Please, Cathy, Johanna's fine. Won't you give me just a few minutes?"

Todd's words were reassuring, perhaps she was overreacting.

"All right, Todd, a few minutes."

Todd led Cathy through broad paths between towering shelves filled with wondrous books. The smell reminded her of the library in the penthouse in Manhattan; it calmed her down a bit more.

"You heard Joanna, Cathy. Are you going to pick out a beautiful and expensive book since I am ordered to give you everything you want?"

She thought things over. Suddenly, something came to her mind. All books that were brought in here were thoroughly examined; no minion secrets could be found here! Then what was she doing here? It was better to leave the palace. Right now! Again she tried to imagine what the minions were doing at this moment in the big palace.

She turned to Todd. The man stood there looking at her with rheumy eyes. It was obvious that he enjoyed her presence: such a beautiful young woman who unexpectedly showed up and dispelled the loneliness of his subterranean existence. She was not afraid of him.

"Todd, there any books here that make mention of minions? Do you know at all what minions are?"

"Of course," he said. "There are many books here about the European Renaissance. The minions are the favorites of the kings and queens, of the nobility and the rich people. . . . Are you interested in minions?"

"Very much. I make a study of them."

Todd nodded.

"Of course! You like to know everything about all facets of history. You will not find much here that you do not know already, but wait! You are in luck! You asked the right question to the right man. How nice is to be able to talk about this with someone who really wants to know all about it."

"What do you mean?"

He came standing closer to her, rubbed his hands and looked up at her.

"You might think that minions were selected from the inner circle of friends of the nobility and the rich. You will find not much or nothing at all about that in the books. But what if I tell you, Cathy, that it was the minions themselves who chose their patrons and patronesses?"

Her heart began to beat faster.

"Are you serious?"

"O yes, I am! And I will tell you some more. Minions. A strange kind of human beings. Very special indeed. Nameless people with special desires and gifts and with strong mutual ties; they never called themselves minions. They are parasites, and their aims have always been very ambitious. Power is what they were after."

"Todd..., how do you know all this?"

She noticed that he was in doubt. Then, suddenly, he heaved a deep sigh.

"All right then. I will give you a book. I know that Johanna approves. It is one of my dearest books. I often take a look in it and try to solve the riddles. But now it is your turn to pore over it. Come, I'll show it to you."

He led the way through long paths and brought her to a low door.

"Everyone is collecting books," he said. "It's the fashion. The palaces of all tycoons are bulging with books! And when they pay a visit to each other, they want to show their excellent taste, how well-read they are and how much they know. And so they give each other the most valuable presents. Books! Behind this door I keep all the Man family's gift books."

He opened the door and gestured her inside.

A moment later, she found herself in a square room. Along the walls stood cast iron figures with their arms spread; they touched each others fingers. On the arms leaned broad bookshelves. On the shoulders of the monsters, half-humans and monstrosities stood other figures who in their turn also carried cast iron creatures. Todd climbed up a ladder and had to stand on tiptoe in order to reach for a particular book. He climbed down with it and put it on a table in the middle of the room.

"Please take a look at this."

Cathy stared with big eyes at the book on the table top.

The cover was of old, cracked leather, and there was no title on it. In the upper right corner was a little hole. A small ribbon was put through it. At the end of the ribbon was a little card. She turned the card and read in a whispering voice:

"A special gift to a special woman. Happy birthday and many happy returns, Johanna Man. With love, Grace Dubois."

Behind her, she could hear Todd snorting scornfully.

"A hole in such a priceless book. It is a sin!"

"Who is Grace Dubois?"

"I really don't know. A lady who wanted to impress someone who is many times richer than herself."

Cathy opened the book and what she saw took her breath away. In a dazed sort of way, she stared at a subtle pen drawing on yellowed, thick paper. What se saw was unmistakably a clever piece of minion art. Men and women stood there in a wide circle and just like the cast iron figures in this room, other men and women were standing on their shoulders. Countless people together formed a tower that reached far into the sky. The artist had worked with short stripes and sharp angles and knew how to evoke a fragile but also macabre atmosphere so palpable that Cathy was afraid to turn the page. What would the next drawing show?

At the foot of the drawing stood a single word in Latin: *Familia*.

"Listen," said Todd while he brought a chair and sat down. "This is what I know. These are the nameless people. They stand on each other's shoulders. They are one big family and pass on all their information to each other. The people standing on the ground possess all knowledge of the ones they carry. If you take a good look at the drawing, you see symbols everywhere. Symbols that are not easy to explain. Look! Little squares, an angry face in a cloud, a waving hand sticking out of the earth, a fish on dry land. All this is even more complicated than the art of the alchemists, and I don't have to tell you how difficult it is to fathom that!"

Finally Cathy had the courage to turn the pages. There were dozens of drawings. Cathy was flabbergasted. She red the short texts:

"*Dies ater. Exitus letalis. Patiente vincit omnia. Non omnis moriar. Lux in tenebris*-- Unlucky day. Fatal accident. Patience overcomes all things. I will not die entirely. Light in the darkness."

Then she read: *Catastropha* and the drawing showed a slender man facing a crowd that fled in panic.

One man against the minions.

"I have looked at this drawing long and often," she heard Todd say. "It is hard to avoid the impression that the lonely hero in the foreground looks very much like Prince Oscar. His face shows up on many a page. Mostly the jester is smiling or even laughing. But on a few other pages, his head is stuck on a pole or cut off by a sword or an ax."

She was also struck by the strong resemblance. She felt a lump rise in her throat, and she did her utmost to keep herself from crying.

"Shall I tell you what I know and what I think?"

She nodded.

Todd rose to his feet and came standing behind her. Slowly he turned the pages.

"These are original drawings. They must be very old! On the backside, you can see notes from all different periods. There is a certain magister Lucas who has written some remarks; every here and there, there are lines from a man who calls himself Aram and more recent text from a man by the name of Jean Galliou. He wrote in French. I think he lived in the middle of the eighteenth century."

This is the book! This is the book! thought Cathy. *"The book everyone was searching for! Nobody knew that it was right here all the time. It was a gift to Johanna and the minions never suspected that it was here underground, right under their feet! This is a miracle--could fate be a power of itself?*

She tried to concentrate on Todd's voice again.

"The last pages of the book contain text only," he said. "But I think that the drawings are of more importance. They have gone from hand to hand so often that one had decided to cut the margins and bind them. They are old. I think they were made at the beginning of the fifteenth century. Up to then, the nameless people had passed on all their secret knowledge by mouth as an oral tradition. But horrible times were bound to come, the inquisition, the time of the witch hunt! The nameless people would suffer a lot. Many of them would die on the rack or be burnt at the stake. One thought that they were witches and wizards working black magic, and because they never ever would yield up their secrets, they already were doomed to death after they had been captured. Therefore, it was wise to put everything about their origin, life, works, goals and prophecies on paper. They did it like the alchemists had done in drawings that are unintelligible for to the layman, but a source of information for the initiate. The Renaissance, between 1450 and 1550, brought them prosperity again. They became the exact likeness of the nobility and the rich people and for the first time they had a name: minions."

He turned over the leaves and showed her a page with text only. Cathy read some lines in Latin and remembered a certain text from the hand of Jean Galliou. Now she was sure. This was the important book the minions wished themselves to have. The book Oscar's life was given to finding.

"Is... is it really mine now? Are you really giving it to me?"

"Ah, poor Cathy," sighed Todd. "Your voice is trembling. You are totally upset about it, aren't you? Yes, of course. It is yours. I know that you will respect it as I do. Now you can actually start a study about minions. Take it along with you. And keep me posted about every discovery you make. Will you promise me that?"

"Oh yes, yes, of course. You... you said you looked at all these pages so many times. Is there more you know about the minions of that period?"

"Actually I do," answered Todd, "Some remarkable things! Wait a minute."

He turned over the pages. Then he pointed at a drawing.

"Here we have a typical example of minion art again. And it is very remarkable that we see the same art in all the modern palaces of the fortunate families." He pointed to the ceiling. "You can see it in the Man palace as well. And right here in this room..."

The drawing showed monsters, creatures and humans standing on each other's shoulders.

"I already gave an explanation about this. One big family. Passing on all their information. Take a good look at it, Cathy. Some of the creatures show their back."

"And what's so special about that?"

"Don't you see the folded wings on their back?"

"Well, yes..., I have seen winged figures of cast iron as well. What are you trying to tell me?"

"What do you think of when you see winged creatures?"

"Birds?" asked Cathy knowing as she said it that it was not the answer. "Vampires? Harpies?" Then she knew. "Angels," she said.

"Right. Angels. There are many kinds of angels. There are different stages. You start here, on the ground." He pointed at the first circle of minions on the drawing standing with their feet in the grass. "The common angels, the well-known messengers. They might be guardian angels. The creatures standing on the shoulders of the angels are figuratively and literally in a higher position. So this could be the so called Powers, angels with many talents. They carry the Thrones on their shoulders, and the Thrones carry the Archangels. And the Archangels, in their turn, carry the Principalities--important guardian angels they are. The principalities carry the Minions..."

"The minions? Are you sure?"

"All I do is make the ranks complete. The Minons carry the Virtues then you see the Cherubins and on top stand the Seraphim. The Seraphim are of the highest order."

Suddenly he started to laugh.

"Don't you look as if you see ghosts, Cathy. This is all the product of very creative thinkers and artists from the past. I must admit that all these creatures don't look nice or friendly. Maybe they are not good guardian angels at all. Imagine..., they might as well be fallen angels. Who can tell? Maybe one of the creatures on top is Lucifer... the devil himself..., for we see how the minions reach to the sky. There are more than nine ranks; they go up and up, and so they bring the devil to heaven, to make war."

Cathy gasped for breath.

Angels. A thousand thoughts came up in her mind. Angels! Fallen angels! Evil creatures of the worst kind. Todd turned the page. She began to feel sick when she saw the jester's head on a stake. There was no mistaking; it was Oscar's face!

Somewhere in the library a door was slammed shut.

"Dawson!" a harsh voice sounded. "Where are you? And who's there with you? Todd Dawson!"

"It's Kenneth Mayfield, Ferdinand's minion," muttered Todd in surprise. "What is he doing here? Wait for me, Cathy, I will be back in a while."

He ran away on his short legs. Cathy picked up the book and left the room. She listened to the fast footsteps of Todd and then went into the opposite direction herself. She tried to make as few sounds as possible. The paths between the bookshelves seemed to be endless.

She heard the same voice again but this time not so far away from her:

"Then where is she? Where is she?"

Todd's voice was too soft to hear what he answered.

Cathy reached a wall and searched for the door of an elevator. She found it between two high bookcases. The door slid open.

Please, she thought, *oh please, let Joanna's code work!*

She touched the black knob with her thumb, and her fingers slid over the keys. The door closed without a sound; the lift came into movement. Perspiring with fear, she stepped out a few moments later, ran through the arriving hall to the platforms. The Bull steamed up, still slowly enough to catch it, but the doors were closed. The end of the platform came in sight. In one of the carriages, a man was standing at the window. She recognized him. She waved at him with her left hand while she pressed the book tightly under her left arm. The man seemed to recognize her as well and opened the window. He had to put a hand on his cylindrical hat when he popped out his head.

"Cathy... Oscar Man's girlfriend..."

"Help me! Let me in!" shouted Cathy.

The man moved quickly.

He ran to the door and opened it. Just before Cathy would fall down at the end of the platform, he lifted her up and pulled her inside. It was only then that Cathy knew where she had seen this man before: in Fenrir City where he had been one of the witnesses in the lawsuit against Oscar. It was Orville Hood the stationmaster.

The train gained speed. Orville plumped down on a soft bench.

"Isn't that an odd coincidence," he sighed. "I just went up and down to the palace on a practice run, and who is my only co-passenger all of a sudden? Oscar's lady."

"His wife, soon, I hope," said Cathy. "If you see to it that I can leave the station unnoticed in a little while, Oscar will reward you handsomely. Believe me, it is a matter of life and death."

Orville gave a short nod.

"At your service, Mrs. Man, at your service!"

* * *

The three generals had taken off their uniform jackets. They sat at a long table in a room on a secret army base somewhere in the state of New York. Despite the throbbing air conditioning, they were all sweating. For three long days, they had listened to the meaning of countless experts who had read the quickly made translation of Cathy's incredible discovery.

All kinds of learned men and women had stood in front of them, spouting their opinions: psychologists, psychiatrists, priests well-versed in Scripture, historians, philosophers, occultists, decode experts, connoisseurs of the secret languages and pictures of alchemists and many, many others. The final result had been predictable; after the final orator had left the room, they were none the wiser.

"Damn! Damn!" shouted Alvin Hodgkinson slamming both fists on the table top. "What a waste of time!"

He looked behind him; Oscar, Cathy and Falcon sat in a dark corner and had heard every word of every speaker.

"Please, who of you will explain it one more time? You seem to be the only ones who are able to come up with some understandable ideas. Come sit down with us; take as much coffee as you want and talk, talk, talk."

It was Oscar who took the word as soon as he had taken place in front of the generals.

"Alvin is right. You wasted your time. You listened to people who know nothing of the entire situation. Allow Cathy to explain things one more time. She has read the translations over and over again and has studied the drawings as long as she was able to keep her eyes open. Cathy, please, tell them what you know, what you think, and after you, Falcon will put in a word as well."

Cathy nodded.

"All right. One more time then, as Oscar said. It was Todd Dawson who drew my attention to the folded wings of creatures in the minion art. Minions standing on each others shoulders are a symbol for passing through information from one generation to the other.

"But there is this another explanation; they could be angels. Starting from the ground up are the common angels. Then we see Powers, Thrones, Archangels, Principalities, Minions, Virtues, Cherubim, Seraphim. At least, that is what Todd was thinking in his innocence. Just by coincidence, he came up with evil angels, with Lucifer the devil... If he only knew how right he was! We are dealing with the dark side of angels. Oh yes, my dear generals, I can still see the disbelief in your eyes.

"Go out in the streets of any city and interview passengers at random. Ask them one simple question: 'Do you believe in angels and have you ever had to deal with one?' You will be astonished by the results! Thousands and thousands, no, millions of people all over the world will tell you about how something bad turned out into something good thanks to the help of a guardian angel. Check it and you will know it. Ask the same people if they have actually seen an angel, and most of them will claim they did. There are good angels, and there are bad angels. Our minions are bad angels. And they are so clever! You never know what is true where they are concerned; you can give a double meaning to all they do. Double! A perfect word for their way of acting.

Their art is one good example. Standing on each other's shoulder; passing through information or reaching the highest order of dark angel knowledge? Who can tell? They double-cross; they are double dealers; they practice double talk. They are the doubles of the rich, the famous, the elite. They act like the puppets of their patrons, but it is they who are pulling the strings. Angels. Falling angels. Servants of

Satan, devils! Angel: the word comes from the Latin *angelus*, which means no more than *messenger*.

"But the message these minions give us is not exactly friendly. What they say, generals, is this: 'We are heavenly creatures, standing high above men. Our goal is to rule the earth. After we have succeeded to suppress all mortals, we will be promoted. We will climb up the shoulders of others and raise above the status of minions, with only Satan above us.' For many a thousand years people have had to deal with angels and still no one can explain who they are, messengers of God, messengers of the Devil.

"Good angels, fallen angels. Try to catch one and you will be no more. I know Algernon Sparks tried to do that, and we all know only too well what happened to him."

The generals nodded.

Cathy looked at Falcon.

Falcon rose to his feet and gestured to Cathy who returned to her chair.

"What Cathy said is right," he said standing in front of the table. "The book she brought with her from the palace of the Man family tells it all. I don't think all angels are creatures of flesh and blood. But the minions are! They are evil in the flesh, take it from me! Lucifer keeps a close eye on them. The Devil himself is their leader. Jean Galliou writes about them; he has seen minions; he has been with them on the path of destruction. Study the translation of the book and you will know that he met them.

"They are here; they have always been here. Forsaken by God, bound to the Devil! You will find no guardian angels among them; they do not know what mercy is or how it feels to do good. We have seen drawings of the jester, looking very much like Oscar, who defeats them. We also saw drawings of a cruelly murdered jester. Also with a face like Oscar's. A smiling jester or a beaten jester. That is what it is all about, gentlemen. Cathy has made an incredible discovery, and now we finally know what minions are: black angels on their way to devilish victory. They fell down from heaven or came straight out of hell. Again, double possibilities. But it does not matter whether they came to us from above or from below. Fact is that they are here and that they are ready to strike. The only one who is able to help us is Oscar Man. Take that for a fact.

"That is all I can tell you about it. Make a thorough study of that book, and concentrate on the symbols in the drawings--not for the present, but for the time to come. Other generations will be only too grateful when they know how to defend themselves when minions come back in the form of creatures who have almost the powers of the Devil himself. And come back they will. We can be sure of that. We ourselves have to concentrate on Faron Hayes and the minions that are with him."

He sat down again. Now the generals looked at Oscar.

"Cathy is right," said Oscar. "Falcon is right. And I will do my utmost to help every man and woman on this earth."

Dean Howe raised his hands and looked up at the high ceiling.

"But the army can't fight the Devil's henchmen!" he sighed. "I... I don't know what to do any more." He turned to Oscar, helpless, beseeching.

It was general Scott James who expressed his feelings in a way everyone

could understand. He covered his face with his hands and cried out:

"O, God, have mercy!"

* * *

The greatest team ever comprised of a businessman and a minion was the headstrong founder of Cabo de Barra Joseph Krocht and his minion Marcus Hayes. During the entire time that they worked together, no one ever suspected that the minion was the brains behind the duo. Marcus Hayes had always remained in the background and during any public occasions was seen only as the faithful follower and imitator of Joseph Krocht.

With his acumen for business, his inventiveness and perseverance, Krocht's leading role was simply a matter of fate. With all he had going for him, he was predestined to become a tycoon. He was so headstrong and conceited that he would never have admitted to anyone that his best ideas were usually the result of in-depth conversations with his minion Marcus, who was actually the person that led Krocht to the realization of his ambitious dreams. Joseph Krocht, the great innovator, took over the helm of his world and never once looked back to see—nor did he care—if any followed him on his wondrous course. Although he was entirely under the spell of his minion without ever once realizing it, he always kept the upper hand over everyone, except Marcus Hayes. Joseph paved the way for his son Walter, the imperator, the emperor of Georgia. Marcus, in turn, knew that he too would be replaced after his own death—by his son, the next generation of Krocht minion Faron Hayes.

The multinationals reached previously unknown heights of perfection. The tycoons were all powerful; they were the rulers of business and government, and behind them all stood the minions, pulling the strings.

Chaos and decadence went hand in hand. The show changed constantly: one day the street would be full of seething, joyous crowds dressed in a myriad of colors and the following day would be a boring, drab affair. What was imposing and refined one day was of no interest at all the next. The tycoons allowed themselves to be led like cattle through the hypnotic atmosphere the minions had created. And they were happy—they were kings! Cabo de Barra got its imperator when Joseph Krocht exchanged his three-cornered hat for the crown he placed on his own head, and then made the title hereditary, guaranteeing that his son would ascend the throne after him.

Meanwhile, his minion had begun a project that would, in time, become the greatest piece of art of all time. Krocht naturally believed it was his own plan and became entirely consumed and so enthusiastic about it that he collaborated on it tirelessly and invested a fabulous fortune. He was convinced that he was busy with the realization of his own dream while in reality he was building on the foundation laid by Marcus Hayes.

Under the command of forty engineers and twenty architects, an enormous army of workers descended on the harbor of a Norwegian fjord. The specialists and technicians came from America, England and the Netherlands and shared a common passion for navigation; specifically, they were enamored with the bygone days of the proud, imposing steamships that had sailed the oceans at the beginning of the twentieth century. So, in the fjord, on the orders of Cabo de Barra, a magnificent ocean steamer was built.

No information about it was ever made public; anyone who was interested had to guess at the total weight of the colossus, as well as its draught and speed. It was said that the *Njord,* as the ship was christened, had a weight of more than thirty-five thousand tons, a draught of thirty-five feet, a height (from keel to top deck) of sixty feet and could reach a speed of more than twenty-five knots. Its length was eight hundred and twenty feet, and it measured eighty-two feet at its widest point. There were nine decks, all made of steel, which could house a crew of one thousand sailors and three thousand passengers—a colossus indeed!

The ship was named for an old Scandinavian god, the ruler of the seas and storms and the protector of all ships. This ship that bore his name was of a style, luxury and grandeur that would have astonished and pleased even the gods themselves.

But alas, even though the *Njord* was an extraordinary work of art, it was a minion work of art, which meant that it was far from a perfect replica of an ocean steamer from the past. Minion art was close to what humans might conceive of and bring forth by their own hands, but it was always bloodcurdling. The basis and stencil of their fantasy never actually caught the spirit or flavor of what once was. The illusions minions created always seemed to have different meanings to everyone who saw them.

In that way, the *Njord,* with its deep black hull, light brown superstructure and three gigantic black smoke stacks adorned with orange stripes, appeared to many people like a Samson sigh—a ship that attempted to show, one final time, the strength generated by an almost forgotten technology. To others it was a piece of art that had to be seen from the inside because the staterooms, staircases and gangways were designed and decorated by architects who had also lent their hands to the construction of the tycoon's palaces. And then there were the gigantic pistons and engines that drove the outer screws and the turbines that brought the mighty central propeller shaft into motion. The designers had opted for steam power created by burning coal, so there was no use for oil or gas. This antiquated method of powering the vessel meant that countless teams of firemen were forced to work themselves into a dripping sweat as they threw tons and tons of coal into outdated stokeholes, behind which lay a blazing, roaring hell.

The interior of the *Njord* was breathtakingly beautiful. There were luxurious staterooms and spacious suites. There were swimming pools, ballrooms, many different dining rooms, bars, shops, cafes, and even covered gardens. The walls were paneled with valuable wood from around the world, and even the staircases were works of art. There were statues everywhere, and the ceilings and floors were lavishly carpeted and decorated.

This, then, was the proud and mighty ship upon which Joseph Krocht had sailed the oceans of the world. From his opulent stateroom, he had conquered the world with his businesses. His son Walter, on inheriting the ship, left everything just as his father had kept it, as a display of his affection and respect for his father. Now, however, the *Njord,* the pride of Cabo de Barra, was owned by the new tycoon who had taken over the crown of the imperator—the mighty minion Faron Hayes.

It was said that many secrets were hidden under the decks of the steamer. Behind antique sliding panels could be found the most modern equipment, just as in homes and offices. There were also persistent rumors about the use of strange, new, unusual technologies in use, although nobody had any details as to what these were. Between the decks, millions of yards of copper wire had been wound, and there was speculation as to the presence of mysterious and incredibly powerful magnetic fields. But since the use of such a thing was completely incomprehensible to anyone, no credibility was attached to these rumors.

Anyone who had ever been a guest on the *Njord* agreed that no more beautiful or imposing piece of art existed anywhere. It was considered to be the pinnacle of human shipbuilding ingenuity, a vessel in which technical ability and art had come together in the perfect symbiotic relationship.

An enormous crowd of spectators had gathered to witness this seagoing palace when it entered New York's lower bay and dropped anchor off the coast of Brooklyn. It had docked away from the pier to keep the more inquisitive onlookers from getting too close. Regardless of their precautions, however, hundreds of pleasure craft of all sizes, filled with people who wanted a closer look, swarmed around the giant ship, waving and cheering--some of them actually close enough for the people aboard to bang on the hull with their hands. Someone on board one of the smaller vessels began to clap his hands in excitement and appreciation of this wondrous vessel, as only other nautical enthusiasts are wont to do. Gradually, all the other visitors took up this tribute, and it continued until the *Njord* responded with a roar from its foghorn that was heard halfway across the borough of Brooklyn.

From the decks of the smaller vessels, everyone looked up along the hull, which rose over twenty feet above the surface of the water and at the light brown superstructure that glimmered in the sun. Small clouds of smoke rose slowly from the tall smokestacks and dissolved in the windless sky.

The *Njord* appeared to be a phantom ship, much like the fabled *Flying Dutchman*: except for the rising smoke and the sound of the ship's horns, there was no sign of life. There was no one on deck leaning over the railings to return the welcome, which seemed especially odd since it was common knowledge that the ship carried many of the leaders of the international corporations.

The *Njord* had been in Europe and had left the port of Rotterdam, Holland, with the tycoons and minions of Dis Pater and Exergue Pertenaires on board. Also on board—besides the usual occupants, Faron Hayes and the staff of Cabo de Barra—were the ranking members of Richthausen Gold, Fenrir International, Syrinx Colorado, Hygnos Hybrid Corporation, Fortuna Fund and Eleventh Emirate, who were taking advantage of this voyage together to exchange views on the quickly changing state of affairs in the world. Now docked in New York, they awaited the arrival of the delegations from Man-Mandate Enterprises, the representatives of Pilgrims Palladium and Prince Oscar Man.

Oscar arrived by helicopter with the smallest of the delegations, for he was accompanied only by Cathy Wheeler and Tony Falcon. The small chopper easily landed on the upper deck and immediately took off again after the three passengers had stepped out. A luxury yacht ferried the representatives of Pilgrims Palladium to the *Njord*, winding its way between the smaller craft in the water.

Queen Lillian DiCampo boarded followed by her minion. They both wore long red coats with white collars, and their gray hair was tied back under their golden crowns. Sven Enlart and his minion Gene Fletcher followed, and behind them came other tycoons, joined by men and women of their royal households and security services.

The Man family entourage arrived from the palace in an enormous zeppelin. The day, being beautiful and calm, allowed the pilot to bring the huge dirigible right above the steamer, floating up toward the foredeck. A gondola was lowered on steel cables, and King Ferdinand and his minion Kenneth Mayfield were the first to step out, clothed identically in green hunting suits and both wearing crowns. Jimmy Man leaped out of the cab as it made a sudden upswing and was caught by one of Cabo de Barra's deckhands. His minion Mike Farland remained close to the gondola to assist Johanna and her minion Tana Rowe as they alit. The gondola was then hoisted up and lowered several more times to deliver the remainder of the retinue.

Shortly the *Njord* left the dock, escorted by tugboats, which came alongside to turning the ship and bring it a mile or two farther out on the water. Then she was cast off; the engines of the behemoth began to thump, and the foghorns boomed. As the *Njord* picked up speed, the little ships that followed it danced in its wake.

While the lesser members of the family were escorted by crew members to their cabins and suites to do the unpacking, the royal guests were being welcomed in a plush salon that opened out onto one of the sun-drenched afterdecks. Faron Hayes, with his large stature, short hair and trimmed beard looking for all the world like Walter Krocht's twin brother, wore a seaman's uniform adorned with golden epaulets and a crown. He indeed looked more impressive than Gregor Knudsen captain of the *Njord*, who was a head smaller and wore a much more simple uniform. The new arrivals were warmly greeted by those on board who had already made such a long voyage.

Oscar was quite surprised when Kim La Croix, the woman who had tortured him so during his trial in Fenrir City, walked up to him, shook his hand heartily and bowed. He recalled that she was the minion of Sascha Krocht, Walter's sister.

"I'm so very glad to see you again," she said as if they were long-lost friends, "I have been hearing so many good things about you."

Not knowing what to say to this, Oscar simply smiled at her. Taking his reaction to her entirely the wrong way, she backed away from him, chagrined and bowing, until she had put some distance between them. She then turned and scurried away as quickly as her long, tight dress would allow.

Oscar's second big surprise came when the queen of Pilgrims Palladium Lillian DiCampo came up to introduce herself to him and kissed one of the rings on his right hand.

"Although we lead a secluded life in Portland, my lord, be assured that we are aware of your power."

He had a sneaking suspicion that her words had been suggested to her by her minion, a proud woman with a hard face, whom he saw standing beside her. The minion's long gray hair, pulled back tightly in a ponytail, did not put him off the scent of her identity, though. He had known her briefly when she was many years younger and her hair was blond. Before him stood Laura Langen, the veiled woman who had held his hand in the Swiss churchyard. He felt how she now tried to probe him with her strong mind, finding no opening. The spiritual essence of Prince Oscar remained untouchable to the gathered minions.

"It is very nice to meet you," he said to Queen Lillian and then offered his hand to her minion saying: "Laura Langen. Why, the last time I saw you, I was but a small boy who had to look up to be able to see your face."

"And now, my prince, it is your right to look down on me," she replied softly, slowly withdrawing her hand. Then, bowing with downcast eyes, she returned to her queen's side.

As Captain Knudsen began his welcome speech, Oscar took Cathy by the hand and walked along the deck enjoying the cool breeze in their faces that had suddenly arisen. Oscar was wearing his fox heads and gray boots while Cathy had chosen a dress of gold brocade and a hat with broad brims.

"I feel a strange pressure in my head," said Cathy. "Is it the oppressive atmosphere in there? Or does it have something to with the minions?"

"Both," replied Oscar. "They are depressed, and there is most definitely something in the air. I noticed it too as soon as we came aboard."

They leaned over the railing and gazed down upon the calm water of the Atlantic Ocean.

An invitation from Faron Hayes had gone out to all the international tycoons. Everyone was invited to sail aboard the *Njord* where there were to be grand parties, and meetings would be held to discuss the future of the major corporations in this rapidly changing world. Everyone had arrived with large retinues, and there were more than three thousand guests on board. Hayes had ordered his captain to handpick only the best and most efficient servants and crewmembers. Each of them, from cook to female companion, must see to it that all the guests had a marvelous time. Various entertainment artists were hired to provide music and to put on spectacular stage shows.

Hayes had stressed the fact, when he sent out his invitations, that it was of the utmost importance that these meetings be held in a place where they could not be disturbed by any outside interference.

And everyone had come.

Except for Oscar Man, Cathy Wheeler and Tony Falcon, no one realized that this entire affair had been organized to bring all the minions together. The kings, tycoons and all their assorted followers were of absolutely no interest to Faron Hayes, and he had gone through great pains to make sure that they were mindlessly entertained and diverted during this voyage. It was the minions who were important now.

Oscar was the only outsider who had received an invitation. A messenger from Cabo had come to the penthouse and handed it to him personally so that no one would consider him a part of King Ferdinand's entourage. Tony Falcon had requested to accompany him, and Oscar had agreed, insisting that he wouldn't have it any other way.

It remained a mystery, though, what was going to happen.

Oscar understood only too well that the minions felt more and more driven to the wall. The highly effective actions of President Angus Sebastian had lately caused the internationals to be forced to deal with a growing number of limitations.

Oscar pointed at the horizon where several dark specks were visible.

"See there?" he said. "That is what bothers the minions. They had hoped to achieve dominance over the entire world, no matter how slow the process, but so far they have not been able to accomplish that. They are still forced to accede to another man's edicts, and that man, as far as they know, is Angus Sebastian. Behind us is a naval squadron that will follow this cruise everywhere; they have been unable to take control of the military."

He began to laugh softly, and she looked at him quizzically.

"General Howe is on board one of those ships. He wants to keep a close eye on any developments and insists on being present personally if something important happens. Actually quite brave for a man who claims to get seasick when he steps into his bathtub!"

"Aren't you at all frightened?" Cathy wanted to know. "You have seemed so relaxed all day, continuously joking."

"Falcon is with us," said Oscar looking serious once again. "He is the man who molded Angus Sebastian into the most important man in the world, throwing dust in the eyes of all the royal families, my own included, and corporations all at the same time. The navy is in the neighborhood, Cathy. Everything can begin now. I'm sure that we must be prepared for anything. You know that I came here voluntarily. There's something in the air. Are you afraid? If so, it may have been a better choice to remain at home."

"Honestly? I am afraid," said Cathy. "Of course, I could have stayed home. Nevertheless, I am obligated to witness events firsthand if I am to be your biographer, and I do want to be that—among other things." She smiled into his eyes and continued, "I saw how Kim La Croix and the minion of Lillian DiCampo bowed to you. How do you explain that?"

"I haven't the faintest idea. By the way, I recognized the minion of Lillian. She tried to probe my mind when I was a child. If she had found out then that I possessed special talents without being a genuine, merciless minion, that I was not a cherished murderer in the making, she probably would have taken me to a deserted spot and broken my neck personally. You ask me if I can explain her behavior, and I must honestly tell you that I cannot."

"The woman from Switzerland you told me about?"

Faron Hayes came on deck with a tray full of glasses.

"Prince Oscar!" he cried. "I see that you have chosen the sun and the sea air over the dull speech of our captain. Let us have a drink!"

He held out the tray to offer them a glass and then, after taking one himself, handed it to a footman to remove. He raised his glass, looked at Oscar and asked, "To what shall we drink, Prince?"

His mouth widened sardonically between the bristly hair of his moustache and beard without actually becoming a real smile.

Oscar remembered the minion Mike Farland asking him the same question in the palace. He nodded in the direction of the approaching naval vessels, which had come a deal closer.

"To the winner of the race?" he said.

"Ah!" exclaimed Hayes glancing at the squadron. "It's not much of a race, now, is it? The *Njord* can do twenty-five knots. Those frigates wouldn't have the slightest difficulty beating that."

"I meant it in a more symbolic way," said Oscar. "A competition for power between the system they represent and the minions."

Faron Hayes emptied his glass in one gulp and threw it overboard. He nodded slowly, his eyes fixed on the spot where the glass had disappeared.

"Believe me, Prince Oscar, you are the last one I would argue with. The last one I would want to make angry. You know better than anyone what is going on."

"Is that so?" asked Oscar.

He looked through the open doors to the bustle in the salon, and thought it strange that no one else was coming out on deck.

"Yes, that is so, Prince," said Hayes. "Inside of you slumbers a knowledge, a power, which must be unprecedentedly great. We all know it. A battle between two minions can last for days, sometimes even weeks. It is like sword fighting with the mind, and every minion knows the game of thrust and parry, strike and withdraw, of dealing out sensitive pricks, ripostes and challenges and all the while saving his breath and waiting for the chance to deliver the death blow! You did something other minions have never been able to do: you went mind to mind with three minions and came out as the victor after only a brief battle--Kenneth Mayfield, Mike Farland, Tana Rowe. Trust me, Prince Oscar, you are the most important guest on board the *Njord*."

Cautiously, he laid one of his huge hands on Oscar's shoulder.

"Let's go for a walk on the deck past the salon. We'll head toward the bridge, which is on the same level." He turned to Cathy and said, "Won't you come with us? In our eyes, Prince Oscar's girlfriend is indeed a true princess."

With his hand still on Oscar's shoulder, he nonchalantly pushed Oscar along.

They crossed the deck, coming to a narrower part that lead past the salon and cabins. On the outside of the railing hung the big lifeboats, and when they looked up, they could see the imposing funnels that blew out blackish-gray smoke.

Faron Hayes stood still for a bit, tapping the toe of his right foot on the metal of the deck.

"Here, under our feet, the dream of my father Marcus Hayes lives on, a dream he shared with Joseph Krocht. Do you feel that light trembling? That is all that we feel of the colossal powers of the engines. The *Njord* is a tribute to the ocean steamers of old, and it is— as everyone knows—also one of the present wonders of the world. You will agree with me after you have taken a walk through the inside of the *Njord*. My father and the elder Krocht must have stood on the bridge together often, and as they looked out over the endless sea, they undoubtedly felt very proud. They loved to be at sea. Here, on board the *Njord*, they discussed all their business plans. Do you know, Prince, what the first, real multinational corporation was?"

"No," replied Oscar shortly.

"The Dutch East India Company," said Hayes. "A Dutch trading company. Founded in 1602; a hundred years later they had a fleet consisting of hundreds of ships and had thousands of permanent employees. They had business dealings all over the world—Indonesia, India, China, Japan, the Caribbean, North America, South America, just to name a few places where they traded. Imagine all those wooden ships, spread across the oceans of the world like tiny vulnerable islands. And on board all those vessels, no matter how far from home, the rigid laws of the company were always enforced; there was no escape from that! Marcus Hayes and Joseph Krocht dreamed of such an imperial realm and actually built it together. They succeeded in their mission, and perhaps the reason they spent so much of their lives at sea was to express their commitment to the memory of that great commercial enterprise from the past."

Now a real smile appeared on his face.

"But their dream did not realize itself as a sailing ship. It became the *Njord,* a veritable wonder of the modern world, on the construction of which neither time nor money was spared. And now it belongs to me! I have the papers to prove that I am the sole and rightful owner."

He stood still with his face inches from Oscar's and looking him right in the eye said, "My signature under a few simple lines, Prince, and the *Njord* is yours. I could arrange it this very day."

Cathy was still thinking over what Hayes had related regarding the Dutch East India Company, about which she herself was quite knowledgeable. As they walked along the deck, she had the opportunity to realize just how enormous the ship really was. All those thoughts, however, disappeared instantly when she heard what the minion was now proposing.

She stood there shocked, not understanding why Oscar did not seem surprised. The largest art treasure in the world had just been offered to him, and he hadn't moved a muscle in his face. In fact, he showed no reaction at all! The value of the *Njord* was incalculable. What had possessed Hayes to even make such a proposal? She began walking again and caught up with the men who strolled along the railing with their hands behind their backs.

They entered the ship's bridge through a steel door. The bridge, as might be expected, was an enormous affair. The front was comprised of twenty rectangular windows and covered the full width of the ship. Various pieces of equipment were placed in cabinets that looked very much like museum showcases and that could be sealed with panels of frosted glass. The first officer was on duty, and near the windows sat a few uniformed men in big leather swivel chairs. Between each pair of windows stood a statue, one of which one was the symbol of Cabo de Barra the sailor who stood with his feet in the water. Cathy was the last one to enter, and she closed the door behind her. No one seemed to notice them, and the officer did not even greet the minion.

Suddenly, Faron Hayes turned toward Oscar and looked at him with the eyes of a madman, his face twisted with anger. His lips parted, and from his throat came an unreal hissing sound. His forehead and cheeks became red, and the veins in his neck looked as if they might explode. He put his hands around Oscar's neck and began shaking him furiously.

"Damn it, man, I'm offering you a fortune!" he hissed. "No ruler at any time in history was ever offered something of such value. Is it not enough? Do you want more? Well, do not worry, you will get more. Don't make it hard on us, Prince Oscar Man!"

His lips kept moving without forming real words. All that escaped his mouth were terrifying, guttural sounds, and his eyes had become huge.

Oscar had remained standing there calmly, but now, as he stared at Hayes with a piercing look, something in the atmosphere of the room began to change. The first officer and crew still had not looked up from their duties, even though a multicolored, flaming energy now crackled all around them. A radiation of the same kind danced around the statues near the windows. Cathy felt the floor shake under her feet, and it seemed to spread throughout the entire ship. Outside, the sun was shining brightly in a steel blue sky, and the sea was calm. Faron Hayes was furious now. He was still holding onto Oscar and emitting those awful demonic sounds. Then, suddenly, he pulled his hands back as if he had burned them and fell down upon his knees. The energy dissipated, and Cathy no longer felt as if everything around her was burning and moving.

"I am so sorry, Prince," said Hayes meekly. "I should never have let myself lose control like that. I beg of you, please forgive my aggressive behavior."

"We won't discuss it any further," said Oscar lightly as if he had not almost been strangled by this big, strong man.

Hayes slowly rose to his feet and said, "Thank you for your understanding. Early tomorrow morning there will be a meeting, and we will be by ourselves. Do you understand what I mean? The minions will make an important decision then. Now I must get back to my guests. Do me a favor, Prince. Take Cathy for a walk throughout the ship, look around. You are free to go anywhere you please. This ship, which will soon be yours, has no doors that shall remain closed to you. Dinner tonight will be served in the grand salon, but if you choose not join us that is fine. Any servant of Cabo de Barra will gladly show you there, if need be. If I do not see you anymore tonight, I wish you a good night. Tomorrow morning we will meet again."

After bowing deeply, he walked out the door and disappeared. As soon as he was gone, Cathy ran to Oscar and gently slid her trembling fingers over his neck.

"Did he hurt you?"

"Hardly," said Oscar. "Come, let's go to our suite and calm you down a little. Later on this evening, we will have a look around the ship and take Falcon with us."

As they walked over to the door through which they had entered, Oscar tapped a man who was leaning back in his chair staring at the control panels in front of him on the shoulder. He did not react to Oscar's touch.

"The power of the minions," he said. "The first officer and his men don't even know that we are here."

"They are acting so strangely," remarked Cathy. "I have not heard them talk to each other, and they have hardly moved at all, besides an occasional slight motion of a head or hand."

"That will all change as soon as we've left the room," said Oscar. "Just watch."

They went out to the side deck and looked back through a window. The officer started to talk to someone, and another man stood up and took something from a cupboard. He said something to his companions, and they all burst out laughing.

"I assume that you understand more of this," said Cathy. "So—they are under the influence of the minions?"

"Yes, that of Faron Hayes, just as my brothers and sister exist under the mental pressure of their minions. That is the minion method of manipulating people. I know that Faron Hayes would love to put you under his mental pressure, also, to be able to learn more about me, but he wouldn't even think about trying it."

"Why not?"

"Because he is afraid of me."

"He made you such a phenomenal proposal. The ship could be all yours, and you didn't react to it at all."

"I shielded myself; I did not allow my emotions or feelings to show."

"But will you agree to it later? I mean, would you like to become the new owner of the *Njord*? And do you have any idea what he will ask for in return? No doubt he will want something."

"Tonight, ladies and gentlemen, Faron Hayes as the devil and Oscar Man as the naive man who sells his soul to him," quipped Oscar. "Are you thinking about a play that goes something like that?"

Cathy held her tongue. She felt that she would not, and could not, get through to the man she loved. At this moment, Oscar had completely shielded himself and would not bare his feelings to her the way she was used to. She had no choice but to accept that, understanding that much was going on that she knew nothing about.

Oscar picked a door at random, and they entered a small room with a wooden floor and wooden walls. Along the ceiling were the carved heads of monsters with human features. A broad staircase led up to a larger room, and another led down. They went downstairs, and Oscar addressed a man in a black uniform with the symbol of Cabo de Barra on his chest.

"I am Prince Oscar Man," said Oscar authoritatively. "Show me the way to my suite."

"Of course, my lord," said the man, bowing slightly. "Will you please be so kind as to follow me?"

Cathy held on tight to Oscar's hand. She wanted desperately to say something about the terrifying behavior of Hayes on the bridge, but she remained silent, walking at the side of her prince and experienced the beauty of the ship and all the special art treasures of the minions.

Once they were in their suite, Oscar sent for Falcon immediately and told him about the behavior of Faron Hayes and about the meeting that was set for the next morning.

"I will come with you," said Falcon decidedly.

"I think only those invited will be admitted."

"Well then, I will make myself known. As soon as they understand that I am part minion, like you, they will have to accept my presence. Believe me, Oscar, I have to stay close to you. You must prepare yourself for a hard fight."

"Do you have any idea what they want?"

"It's fairly obvious. They feel as if they have been backed into a corner. Now they have been forced to acknowledge your superiority, and that is how they want to accept you."

"Can you be a bit more specific?"

"They see in you their liberator, or their leader. If you can show them the path to the top, the ship will be a very reasonable price to pay."

"What am I supposed to do, Falcon?"

Falcon looked at him for a moment. Oscar could never get used to the look in those mysterious eyes. His face showed resoluteness now.

"You turn down all their proposals," he said.

Oscar nodded, and the conversation was done.

He had a dinner for three set up in one of the rooms of his suite. Afterward, they went, as Hayes had suggested, for a walk through the ship. It struck them that no one paid any attention to them, as if they were invisible. They walked past crewmen, guards and servants without any of them reacting to their presence. Only the one time when they met a minion were they greeted in a friendly way. It was Gene Fletcher of Pilgrims Palladium, and even he stopped and bowed to Oscar.

Falcon walked in front and opened the doors everywhere they went. Cathy and Oscar walked behind him hand in hand, staring at everything.

As in the Man palace, not a room, hall or corridor was like any other. The staterooms, salons and halls were all different in size, layout and furnishings. In a ballroom large enough to hold more than five hundred people, a small string orchestra played. The minions, tycoons and other guests had enjoyed an extensive dinner and then come here to talk, drink and dance. Oscar looked in and saw Ferdinand, Jimmy and Johanna Man walking through the room, accompanied, naturally, by their minions.

Faron Hayes, however, was not there. Much to their surprise, when they did see him, it was in the bowels of the ship. They had gone all the way down to see firsthand the huge stokeholes where the coal was fed into the furnaces, where sweating, panting men ran back and forth with heavy wheelbarrows full of fuel to feed the behemoth. The trimmers stood constantly at the ready to fill the wheelbarrows again. It was the firemen, though, who had to throw the red-hot coals from the furnace plates into the fire holes. The current shift was on a break, and the men were leaning against a wall as they tried to catch their breath. Their bare chests were shining from the sweat, and as they rested, Faron Hayes was doing the work all by himself. He was wildly shoveling up the coals so intensely that sparks flew about, and then he flung them into the hole. No one dared come close to him. Only when he had turned around to the stokehole behind which the fire was roaring, to feed the ever-hungry flames with new, red-hot coals, did the men have the courage to approach in order to remove the incombustible cinders from the plates. The heat in the boiler room was unbearable, but it did not deter Hayes from wielding the enormous shovel with unabated energy.

"Let us take over again," cried a fireman suddenly. "You've been working the hole too long now."

Hayes stopped for a moment, the sweat dripping and gleaming off his beard. His huge, bare, upper body was soaking wet, and the veins on his arms were swollen blue tracks that contrasted sharply against his shining white skin. He emitted a short roar, shook his head so fiercely that drops of sweat splattered around and then continued working with renewed energy.

"Get away from here," panted Falcon. "You won't be able to stand it!"

They left the boiler room, and when they had returned to the deck above it, they felt the ship tremble from the awesome power of the engines.

"Faron Hayes," said Cathy softly. "One of the most important men in the world and perhaps the richest. Why would he be exhausting himself in that hell? Everything I have seen here is so strange. The strangest, however, is that I am no longer afraid."

"We can imagine many different reasons for Hayes's behavior," said Oscar as they walked through one of the lower decks. The deck was lined with statues of half-human male and female monsters. The creatures on either side held their arms above their heads and supported on their hands the curved arch of the metal ceiling.

"We can speculate that he enjoys keeping his ship at top speed by doing the work of twenty men, or perhaps it is his idea of a workout, and this is how he stays in shape. Or perhaps he's trying to wear himself out so that he can get a good night's sleep. But we both know better, don't we, Falcon?"

"He is frustrated," replied Falcon. "He's at his wit's end."

"Exactly," said Oscar. "And, Cathy, I can also explain why your feelings of fear have been so greatly diminished. An outside power is making all this much easier for you."

"The minions?" she asked surprised.

"No. Mine. I'm keeping an eye on you to make sure that you don't panic. You say that you want to put everything down on paper later. Well, I'm giving you the opportunity to get a realistic view of all that may transpire."

When Cathy and Oscar returned to their suite after roaming around the ship for more than an hour, they hadn't even seen a quarter of it. Falcon had gone back to his own stateroom; he wanted to turn in early.

"There will be some intense arguments tomorrow," he had said. "When you refuse to accept their proposals, Oscar, they'll probably sail into the nearest harbor and put an abrupt end to their hospitality."

After Cathy had gone to sleep, Oscar left their suite. He returned to the big ballroom and opened one of the doors. It was still alive with the bustle of the party. Most of the guests were dancing, and no one paid any attention to him when he walked in. His half sister Johanna spun around him in the arms of Sven Enlart, the tycoon from Pilgrims Palladium.

Ferdinand Man paced up and down with his hands behind his back, followed by a number of ladies from his court and Hugh Willis, one of Man-Mandate Enterprises most wealthy stockholders. Jimmy Man was dancing with Margaret Sharpe, whom Oscar had not realized was even on board. He noticed that the minions had left the room.

Just as he had taken Cathy's fear away using the power of his mind, the minions held their guests firmly in their grip and saw to it that they were having a good time and would remember later on that their stay on board the *Njord* had been wonderful. Oscar made his way through the crush of revelers who were dancing, doing cartwheels and turning somersaults. He walked over to a table and filled a sterling silver goblet with wine. He could feel the mental strength of the minions. Their collective power had taken possession of the entire ship, and it was perceptible from the biggest down to the smallest room, manifesting itself on all the decks and penetrating every rivet.

But Oscar did not fear that power.

He leisurely emptied the silver chalice and calmly strolled out of the ballroom. It was time for him, too, to get to bed. He wanted to feel well-rested when he woke up in the morning.

He returned to his suite, playing with the idea of being the new owner of the *Njord*.

Slowly, he shook his head.

He already thought his penthouse in New York City was too big.

Chapter Thirteen

Battle

It seemed to be just another day for the crews aboard the naval vessels. The frigates followed the giant *Njord* from a respectable distance across the calm sea. The sun shone down on the water and played a game with its radiant beams behind the *Njord* where it made the foaming backwash sparkle. Everyone assumed that the minions and their guests would stop at some European harbor before making the return trip to America. Never before had so many important people been gathered on board one ship.

What should have been an exercise in harassment and flexing of military might, as Tony Falcon had advised and General Dean Howe had requested, was not that at all. What was happening here was comparable to a school of herrings chasing a whale.

Howe had breakfast with Admiral Irvin Hernandez a man who carefully wiped his imposing moustache after every bite or drink and frequently used his fork to emphasize his words. He explained, in detail, how much money he asked for each year from the government and how he intended to spend it modernizing the fleet. The general listened with half an ear and wished he was somewhere far away from here, on firm ground where he could see more than gray painted steel in a gray sea.

After breakfast he went up to take a look on the bridge of the frigate. Staring at the high bow in front of him, he wondered if it was as quiet on board the *Njord* as it was here.

He would sacrifice anything to be able to look through the ship's plating and see what the minions and tycoons were up to.

On the *Njord,* breakfast was also being served. There were two gigantic dining rooms on board; the tycoons had gathered in the most luxurious of the two and cheerfully discussed last night's party, which had lasted until late in the evening. Cathy Wheeler was also present and was seated with the Man family. She was sitting between Johanna Man and Margaret Sharpe and feeling totally at ease. There was a carefree atmosphere in the dining saloon.

As if she had known Cathy for a long time, Margaret, whose eyes had a dreamy glaze to them, leaned over to her and said, "This is all so exciting. In just a short while, we'll all be sitting in a beautiful theater. We are to be treated to a grand spectacle! Even the people of Fenrir International have to admit, although reluctantly, that the various artists who are to perform for us prefer the ship over Las Vegas."

"The acoustic qualities of the *Njord*'s theater are said to be quite unique," Johanna chimed in. "Everyone says that there is nowhere else where a choir can perform not only extraordinarily as a whole, but each individual voice be can distinguished."

Cathy nodded, smiled and felt happy. Nobody seemed to think it odd or wonder about the fact that they were going to the theater right after breakfast. There was something in the air, a hardly perceptible buzzing. Everyone in the room was talking in an undertone. No voices were raised, and any laughter was done in a hushed refined manner, although there was an overall atmosphere of modest mirth in the room. The royalty discussed art and poetry, and none of the tycoons talked about business, as they usually did. The servants made their ways silently across the room delivering food to the tables as if they were floating above the thick, red carpet.

After they had finished their meal, the entire company stood and headed toward the exits. Guards in the employ of the different companies now joined them, and everyone was escorted to the theater by the ship's stewards. Once inside, everyone settled into luxurious leather armchairs.

From within this room, the outside world was not visible, and the sea was so calm that the assembled company seemed to forget that they were even on a ship.

The remaining guards stayed in their cabins, and the ship's crew also relaxed, waiting in the kitchens, resting in their cabins or sitting silently by the swimming pools. Only in the boiler room did the ship's work continue as the crew below sweated and slaved to keep the *Njord* up to speed.

While all this was going on, the minions had gathered in Faron Hayes's suite. There they sat on wooden chairs along the walls. With drawn, serious faces they waited in silence for the arrival of Oscar Man, their eyes focused on the door that led to the reception hall.

At long last the door opened, and Oscar Man, dressed in gray with gold trim, entered, followed by Tony Falcon. The door closed behind them. Oscar and his companion remained standing. On his way to this meeting, as Oscar had walked through the ship, he had felt the peculiar atmosphere that was all around as a tingling on his skin and a pressure on his brain.

The *Njord* was a world in itself, a speck on the endless waters, the autonomous territory of the minions who had combined their powers to impose their will on all the others present.

"I suppose you expected me to come alone," said Oscar in a clear, untrembling voice. "But I have brought my good friend Tony Falcon with me, and it is my wish that he stay."

The minions all stood and bowed to him. Faron Hayes, dressed in an imaginative captain's uniform covered with gold braid and lavishly adorned with many medals for his accomplishments in the business world, took off his hat and said, "Prince Oscar, your will is law."

They all sat down again on the chairs that had now been drawn to the center table in a horseshoe shape. Oscar took a seat near the door through which he had just entered. A chair was hastily fetched for Falcon, and he too took a seat.

Oscar looked down the row, recognizing most of the men and women. The minions of his half-brothers and half-sister, Kenneth Mayfield, Mike Farland and Tana Rowe were present. Also in attendance were Albert Herr from Dis Pater, the lawyer Kim La Croix- -the minion of Sascha Krocht, sister of the murdered Walter--and Gene Fletcher from Pilgrims Palladium. He spied Iris Warburg, whom he had once met in the palace of the Man family; she was a minion of an important tycoon of the European Exergue Pertenaires. He saw that Laura Langen the minion of the queen of Pilgrims Palladium was also there. As he looked at her, strong memories of his youth in Switzerland came back, and he had to hold on to the armrests of the chair very firmly, for he felt as if he were suddenly about to fall into an abyss. But then, somewhere in his mind, came the calm, reassuring voice of Emlyn Gray, and he knew his ancestors would stand by him.

"Welcome, Prince Oscar," said Hayes. "I have arranged this room especially for this meeting. To the captain the bridge may be the most important part of the ship, but in reality, this is the soul of the ship and where the most important decisions are made. We all greet you as one of our own, or if I do you an injustice with that, one whose power is greater than our own—for we have all experienced it. May I assume that Mr. Falcon also belongs to us?"

It was Falcon himself who responded.

"Aye, cast in the same mold."

Hayes stared at him searchingly but lowered his eyes in disbelief after looking into Falcon's, for he had caught a glimpse of the terrifying world behind the gray eyes. He turned to Oscar once again.

"We receive you with all soberness and acknowledge that you are the one who shines like the brightest star in the dark firmament. Much too late have we acknowledged and accepted your superiority. If anyone of us ever caused you any grief, Prince, we will take the blame collectively. We have all come a long way and have achieved much. But unfortunately, it is not enough. We had absolute dominance simply for the asking, but we did not succeed in drawing the power toward ourselves.

"I have already offered you the *Njord,* our most important work of art. The ship, however, means nothing at all compared to that which is yet to be offered to you.

"From generation to generation, we have worked toward the realization of a dream. In every successor, in every talented descendant, something more has become visible of this ultimate destination. A deep, hidden knowledge has been drawn up from the great well of time. The generations have all stood on each other's shoulders so that the last ones may reach the top."

Oscar immediately thought back to the works of art in Ferdinand's palace that depicted all those creatures standing atop one another, supporting the cast iron dome.

"But the topmost one did not seem to be able to reach high enough, and now it is of the greatest importance that we all don't come tumbling down. All of our efforts have not been for nothing, have they? Countless civilizations have risen and disappeared again under the eternal sun and moon, and now it is our time, and we will appropriate everything we need for our own use. You have the power to lead us, Prince Oscar. We acknowledge your superiority, and we will follow you. Will you show us the way? There is a crown in the making for you and with it comes absolute power and immense wealth."

Faron Hayes donned his hat again, backed toward his chair and sat down. All eyes were turned toward Oscar now. He rose to his feet and stretched out his arm. He extended his finger and slowly pointed at everyone, moving horizontally from the left to the right.

"From generation to generation has the venom trickled inside!" he said loudly, and everyone looked up with a start. "Everything that could have, and should have, been used for the good of the world has been used instead to fan the fires of hate. And now the temperature has been reached that it must be in hell, and you are prepared to burn down the entire world if need be, to wipe out everything and everyone, in order to make room for none other than yourselves. I don't want to go to deeply into your sick ways of thinking. Perhaps I do indeed have the power to lead you to the paradise of which you are dreaming, but I know that the road to it would be a bloody one. Too often have I seen my ancestors in thoughts, wading through a lake of blood, craving power. All the terrible forms death can take have paraded before my mind's eye. And I spit on it!"

Something suddenly changed in the atmosphere of the spacious stateroom. Oscar felt a heavy weight on his eyes and temples and perceived an ominous rustling that did not reach him through his ears, but entered directly into his mind. But he was not a man easily daunted.

"My whole life I have tried to stand aside as much as possible," he continued. "I saw things happening without being a part of it myself. I wouldn't get involved in anything. And so it is still: I am not here to take part in something that stands so far away from me. I will not judge what you have done and brought about. You changed the world in your own favor, had it all your way, and it never occurred to you how much damage this could do to others. I don't even want to discuss the horrible murders of Walter Krocht, Carl Holdorf, Roberta Rodriguez and others. But I will always remain protective of my family--Ferdinand, Jimmy and Johanna. I cannot, and will not, mean anything to you. The death of my faithful guards Richard and Jay Jay Wright presses hard on my soul, and if I were ever to use my power for anything, then it would be to have my revenge on you for them."

He moved his head slowly, looking at everyone in turn.

"This is all I have to say. A crown from your hands is the last thing I want."

Faron Hayes made a hopeless gesture with his hands.

"Please, Prince, take some time and think about it."

"Probe my thoughts, minion, and you will know that my decision is final," was Oscar's answer.

Faron Hayes stood up, as did all the others. Oscar knew that they were receiving his train of thought and opened his mind to them and just as quickly shut them down again. The steel walls of the stateroom began to tremble. A crackling sound came from all corners of the room, and transparent blue balls appeared in the centers of which vivid yellow flashes of lightning hissed. The minions had combined their powers and decided that Oscar Man must be forced to acquiesce to their desires now that he had clearly shown them that he had absolutely no intention of leading them of his own free will. Oscar, in turn, understood that this was to be a battle to the death, for he would never bend or surrender to their collective attack.

Emlyn Gray and his followers appeared in his mind. Stamping boots caused a swell in the lake of blood. It dawned on Oscar that Emlyn Gray had been a genuine minion and that it just might have been that he, symbolically standing on Gray's shoulders, might have brought the false arts to perfection. But things had turned out differently. Oscar was not the same as his ancestors, and now he made use of all the knowledge and skills that had been passed on to him to resist the superior power of the minions.

He spread his arms, and streams of energy flew from his fingertips. Faron Hayes produced a gargling sound as if he were about to choke.

Laura Langen let loose a long-drawn hiss. Without speaking, she made it clear to Oscar that she thought he should have died as a child in Switzerland and should never have been allowed to come to the palace of the Man family in New York. A rain of impulses hit Oscar, and he made staggered backward.

An energy exploded in the stateroom that washed over the entire ship.

The *Njord* slid across the calm waters, but inside the ship a terrible hurricane raged.

In the theater, the guests sat bewildered and terrified in their plush armchairs. Everything around them was moving and churning. The forty or so dancers that had been on stage fled in panic when the ship began to tremble. It felt as if the *Njord* were not only lifted up from the water and then smashed down again by mountainous waves but also as if it were being spun around on its axis from left to right.

The people clung to their chairs as they were thrown past each other, bumping and slamming into everything. With a deafening crash, the chandeliers freed themselves from the ceiling, the lamps bursting apart as they fell.

"The ship is going down!" cried Johanna Man. "We will all die!"

Now everyone gave voice to their fear and began screaming and crying.

Ferdinand Man leaped from his chair and ran unevenly to a door. The other guests also got to their feet and tried to reach the exits. Dancers, musicians, guardsmen, cast members, crew members, tycoons, kings and queens, all jostled each other and cried out in unbridled fear. Cathy Wheeler, completely in a panic, was pushed and fell headlong onto the quaking floor. Trying to keep herself from being trampled to death, she rolled aside and tried to stand up again.

"Come!" she heard someone say.

Margaret Sharpe reached out her hand to her.

And together they ran for their lives. The floor underneath them was going up and down in such way that they were thrown in every direction. Sascha Krocht tumbled across the floor with blood streaming from her mouth until Queen Lillian DiCampo took pity on her and assisted her; the women staggered along together.

Sven Enlart of Pilgrims Palladium managed to reach his queen and help her support Sascha. They got the doors open, fled along the long hallways and climbed the broad staircases. Still screaming in mortal terror and moaning with pain as they were ferociously smashed against the walls, they tried to reach the upper decks.

"What are we supposed to do?" asked Cathy aloud.

Her voice was lost in the chaos and noise, but Margaret Sharpe shouted in her ear, "We must find Captain Knudsen. He will tell us what to do. Is the ship lost? What is happening?"

"It must be a freak of weather!" screamed Cathy. "Maybe we should stay inside instead. Outside the storm is raging. There must be towering waves out there!"

More and more guards joined them. They protected the tycoons and kings as best they could by taking them in their midst. The colossal ship, the wonder of the modern world, continued to be lifted up and smashed from side to side. The splashing of gigantic waves and the roaring of the storm was heard everywhere.

A door opened that gave entry to the upper decks, and Captain Knudsen appeared in front of the fleeing crowd making frenzied gestures.

"Come along! All of you! Into the lifeboats!" he yelled.

He pressed both hands against his head and closed his eyes. Everyone was suffering from a terrible, stinging headache. It was as if the *Njord* had tired of its guests and shook and stamped herself to be rid of them. The captain managed to calm himself down, and now he cried out, "Please! Stay in line and wait until someone comes for you. There is enough room for everyone. The *Njord* is sinking. My men will get you all into the lifeboats and get you to the navy's ships. If everyone remains calm, we'll all be okay soon."

A guard from Cabo de Barra took Cathy by the arm, and she let herself be guided to the deck. The storm cut off her breath. The rain beat her face and soaked her clothes. The deck turned around and around. The man held her tight and shouted above the screaming of the wind that everything would be all right. Above her the sky was jet black. She thought it was very strange that she could still see clearly, just as she had been able to see everything in the windowless theater when the lamps had burst. The next moment, she was thinking about something else: she began to shout for Oscar and tried to free herself from the grip of the guard.

"Don't struggle!" she heard him shout, the fear in his voice extremely evident. "Don't make it more difficult than it already is. You must get away from here as soon as possible. The ship is lost!"

"Oscar! Oscar is still on board!" cried Cathy.

She managed to free herself from his grip, and when he tried to catch her again, she hit him in the face—hard.

"Oscar!" she cried out one more time.

The giant ocean steamer shot up so fast that she was flattened against the deck, the breath pressed out of her lungs. The *Njord* came down in a deep, watery valley, surrounded by hissing waves.

"I'm not going to let you go again," a voice said in her ear, and she thought she recognized it as Oscar's.

She spit seawater and took a deep breath.

Both the world, and her head, were spinning out of control.

Dean Howe stood next to Admiral Irvin Hernandez on the bridge of the frigate and stared through a spyglass at the *Njord*. Everyone who was not busy with the ship's necessities had come on deck to see what was happening on the *Njord*. It was still a clear, windless day with visibility from horizon to horizon and long white clouds slowly floating through the sky.

"It looks like people are running up and down, crazy with terror," said Dean Howe. "They're jumping into the lifeboats. They are fighting with each other for a place—no doubt someone is going to get hurt. Is it still impossible to make contact with them?"

"It's not impossible," said the admiral scornfully. "It's simply that the *Njord* refuses to respond."

"Shouldn't you take some action?"

Irvin put his spyglass down and looked at the general.

"What can I do? And why should I do anything, anyway? They are playing an insane game over there that I don't understand at all. And besides, what instructions am I to give my men if I send them over there? Do you have any ideas? If you can give me some good advice—"

The general shook his head so that everything he saw through his spyglass began to move.

"No, I don't know either. You are right. It is better to wait. I'll bet you anything that the lifeboats will come to us. The navy is getting visitors."

He was right. The big lifeboats headed for the frigates. The sailors had a great deal of trouble getting the now apathetic passengers of the *Njord* on board. They launched boats to pick up swimmers who had jumped into the sea.

Cathy felt that the storm was over, that it was no longer raining and that the waves had abated. General Howe had discovered her among all the others and had taken pity on her. He took her with him to the bridge and sat her down in a comfortable chair. She stared blankly in front of her and showed no reaction to any of the questions he asked her. Then suddenly she seemed to come to her senses, as if she had awakened from a dream, and looked round in surprise. It took another few moments before she realized that she was on a naval vessel, and then she recognized the general.

"Oscar—" she whispered softly.

Oscar Man felt himself growing weaker and weaker; his powers were no match for the united hate of the minions gathered before him. Their psychic bursts made the entire ship resonate. It was as if the *Njord* had come to life. Oscar received flashing images of terrified people fleeing the ship. It was as if the giant ship of steel were shaking like a wet dog trying to rid itself of fleas. Once again, the minions reached out their hands to him, and waves of energy splashed around him, weakening him still further. They were very busy trying to kill him. Bit by bit, they wrenched the life out of his mind and body.

At the very moment Oscar was about to succumb to their efforts, a new source of powerful, unbridled energy came to his rescue. For a moment he thought it originated from within himself, but then it flashed on him that it must have an external source.

Alongside him, Tony Falcon had risen to his feet. With a powerful gesture of his hand, he forced the minions backward. Heavy wooden chairs turned over. Faron Hayes was thrown into the wall with incredible force. Falcon clenched his fists, and the stateroom was lit up by flames that licked the walls and crawled over the bodies of the minions. Oscar called upon his ancestors and pleaded for more power. Emlyn Gray appeared in front of him and spoke, but he couldn't understand him. The voice of Falcon reached his ears instead.

"I am here to help you, Oscar. You know that, don't you? Together we will stand up to them. We will even defeat them. Let me warn you, they will not spare you. Remember who they are... the devil's henchmen!"

Oscar pushed his hands to his ears as if he was able to close his mind that way to the everlasting pressure the minions exerted in it.

"Oscar!" it droned in his head.

He could not tell if it still was Falcon who tried to communicate with him.

While he slowly sank down on his knees, a horrible idea came to his mind--in another place, probably even in one of their palaces, he could have been able to cope with the spiritual powers of the minions. But here, on board the ship, an extra power was present, generated by minion technology--it was the giant *Njord* that transmitted an energy that weakened him and made the minions stronger and stronger. He remembered the millions of yards of copper wire were hidden under the decks to generate magnetic fields.

The next moment, he was no longer able to think about such things at all. He had a feeling as if his head was leaking, like a punctured balloon. Thoughts and feelings disappeared; his mind left his body and floated through the suite in panic. The minions stretched out flaming tentacles to his mind, got hold of it and tried to squeeze it together. The feelings came back.

Oscar felt a stunning pain. Only now he became aware of his body, which was not of flesh and blood. He jumped up and down in white terror, and all of a sudden, he found himself standing opposite his own kneeling body and stared into his own eyes; his mouth was wide open and a rasping sound came up from his throat. He wanted to slip back into that body, give it new strength and make it stand up. Instead of that, he was driven backward.

"Leave us, false prince, leave us for ever!" cried all minions at the same time.

Emlyn Grey appeared swollen into a gigantic monster and almost exploded. Then Falcon materialized next to his kneeling body; behind him were his own ancestors who had come to support him in his battle.

Just when Oscar had almost managed to slip back into his stiffened body, he was forced out again. He came close to a steel wall of the suite. When he actually touched it, a shock went right through him as if the *Njord* was electrically charged; then he fell through the wall and hurtled down through the ship.

"You will die, Oscar Man!" he heard the minions chant from far away. "Now it all ends for you!"

Oscar was bounced over a deck as if his entire being was squeezed together into a ball. He was not able to stop the movement. He fell through a deck and then flew through cabins, restaurants and theatres as if there were no walls at all. He went down and down, through all decks, and then he floated above red-hot coals. Now pain dominated all other feelings. He went right through the stamping engines of the *Njord* and suddenly his spirit got enwrapped by something that was almost body-like, and he stood still in a hold that was filled with boxes and crates. Faron Hayes was there too, taking off his hat and making a bow. He spoke and his voice sounded as thought he spoke from a cavern.

"We're going to destroy you, Oscar Man. Nothing will be left of you. You'll have to deal with all terrors of hell, you hear? Ah, but first we'll make the jester dance..."

Suddenly Hayes had a huge shovel in his hands. He held it high above his head and brought it down with force. Oscar was stunned. He flew through the hold--through the entire ship --and everywhere he heard Minion voices:

"I should have put an end to your miserable life in Switzerland," repeated Laura Langen.

"You are damned, Oscar Man! I spit on you! And I know a place where you can burn eternally."

"It's all over for you. Your spirit is separated from your body. They will never again me united!"

He bounced against a wall, went through a deck, got hit by an invisible force and rushed on faster and faster.

"Spirit and body. Separated forever and a day! We need not do any more. Now it all becomes very easy!"

A chorus of minion voices, steeped in hatred, sounded from all sides.

"All we have to do is behead you!"

The voices grew louder.

Again laughter.

Twenty, thirty excited voices together:

"Chop his head off! Chop his head off!"

But Oscar's fear had reached its limit final bounds and became a parody of fear--and that was something the jester could handle; suddenly he feared nothing and no one any more and was filled with feelings of empowerment. He took new strength from his own minion source and called up all his ancestors to fight at his side.

"Emlyn Grey!" he heard himself cry.

Oscar had to hurry. He knew that his body was still in Faron Hayes's suite, motionless, in a kneeling position. All one needed to separate his head from his body was a blade sharp enough to cut through flesh and bone.

His ancestors gathered and lined up behind him.

"We are ready, Oscar."

"Let's go then."

They floated across the *Njord*, and no iron wall could stop them. Their howling rose to a deafening roar. Right before they reached the suite, Falcon and his ancestors joined them.

"Faster! Faster!" shouted Oscar. "They are going to destroy my body!"

The ship began to move heavily. It shook like a harpooned whale.

"The *Njord* hates us!" cried Falcon. "The ship would rather spit us out!"

Oscar reached the suite. The minions who had kept him on the run entered as well and came standing next to each other.

The body of Falcon was pressed up high against a wall, the arms and legs spread. Oscar looked down on himself. There he still knelt, waiting for the end. Laura Langen was the one who should execute him. She held a long sword in her hands. The shining steel blade chased with minion art.

"Farewell, Oscar Man!" she said resolutely while she lifted up the sword.

Oscar made a despairing attempt to return into that lifeless body. Behind him positive powers were built up, and he could hear his ancestors murmur..

"Now! Now!" cried the minions. "The moment of truth has come! Let the head of the jester roll!"

Suddenly the body of Falcon came loose from the wall. Just before it would strike the ground, it came to life. Falcon took a tumble, seized Oscars' waist and pulled him down. The sword came down: it cut through the air and threw Laura Langen off her balance. During her fall, she swung the weapon away from her, and the sharp point pierced Faron Hayes's breast.

The captain gave a cry, which was drowned by the shouting of all other minions. They stepped backward. Falcon spread his arms. Fiery tentacles twisted from his fingertips through the suite.

Faron Hayes fell forward. When he was lying on the floor full length, the sword tip shone through the back of his uniform jacket. The noise the minions made went above the limit of audibility. They stood there with their mouths open and there was panic, desperation in their eyes.

Oscar scrambled up. The reunion of spirit and body gave him a short, odd sensation, but then he was himself again, in control of his body.

"Falcon! What is happening?"

"Don't wait for the minions to recover!"

"What do you mean? I don't understand you, I..."

"Listen and obey, Oscar Man! For there is no time to tell it to you a second time. Go now, while you still have the strength. Are you listening? Leave the ship! Now!"

"Falcon!" cried Oscar. "I won't leave you alone!"

"You heard what I said!" echoed the compelling, powerful voice of the man. "Disappear! There is not much time!"

Oscar groped his way to the door, found the knob and turned it. Slipping outside, he was surprised by the hellish storms of energy that blew through the ship. Bending forward, his long hair flying, he went through the deserted gangways of the *Njord*. Behind him, he heard a horrible screaming, and he knew that the minions had fallen upon the brave Falcon with renewed and united power. He quickened his pace along the rows of monstrous images and heard the foghorns roar.

Oscar was exhausted when he finally came on deck and looking over the railing saw the calm ocean far below. He had great difficulty getting his thoughts in order. He jumped up and down on the deck as if it were electrically charged, and then he climbed up on the rail and let himself fall. His body reached a very high speed on his descent, and when he hit the water, he sank yards below the surface before he was able to swim back up.

He had been swimming for no longer than two minutes when a naval gunboat came close enough to rescue him. A sailor grabbed for him and pulled him out of the water. The man was about to say something to him. His mouth opened wide, but he didn't say a word. Instead, he pointed straight in front of him. Oscar stood up and turned around. Standing in the softly swaying boat, his feet apart, he wrung the water out of the sleeves of his shirt and stared at the mighty *Njord*.

"The ship is disappearing!" said the awestruck sailor.

It all happened in the space of a few seconds.

The tall black hull and superstructure seemed to become transparent. Big holes in her sides showed the blue of the sky as they grew wider and overlapped. The surge of the wash disappeared, and the sea became smooth and deserted. The *Njord* along with the minions, the crew and all others remaining aboard vanished into thin air.

The sailor sank to the bottom of the boat on his knees, folded his hands and began to jabber unintelligibly.

On board the naval frigates, everyone had witnessed the incident with their eyes, just as the *Njord* had also disappeared from the radar screens. Cathy Wheeler began to scream hysterically, and a doctor was called to sedate her.

Before she fell asleep, she whispered softly, "Oscar, . . ."

* * *

"If I had agreed to Hayes's proposal," said Oscar Man, "I would have been joining forces with the minions. We would have had all the tycoons—and the world—in a stranglehold. Once we were back on dry land, they would have been ours to control like robots."

He stood with Cathy Wheeler on the terrace of his penthouse in New York City and leaned over the railing. Cathy stroked his hair and shoulders and stared out in front of her. Big gray clouds floated in from the river over the skyscrapers of Manhattan. The wind gathered strength. It was going to rain.

"Tell me something about the past," said Oscar when she didn't react to what he had just said.

"About Manhattan? About America?" she asked.

"The *Flying Dutchman*."

"Oh," said Cathy. "That is quite a different story from that of the *Njord*."

Now it was Oscar who kept silent.

"The ship that later became known as the *Flying Dutchman* belonged to the East India Company and left Amsterdam destined for Batavia. That was, if I am not mistaken, in the year 1680. The ship never reached Batavia. The weather was so bad that the captain was not able to round the Cape of Good Hope. Not knowing what to do, he called on the devil for help, who made him swear a horrible oath. The punishment for his reckless deed was hard. He was to sail the oceans of the world until the end of time. Every now and then, the ship is seen by sailors or by people standing along the coast looking out over the sea. The masts, the sails, the rigging, but especially the high stern of the wooden ship, give it away that it has to be an East Indian. For long periods of time, the ship remains unseen. Then, all of a sudden, it seems to reappear again."

Oscar nodded, turned toward her and gave her a kiss.

"Come," he said, "we have to change."

Not much later, they stepped into a taxi. Eddie Brooks, the man who had first brought Oscar into contact with Tony Falcon, was at the wheel. They drove off as Eddie Brooks expressed his amazement over the news he had heard about the disappearance of the *Njord*.

"How can such a big, majestic ship disappear, just like that?" he asked aloud. "I often wonder if this could be another one of Falcon's stunts."

"You might be right about that, Eddie," said Oscar.

They arrived at the station of the Man palace where Orville and Phoebe Hood and their adopted daughter Angelina stood waiting for them. As the taxi drove away, they greeted each other.

Angelina embraced her half-brother as if she never would let him go again and said, with tears in her eyes, "You were already a prince, but now you are so famous, too. If you only knew how high your star rose after you saved President Sebastian."

"Hopefully, that will be my own salvation as well," said Oscar. "My new status makes it difficult, perhaps even impossible, to make me do things I absolutely don't want to do. I will explain what I mean by that later. I am just about the last survivor of a dark breed, and I know a few men in the army who are eager to spend a year or so examining me. I must have a long talk with our president."

As they walked to the station building, Oscar tapped Orville on his arm.

"A promise is a debt, Orville. But when I promised you that we would take a couple of rounds together on the Ferris wheel, I could not have possibly known how much I would have to tell you."

"You should tell me about Europe."

"Tomorrow we go on the wheel, and of course, I will tell you all about my stay in Europe. What I have to tell you after that will surprise you so much that at first you will think that my imagination has run away with me. And as we talk and go around, we will look out on the palace of my family, one of the many heritages left from an era that was so recently closed, and slowly but surely you will come to find that building even more astounding than you do now."

"All this makes me even more curious," muttered Orville. "But first we go home. Phoebe and I have prepared a terrific meal, Oscar. For one cannot put just anything in front of a prince."

When they were inside, Oscar felt cheerful and relaxed.

He felt as if he had come home. From now on, things would be changing quickly in the world. As far as that was concerned, there was another challenge waiting for Cathy after she had finished his biography. Then she could start to describe the more recent developments.

"We can only consider the future in the light of the past my teachers always drummed into my head," was one of her regular statements.

And few people had been more involved in recent history than she.

"Can you ever look at the sea again without thinking about the *Njord* and its passengers?" she had asked him the day before.

His answer had been short and came with a very deep sigh.

"No."

"I love you, Oscar."

"I know that. And I love you."

"Do you know what you are?"

"Please tell me. Or whisper it to me."

She brought her lips to his ear. He felt her warm breath when she said in a soft tone:

"You're my personal guardian angel."

About the Author

Koos, a 'Dutchy' with spunk and an inexhaustible drive and fathomless imagination, is one of the most prolific authors of sci-fi and children's books in The Netherlands. His novels, All-Father and Wolf Tears, earned him the moniker, the Dutch Stephen King.

He wrote his first sci-fi novel, Adolar, in one weekend when he was 18 years old and the manuscript was published shortly thereafter.

Koos has published over 60 books, both children's books and novels, hundreds of comic scripts, and he has worked as a copywriter. He is currently working on several screenplays and new novels.

To read more about Koos and his work visit his website at www.koosverkaik.com or follow him on Facebook at https,//www.facebook.com/koos.verkaik.5

Also by Koos Verkaik

Novels in Dutch

Adolar

Terug naar het Dorp

Conflict Afrika

Mana, en Toen Brak de Hel los

Dans van de Nar Grapstad

De Meesterparasiet

Psycho Park

Alvader

Wolfstranen

Neanderthaler Dromen De

Children's Book Series

Saladin Series

Saladin het Wonderpaard
Spookpaard

Saladin en Silver

Silver en het

De Nar van Nottingham

Slimmetje Series

Het Konijn uit de Hoed

De Boze Beer

Schipbreuk

De Hoge Hoed is weg
Kabouterland

Ridder Joris

De Schat van Kabouter Bollewijn

Professor in Paniek

De Tovertrein

De Verdwaalde Walvis

Sneeuwmannen in

Otto de Otter

Krimpende Paddestoelen

Wolpertinger series

De Monsterherberg	Drie Dolle Prinsen
De Onderlanden	Koning Leo Lawaai
Het Land van Franje	Alex de Grote
De Drakentuin	Heros de Haas
Roest IJzervreter	

Novels in English

The Nibelung Gold	Heavenly Vision
All-Father	Neanderthal Dreams
Dance of the Jester	HIM, After the UFO Crash

Children's Book Series

Wolpertinger Series

The Monster Inn	The Dragon Garden
The Downhills	Rusty Iron
Uncle Balloon	Three Mad Princes
The Land of Fringe	

Saladin Series

Saladin the Wonder Horse	Silver and the Ghost Horse
Saladin and Silver	The Jester of Nottingham